P9-CLW-816

VOLUME
TWO

SKYW

SKYWARD, VOL. 2. First printing. February 2019. Published by Image Comics, Inc. Office of publication: 2701 NW Vaughn St., Suite 780, Portland, OR 97210. Copyright © 2019 Joe Henderson & Lee Garbett. All rights reserved. Contains material originally published in single magazine form as SKYWARD #6-10. "SKYWARD," its logos, and the likenesses of all characters herein are trademarks of Joe Henderson & Lee Garbett, unless otherwise noted. "Image" and the Image Comics logos are registered trademarks of Image Comics, Inc. No part of this publication may be reproduced or transmitted, in any form or by any means (except for short excerpts for journalistic or review purposes), without the express written permission of Joe Henderson & Lee Garbett, or Image Comics, Inc. All names, characters, events, and locales in this publication are entirely fictional. Any resemblance to actual persons (living or dead), events, or places, without satirical intent, is coincidental. Printed in the USA. For information regarding the CPSIA on this printed material call: 203-595-3636. For international rights, contact: foreignlicensing@imagecomics.com. ISBN: 978-1-5343-0881-7

VARD

'HERE THERE BE DRAGONFLIES'

WRITER
JOE HENDERSON

ART & COVER
LEE GARBETT

COLORIST
ANTONIO FABELA

LETTERER
SIMON BOWLAND

ART & COVER
LEE GARBETT

EDITOR
RICK LOPEZ Jr.

PRODUCTION
CAREY HALL

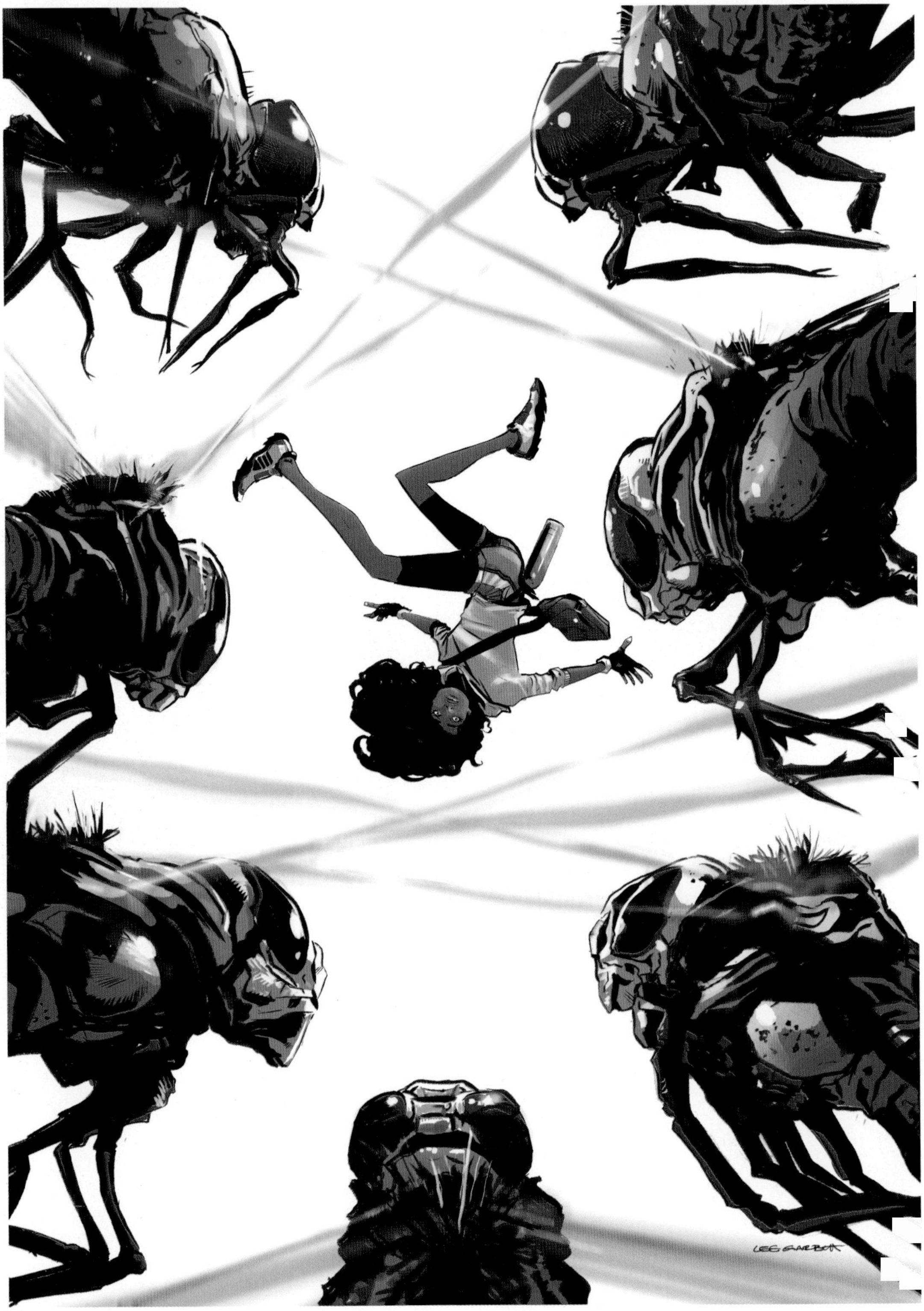

CHAPTER SIX

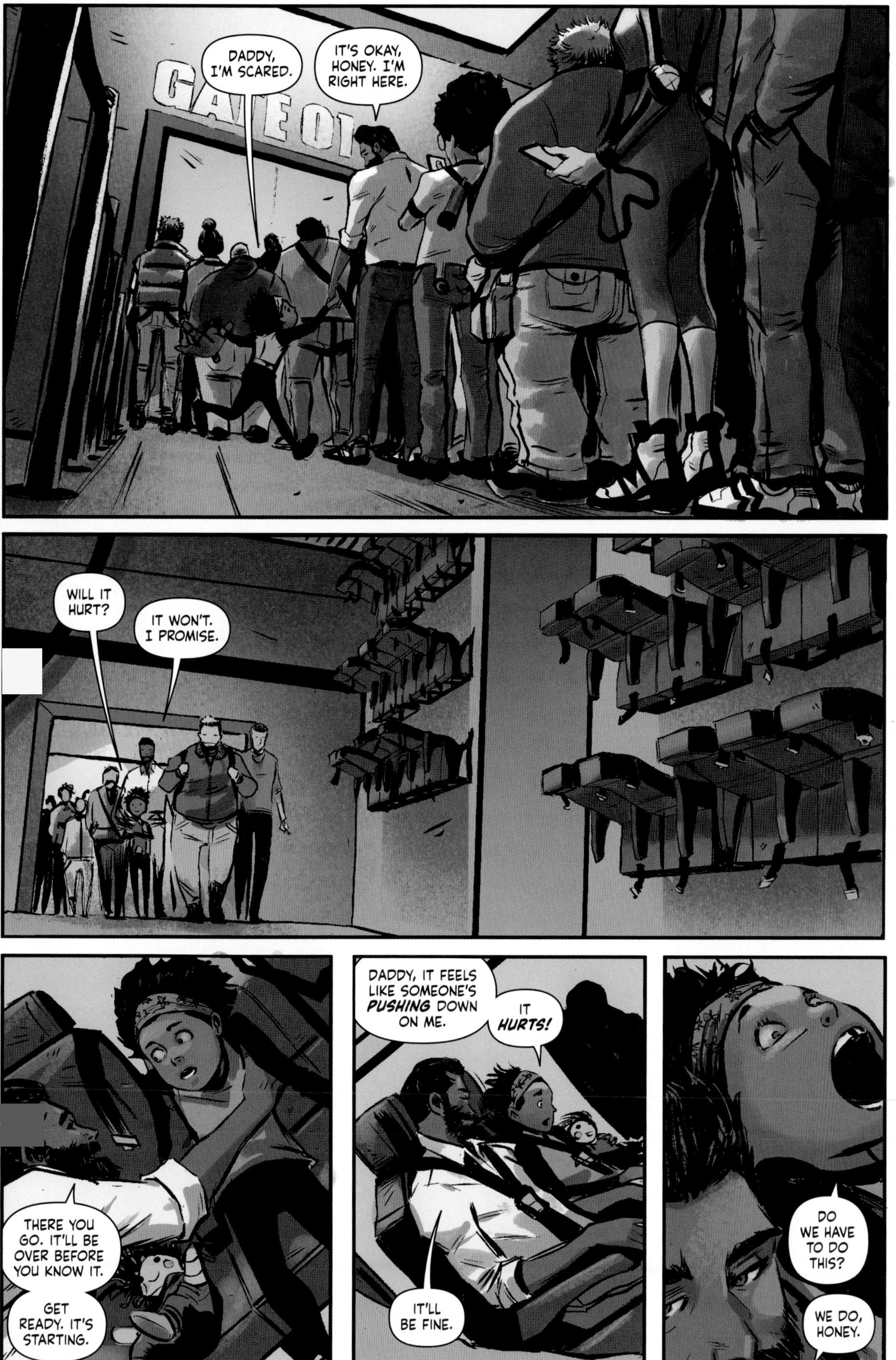
DADDY, I'M SCARED.
IT'S OKAY, HONEY. I'M RIGHT HERE.
GATE 01
WILL IT HURT?
IT WON'T. I PROMISE.
THERE YOU GO. IT'LL BE OVER BEFORE YOU KNOW IT.
GET READY. IT'S STARTING.
DADDY, IT FEELS LIKE SOMEONE'S *PUSHING* DOWN ON ME.
IT *HURTS!*
IT'LL BE FINE.
DO WE HAVE TO DO THIS?
WE DO, HONEY.

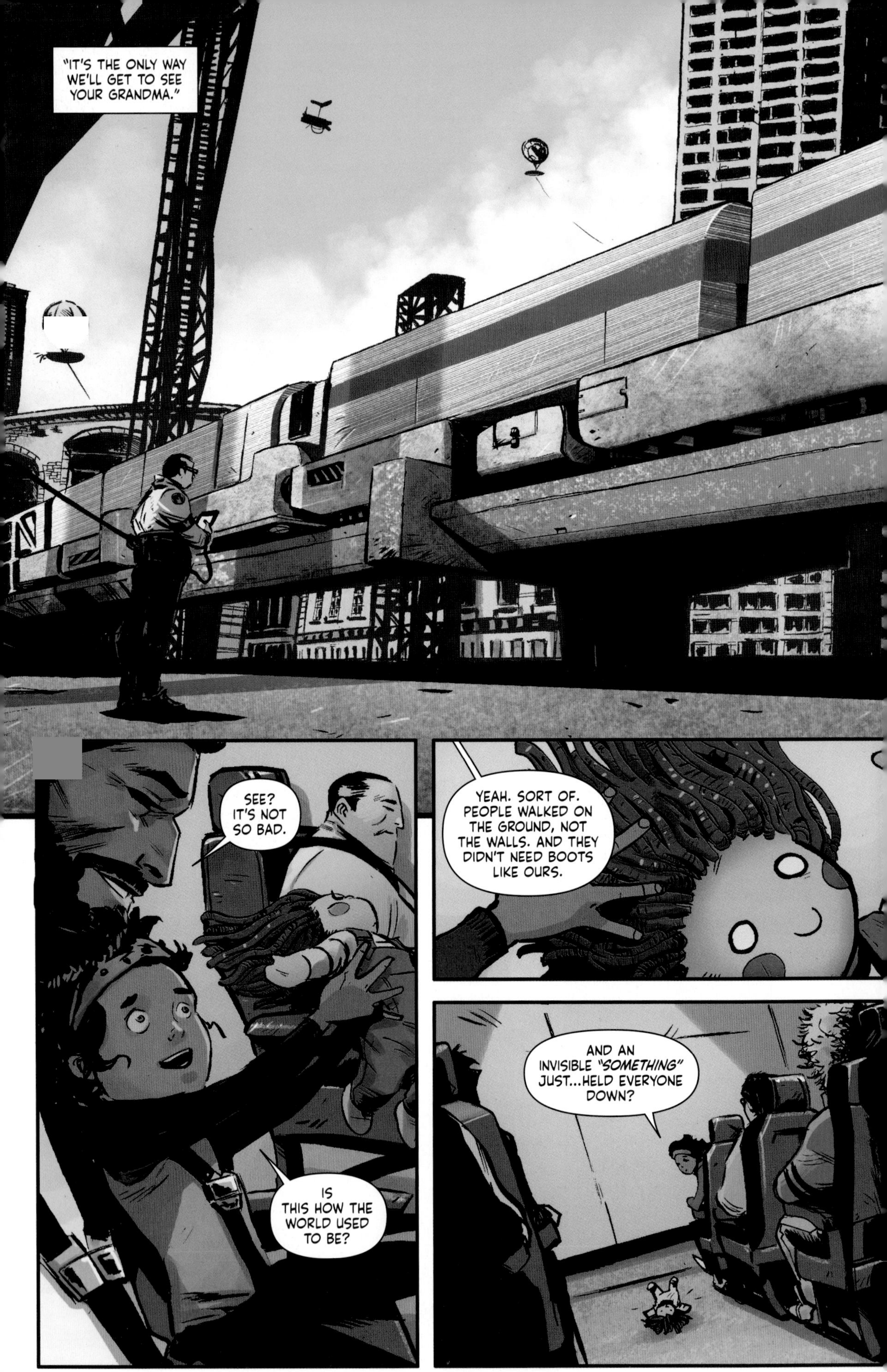
"IT'S THE ONLY WAY WE'LL GET TO SEE YOUR GRANDMA."
SEE? IT'S NOT SO BAD.
IS THIS HOW THE WORLD USED TO BE?
YEAH. SORT OF. PEOPLE WALKED ON THE GROUND, NOT THE WALLS. AND THEY DIDN'T NEED BOOTS LIKE OURS.
AND AN INVISIBLE "SOMETHING" JUST...HELD EVERYONE DOWN?

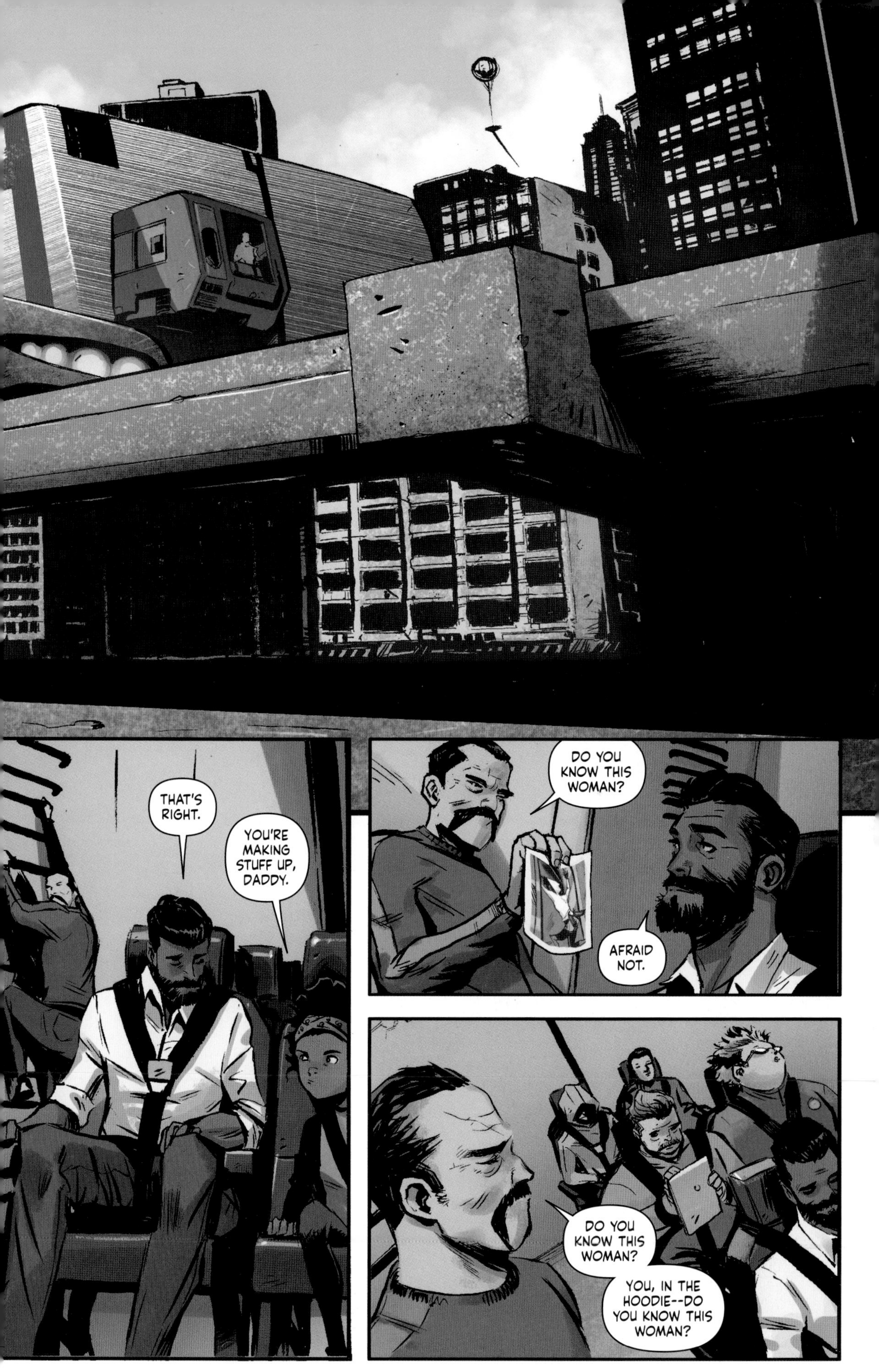
THAT'S RIGHT.
YOU'RE MAKING STUFF UP, DADDY.
DO YOU KNOW THIS WOMAN?
AFRAID NOT.
DO YOU KNOW THIS WOMAN?
YOU, IN THE HOODIE--DO YOU KNOW THIS WOMAN?

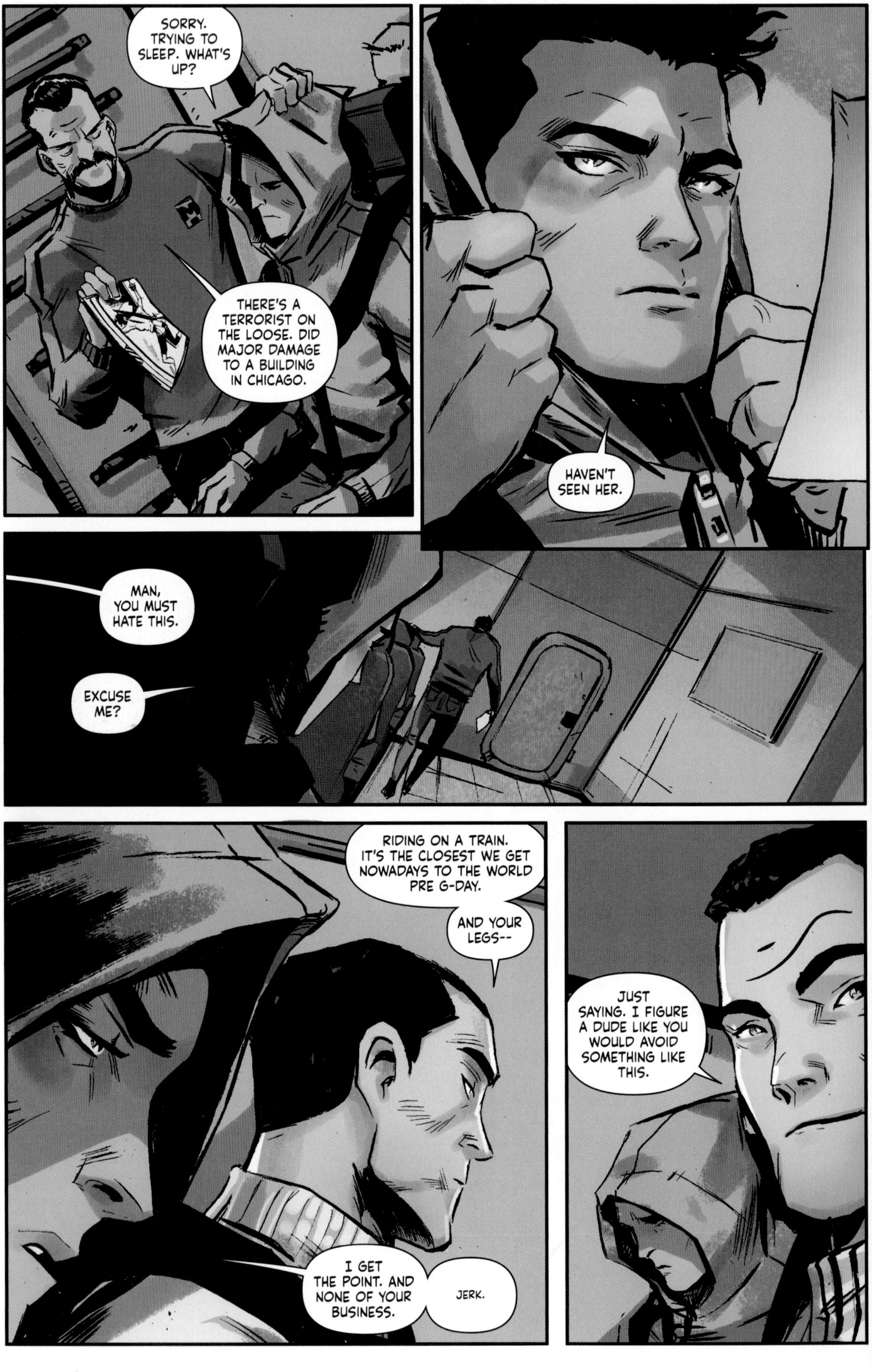
SORRY. TRYING TO SLEEP. WHAT'S UP?
THERE'S A TERRORIST ON THE LOOSE. DID MAJOR DAMAGE TO A BUILDING IN CHICAGO.
HAVEN'T SEEN HER.
MAN, YOU MUST HATE THIS.
EXCUSE ME?
RIDING ON A TRAIN. IT'S THE CLOSEST WE GET NOWADAYS TO THE WORLD PRE G-DAY.
AND YOUR LEGS--
I GET THE POINT. AND NONE OF YOUR BUSINESS.
JERK.
JUST SAYING. I FIGURE A DUDE LIKE YOU WOULD AVOID SOMETHING LIKE THIS.

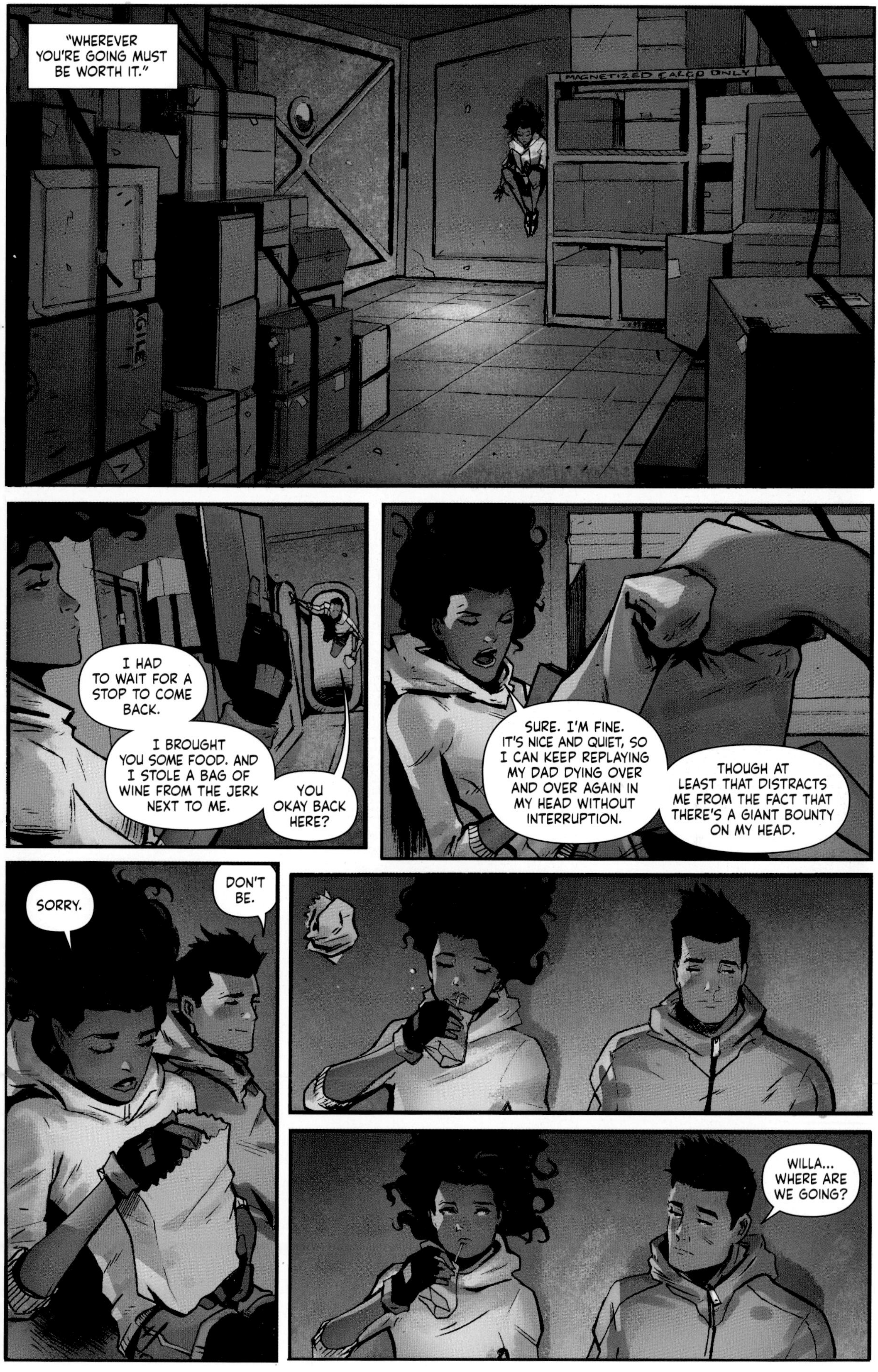
"WHEREVER YOU'RE GOING MUST BE WORTH IT."
MAGNETIZED CARGO ONLY
I HAD TO WAIT FOR A STOP TO COME BACK.
I BROUGHT YOU SOME FOOD. AND I STOLE A BAG OF WINE FROM THE JERK NEXT TO ME.
YOU OKAY BACK HERE?
SURE. I'M FINE. IT'S NICE AND QUIET, SO I CAN KEEP REPLAYING MY DAD DYING OVER AND OVER AGAIN IN MY HEAD WITHOUT INTERRUPTION.
THOUGH AT LEAST THAT DISTRACTS ME FROM THE FACT THAT THERE'S A GIANT BOUNTY ON MY HEAD.
SORRY.
DON'T BE.
WILLA... WHERE ARE WE GOING?

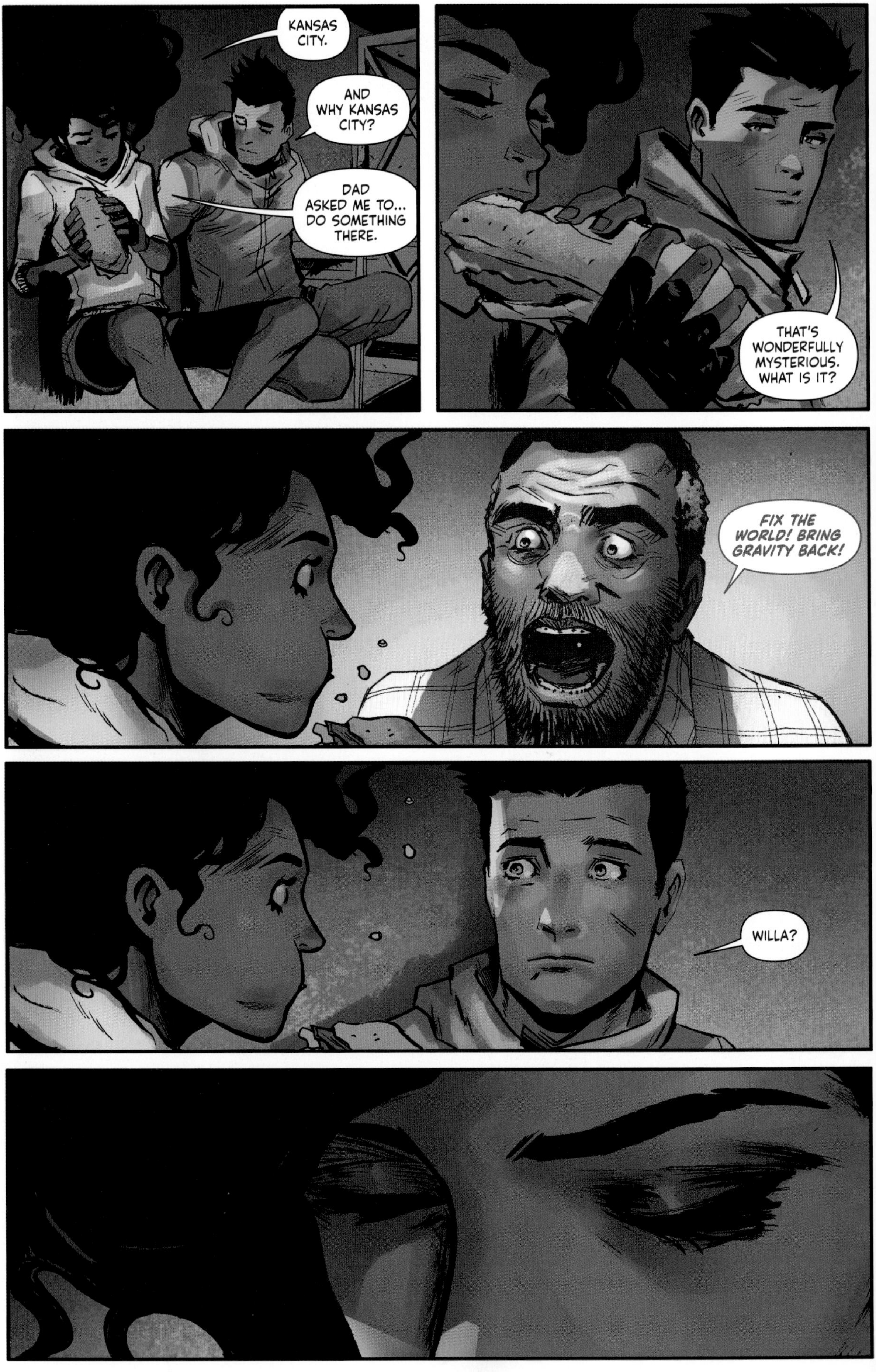
KANSAS CITY.
AND WHY KANSAS CITY?
DAD ASKED ME TO... DO SOMETHING THERE.
THAT'S WONDERFULLY MYSTERIOUS. WHAT IS IT?
FIX THE WORLD! BRING GRAVITY BACK!
WILLA?

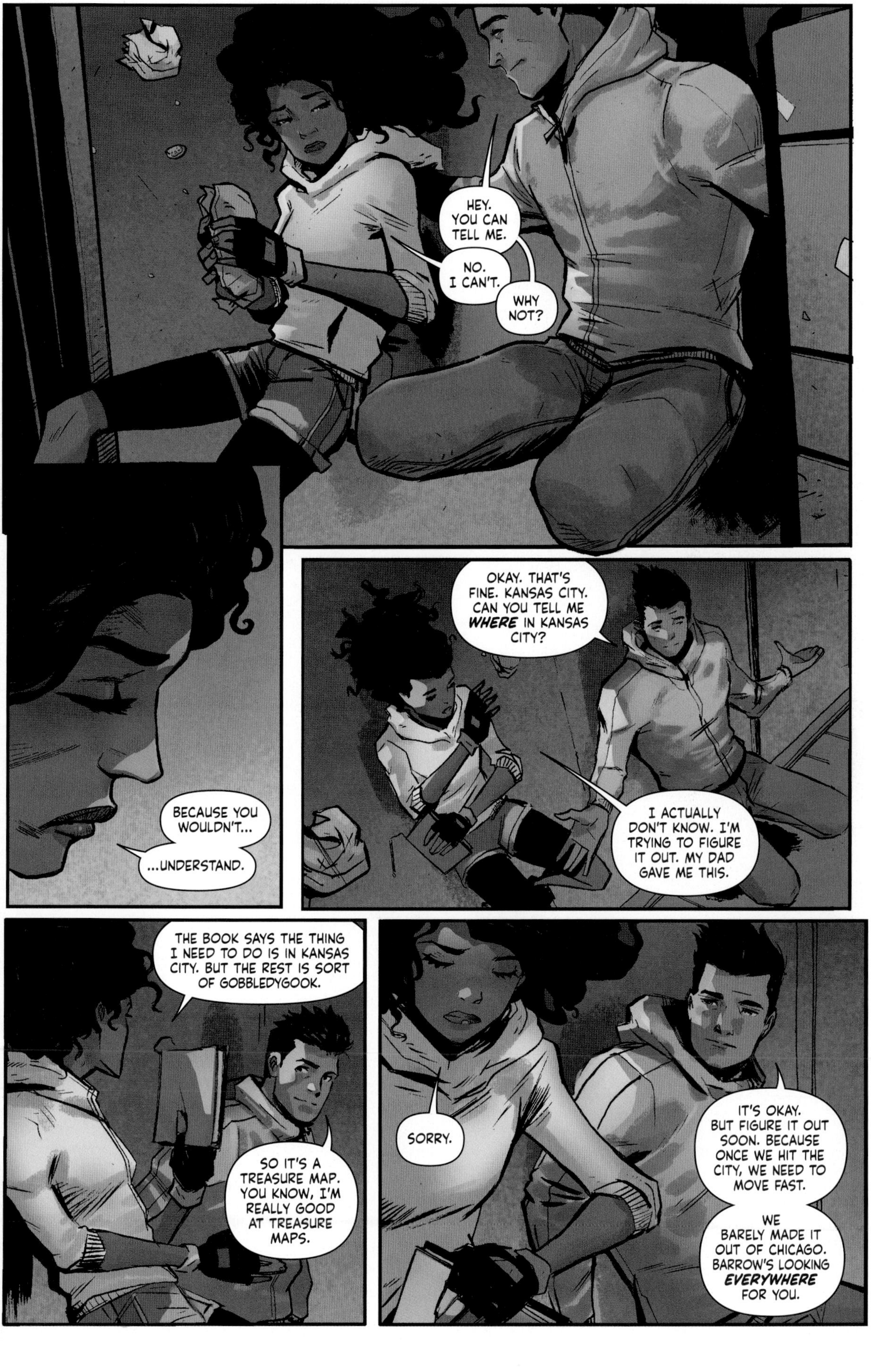
HEY. YOU CAN TELL ME.
NO. I CAN'T.
WHY NOT?
BECAUSE YOU WOULDN'T...
...UNDERSTAND.
OKAY. THAT'S FINE. KANSAS CITY. CAN YOU TELL ME *WHERE* IN KANSAS CITY?
I ACTUALLY DON'T KNOW. I'M TRYING TO FIGURE IT OUT. MY DAD GAVE ME THIS.
THE BOOK SAYS THE THING I NEED TO DO IS IN KANSAS CITY. BUT THE REST IS SORT OF GOBBLEDYGOOK.
SO IT'S A TREASURE MAP. YOU KNOW, I'M REALLY GOOD AT TREASURE MAPS.
SORRY.
IT'S OKAY. BUT FIGURE IT OUT SOON. BECAUSE ONCE WE HIT THE CITY, WE NEED TO MOVE FAST.
WE BARELY MADE IT OUT OF CHICAGO. BARROW'S LOOKING *EVERYWHERE* FOR YOU.

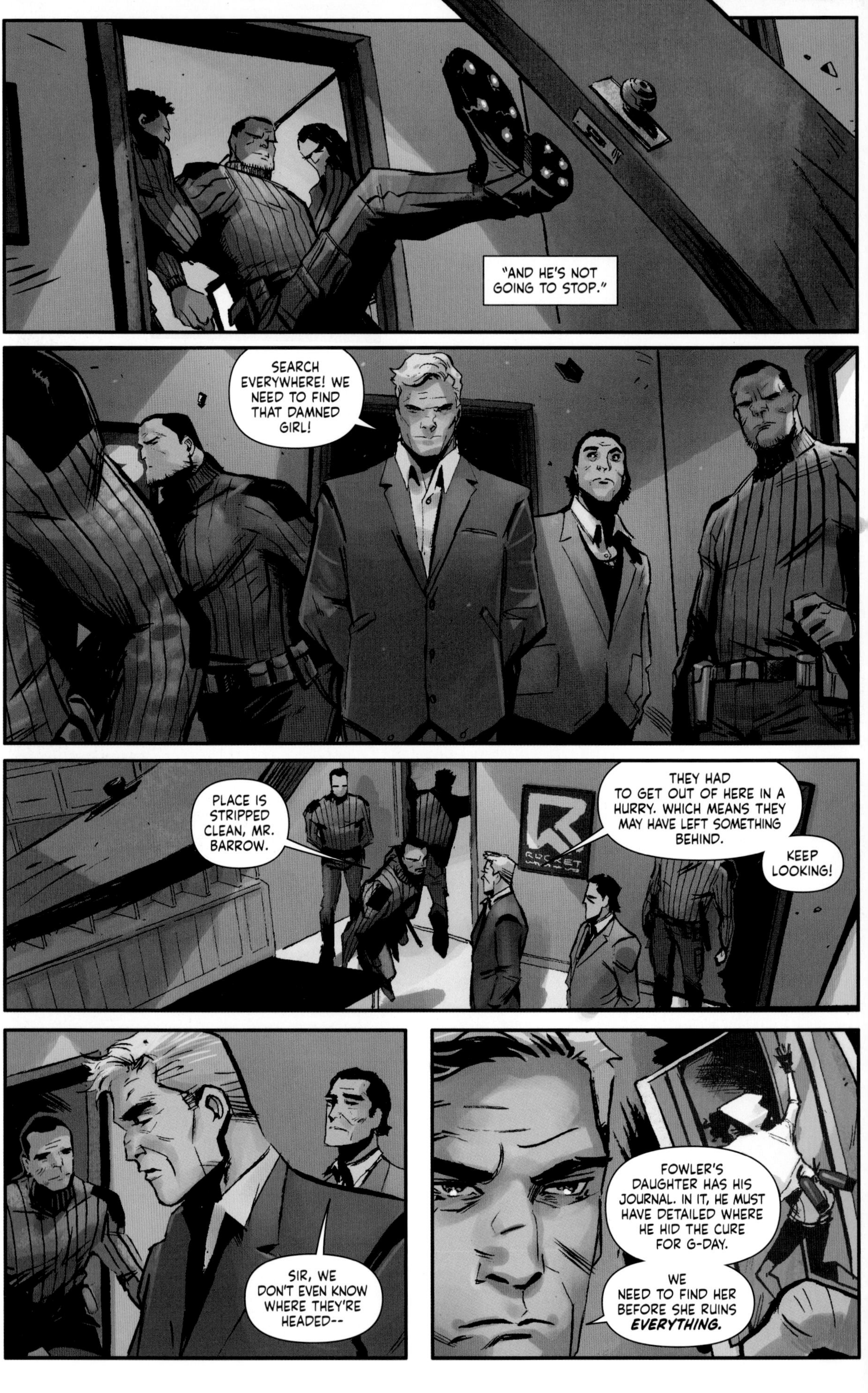
"AND HE'S NOT GOING TO STOP."
SEARCH EVERYWHERE! WE NEED TO FIND THAT DAMNED GIRL!
PLACE IS STRIPPED CLEAN, MR. BARROW.
THEY HAD TO GET OUT OF HERE IN A HURRY. WHICH MEANS THEY MAY HAVE LEFT SOMETHING BEHIND.
KEEP LOOKING!
ROCKET
SIR, WE DON'T EVEN KNOW WHERE THEY'RE HEADED--
FOWLER'S DAUGHTER HAS HIS JOURNAL. IN IT, HE MUST HAVE DETAILED WHERE HE HID THE CURE FOR G-DAY.
WE NEED TO FIND HER BEFORE SHE RUINS *EVERYTHING.*

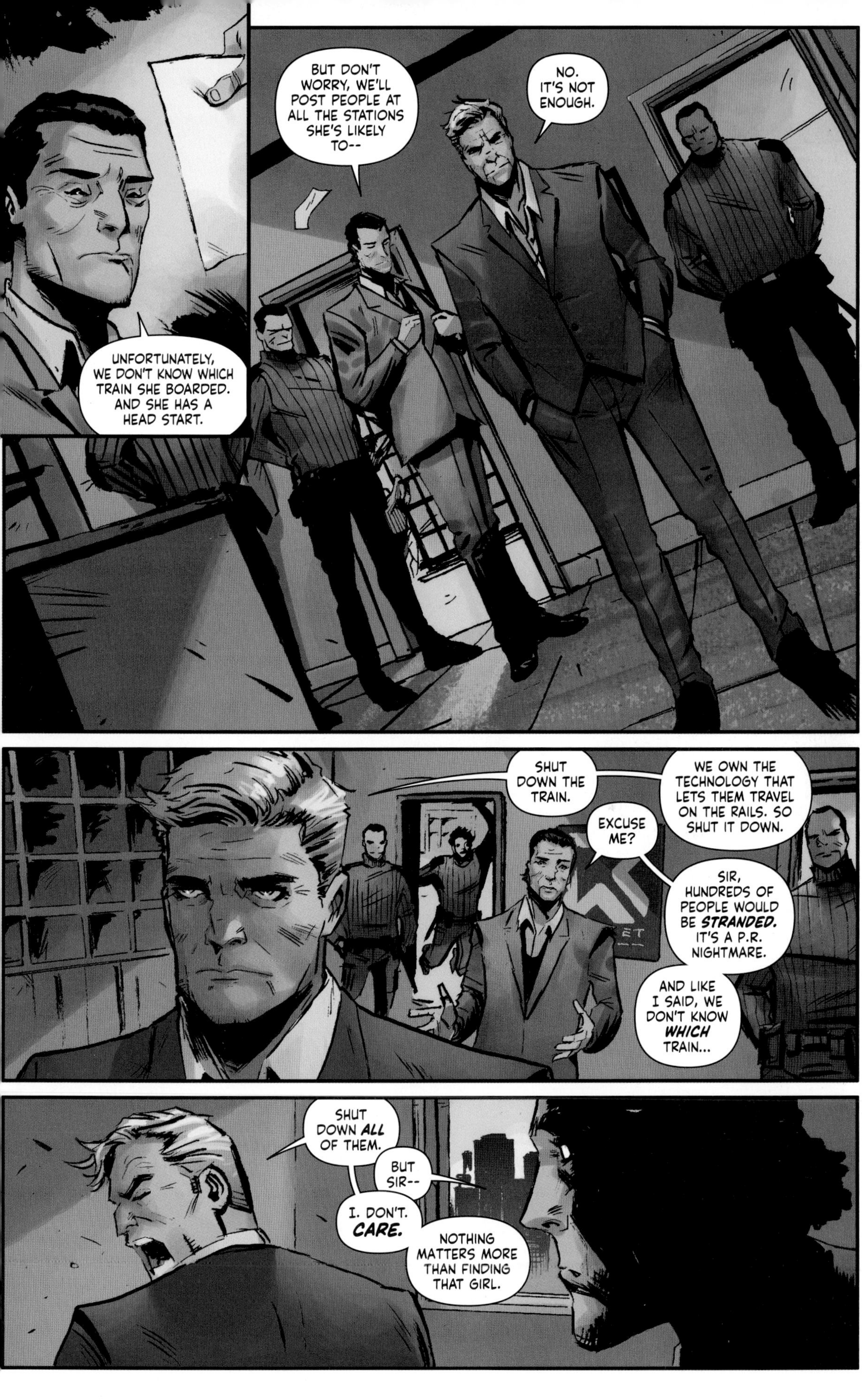
UNFORTUNATELY, WE DON'T KNOW WHICH TRAIN SHE BOARDED. AND SHE HAS A HEAD START.
BUT DON'T WORRY, WE'LL POST PEOPLE AT ALL THE STATIONS SHE'S LIKELY TO--
NO. IT'S NOT ENOUGH.
SHUT DOWN THE TRAIN.
WE OWN THE TECHNOLOGY THAT LETS THEM TRAVEL ON THE RAILS. SO SHUT IT DOWN.
EXCUSE ME?
SIR, HUNDREDS OF PEOPLE WOULD BE **STRANDED.** IT'S A P.R. NIGHTMARE.
AND LIKE I SAID, WE DON'T KNOW ***WHICH*** TRAIN...
SHUT DOWN ***ALL*** OF THEM.
BUT SIR--
I. DON'T. ***CARE.***
NOTHING MATTERS MORE THAN FINDING THAT GIRL.

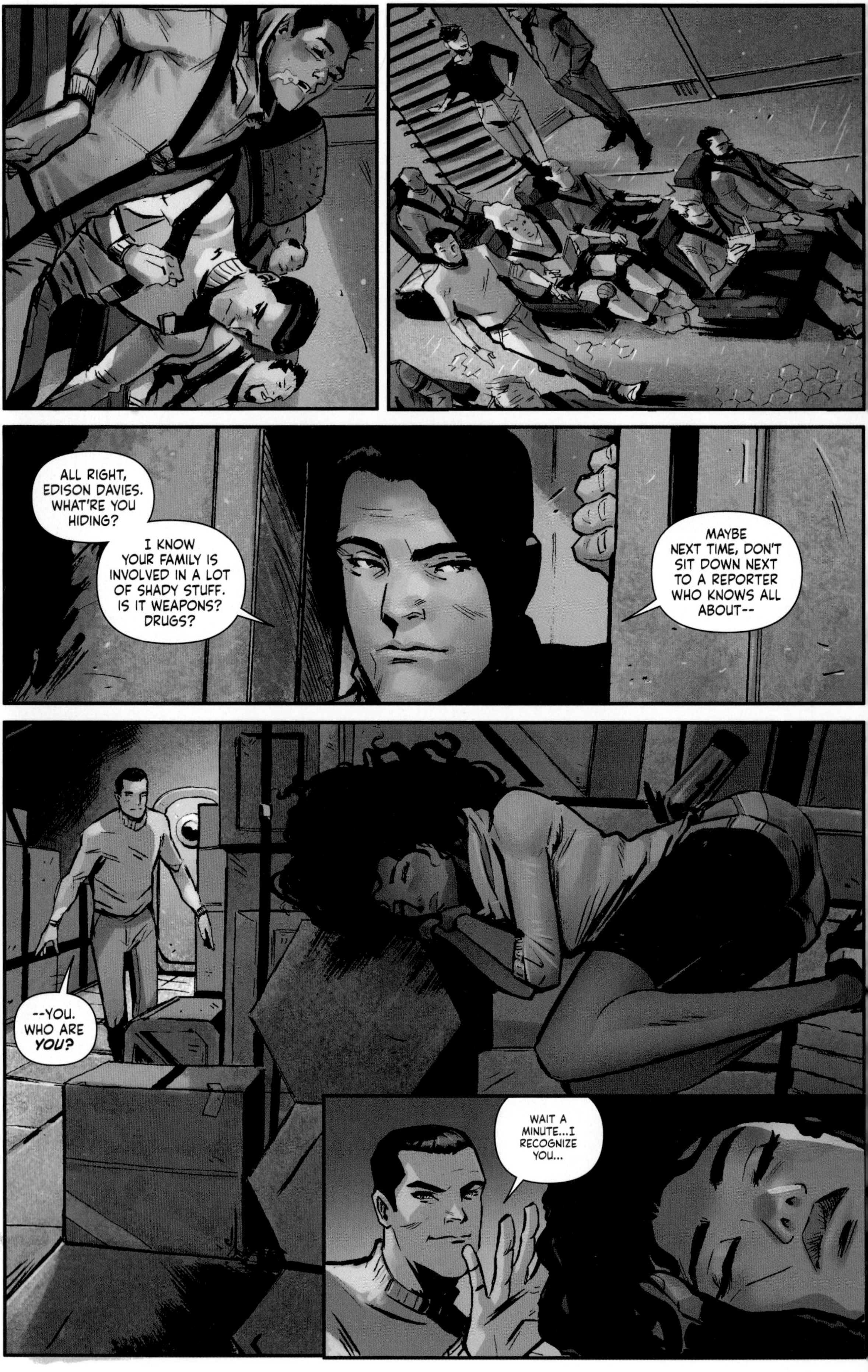
ALL RIGHT, EDISON DAVIES. WHAT'RE YOU HIDING?
I KNOW YOUR FAMILY IS INVOLVED IN A LOT OF SHADY STUFF. IS IT WEAPONS? DRUGS?
MAYBE NEXT TIME, DON'T SIT DOWN NEXT TO A REPORTER WHO KNOWS ALL ABOUT--
--YOU. WHO ARE *YOU?*
WAIT A MINUTE...I RECOGNIZE YOU...

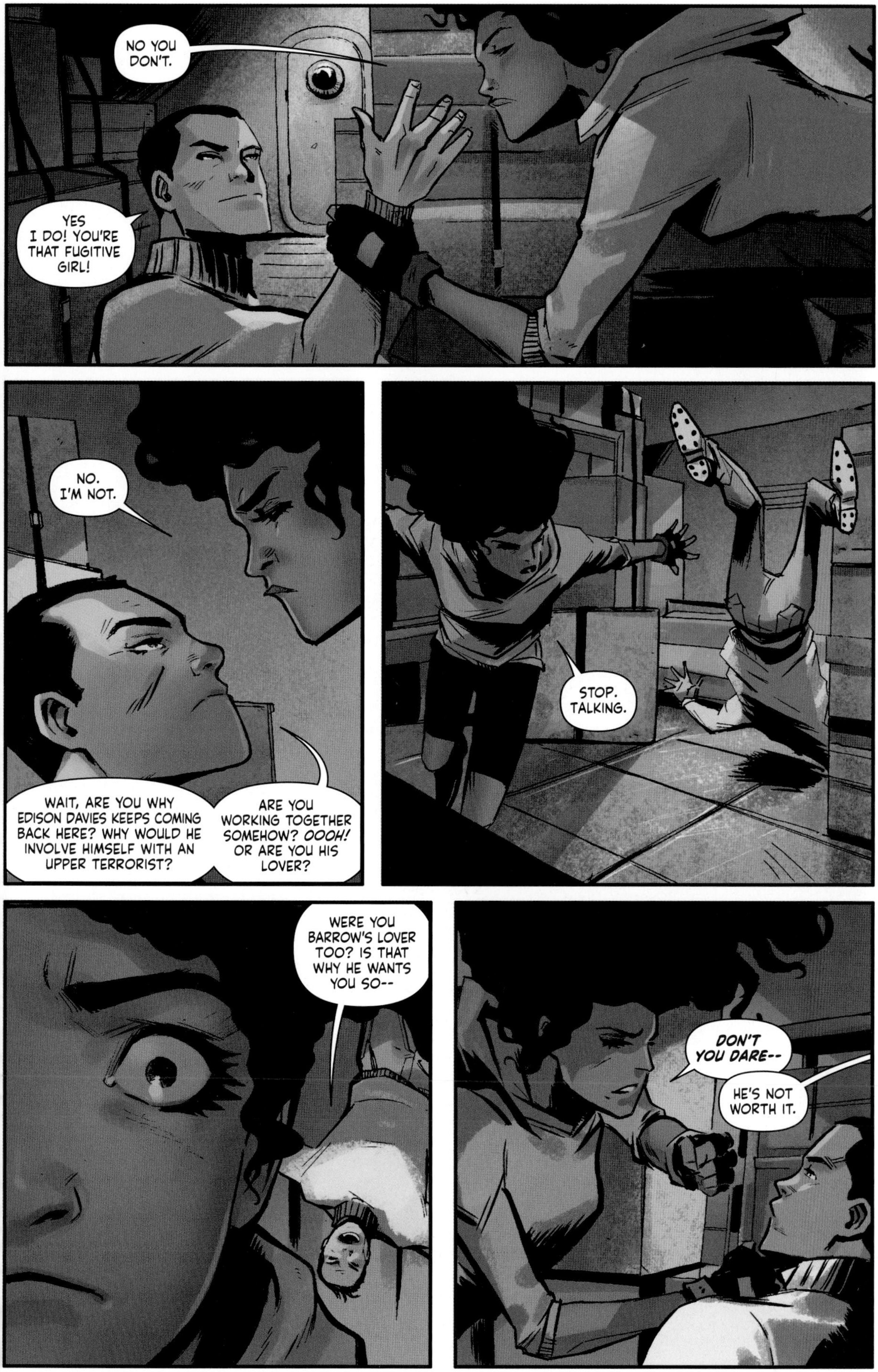
NO YOU DON'T.
YES I DO! YOU'RE THAT FUGITIVE GIRL!
NO. I'M NOT.
WAIT, ARE YOU WHY EDISON DAVIES KEEPS COMING BACK HERE? WHY WOULD HE INVOLVE HIMSELF WITH AN UPPER TERRORIST?
ARE YOU WORKING TOGETHER SOMEHOW? OOOH! OR ARE YOU HIS LOVER?
STOP. TALKING.
WERE YOU BARROW'S LOVER TOO? IS THAT WHY HE WANTS YOU SO--
DON'T YOU DARE--
HE'S NOT WORTH IT.

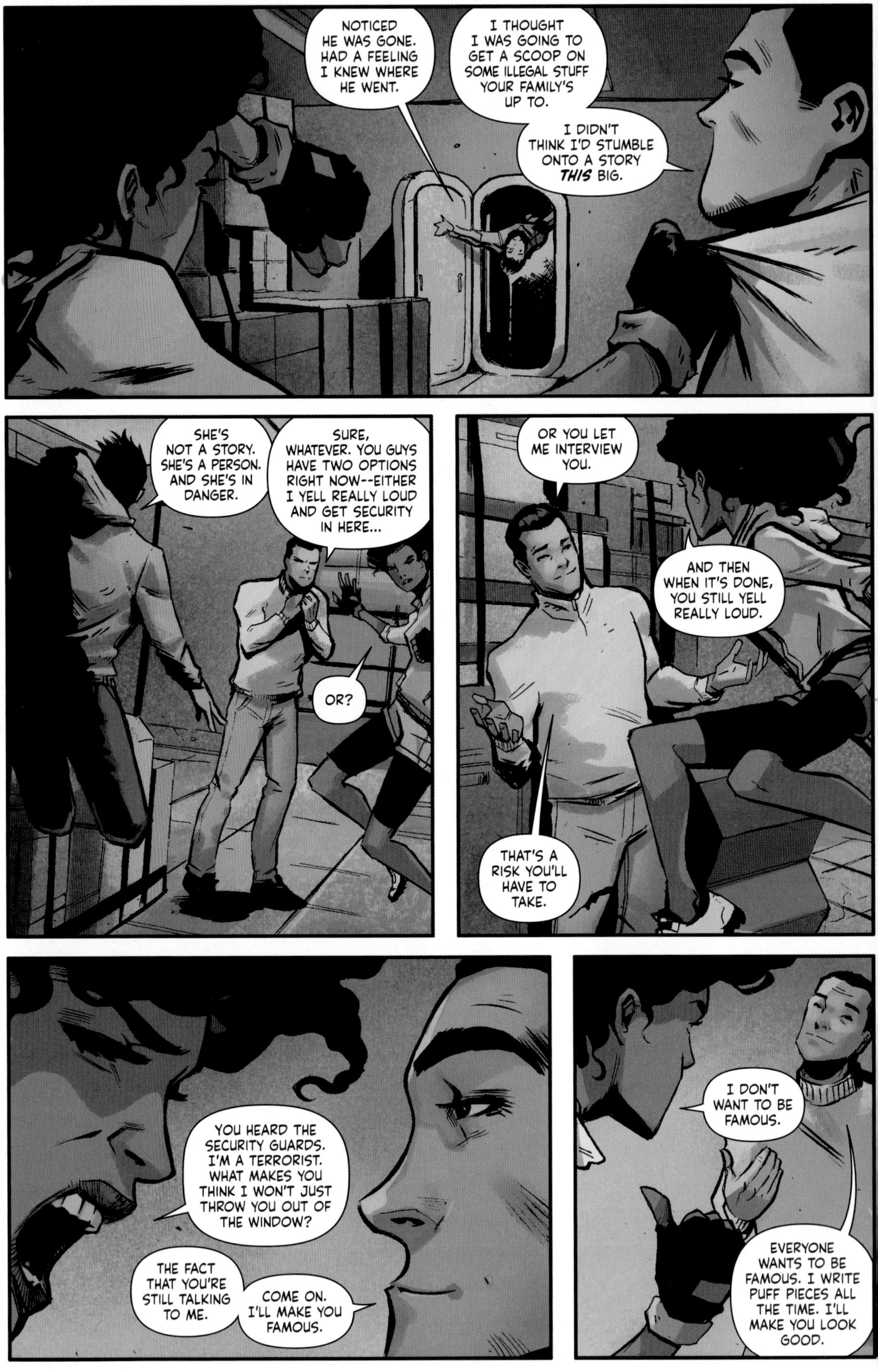
NOTICED HE WAS GONE. HAD A FEELING I KNEW WHERE HE WENT.
I THOUGHT I WAS GOING TO GET A SCOOP ON SOME ILLEGAL STUFF YOUR FAMILY'S UP TO.
I DIDN'T THINK I'D STUMBLE ONTO A STORY THIS BIG.
SHE'S NOT A STORY. SHE'S A PERSON. AND SHE'S IN DANGER.
SURE, WHATEVER. YOU GUYS HAVE TWO OPTIONS RIGHT NOW--EITHER I YELL REALLY LOUD AND GET SECURITY IN HERE...
OR?
OR YOU LET ME INTERVIEW YOU.
AND THEN WHEN IT'S DONE, YOU STILL YELL REALLY LOUD.
THAT'S A RISK YOU'LL HAVE TO TAKE.
YOU HEARD THE SECURITY GUARDS. I'M A TERRORIST. WHAT MAKES YOU THINK I WON'T JUST THROW YOU OUT OF THE WINDOW?
THE FACT THAT YOU'RE STILL TALKING TO ME.
COME ON. I'LL MAKE YOU FAMOUS.
I DON'T WANT TO BE FAMOUS.
EVERYONE WANTS TO BE FAMOUS. I WRITE PUFF PIECES ALL THE TIME. I'LL MAKE YOU LOOK GOOD.

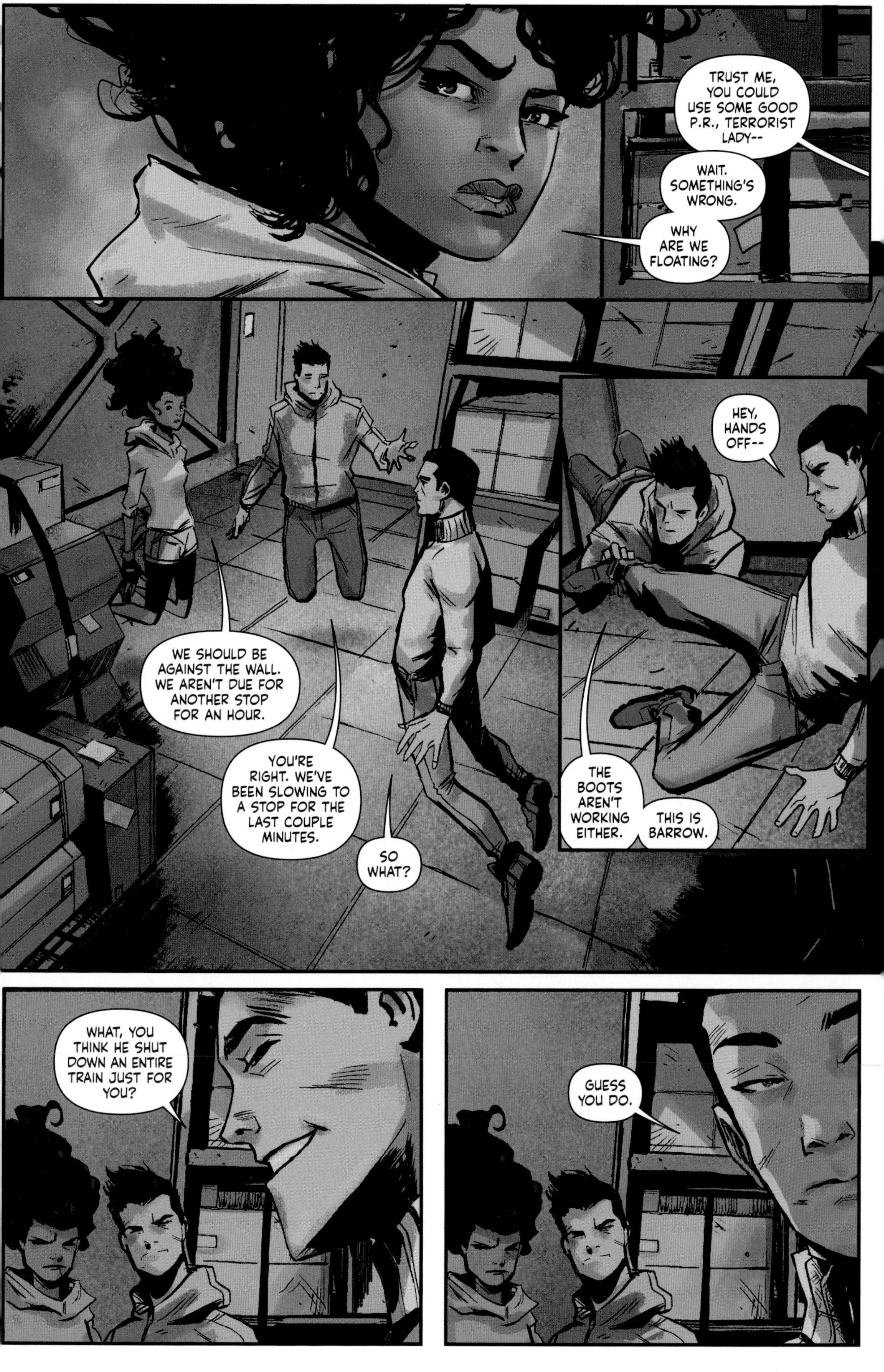

TRUST ME, YOU COULD USE SOME GOOD P.R., TERRORIST LADY--
WAIT. SOMETHING'S WRONG.
WHY ARE WE FLOATING?
WE SHOULD BE AGAINST THE WALL. WE AREN'T DUE FOR ANOTHER STOP FOR AN HOUR.
YOU'RE RIGHT. WE'VE BEEN SLOWING TO A STOP FOR THE LAST COUPLE MINUTES.
SO WHAT?
HEY, HANDS OFF--
THE BOOTS AREN'T WORKING EITHER.
THIS IS BARROW.
WHAT, YOU THINK HE SHUT DOWN AN ENTIRE TRAIN JUST FOR YOU?
GUESS YOU DO.

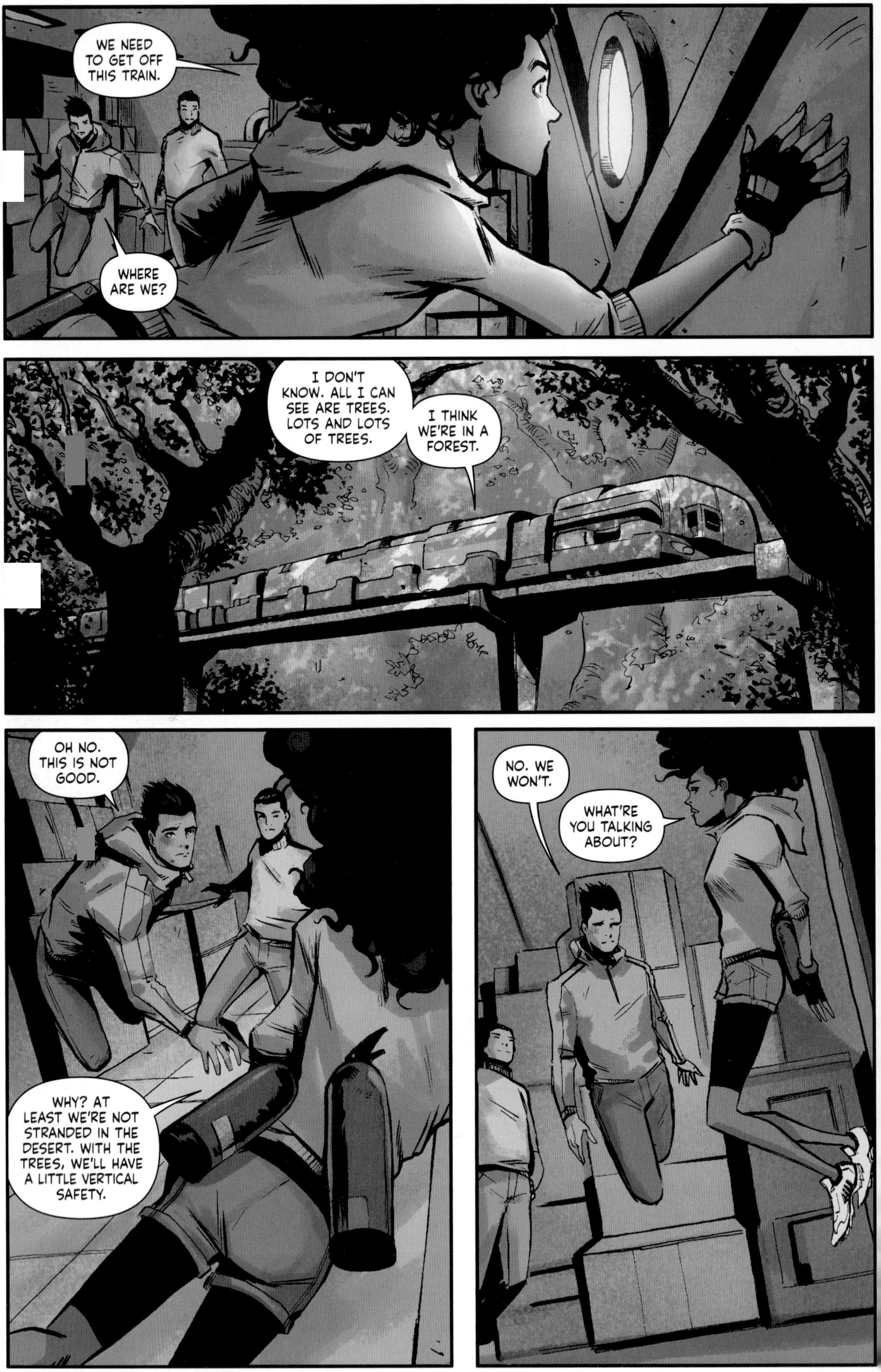
WE NEED TO GET OFF THIS TRAIN.
WHERE ARE WE?
I DON'T KNOW. ALL I CAN SEE ARE TREES. LOTS AND LOTS OF TREES.
I THINK WE'RE IN A FOREST.
OH NO. THIS IS NOT GOOD.
WHY? AT LEAST WE'RE NOT STRANDED IN THE DESERT. WITH THE TREES, WE'LL HAVE A LITTLE VERTICAL SAFETY.
NO. WE WON'T.
WHAT'RE YOU TALKING ABOUT?

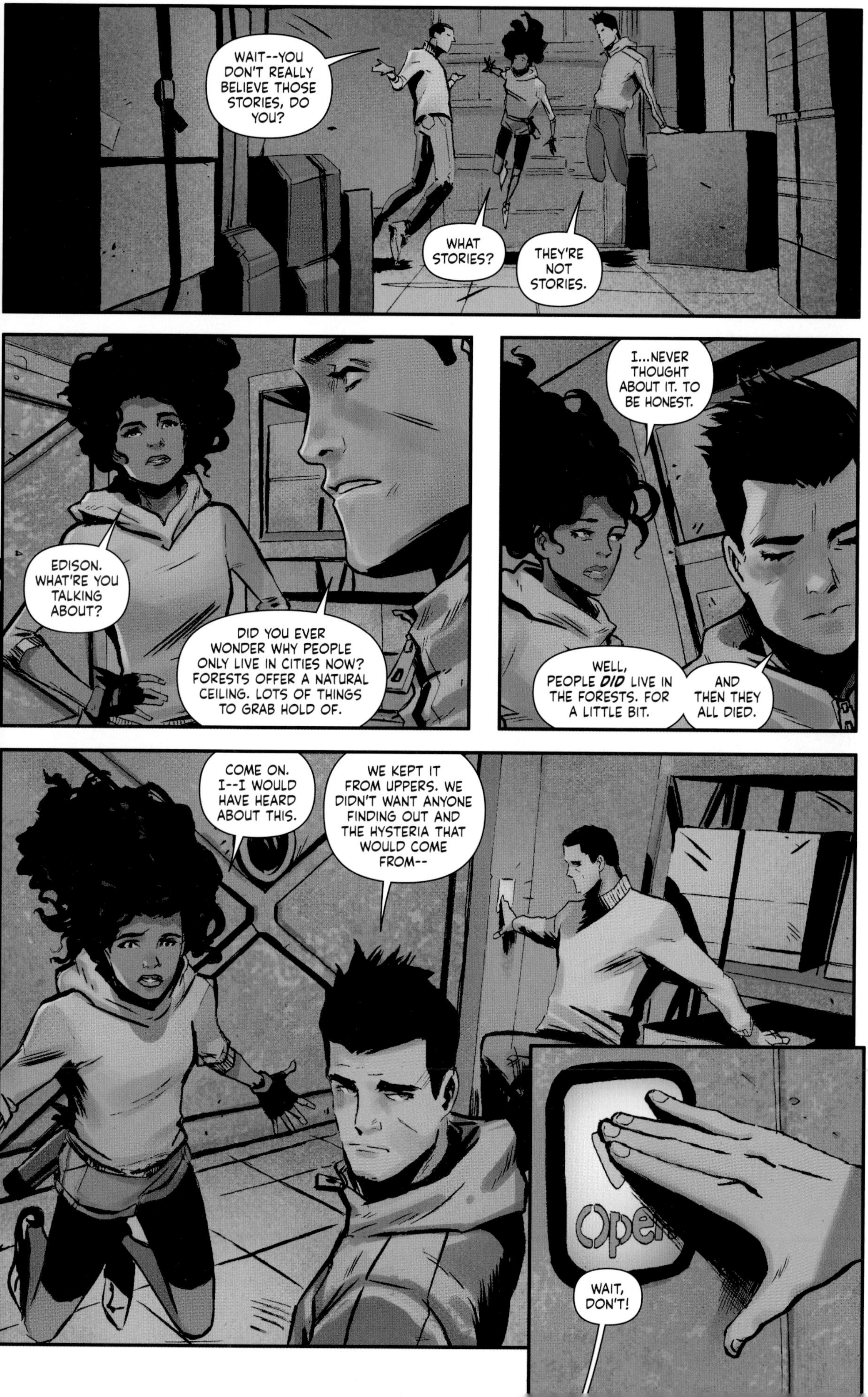
WAIT--YOU DON'T REALLY BELIEVE THOSE STORIES, DO YOU?
WHAT STORIES?
THEY'RE NOT STORIES.
EDISON. WHAT'RE YOU TALKING ABOUT?
DID YOU EVER WONDER WHY PEOPLE ONLY LIVE IN CITIES NOW? FORESTS OFFER A NATURAL CEILING. LOTS OF THINGS TO GRAB HOLD OF.
I...NEVER THOUGHT ABOUT IT. TO BE HONEST.
WELL, PEOPLE *DID* LIVE IN THE FORESTS. FOR A LITTLE BIT.
AND THEN THEY ALL DIED.
COME ON. I--I WOULD HAVE HEARD ABOUT THIS.
WE KEPT IT FROM UPPERS. WE DIDN'T WANT ANYONE FINDING OUT AND THE HYSTERIA THAT WOULD COME FROM--
WAIT, DON'T!

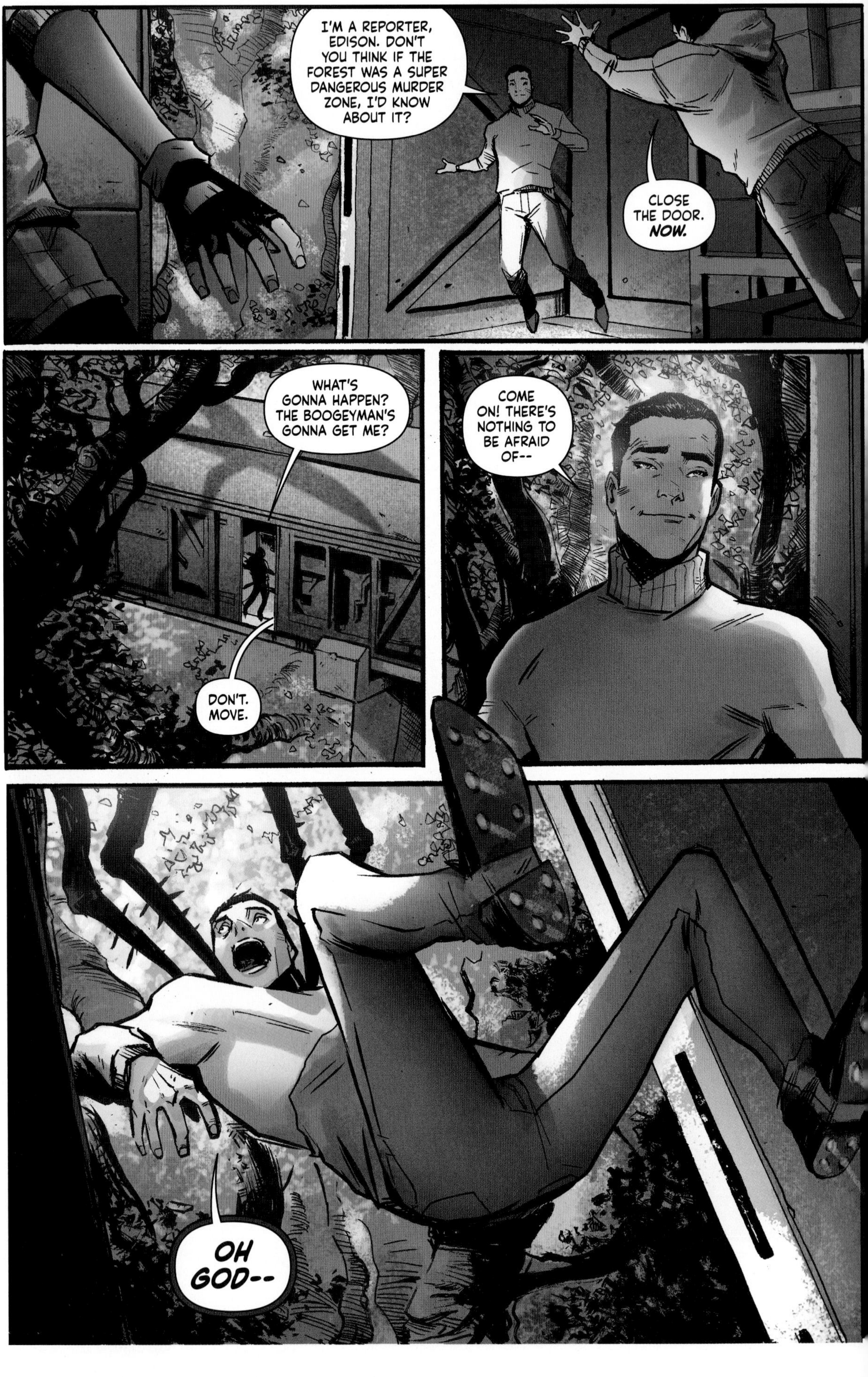
I'M A REPORTER, EDISON. DON'T YOU THINK IF THE FOREST WAS A SUPER DANGEROUS MURDER ZONE, I'D KNOW ABOUT IT?
CLOSE THE DOOR. *NOW.*
WHAT'S GONNA HAPPEN? THE BOOGEYMAN'S GONNA GET ME?
DON'T. MOVE.
COME ON! THERE'S NOTHING TO BE AFRAID OF--
OH GOD--

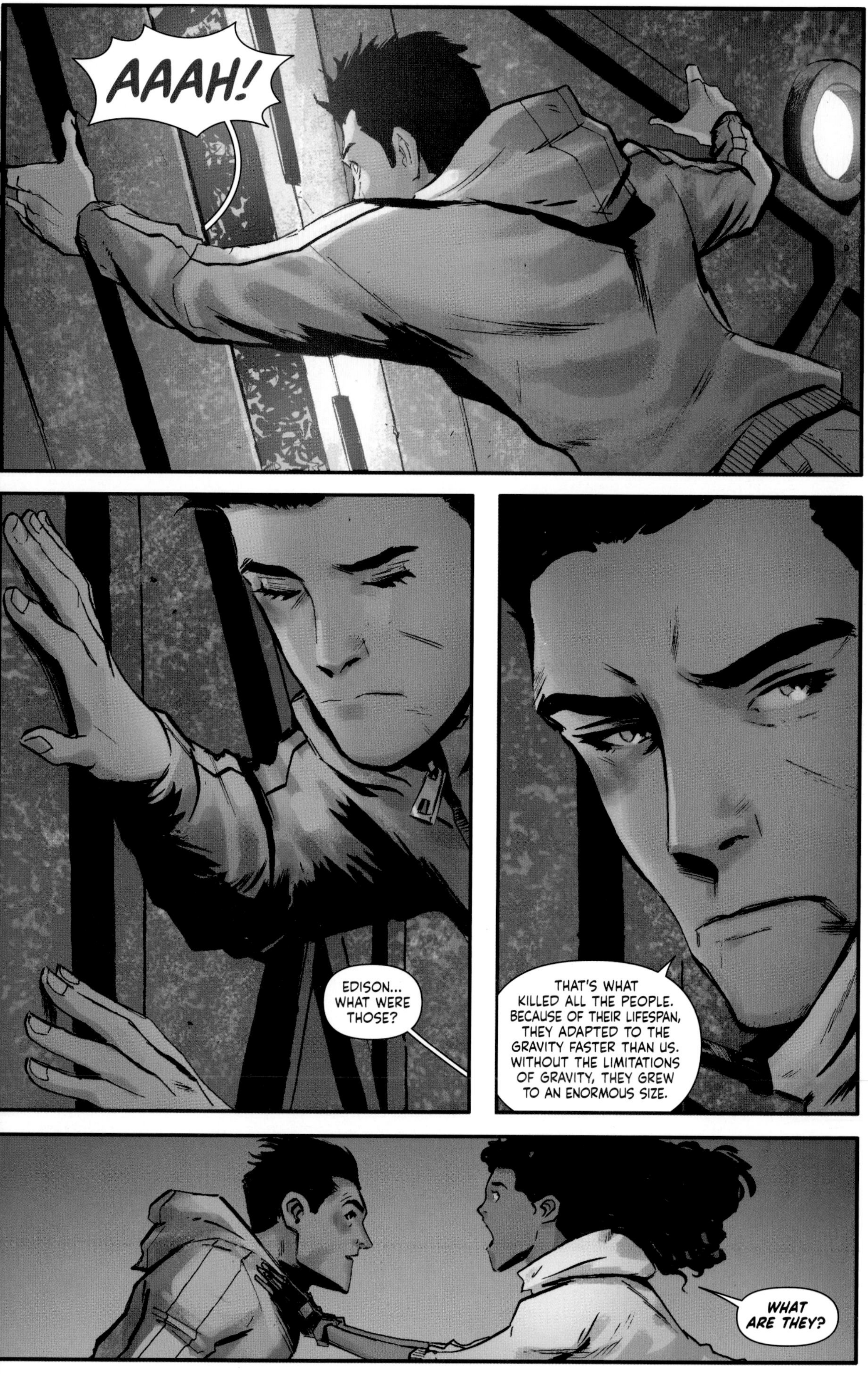
AAAH!
EDISON... WHAT WERE THOSE?
THAT'S WHAT KILLED ALL THE PEOPLE. BECAUSE OF THEIR LIFESPAN, THEY ADAPTED TO THE GRAVITY FASTER THAN US. WITHOUT THE LIMITATIONS OF GRAVITY, THEY GREW TO AN ENORMOUS SIZE.
WHAT ARE THEY?

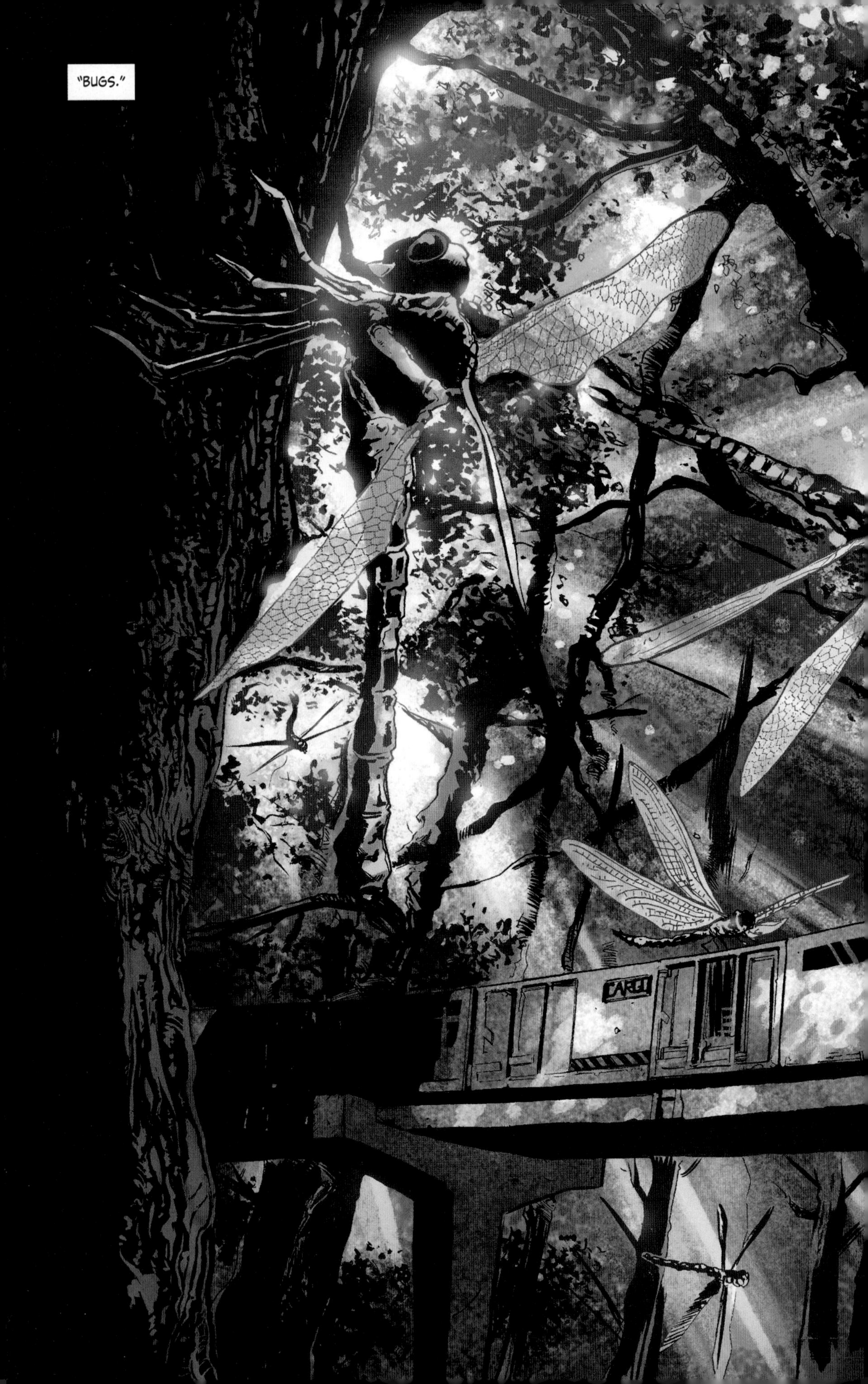
"BUGS."
CARGO

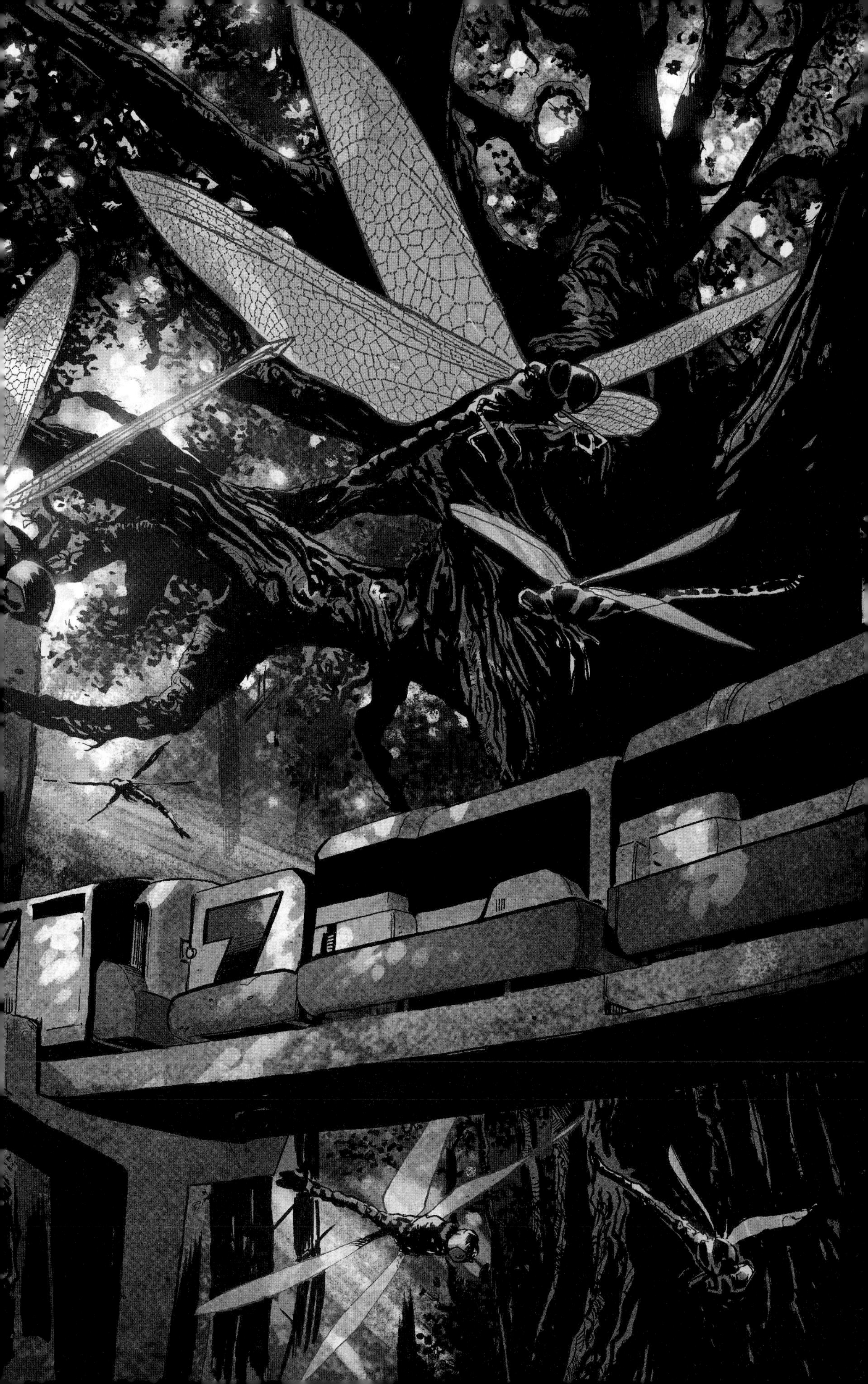
7

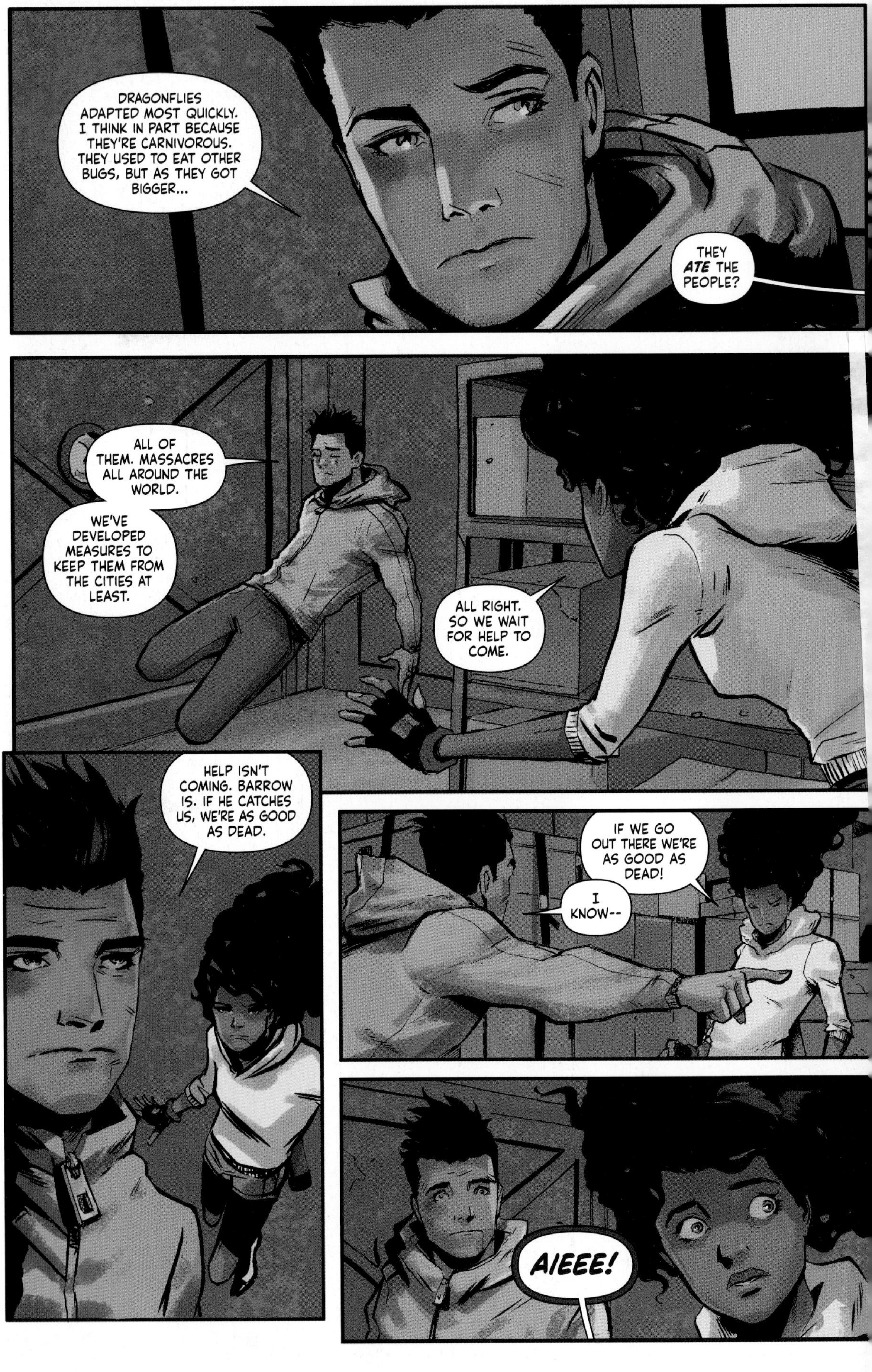
DRAGONFLIES ADAPTED MOST QUICKLY. I THINK IN PART BECAUSE THEY'RE CARNIVOROUS. THEY USED TO EAT OTHER BUGS, BUT AS THEY GOT BIGGER...
THEY *ATE* THE PEOPLE?
ALL OF THEM. MASSACRES ALL AROUND THE WORLD.
WE'VE DEVELOPED MEASURES TO KEEP THEM FROM THE CITIES AT LEAST.
ALL RIGHT. SO WE WAIT FOR HELP TO COME.
HELP ISN'T COMING. BARROW IS. IF HE CATCHES US, WE'RE AS GOOD AS DEAD.
IF WE GO OUT THERE WE'RE AS GOOD AS DEAD!
I KNOW--
AIEEE!

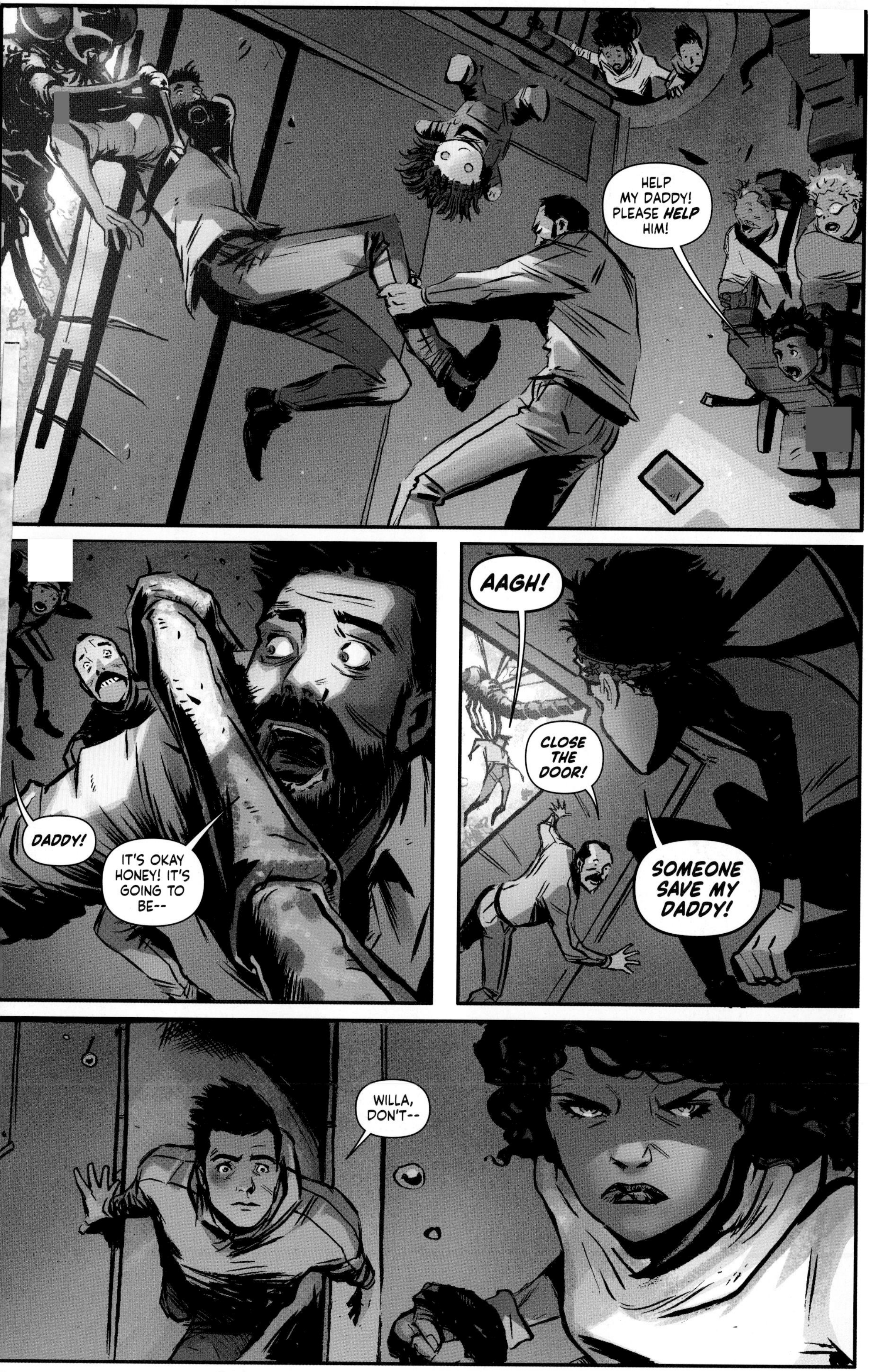
HELP MY DADDY! PLEASE HELP HIM!
DADDY!
IT'S OKAY HONEY! IT'S GOING TO BE--
AAGH!
CLOSE THE DOOR!
SOMEONE SAVE MY DADDY!
WILLA, DON'T--

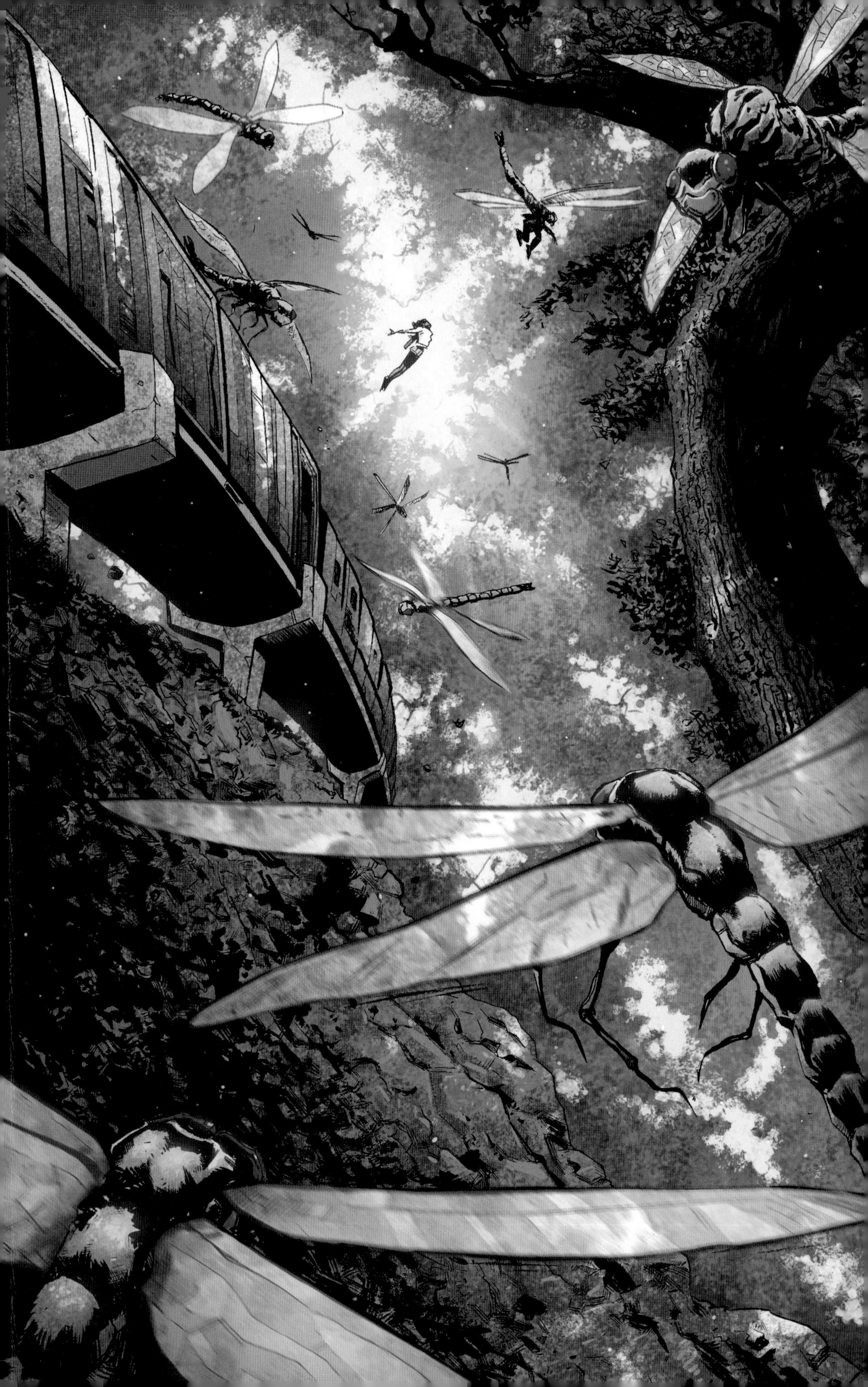

END CHAPTER SIX

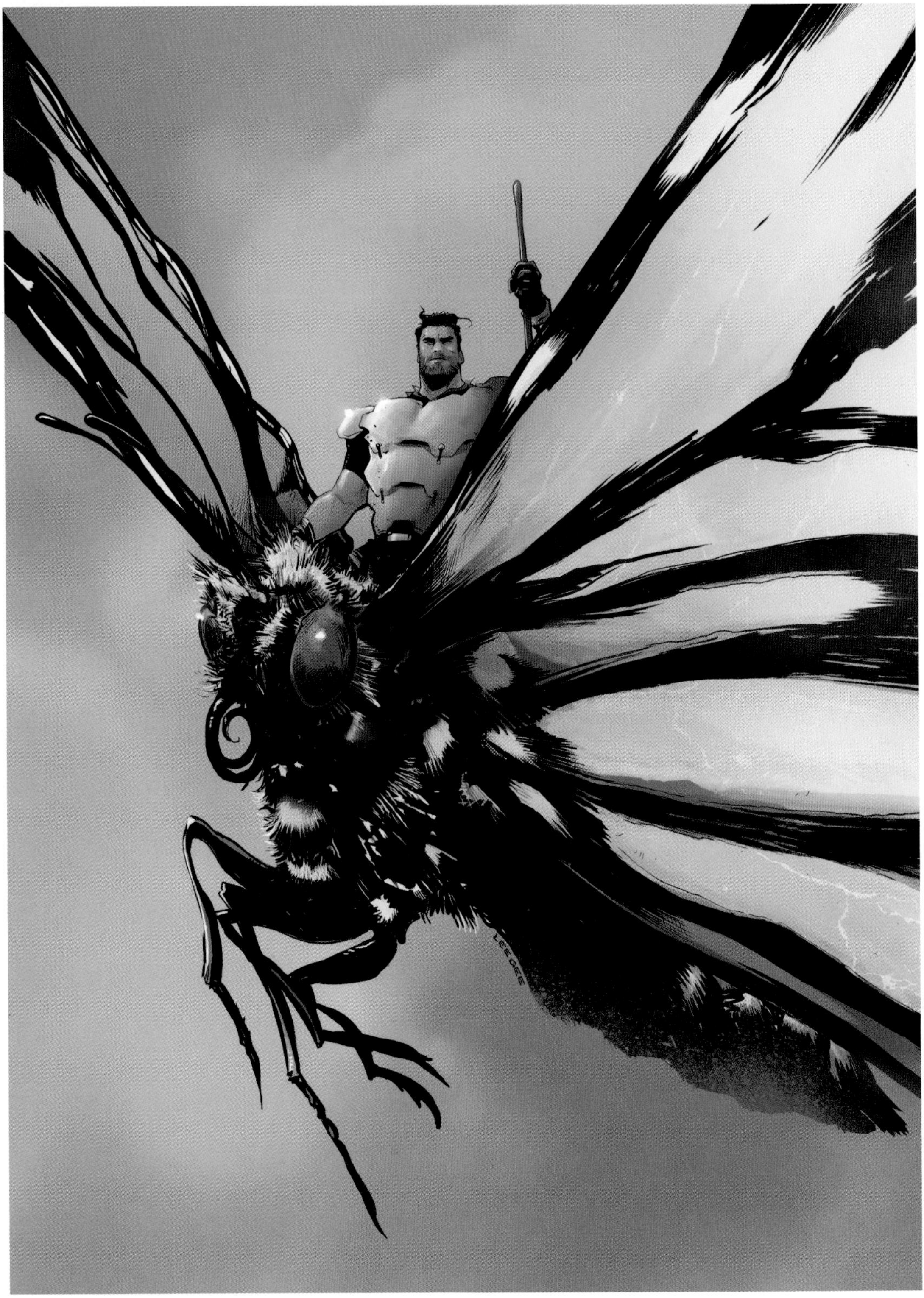

CHAPTER SEVEN

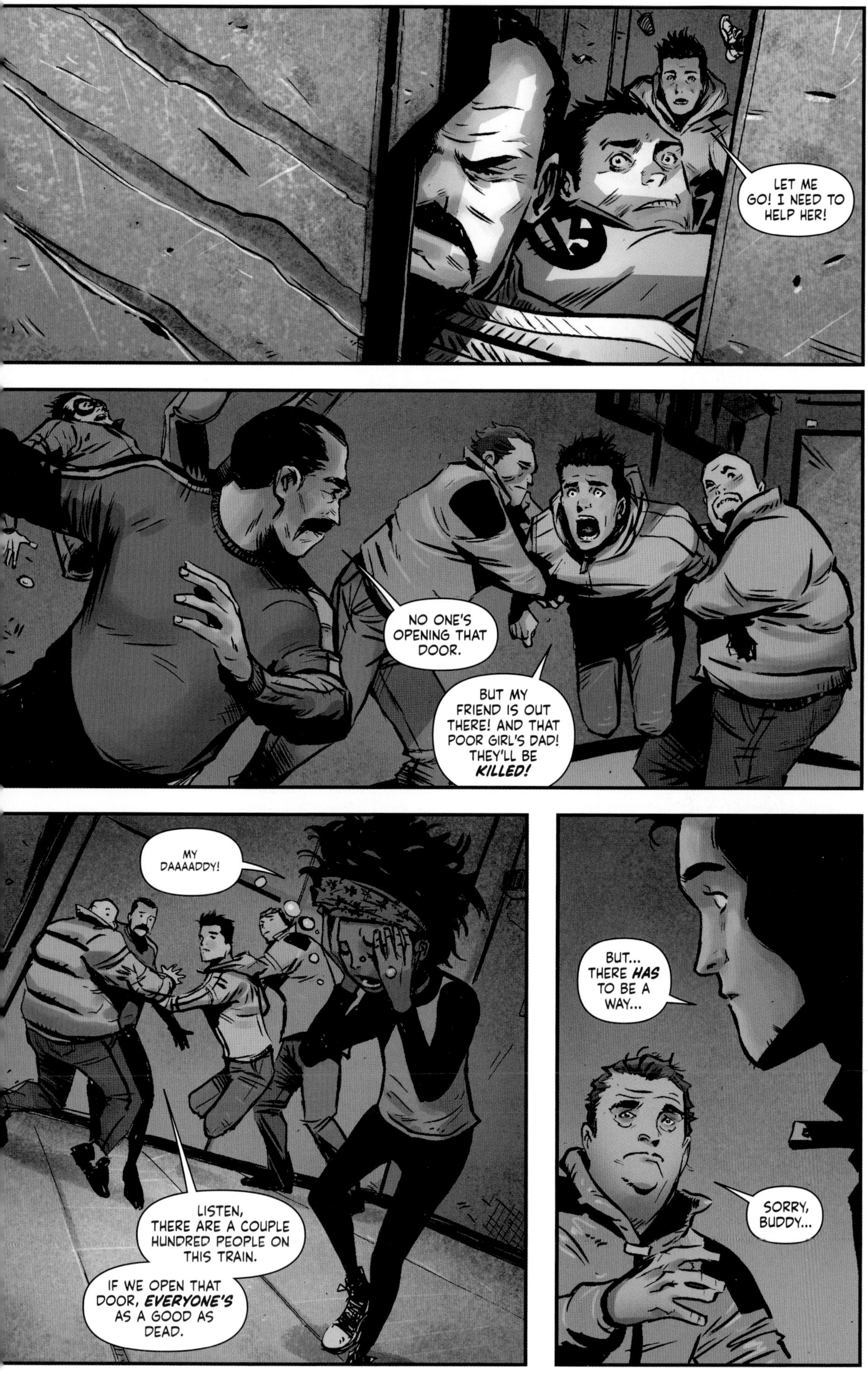
LET ME GO! I NEED TO HELP HER!
NO ONE'S OPENING THAT DOOR.
BUT MY FRIEND IS OUT THERE! AND THAT POOR GIRL'S DAD! THEY'LL BE KILLED!
MY DAAAADDY!
LISTEN, THERE ARE A COUPLE HUNDRED PEOPLE ON THIS TRAIN.
IF WE OPEN THAT DOOR, EVERYONE'S AS A GOOD AS DEAD.
BUT... THERE HAS TO BE A WAY...
SORRY, BUDDY...

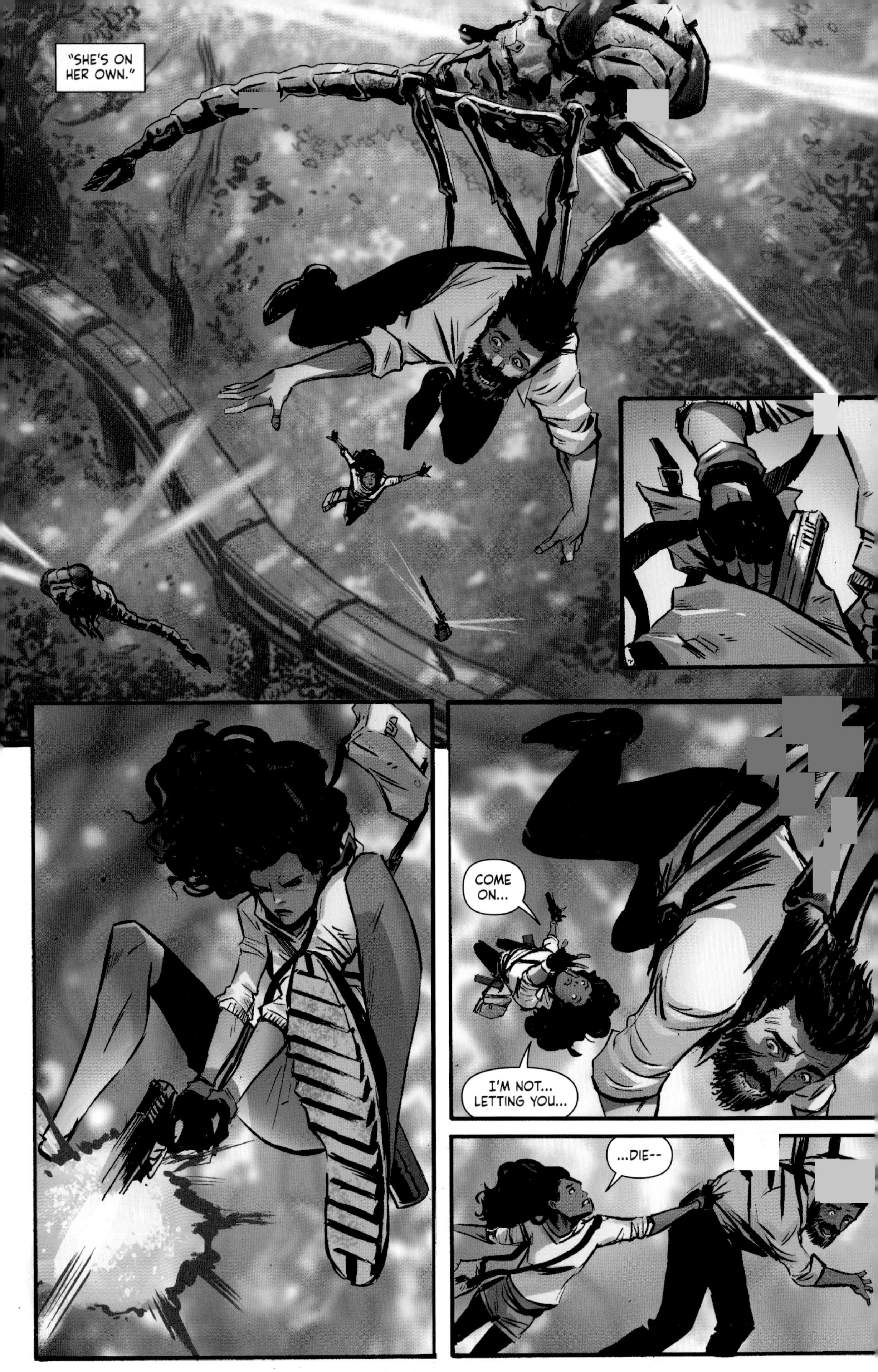
"SHE'S ON HER OWN."
COME ON...
I'M NOT... LETTING YOU...
...DIE--

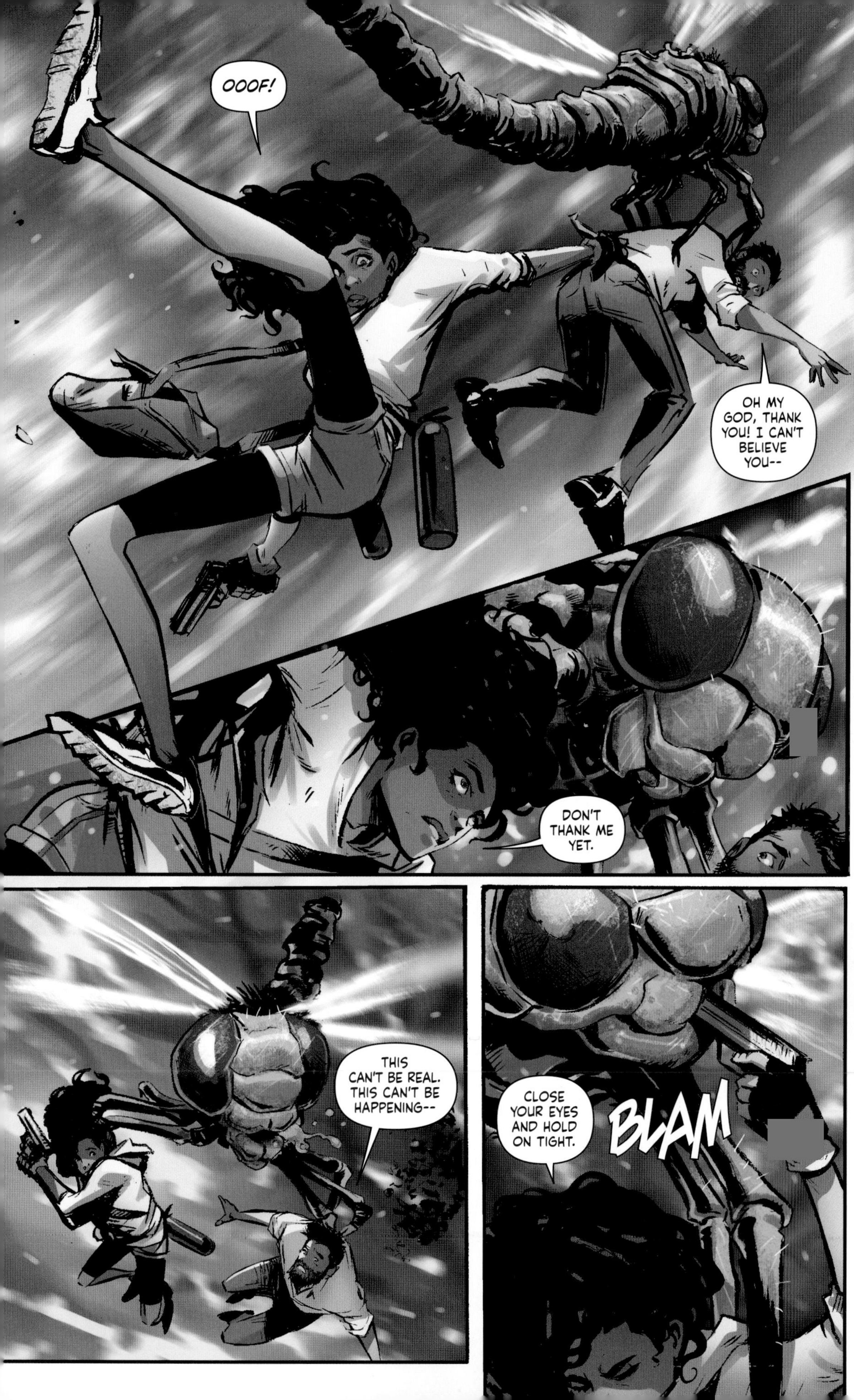
OOOF!
OH MY GOD, THANK YOU! I CAN'T BELIEVE YOU--
DON'T THANK ME YET.
THIS CAN'T BE REAL. THIS CAN'T BE HAPPENING--
CLOSE YOUR EYES AND HOLD ON TIGHT.
BLAM

OKAY, NOW--

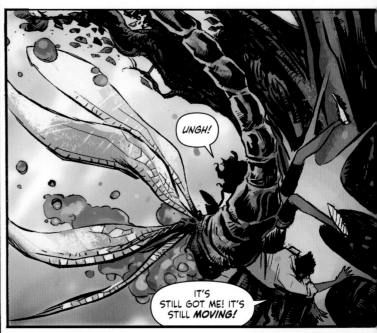

UNGH!

IT'S STILL GOT ME! IT'S STILL *MOVING!*

BLAM

COME ON! YOU DON'T HAVE A HEAD! THAT'S NOT FAIR!

OKAY. WELL AT LEAST WE'RE...

...SCREWED.

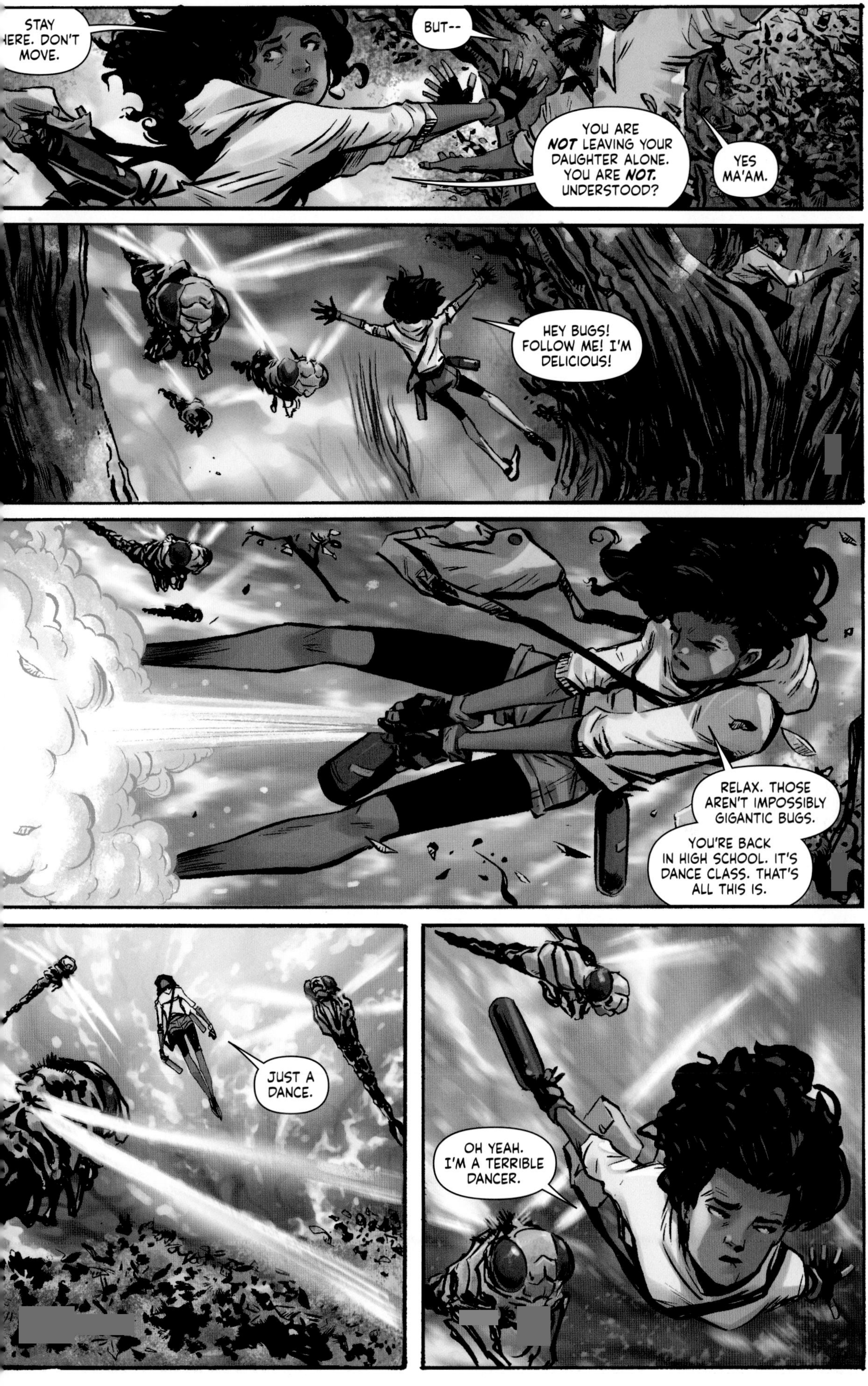
STAY HERE. DON'T MOVE.
BUT--
YOU ARE NOT LEAVING YOUR DAUGHTER ALONE. YOU ARE NOT. UNDERSTOOD?
YES MA'AM.
HEY BUGS! FOLLOW ME! I'M DELICIOUS!
RELAX. THOSE AREN'T IMPOSSIBLY GIGANTIC BUGS.
YOU'RE BACK IN HIGH SCHOOL. IT'S DANCE CLASS. THAT'S ALL THIS IS.
JUST A DANCE.
OH YEAH. I'M A TERRIBLE DANCER.

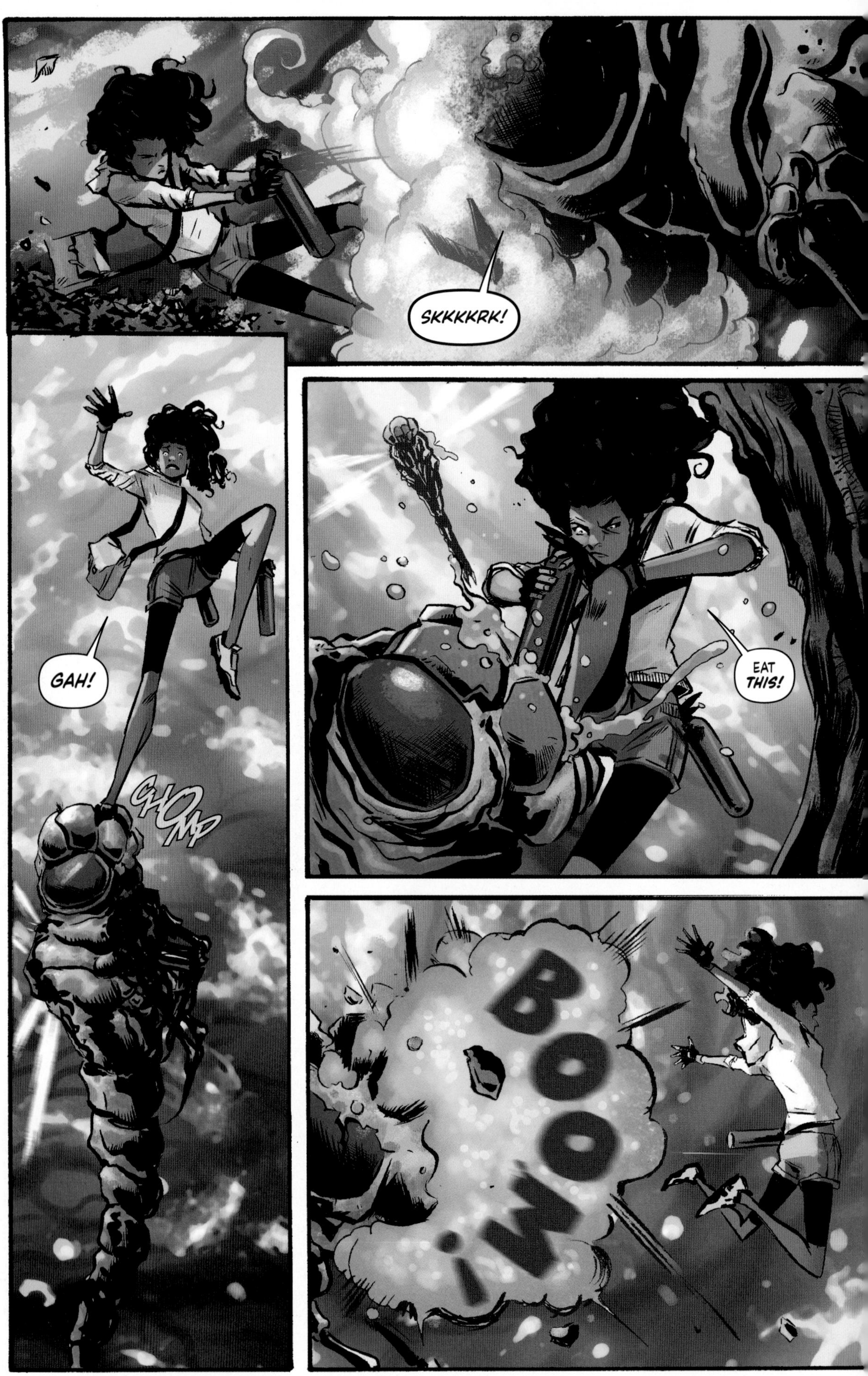
SKKKKRK!
GAH!
CHOMP
EAT THIS!
BOOM!

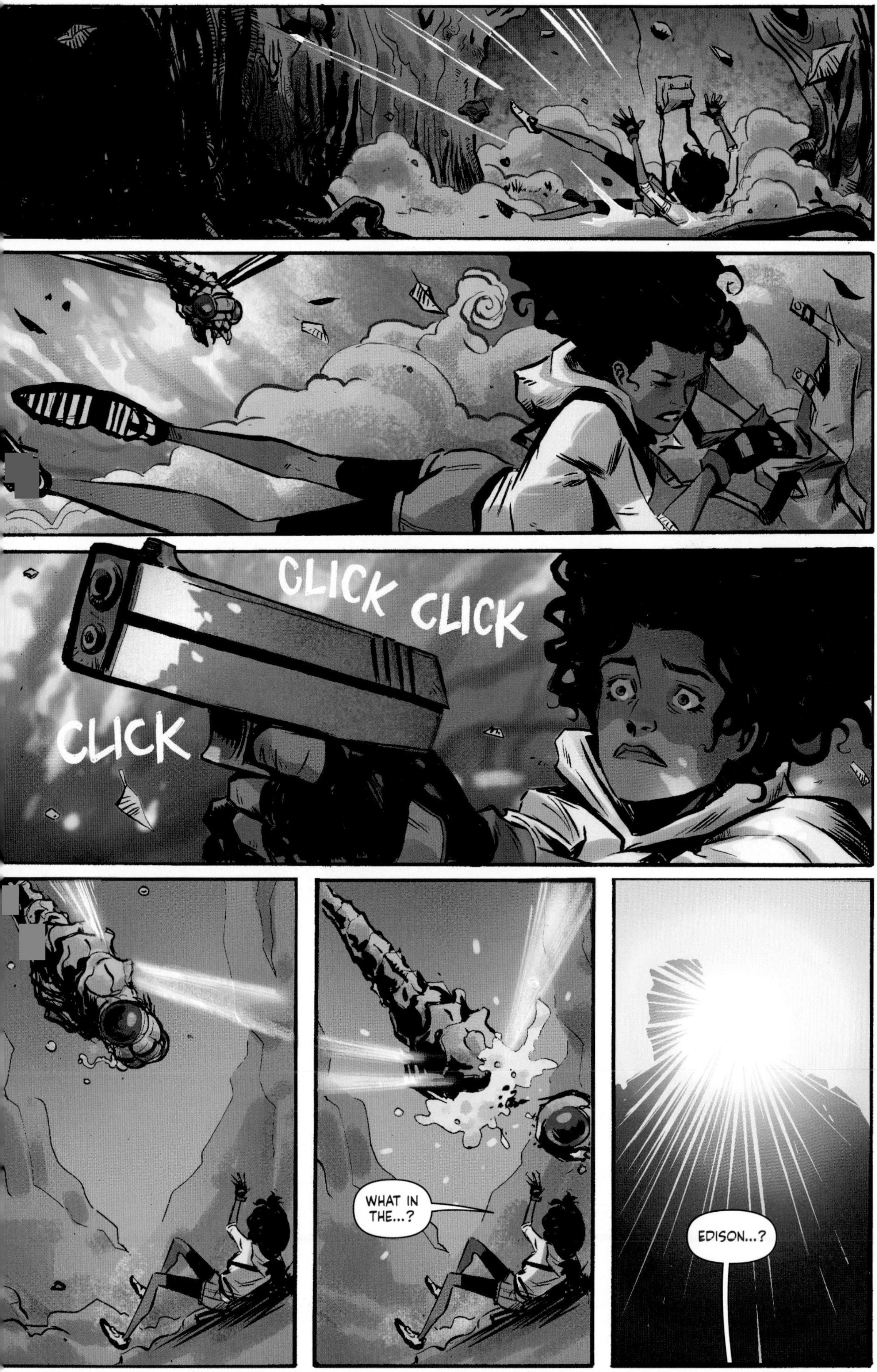
CLICK CLICK
CLICK
WHAT IN THE...?
EDISON...?

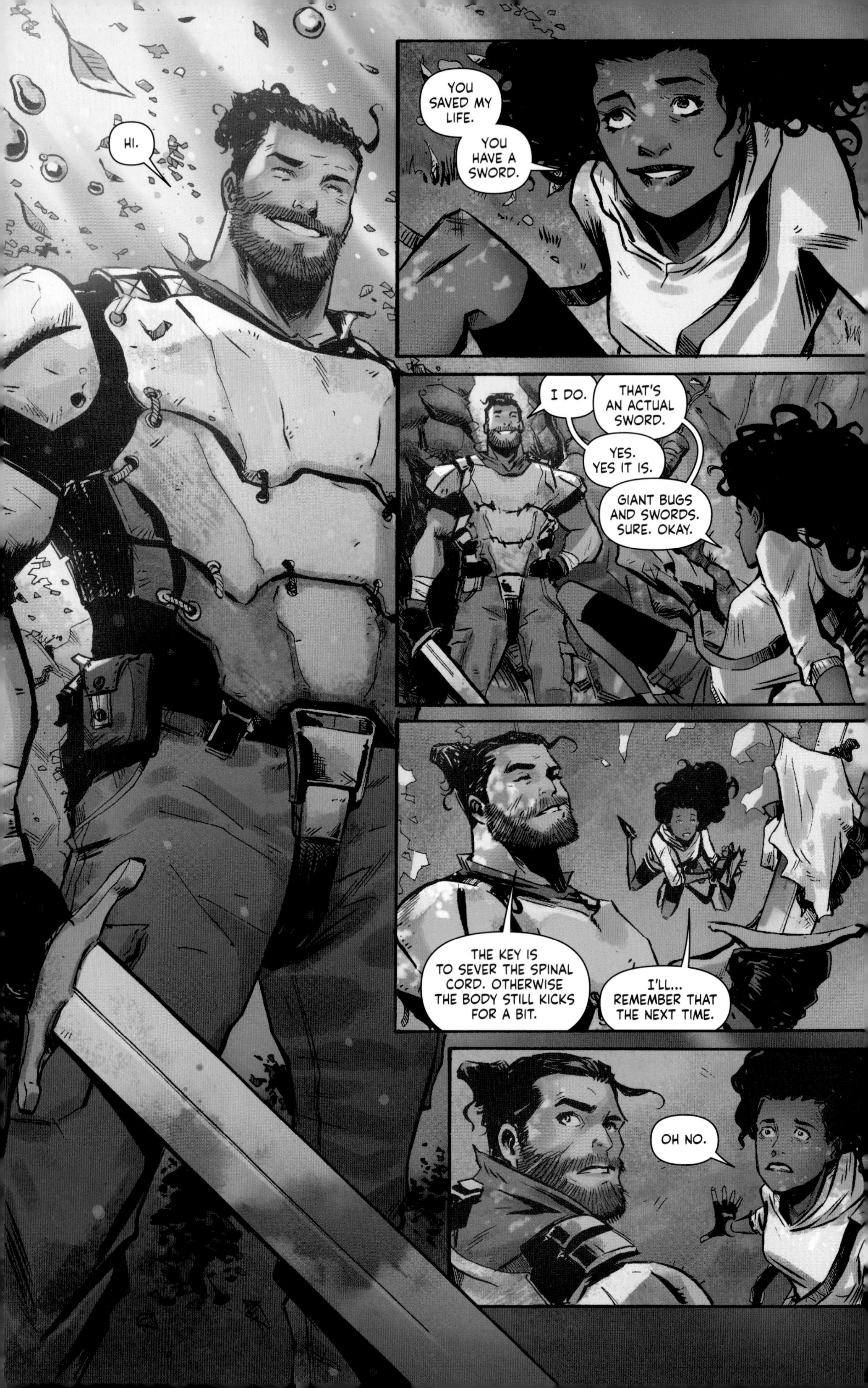
HI.
YOU SAVED MY LIFE.
YOU HAVE A SWORD.
I DO.
THAT'S AN ACTUAL SWORD.
YES. YES IT IS.
GIANT BUGS AND SWORDS. SURE. OKAY.
THE KEY IS TO SEVER THE SPINAL CORD. OTHERWISE THE BODY STILL KICKS FOR A BIT.
I'LL... REMEMBER THAT THE NEXT TIME.
OH NO.

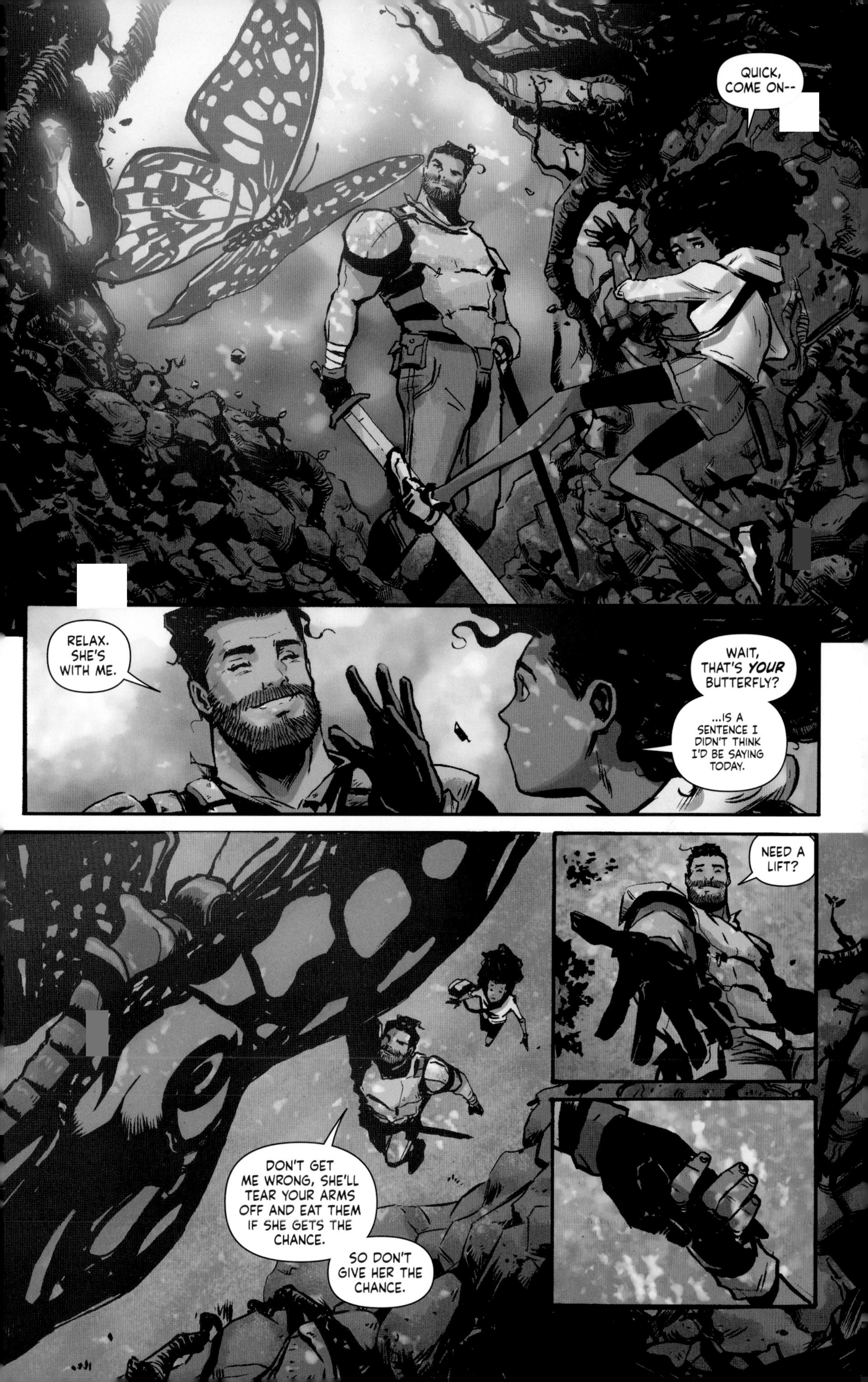
QUICK, COME ON--
RELAX. SHE'S WITH ME.
WAIT, THAT'S *YOUR* BUTTERFLY?
...IS A SENTENCE I DIDN'T THINK I'D BE SAYING TODAY.
DON'T GET ME WRONG, SHE'LL TEAR YOUR ARMS OFF AND EAT THEM IF SHE GETS THE CHANCE.
SO DON'T GIVE HER THE CHANCE.
NEED A LIFT?

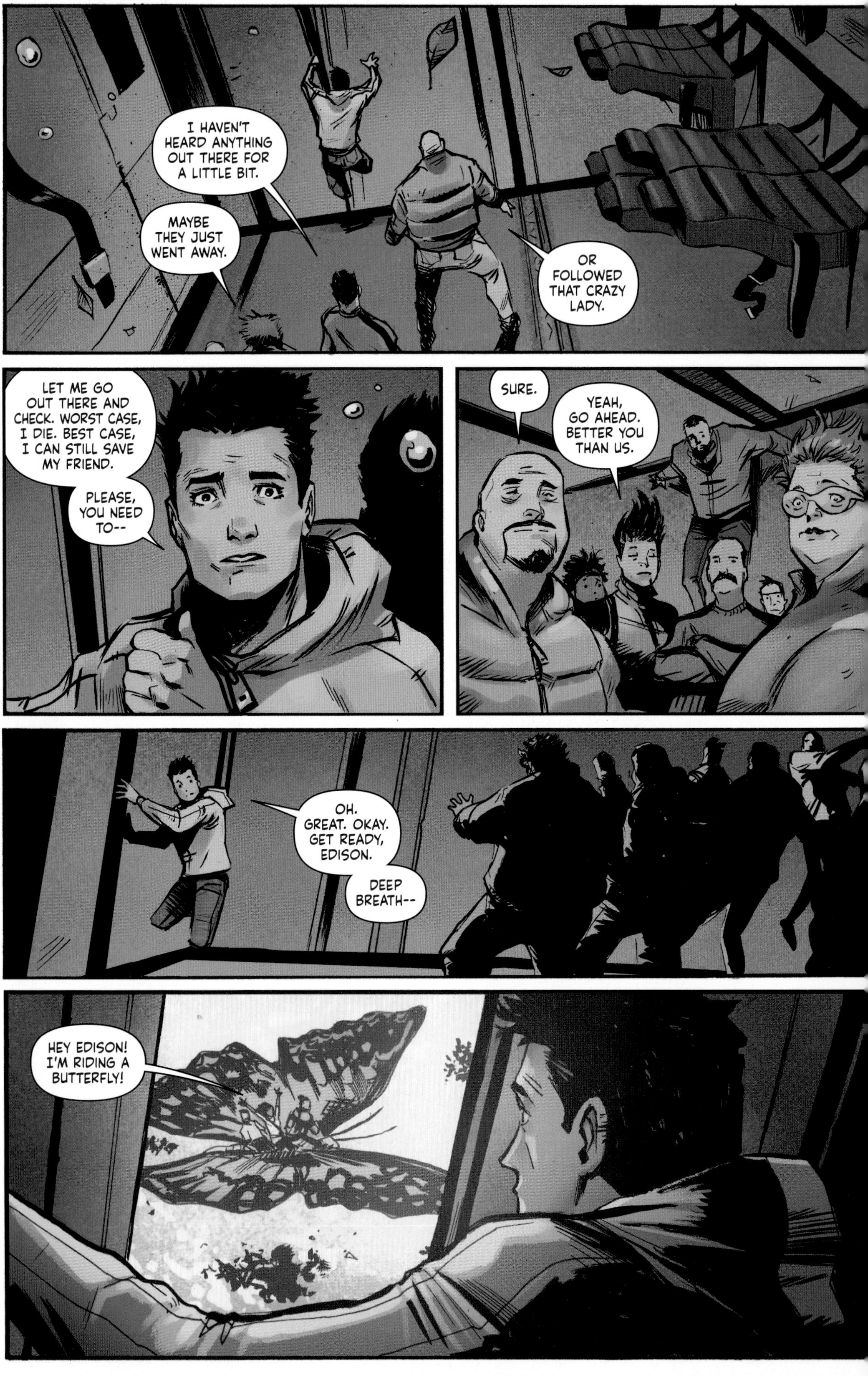
I HAVEN'T HEARD ANYTHING OUT THERE FOR A LITTLE BIT.
MAYBE THEY JUST WENT AWAY.
OR FOLLOWED THAT CRAZY LADY.
LET ME GO OUT THERE AND CHECK. WORST CASE, I DIE. BEST CASE, I CAN STILL SAVE MY FRIEND.
PLEASE, YOU NEED TO--
SURE.
YEAH, GO AHEAD. BETTER YOU THAN US.
OH. GREAT. OKAY. GET READY, EDISON.
DEEP BREATH--
HEY EDISON! I'M RIDING A BUTTERFLY!

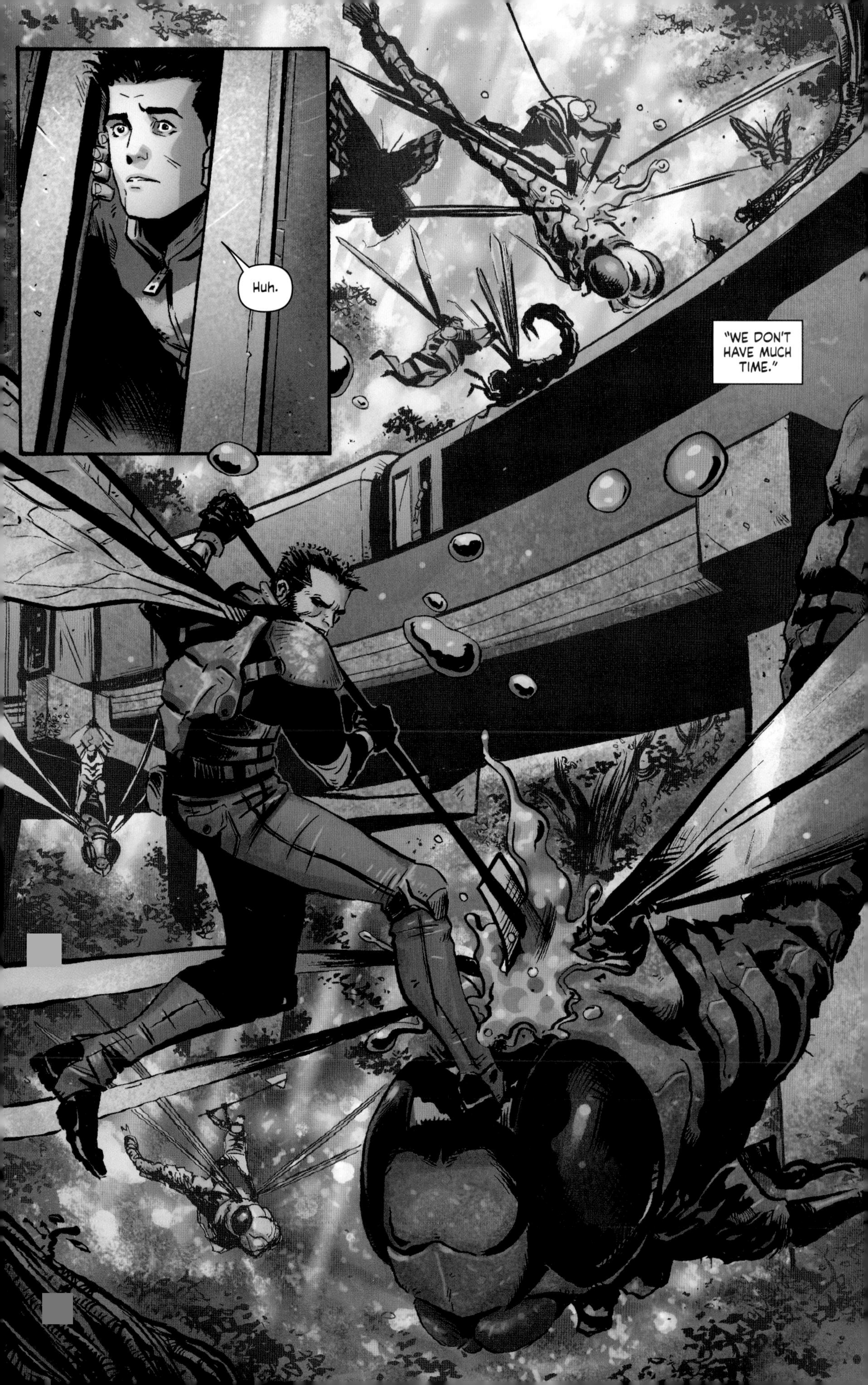
Huh.
"WE DON'T HAVE MUCH TIME."

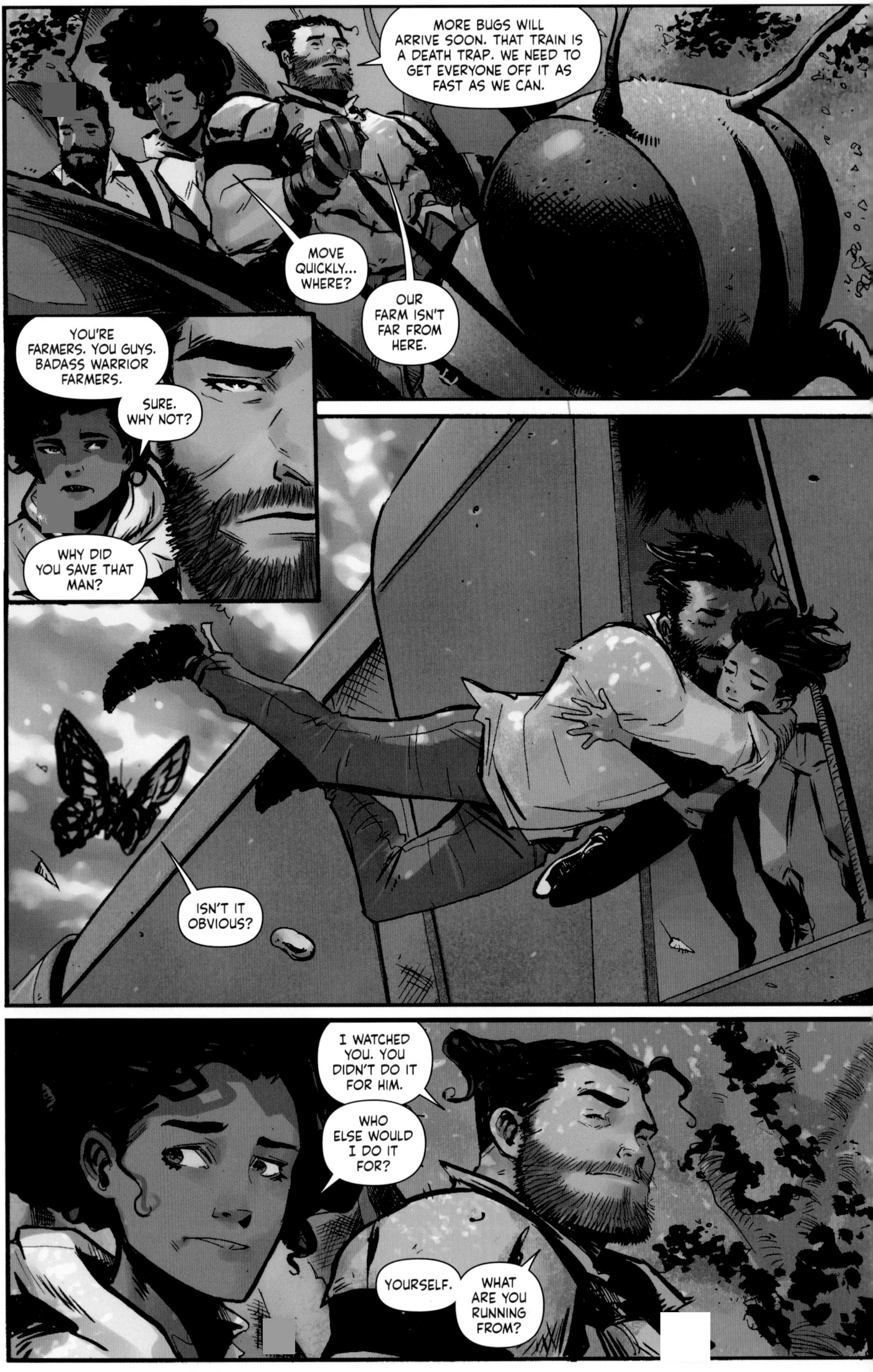
MORE BUGS WILL ARRIVE SOON. THAT TRAIN IS A DEATH TRAP. WE NEED TO GET EVERYONE OFF IT AS FAST AS WE CAN.
MOVE QUICKLY... WHERE?
OUR FARM ISN'T FAR FROM HERE.
YOU'RE FARMERS. YOU GUYS. BADASS WARRIOR FARMERS.
SURE. WHY NOT?
WHY DID YOU SAVE THAT MAN?
ISN'T IT OBVIOUS?
I WATCHED YOU. YOU DIDN'T DO IT FOR HIM.
WHO ELSE WOULD I DO IT FOR?
YOURSELF.
WHAT ARE YOU RUNNING FROM?

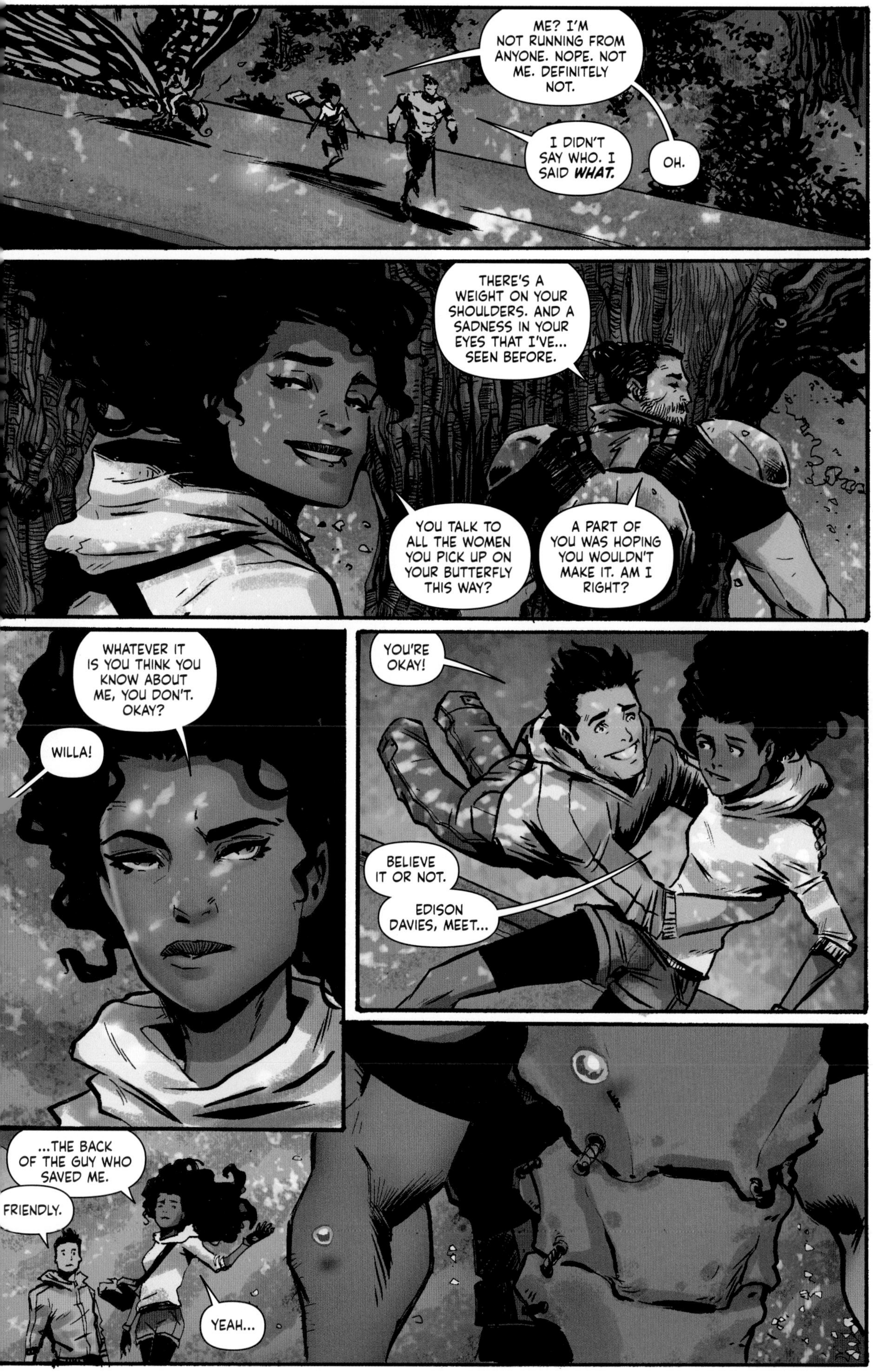
ME? I'M NOT RUNNING FROM ANYONE. NOPE. NOT ME. DEFINITELY NOT.
I DIDN'T SAY WHO. I SAID WHAT.
OH.
THERE'S A WEIGHT ON YOUR SHOULDERS. AND A SADNESS IN YOUR EYES THAT I'VE... SEEN BEFORE.
A PART OF YOU WAS HOPING YOU WOULDN'T MAKE IT. AM I RIGHT?
YOU TALK TO ALL THE WOMEN YOU PICK UP ON YOUR BUTTERFLY THIS WAY?
WHATEVER IT IS YOU THINK YOU KNOW ABOUT ME, YOU DON'T. OKAY?
WILLA!
YOU'RE OKAY!
BELIEVE IT OR NOT.
EDISON DAVIES, MEET...
...THE BACK OF THE GUY WHO SAVED ME.
FRIENDLY.
YEAH...

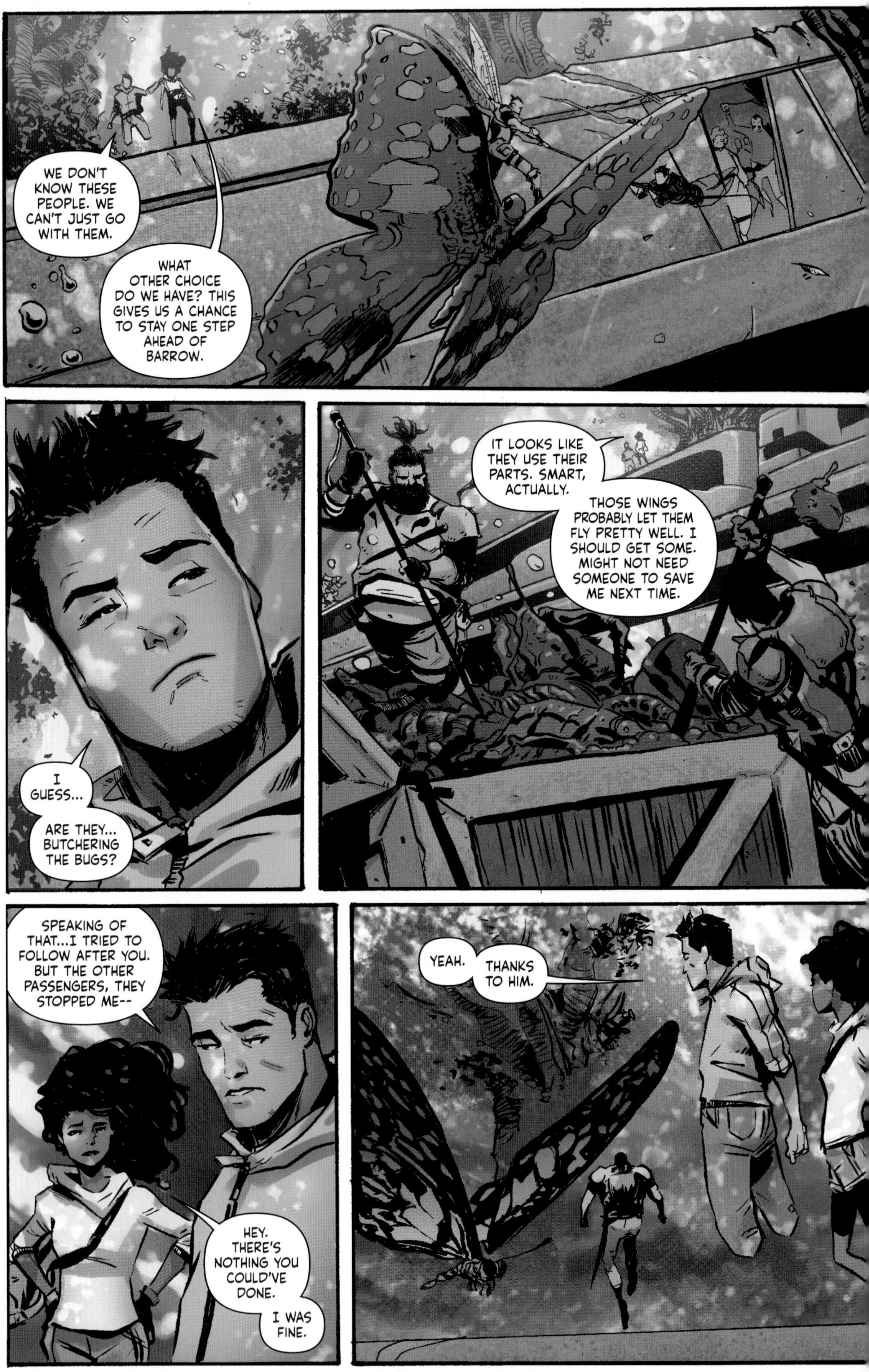
WE DON'T KNOW THESE PEOPLE. WE CAN'T JUST GO WITH THEM.
WHAT OTHER CHOICE DO WE HAVE? THIS GIVES US A CHANCE TO STAY ONE STEP AHEAD OF BARROW.
I GUESS...
ARE THEY... BUTCHERING THE BUGS?
IT LOOKS LIKE THEY USE THEIR PARTS. SMART, ACTUALLY.
THOSE WINGS PROBABLY LET THEM FLY PRETTY WELL. I SHOULD GET SOME. MIGHT NOT NEED SOMEONE TO SAVE ME NEXT TIME.
SPEAKING OF THAT...I TRIED TO FOLLOW AFTER YOU. BUT THE OTHER PASSENGERS, THEY STOPPED ME--
HEY. THERE'S NOTHING YOU COULD'VE DONE.
I WAS FINE.
YEAH.
THANKS TO HIM.

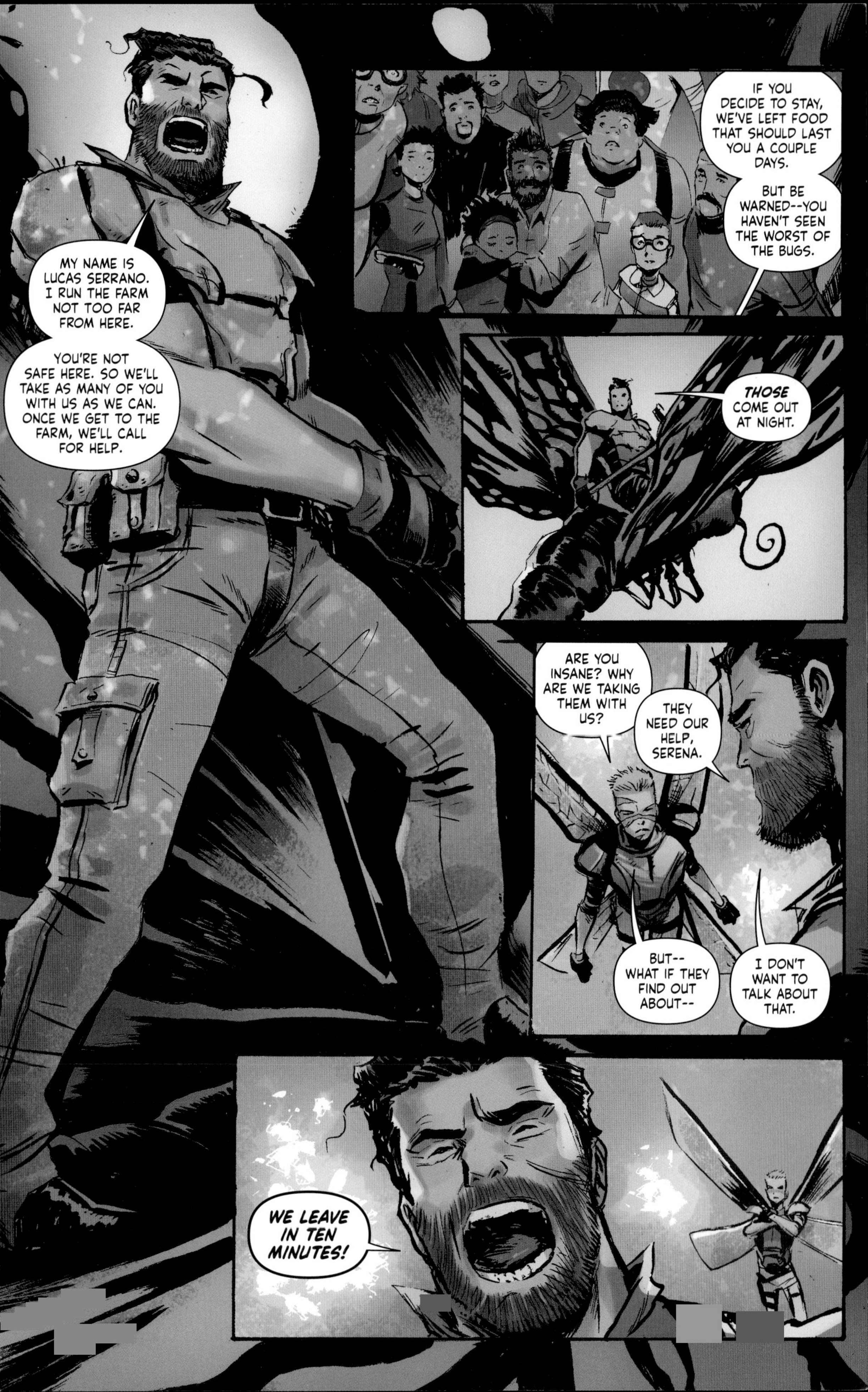
MY NAME IS LUCAS SERRANO. I RUN THE FARM NOT TOO FAR FROM HERE.
YOU'RE NOT SAFE HERE. SO WE'LL TAKE AS MANY OF YOU WITH US AS WE CAN. ONCE WE GET TO THE FARM, WE'LL CALL FOR HELP.
IF YOU DECIDE TO STAY, WE'VE LEFT FOOD THAT SHOULD LAST YOU A COUPLE DAYS.
BUT BE WARNED--YOU HAVEN'T SEEN THE WORST OF THE BUGS.
THOSE COME OUT AT NIGHT.
ARE YOU INSANE? WHY ARE WE TAKING THEM WITH US?
THEY NEED OUR HELP, SERENA.
BUT--WHAT IF THEY FIND OUT ABOUT--
I DON'T WANT TO TALK ABOUT THAT.
WE LEAVE IN TEN MINUTES!

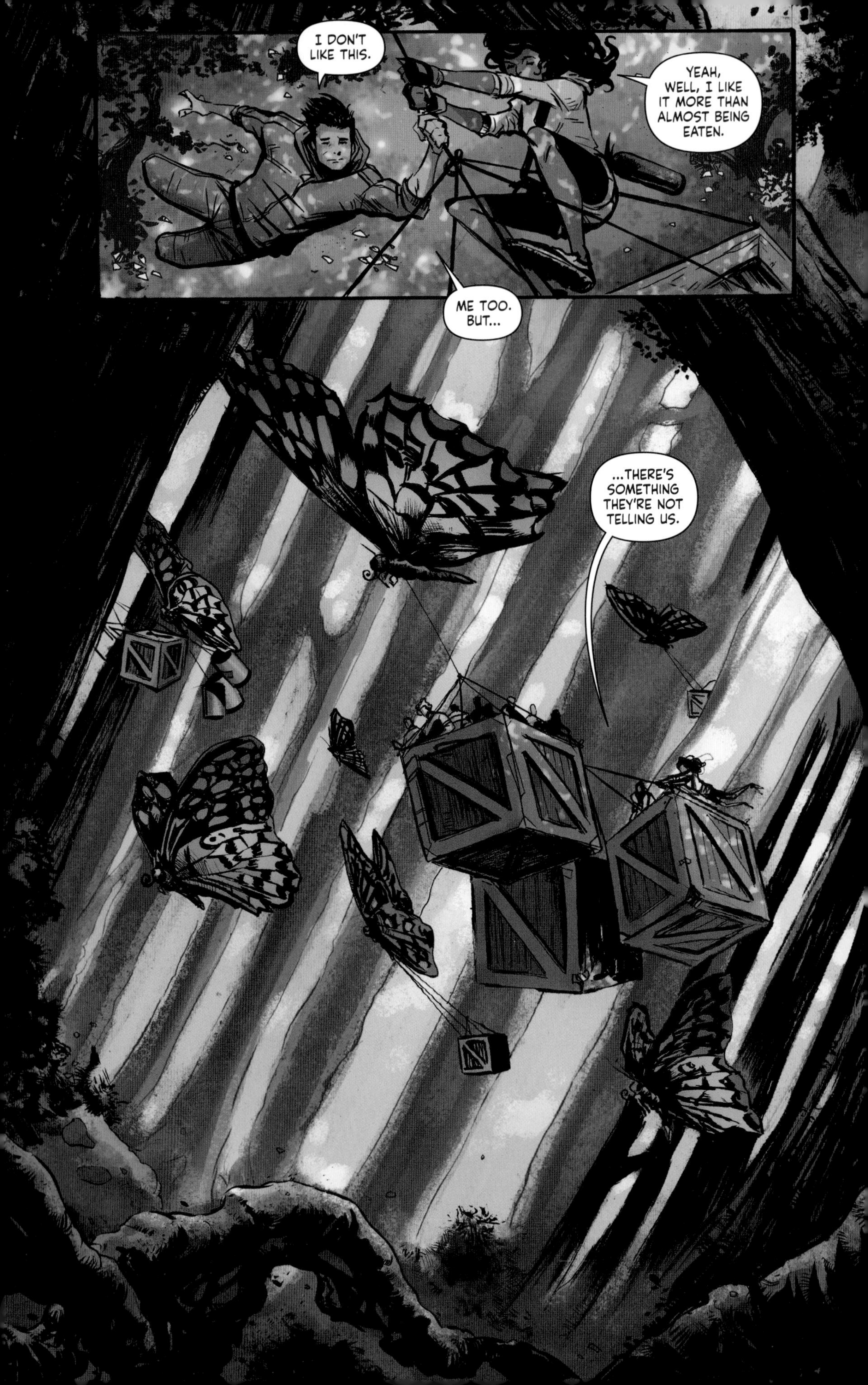
I DON'T LIKE THIS.
YEAH, WELL, I LIKE IT MORE THAN ALMOST BEING EATEN.
ME TOO. BUT...
...THERE'S SOMETHING THEY'RE NOT TELLING US.

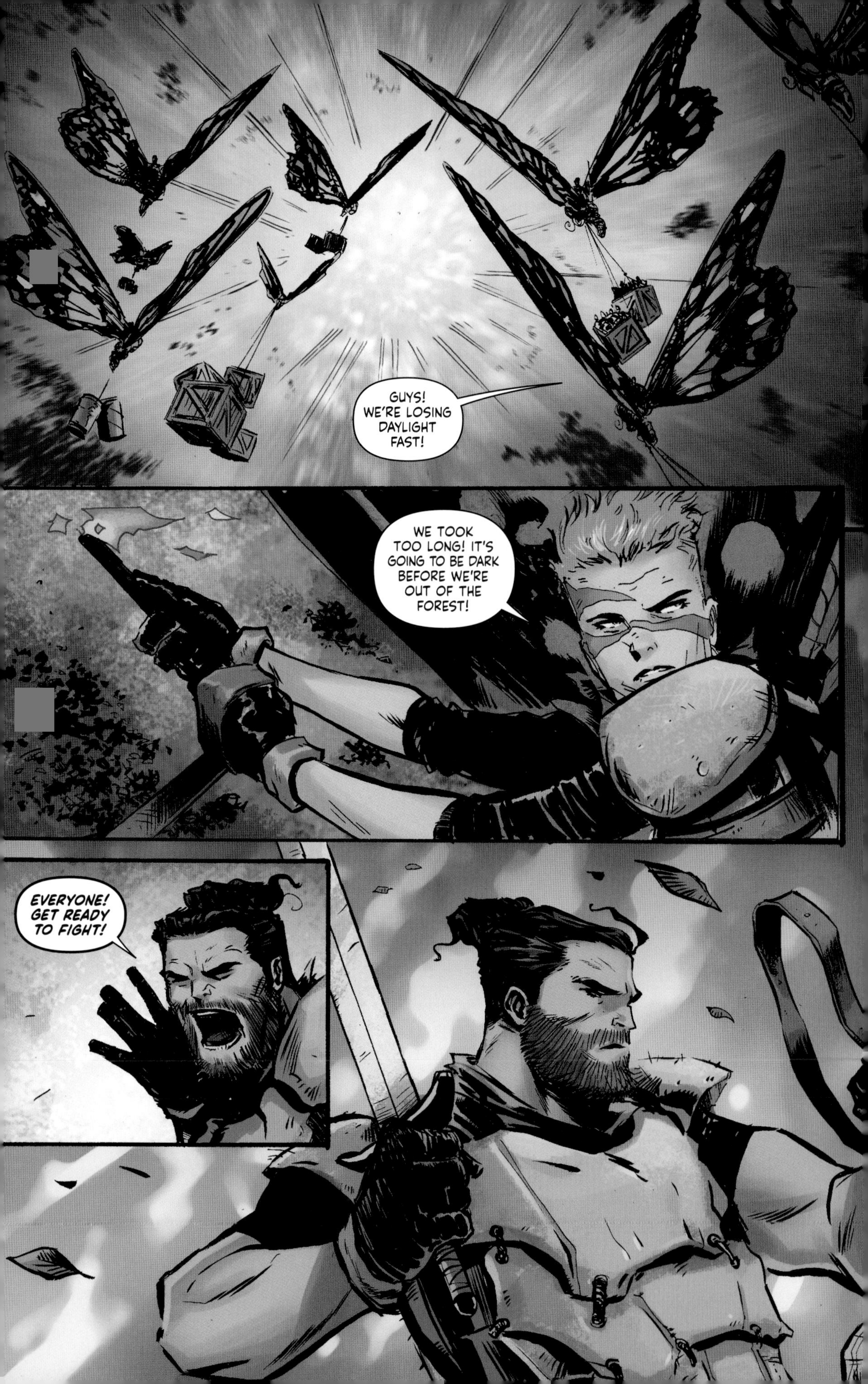
GUYS! WE'RE LOSING DAYLIGHT FAST!
WE TOOK TOO LONG! IT'S GOING TO BE DARK BEFORE WE'RE OUT OF THE FOREST!
EVERYONE! GET READY TO FIGHT!

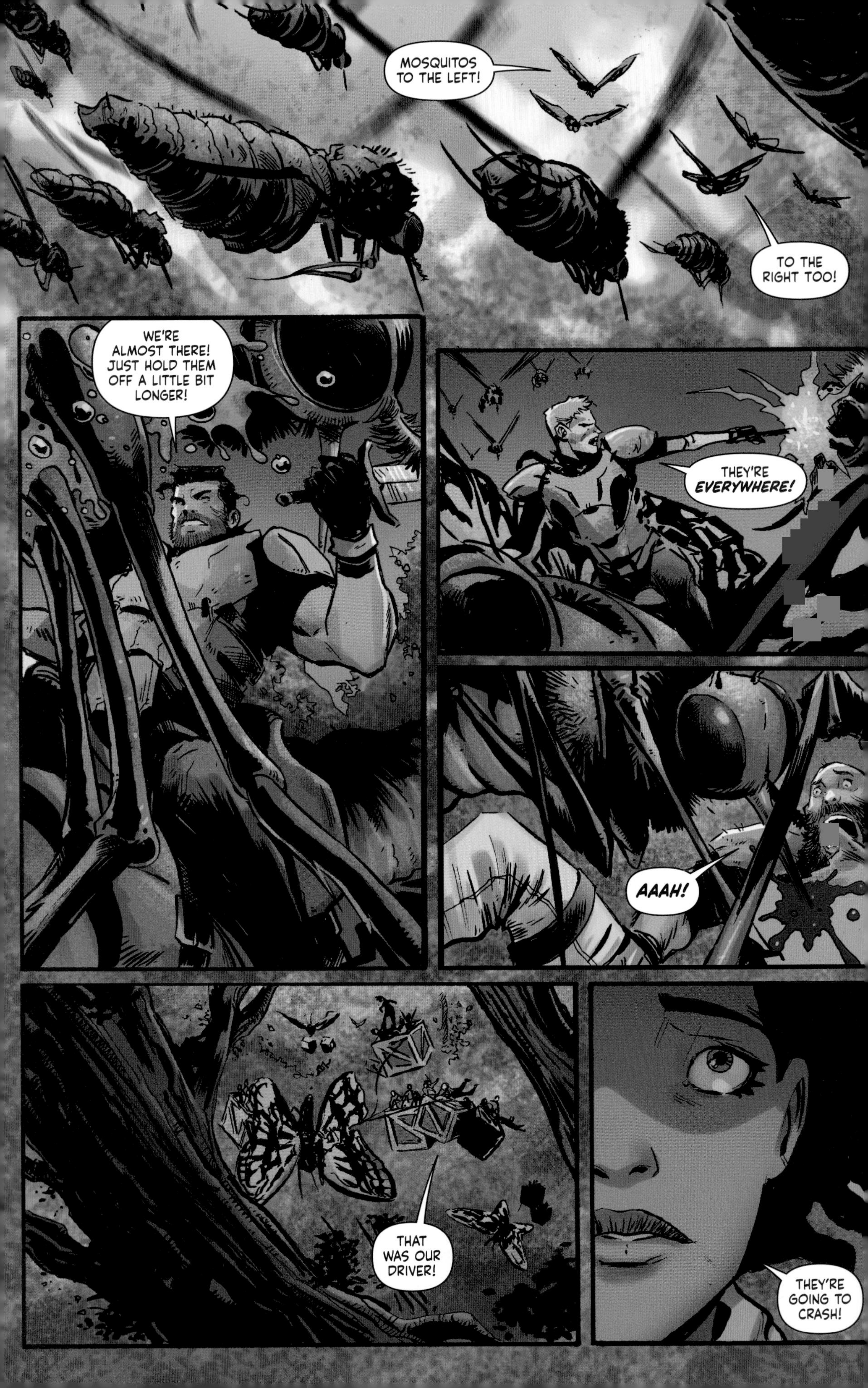
MOSQUITOS TO THE LEFT!
TO THE RIGHT TOO!
WE'RE ALMOST THERE! JUST HOLD THEM OFF A LITTLE BIT LONGER!
THEY'RE *EVERYWHERE!*
AAAH!
THAT WAS OUR DRIVER!
THEY'RE GOING TO CRASH!

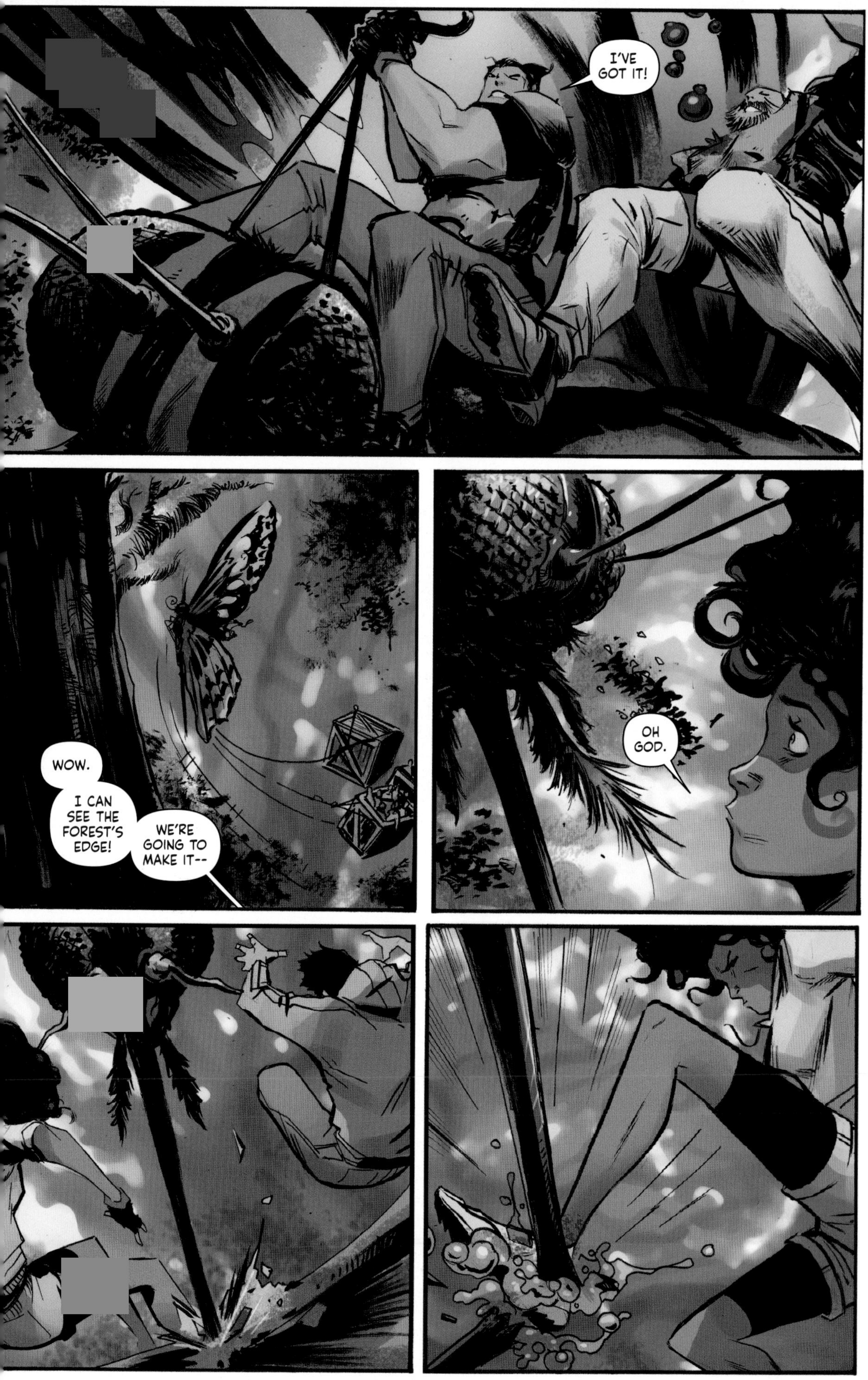
I'VE GOT IT!
WOW.
I CAN SEE THE FOREST'S EDGE!
WE'RE GOING TO MAKE IT--
OH GOD.

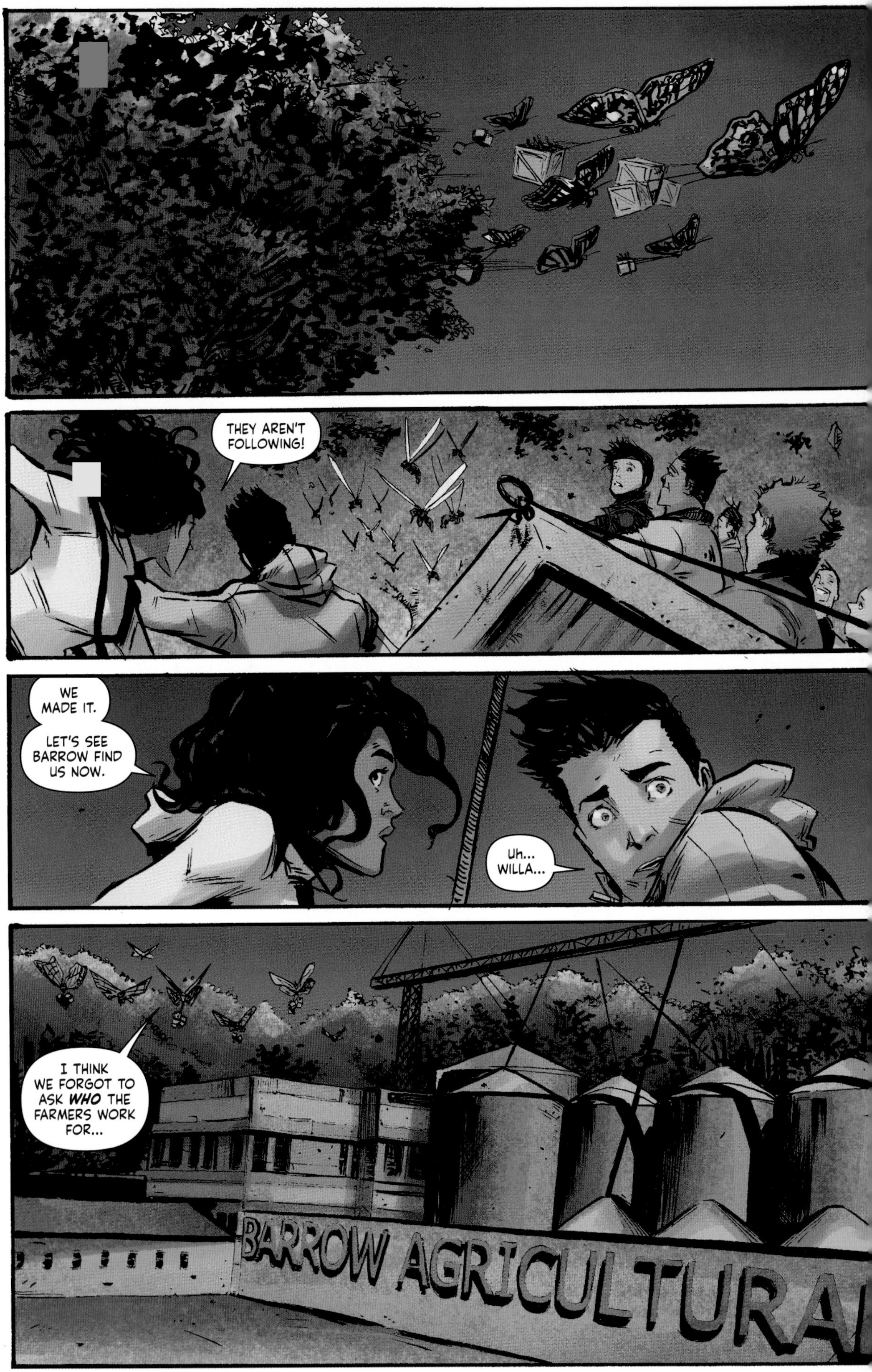
THEY AREN'T FOLLOWING!
WE MADE IT.
LET'S SEE BARROW FIND US NOW.
Uh... WILLA...
I THINK WE FORGOT TO ASK **WHO** THE FARMERS WORK FOR...
BARROW AGRICULTURA

END CHAPTER SEVEN

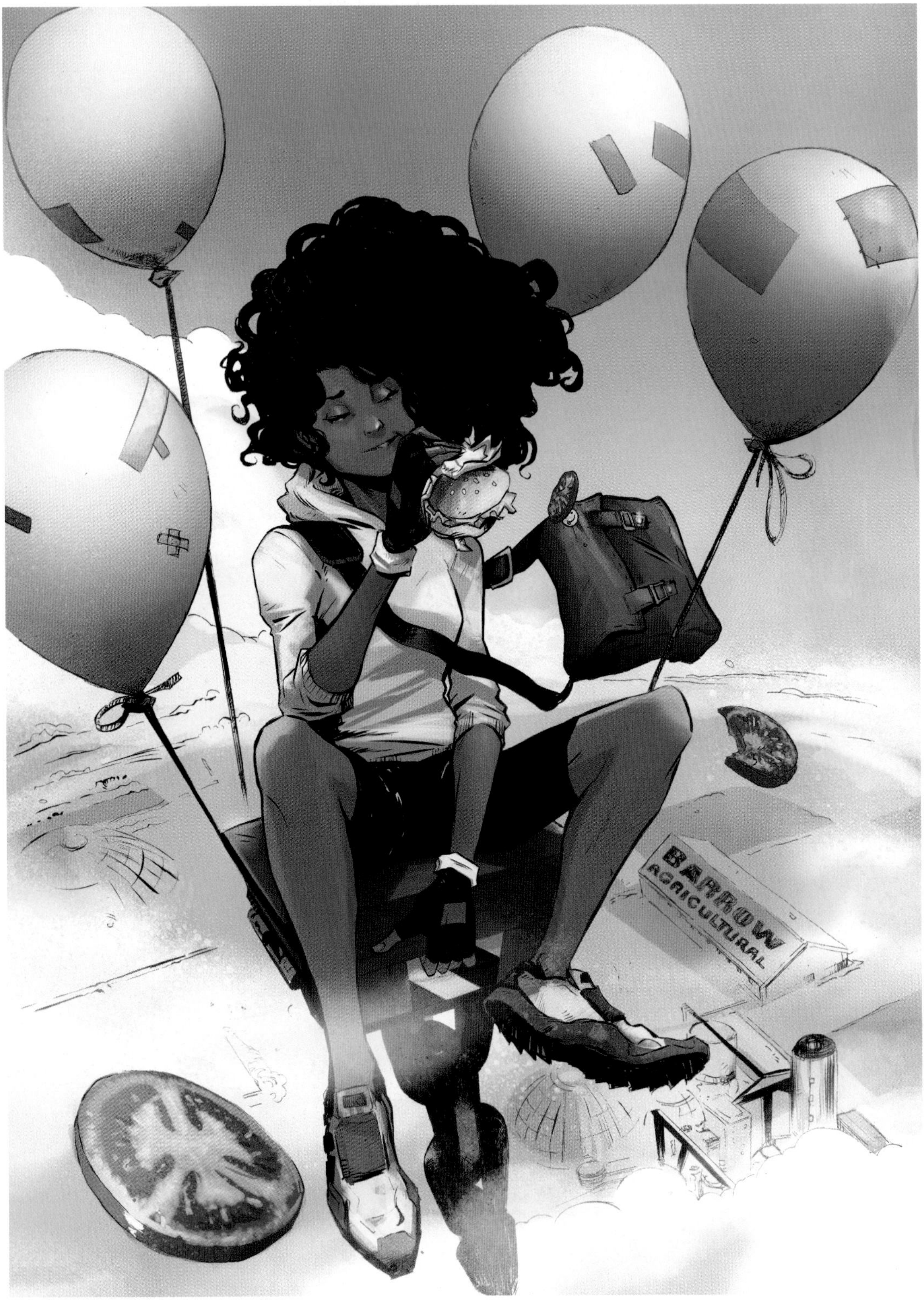
BARROW
AGRICULTURAL

CHAPTER EIGHT

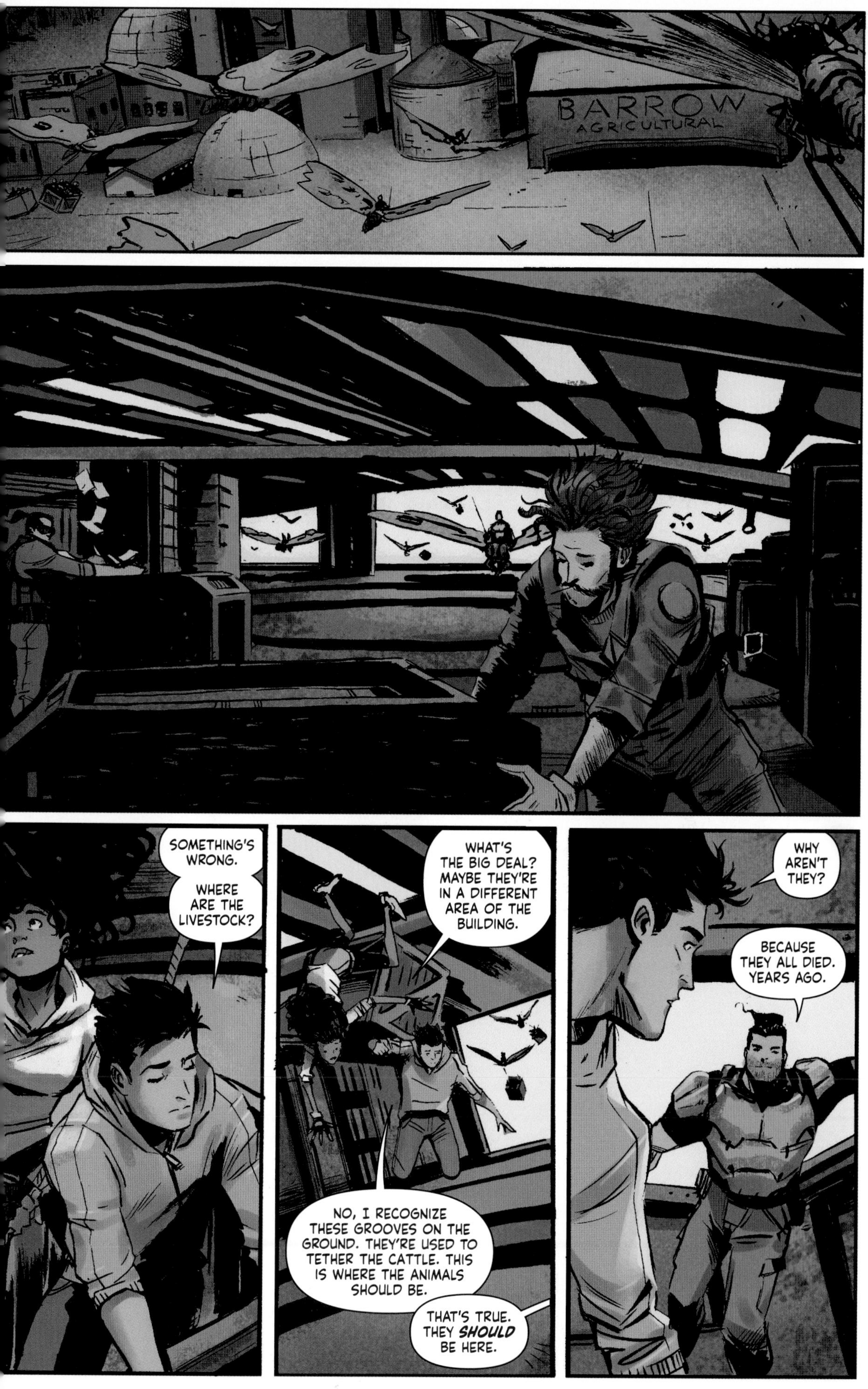
BARROW
AGRICULTURAL
SOMETHING'S WRONG.
WHERE ARE THE LIVESTOCK?
WHAT'S THE BIG DEAL? MAYBE THEY'RE IN A DIFFERENT AREA OF THE BUILDING.
NO, I RECOGNIZE THESE GROOVES ON THE GROUND. THEY'RE USED TO TETHER THE CATTLE. THIS IS WHERE THE ANIMALS SHOULD BE.
THAT'S TRUE. THEY SHOULD BE HERE.
WHY AREN'T THEY?
BECAUSE THEY ALL DIED. YEARS AGO.

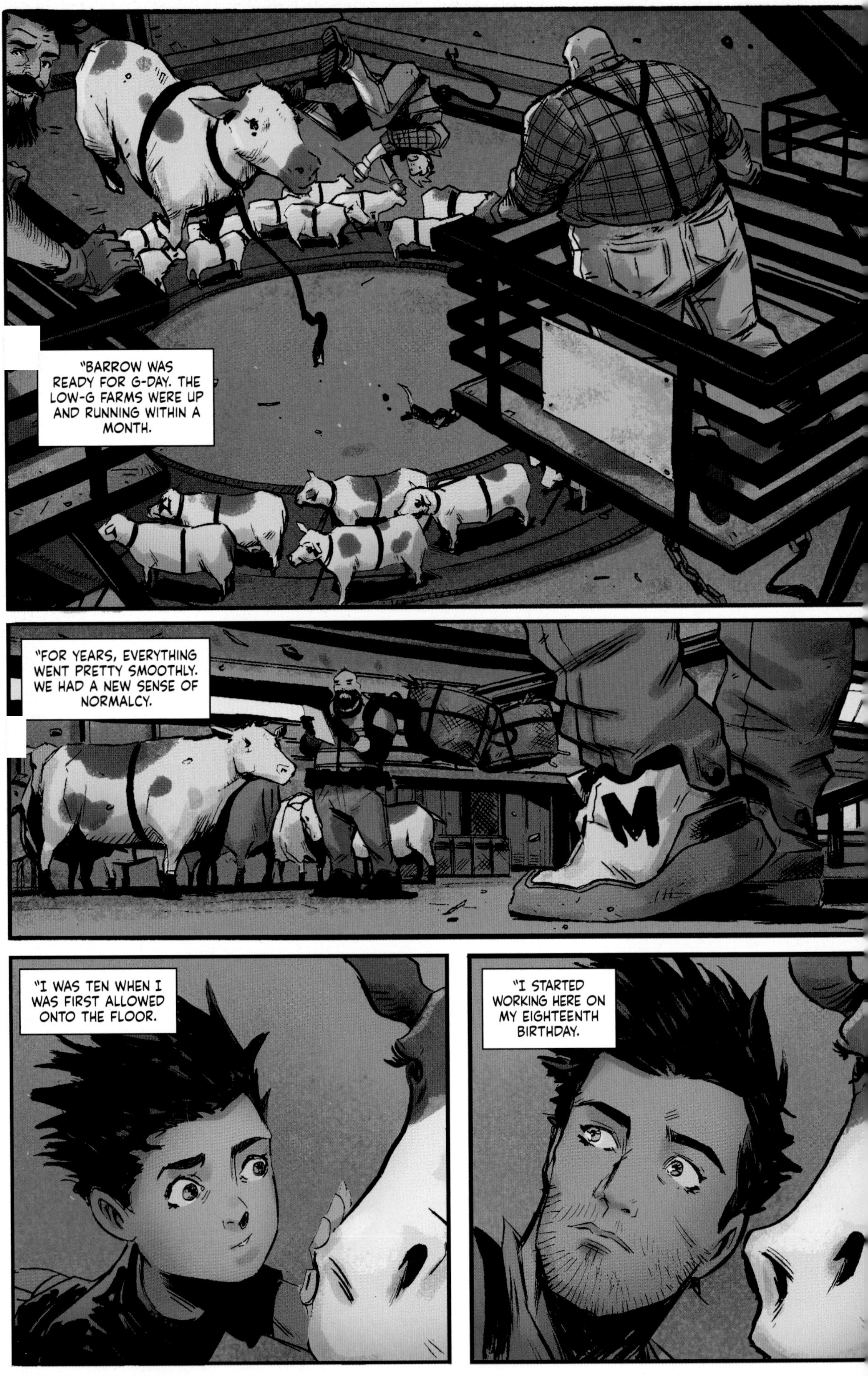
"BARROW WAS READY FOR G-DAY. THE LOW-G FARMS WERE UP AND RUNNING WITHIN A MONTH.
"FOR YEARS, EVERYTHING WENT PRETTY SMOOTHLY. WE HAD A NEW SENSE OF NORMALCY.
M
"I WAS TEN WHEN I WAS FIRST ALLOWED ONTO THE FLOOR.
"I STARTED WORKING HERE ON MY EIGHTEENTH BIRTHDAY.

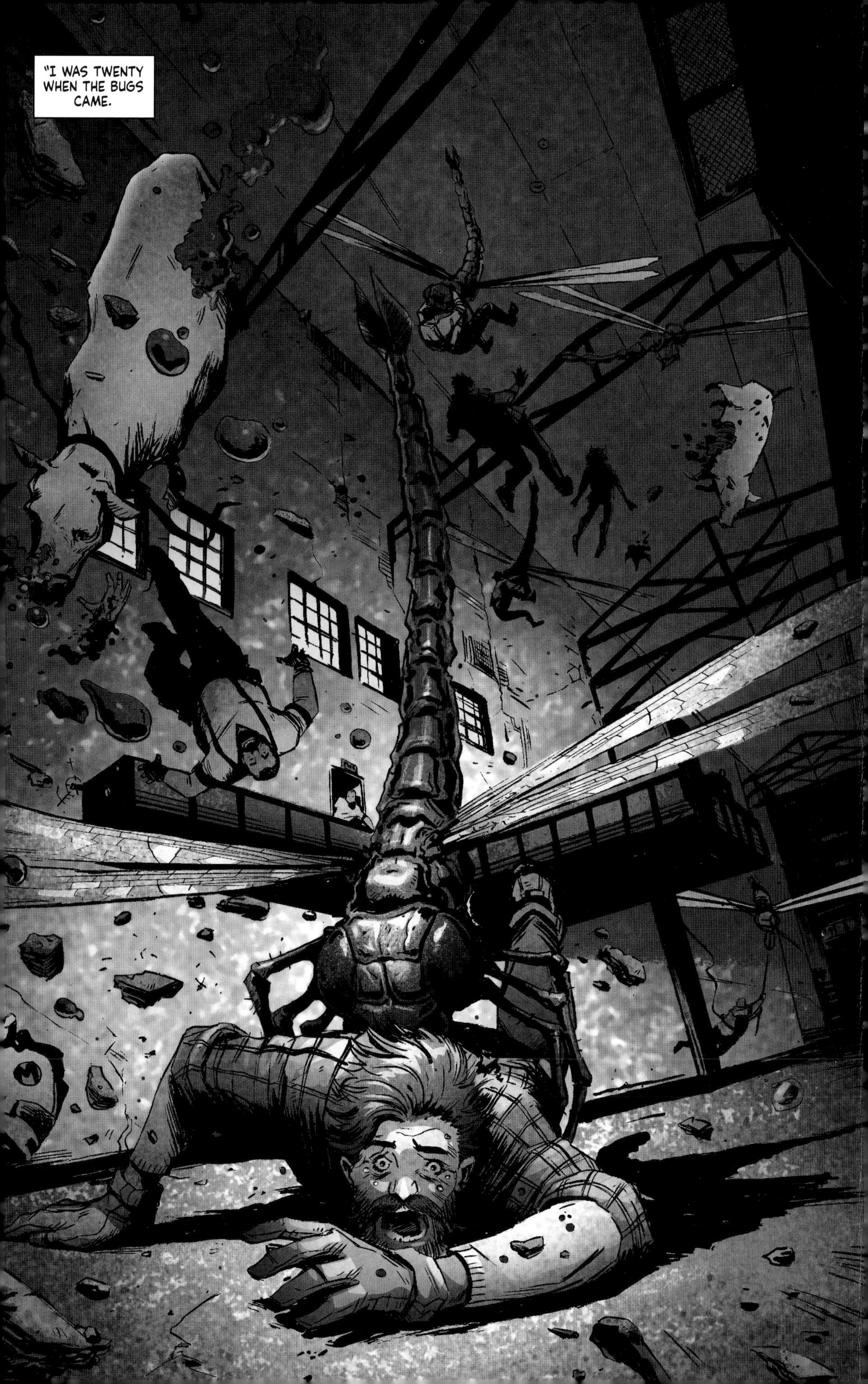
"I WAS TWENTY WHEN THE BUGS CAME.

"WE BARELY SURVIVED. ALL OF OUR LIVESTOCK WAS KILLED.

"ALL THE FARMS IN THE AREA WERE HIT. IN RETROSPECT, IT WAS INEVITABLE. LIKE WE'D SET OUT GIANT BUFFETS FOR THE BUGS.

"BY THE TIME BARROW FIGURED OUT HOW TO KEEP THEM AT BAY, IT WAS TOO LATE.

"THE ORDERS CAME DOWN FROM ON HIGH--THE CITIES STILL NEEDED FOOD.

"OUR JOB WAS TO PROVIDE IT. TO FARM THE LAND.

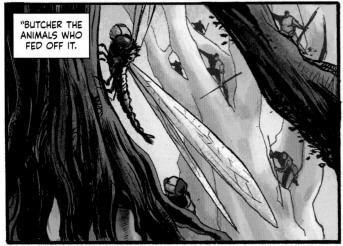

"BUTCHER THE ANIMALS WHO FED OFF IT.

"SO WE DID."

"WAIT A SECOND.

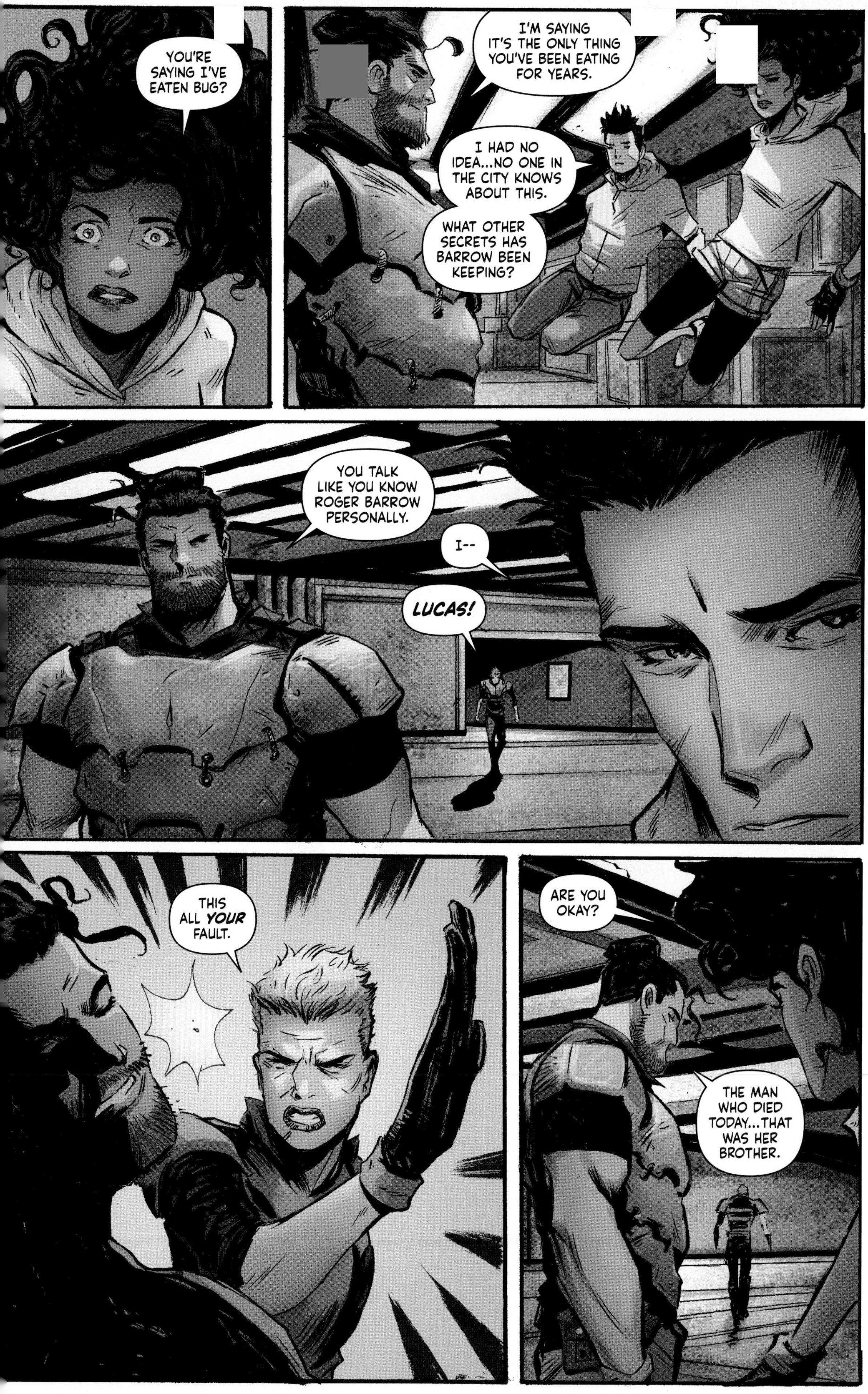
YOU'RE SAYING I'VE EATEN BUG?
I'M SAYING IT'S THE ONLY THING YOU'VE BEEN EATING FOR YEARS.
I HAD NO IDEA...NO ONE IN THE CITY KNOWS ABOUT THIS.
WHAT OTHER SECRETS HAS BARROW BEEN KEEPING?
YOU TALK LIKE YOU KNOW ROGER BARROW PERSONALLY.
I--
LUCAS!
THIS ALL YOUR FAULT.
ARE YOU OKAY?
THE MAN WHO DIED TODAY...THAT WAS HER BROTHER.

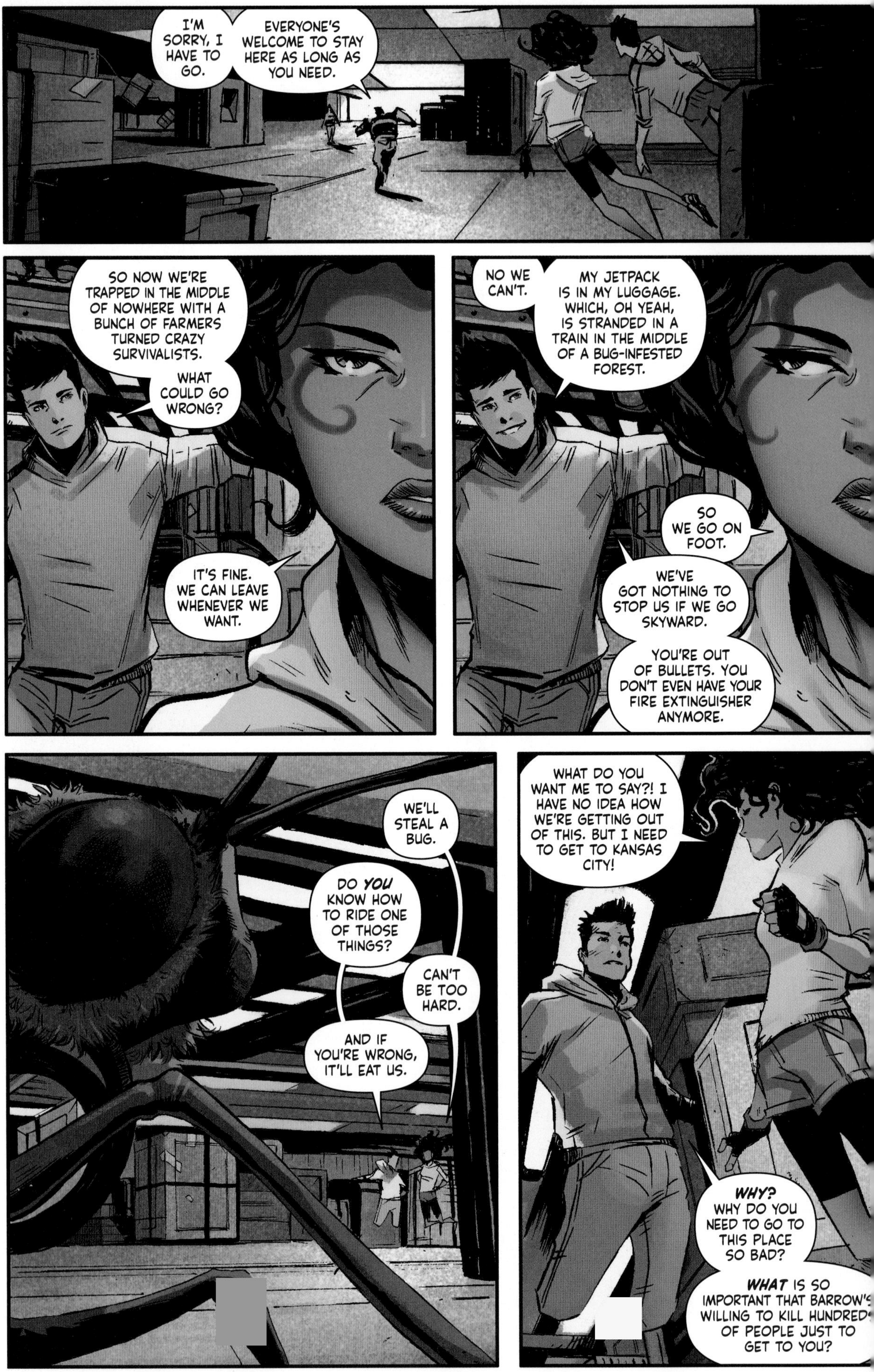
I'M SORRY, I HAVE TO GO.
EVERYONE'S WELCOME TO STAY HERE AS LONG AS YOU NEED.
SO NOW WE'RE TRAPPED IN THE MIDDLE OF NOWHERE WITH A BUNCH OF FARMERS TURNED CRAZY SURVIVALISTS.
WHAT COULD GO WRONG?
IT'S FINE. WE CAN LEAVE WHENEVER WE WANT.
NO WE CAN'T.
MY JETPACK IS IN MY LUGGAGE. WHICH, OH YEAH, IS STRANDED IN A TRAIN IN THE MIDDLE OF A BUG-INFESTED FOREST.
SO WE GO ON FOOT.
WE'VE GOT NOTHING TO STOP US IF WE GO SKYWARD.
YOU'RE OUT OF BULLETS. YOU DON'T EVEN HAVE YOUR FIRE EXTINGUISHER ANYMORE.
WE'LL STEAL A BUG.
DO YOU KNOW HOW TO RIDE ONE OF THOSE THINGS?
CAN'T BE TOO HARD.
AND IF YOU'RE WRONG, IT'LL EAT US.
WHAT DO YOU WANT ME TO SAY?! I HAVE NO IDEA HOW WE'RE GETTING OUT OF THIS. BUT I NEED TO GET TO KANSAS CITY!
WHY? WHY DO YOU NEED TO GO TO THIS PLACE SO BAD?
WHAT IS SO IMPORTANT THAT BARROW'S WILLING TO KILL HUNDRED OF PEOPLE JUST TO GET TO YOU?

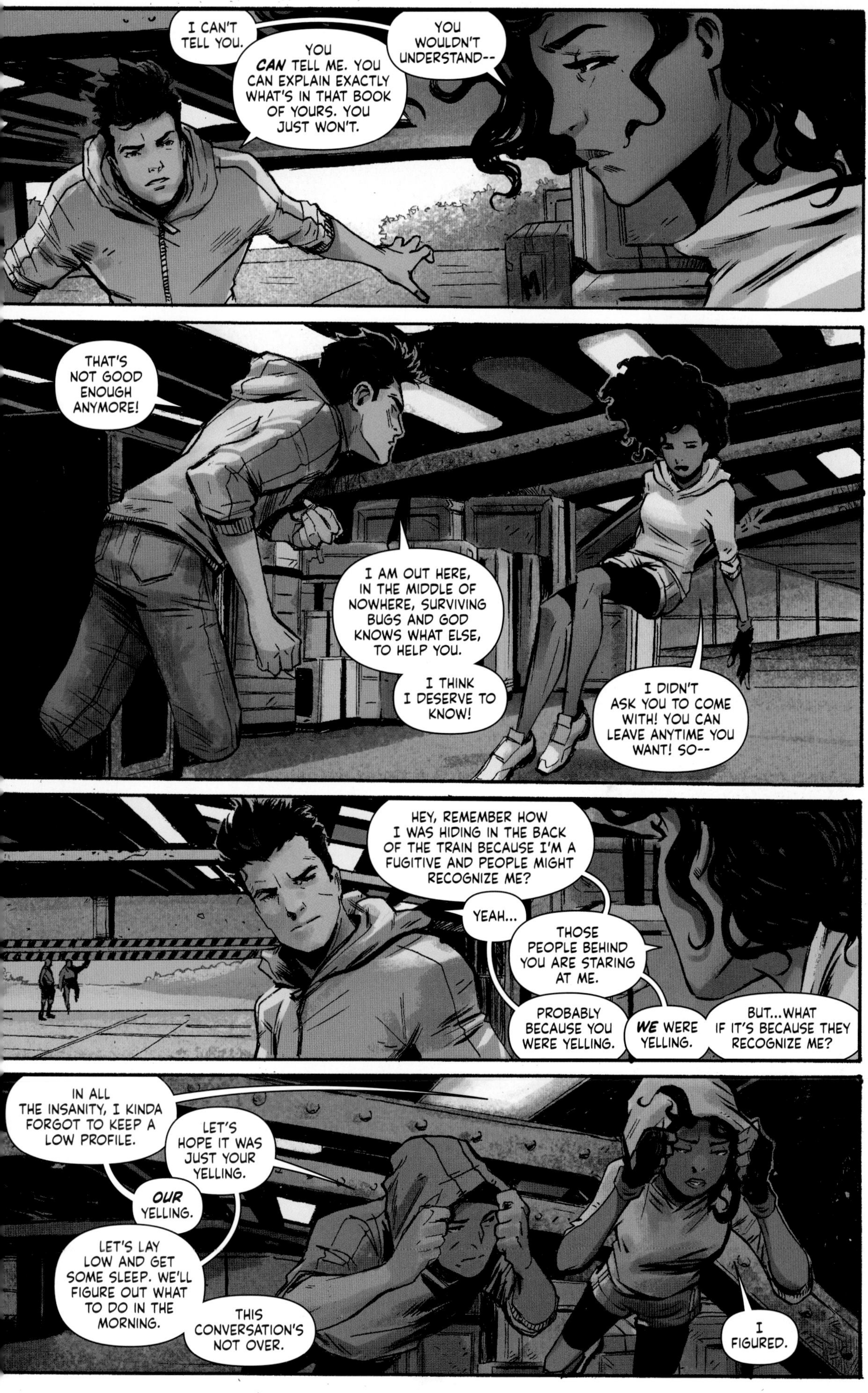
I CAN'T TELL YOU.
YOU WOULDN'T UNDERSTAND--
YOU *CAN* TELL ME. YOU CAN EXPLAIN EXACTLY WHAT'S IN THAT BOOK OF YOURS. YOU JUST WON'T.
THAT'S NOT GOOD ENOUGH ANYMORE!
I AM OUT HERE, IN THE MIDDLE OF NOWHERE, SURVIVING BUGS AND GOD KNOWS WHAT ELSE, TO HELP YOU.
I THINK I DESERVE TO KNOW!
I DIDN'T ASK YOU TO COME WITH! YOU CAN LEAVE ANYTIME YOU WANT! SO--
HEY, REMEMBER HOW I WAS HIDING IN THE BACK OF THE TRAIN BECAUSE I'M A FUGITIVE AND PEOPLE MIGHT RECOGNIZE ME?
YEAH...
THOSE PEOPLE BEHIND YOU ARE STARING AT ME.
PROBABLY BECAUSE YOU WERE YELLING.
WE WERE YELLING.
BUT...WHAT IF IT'S BECAUSE THEY RECOGNIZE ME?
IN ALL THE INSANITY, I KINDA FORGOT TO KEEP A LOW PROFILE.
LET'S HOPE IT WAS JUST YOUR YELLING.
OUR YELLING.
LET'S LAY LOW AND GET SOME SLEEP. WE'LL FIGURE OUT WHAT TO DO IN THE MORNING.
THIS CONVERSATION'S NOT OVER.
I FIGURED.

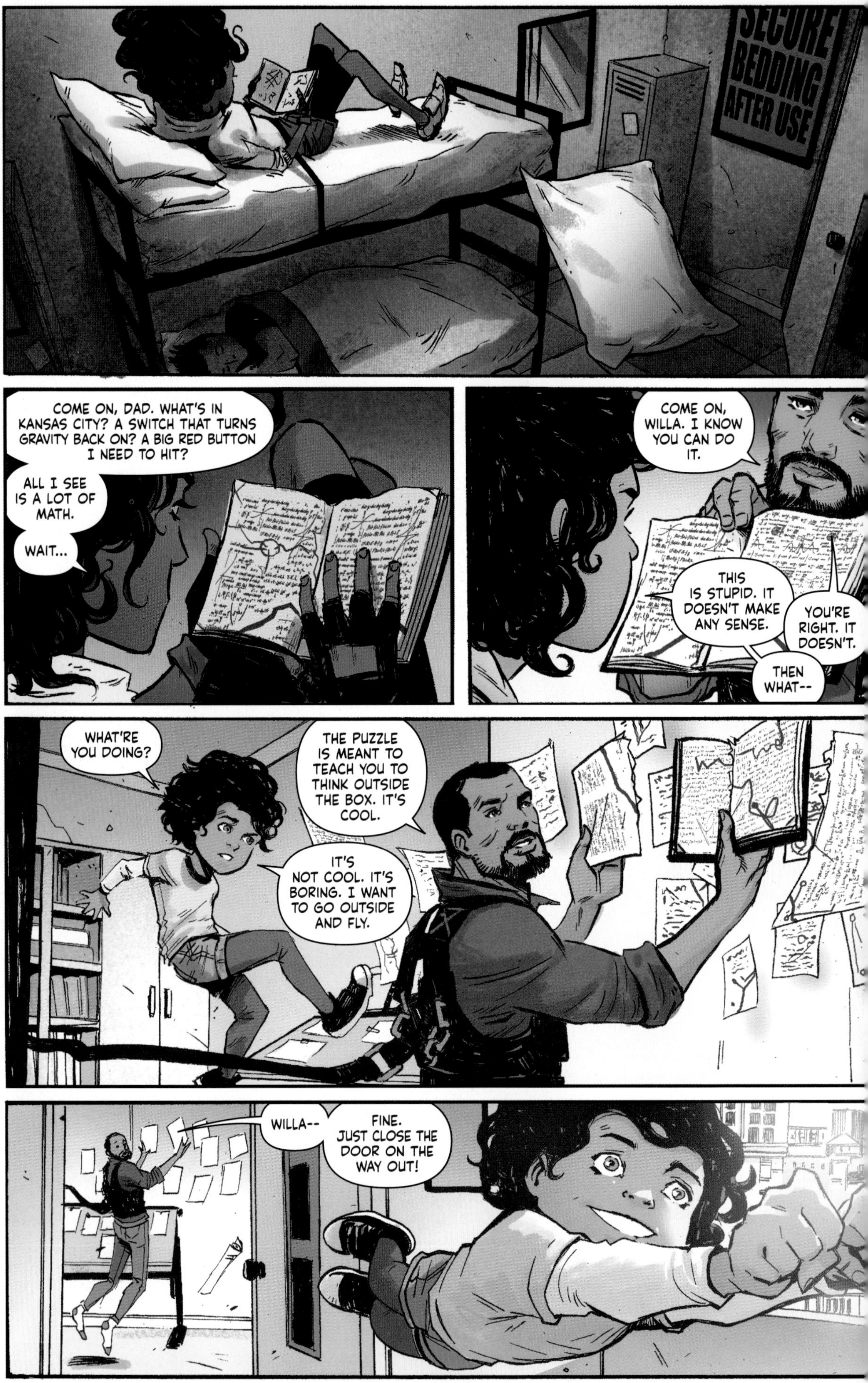
SECURE BEDDING AFTER USE
COME ON, DAD. WHAT'S IN KANSAS CITY? A SWITCH THAT TURNS GRAVITY BACK ON? A BIG RED BUTTON I NEED TO HIT?
ALL I SEE IS A LOT OF MATH.
WAIT...
COME ON, WILLA. I KNOW YOU CAN DO IT.
THIS IS STUPID. IT DOESN'T MAKE ANY SENSE.
YOU'RE RIGHT. IT DOESN'T.
THEN WHAT--
WHAT'RE YOU DOING?
THE PUZZLE IS MEANT TO TEACH YOU TO THINK OUTSIDE THE BOX. IT'S COOL.
IT'S NOT COOL. IT'S BORING. I WANT TO GO OUTSIDE AND FLY.
WILLA--
FINE. JUST CLOSE THE DOOR ON THE WAY OUT!

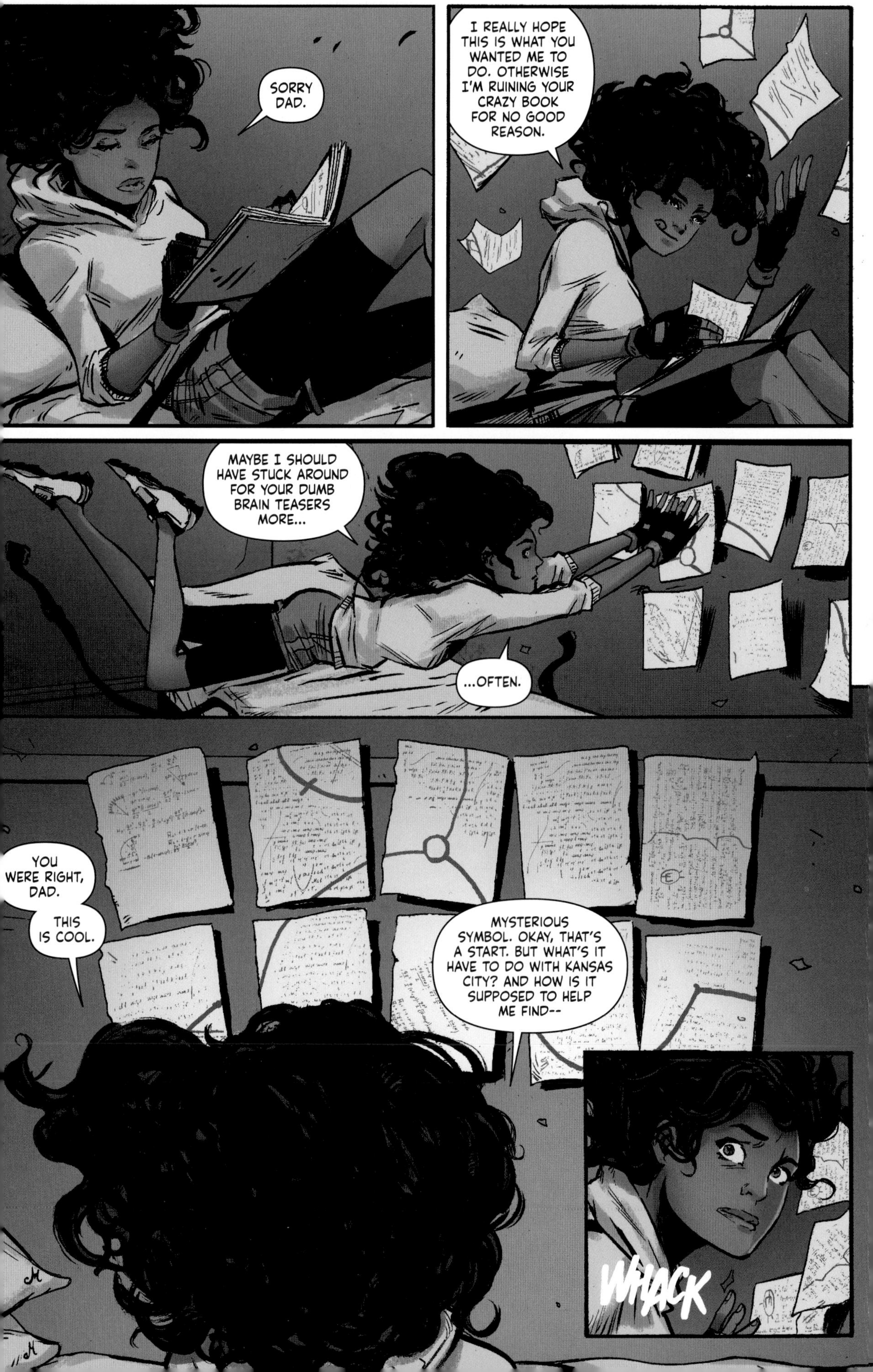
SORRY DAD.
I REALLY HOPE THIS IS WHAT YOU WANTED ME TO DO. OTHERWISE I'M RUINING YOUR CRAZY BOOK FOR NO GOOD REASON.
MAYBE I SHOULD HAVE STUCK AROUND FOR YOUR DUMB BRAIN TEASERS MORE...
...OFTEN.
YOU WERE RIGHT, DAD.
THIS IS COOL.
MYSTERIOUS SYMBOL. OKAY, THAT'S A START. BUT WHAT'S IT HAVE TO DO WITH KANSAS CITY? AND HOW IS IT SUPPOSED TO HELP ME FIND--
WHACK

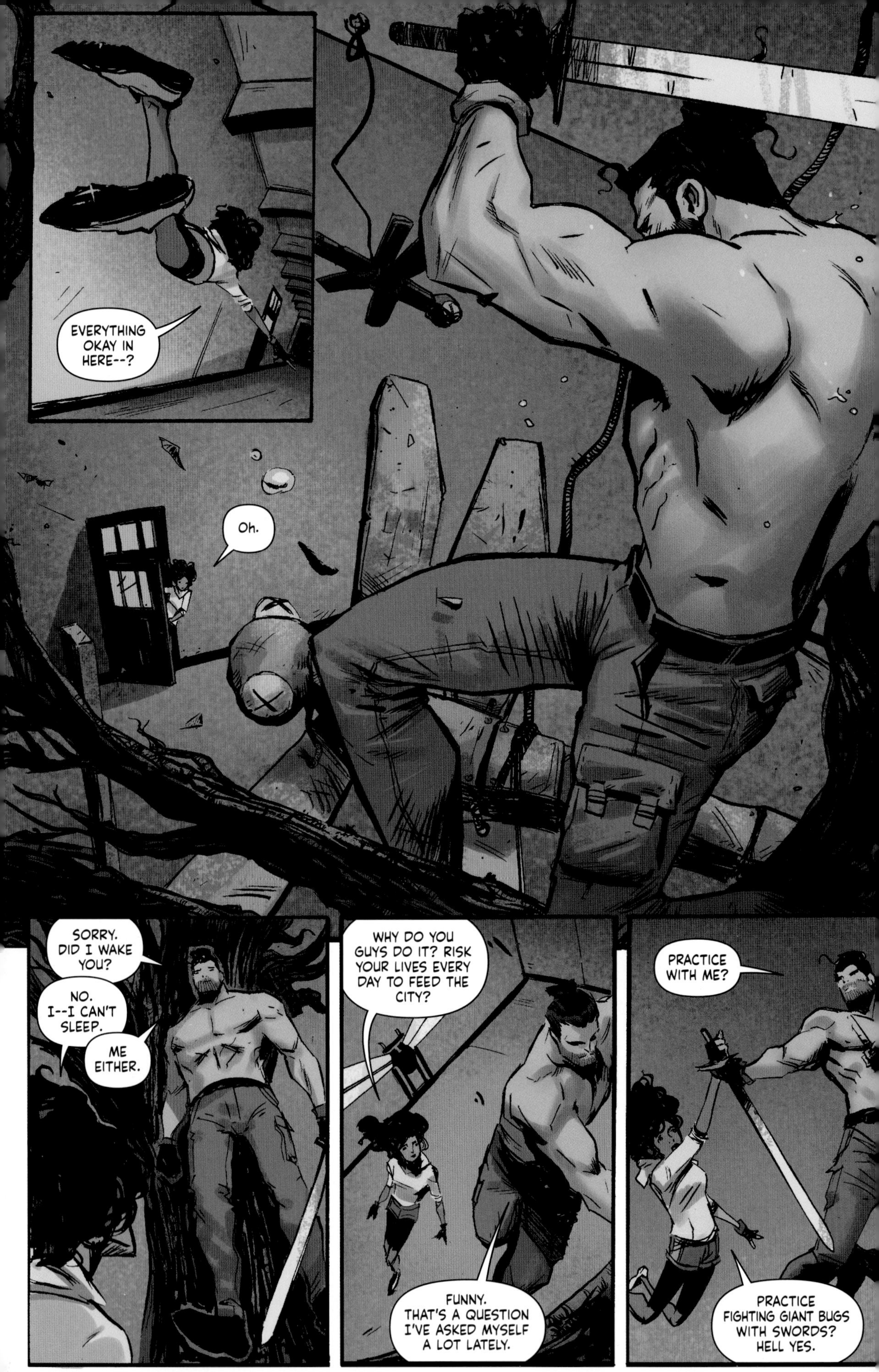
EVERYTHING OKAY IN HERE--?
Oh.
SORRY. DID I WAKE YOU?
NO. I--I CAN'T SLEEP.
ME EITHER.
WHY DO YOU GUYS DO IT? RISK YOUR LIVES EVERY DAY TO FEED THE CITY?
FUNNY. THAT'S A QUESTION I'VE ASKED MYSELF A LOT LATELY.
PRACTICE WITH ME?
PRACTICE FIGHTING GIANT BUGS WITH SWORDS? HELL YES.

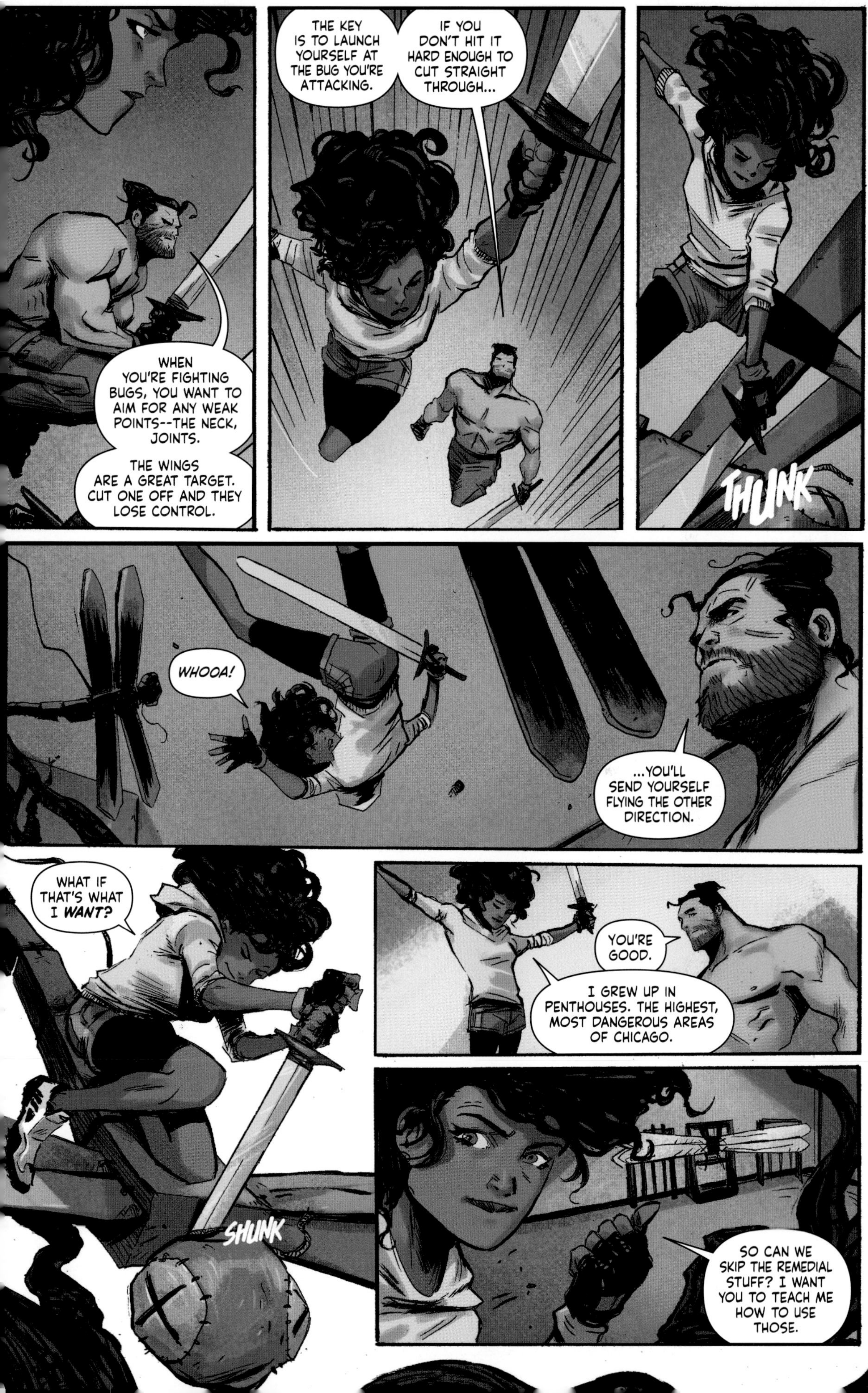

WHEN YOU'RE FIGHTING BUGS, YOU WANT TO AIM FOR ANY WEAK POINTS--THE NECK, JOINTS.
THE WINGS ARE A GREAT TARGET. CUT ONE OFF AND THEY LOSE CONTROL.
THE KEY IS TO LAUNCH YOURSELF AT THE BUG YOU'RE ATTACKING.
IF YOU DON'T HIT IT HARD ENOUGH TO CUT STRAIGHT THROUGH...
THUNK
WHOOA!
...YOU'LL SEND YOURSELF FLYING THE OTHER DIRECTION.
WHAT IF THAT'S WHAT I *WANT?*
SHUNK
YOU'RE GOOD.
I GREW UP IN PENTHOUSES. THE HIGHEST, MOST DANGEROUS AREAS OF CHICAGO.
SO CAN WE SKIP THE REMEDIAL STUFF? I WANT YOU TO TEACH ME HOW TO USE THOSE.

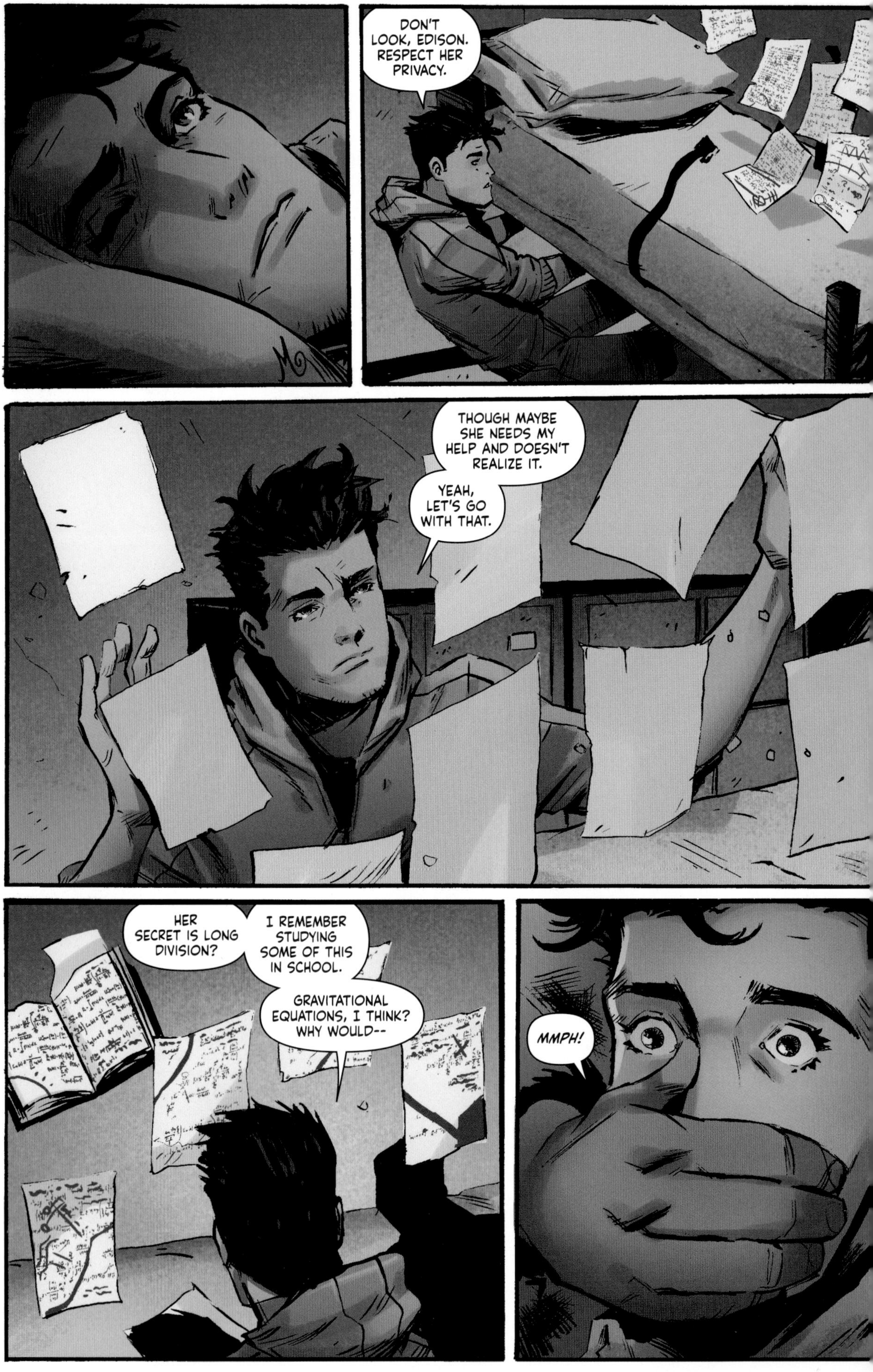
DON'T LOOK, EDISON. RESPECT HER PRIVACY.
THOUGH MAYBE SHE NEEDS MY HELP AND DOESN'T REALIZE IT.
YEAH, LET'S GO WITH THAT.
HER SECRET IS LONG DIVISION?
I REMEMBER STUDYING SOME OF THIS IN SCHOOL.
GRAVITATIONAL EQUATIONS, I THINK? WHY WOULD--
MMPH!

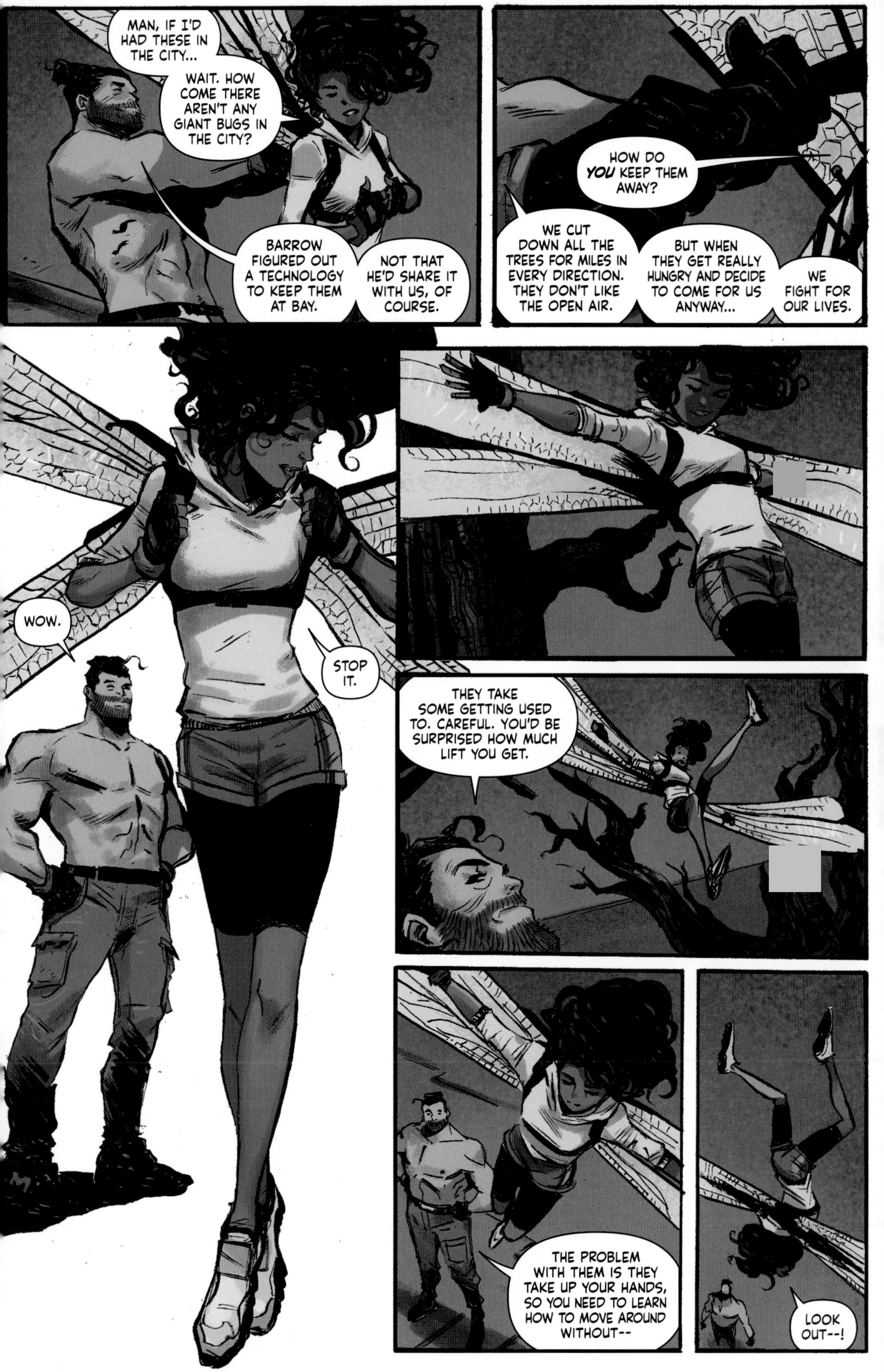

MAN, IF I'D HAD THESE IN THE CITY...
WAIT. HOW COME THERE AREN'T ANY GIANT BUGS IN THE CITY?
BARROW FIGURED OUT A TECHNOLOGY TO KEEP THEM AT BAY.
NOT THAT HE'D SHARE IT WITH US, OF COURSE.
HOW DO *YOU* KEEP THEM AWAY?
WE CUT DOWN ALL THE TREES FOR MILES IN EVERY DIRECTION. THEY DON'T LIKE THE OPEN AIR.
BUT WHEN THEY GET REALLY HUNGRY AND DECIDE TO COME FOR US ANYWAY...
WE FIGHT FOR OUR LIVES.
WOW.
STOP IT.
THEY TAKE SOME GETTING USED TO. CAREFUL. YOU'D BE SURPRISED HOW MUCH LIFT YOU GET.
THE PROBLEM WITH THEM IS THEY TAKE UP YOUR HANDS, SO YOU NEED TO LEARN HOW TO MOVE AROUND WITHOUT--
LOOK OUT--!

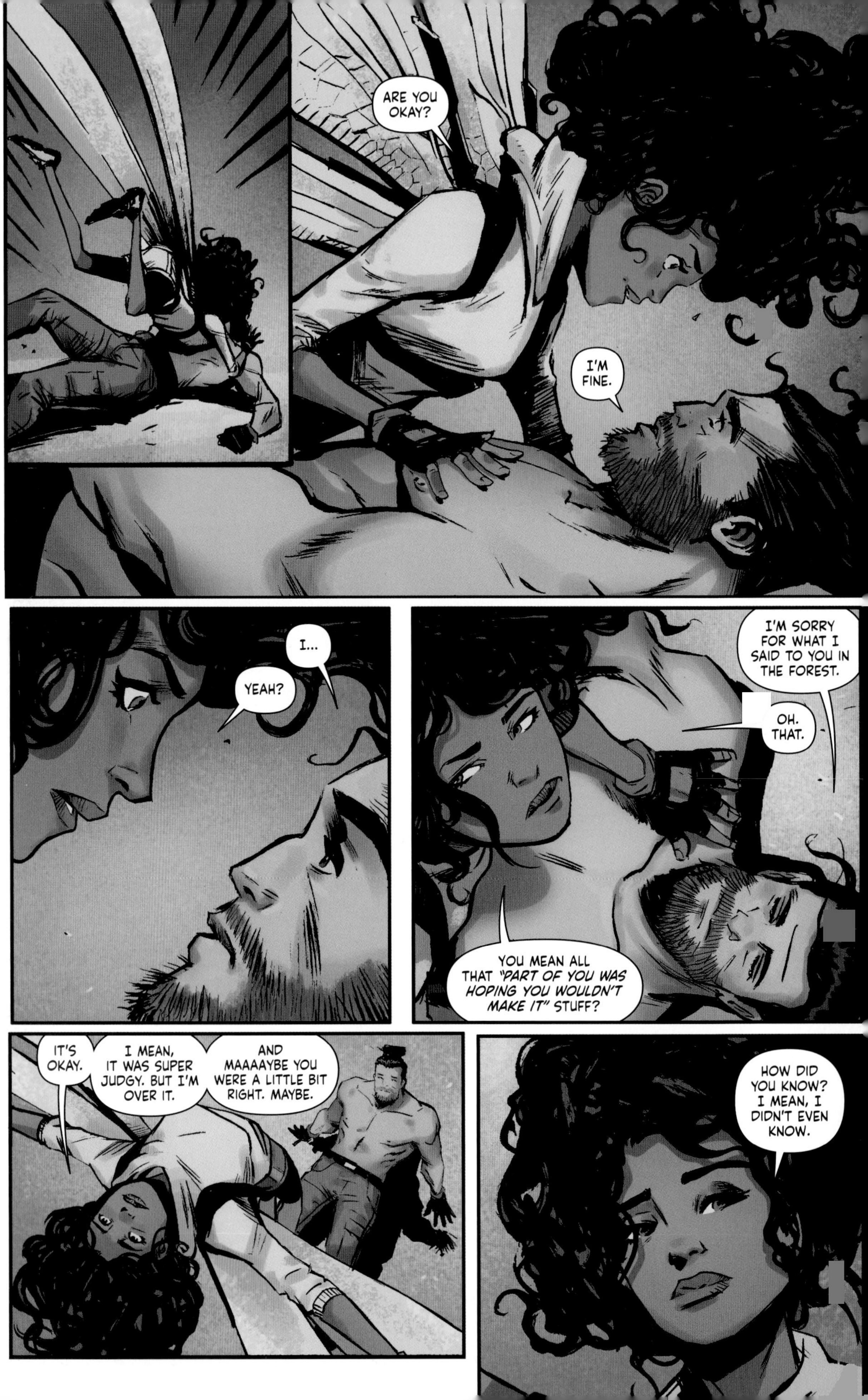
ARE YOU OKAY?
I'M FINE.
I...
YEAH?
I'M SORRY FOR WHAT I SAID TO YOU IN THE FOREST.
OH. THAT.
YOU MEAN ALL THAT *"PART OF YOU WAS HOPING YOU WOULDN'T MAKE IT"* STUFF?
IT'S OKAY.
I MEAN, IT WAS SUPER JUDGY. BUT I'M OVER IT.
AND MAAAAYBE YOU WERE A LITTLE BIT RIGHT. MAYBE.
HOW DID YOU KNOW? I MEAN, I DIDN'T EVEN KNOW.

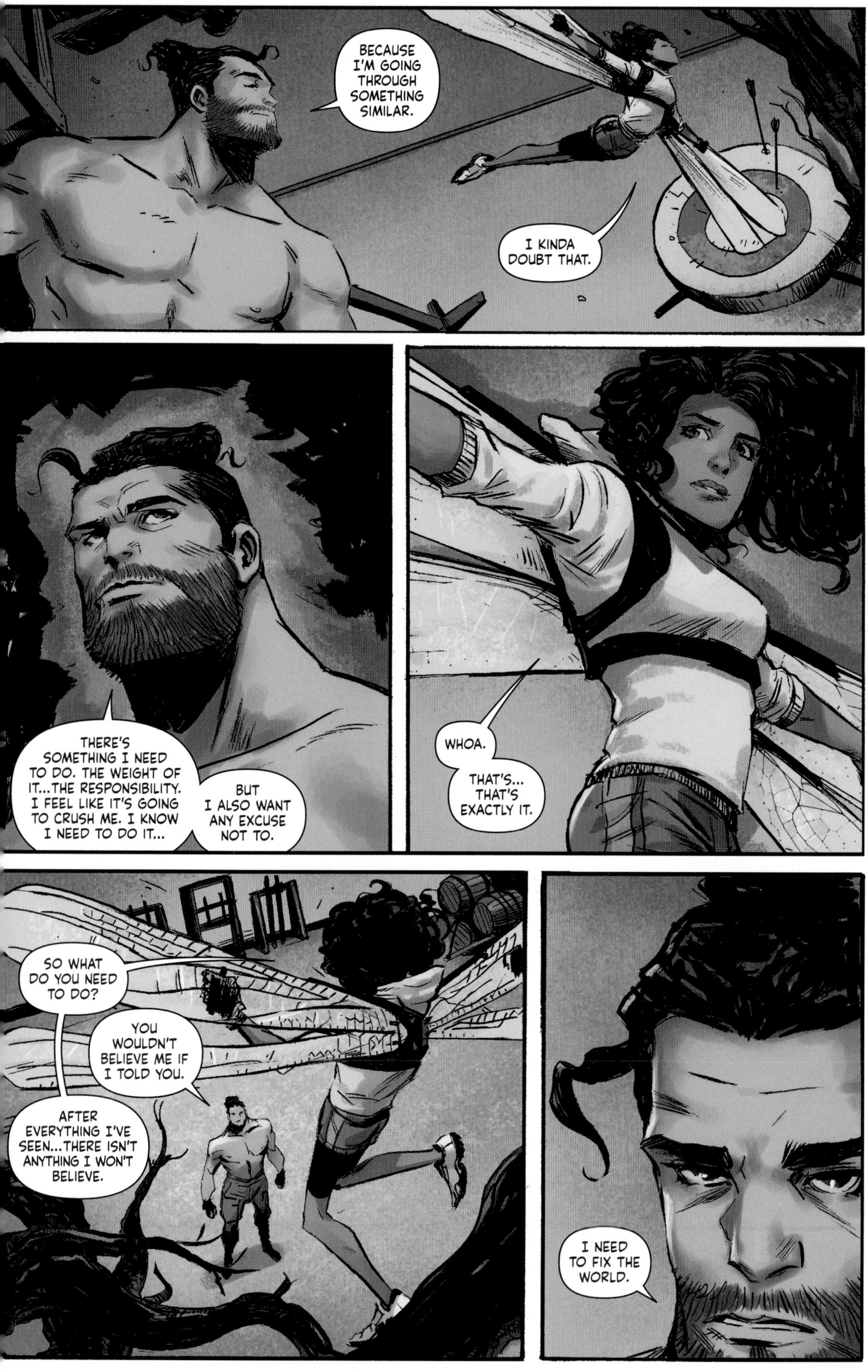
BECAUSE I'M GOING THROUGH SOMETHING SIMILAR.
I KINDA DOUBT THAT.
THERE'S SOMETHING I NEED TO DO. THE WEIGHT OF IT...THE RESPONSIBILITY. I FEEL LIKE IT'S GOING TO CRUSH ME. I KNOW I NEED TO DO IT...
BUT I ALSO WANT ANY EXCUSE NOT TO.
WHOA.
THAT'S... THAT'S EXACTLY IT.
SO WHAT DO YOU NEED TO DO?
YOU WOULDN'T BELIEVE ME IF I TOLD YOU.
AFTER EVERYTHING I'VE SEEN...THERE ISN'T ANYTHING I WON'T BELIEVE.
I NEED TO FIX THE WORLD.

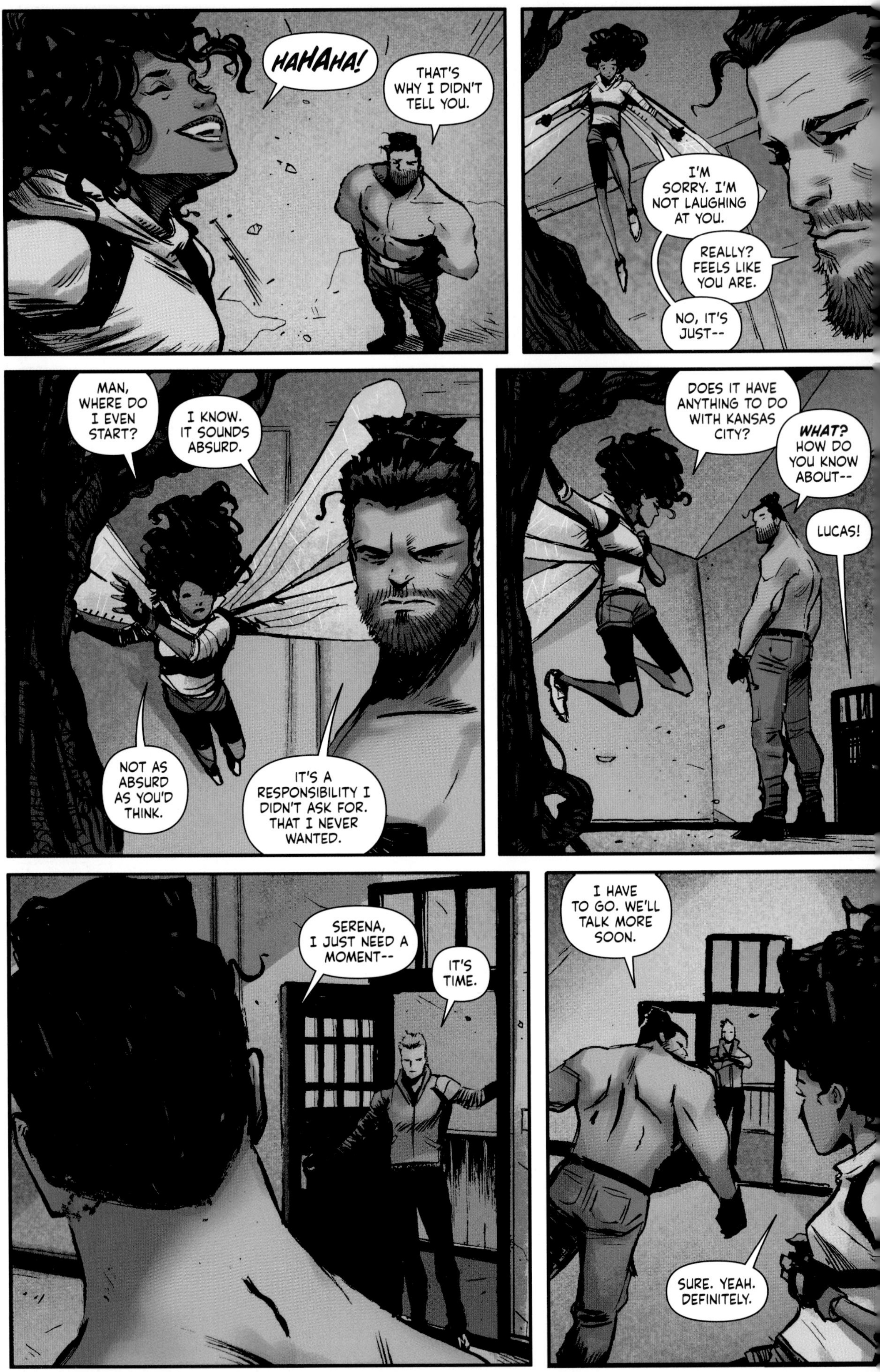
HAHAHA!
THAT'S WHY I DIDN'T TELL YOU.
I'M SORRY. I'M NOT LAUGHING AT YOU.
REALLY? FEELS LIKE YOU ARE.
NO, IT'S JUST--
MAN, WHERE DO I EVEN START?
I KNOW. IT SOUNDS ABSURD.
NOT AS ABSURD AS YOU'D THINK.
IT'S A RESPONSIBILITY I DIDN'T ASK FOR. THAT I NEVER WANTED.
DOES IT HAVE ANYTHING TO DO WITH KANSAS CITY?
WHAT? HOW DO YOU KNOW ABOUT--
LUCAS!
SERENA, I JUST NEED A MOMENT--
IT'S TIME.
I HAVE TO GO. WE'LL TALK MORE SOON.
SURE. YEAH. DEFINITELY.

OKAY. THAT WAS NORMAL. TOTALLY NORMAL AND NOT AT ALL WEIRDLY SEXY.

MAGNETIZE & SAVE LIVES

ANOTHER DAY WITH THOSE WINGS AND I THINK I CAN--

WAITAMINUTE--

NICE TRY, WHOEVER YOU--

HEY! *ET TU*, DUDE WHOSE LIFE I SAVED?

YOU'RE IN DANGER!

THEY KNOW WHO YOU ARE.

WHO? THE OTHER PASSENGERS?

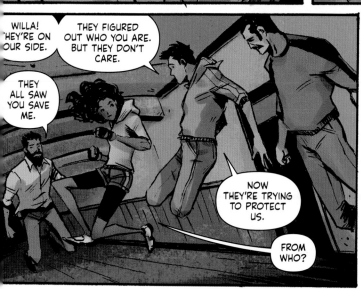

WILLA! THEY'RE ON OUR SIDE.

THEY FIGURED OUT WHO YOU ARE. BUT THEY DON'T CARE.

THEY ALL SAW YOU SAVE ME.

NOW THEY'RE TRYING TO PROTECT US.

FROM WHO?

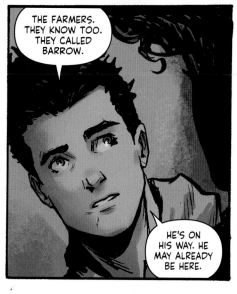

THE FARMERS. THEY KNOW TOO. THEY CALLED BARROW.

HE'S ON HIS WAY. HE MAY ALREADY BE HERE.

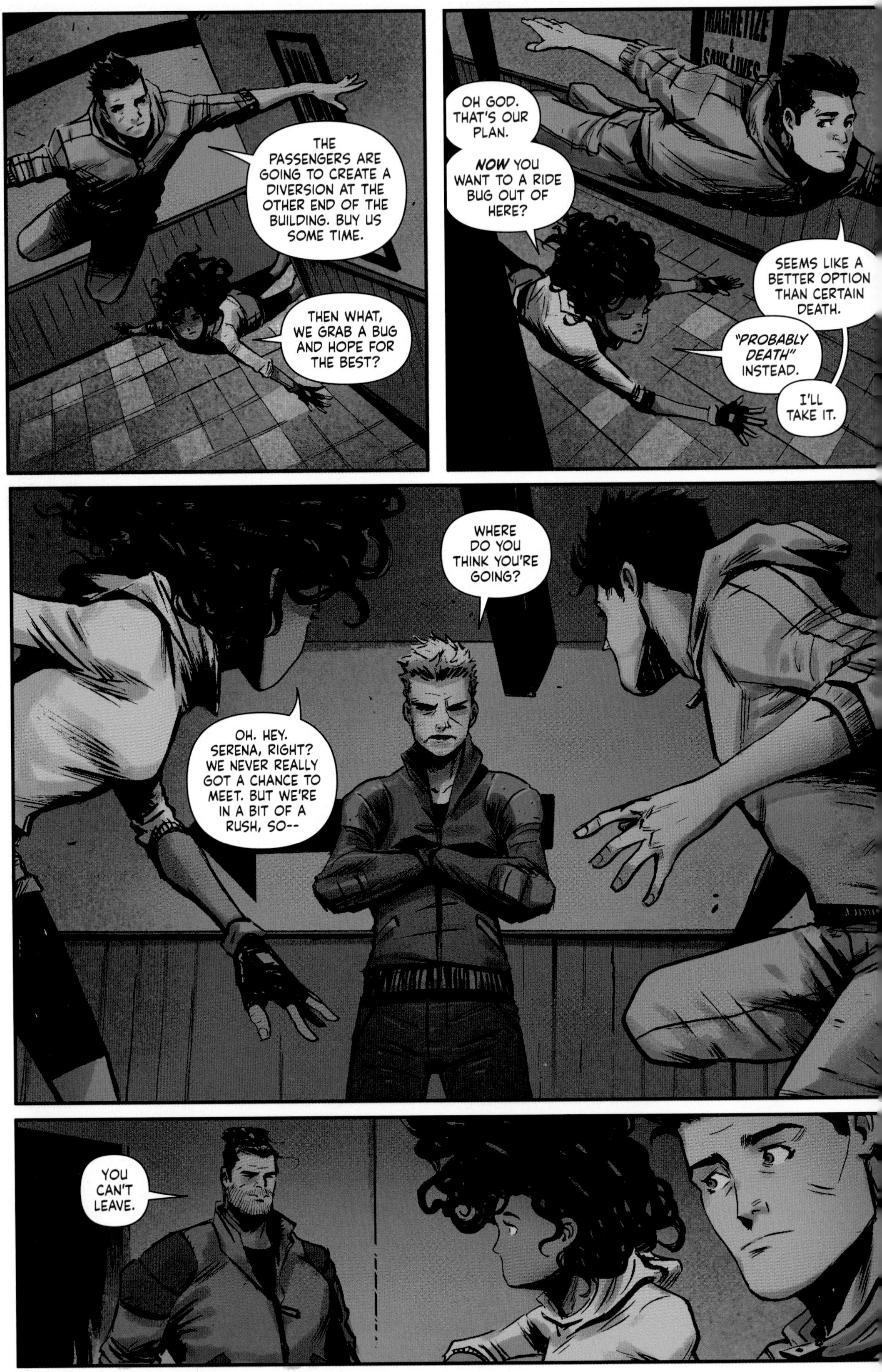
THE PASSENGERS ARE GOING TO CREATE A DIVERSION AT THE OTHER END OF THE BUILDING. BUY US SOME TIME.
THEN WHAT, WE GRAB A BUG AND HOPE FOR THE BEST?
OH GOD. THAT'S OUR PLAN.
NOW YOU WANT TO A RIDE BUG OUT OF HERE?
SEEMS LIKE A BETTER OPTION THAN CERTAIN DEATH.
"PROBABLY DEATH" INSTEAD.
I'LL TAKE IT.
WHERE DO YOU THINK YOU'RE GOING?
OH. HEY. SERENA, RIGHT? WE NEVER REALLY GOT A CHANCE TO MEET. BUT WE'RE IN A BIT OF A RUSH, SO--
YOU CAN'T LEAVE.

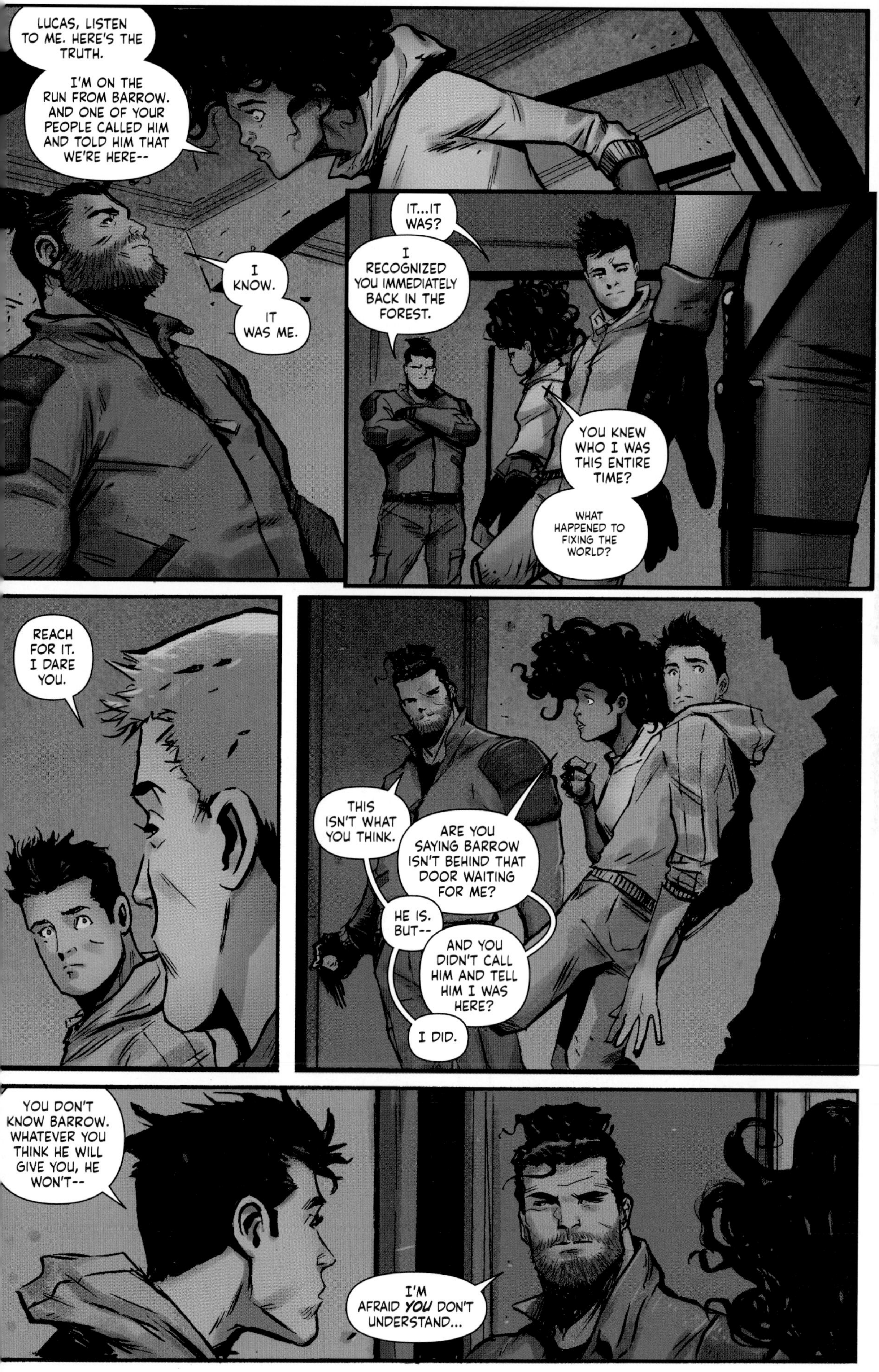
LUCAS, LISTEN TO ME. HERE'S THE TRUTH.
I'M ON THE RUN FROM BARROW. AND ONE OF YOUR PEOPLE CALLED HIM AND TOLD HIM THAT WE'RE HERE--
I KNOW.
IT WAS ME.
IT...IT WAS?
I RECOGNIZED YOU IMMEDIATELY BACK IN THE FOREST.
YOU KNEW WHO I WAS THIS ENTIRE TIME?
WHAT HAPPENED TO FIXING THE WORLD?
REACH FOR IT. I DARE YOU.
THIS ISN'T WHAT YOU THINK.
ARE YOU SAYING BARROW ISN'T BEHIND THAT DOOR WAITING FOR ME?
HE IS. BUT--
AND YOU DIDN'T CALL HIM AND TELL HIM I WAS HERE?
I DID.
YOU DON'T KNOW BARROW. WHATEVER YOU THINK HE WILL GIVE YOU, HE WON'T--
I'M AFRAID *YOU* DON'T UNDERSTAND...

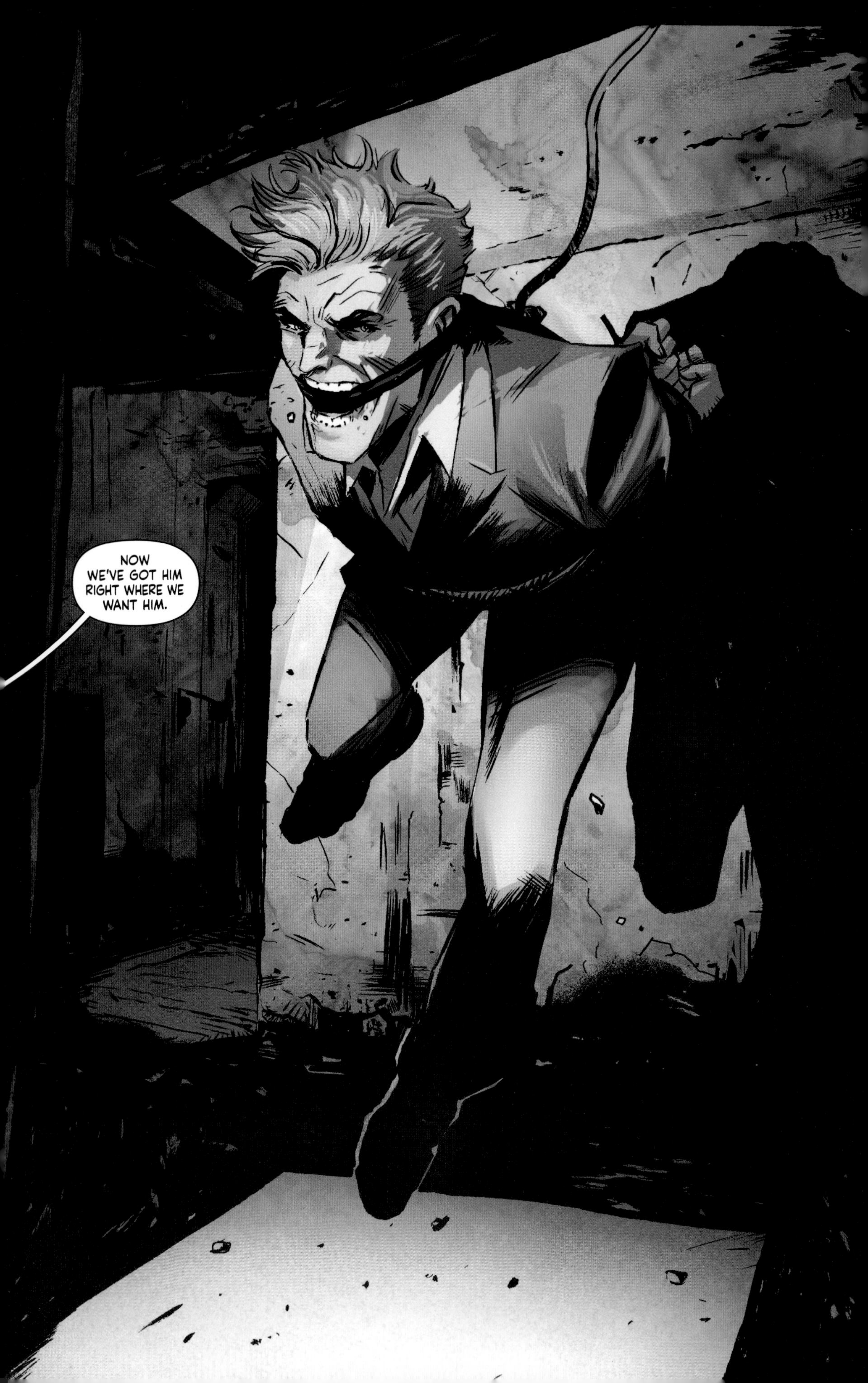
NOW WE'VE GOT HIM RIGHT WHERE WE WANT HIM.

END CHAPTER EIGHT

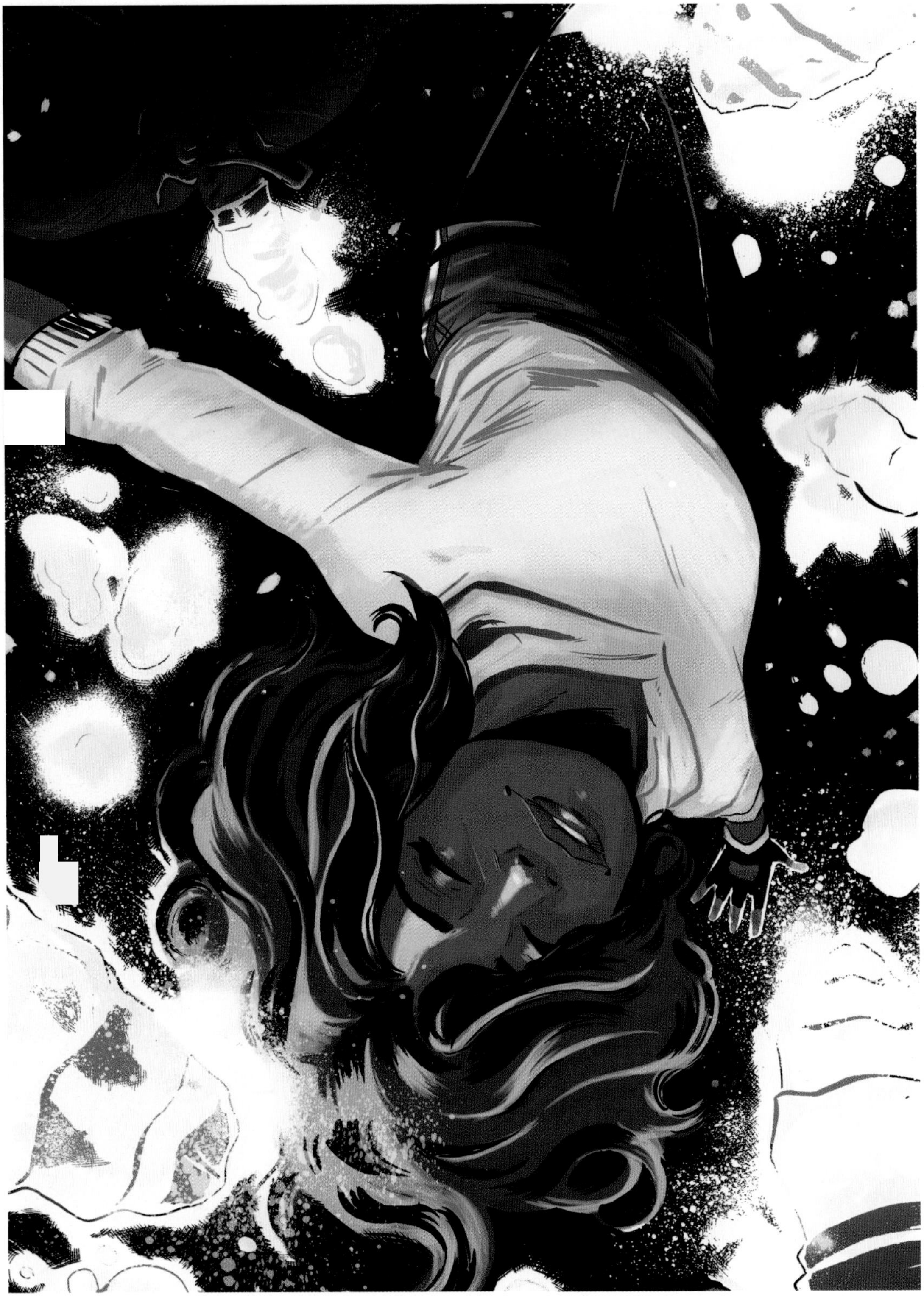

CHAPTER NINE

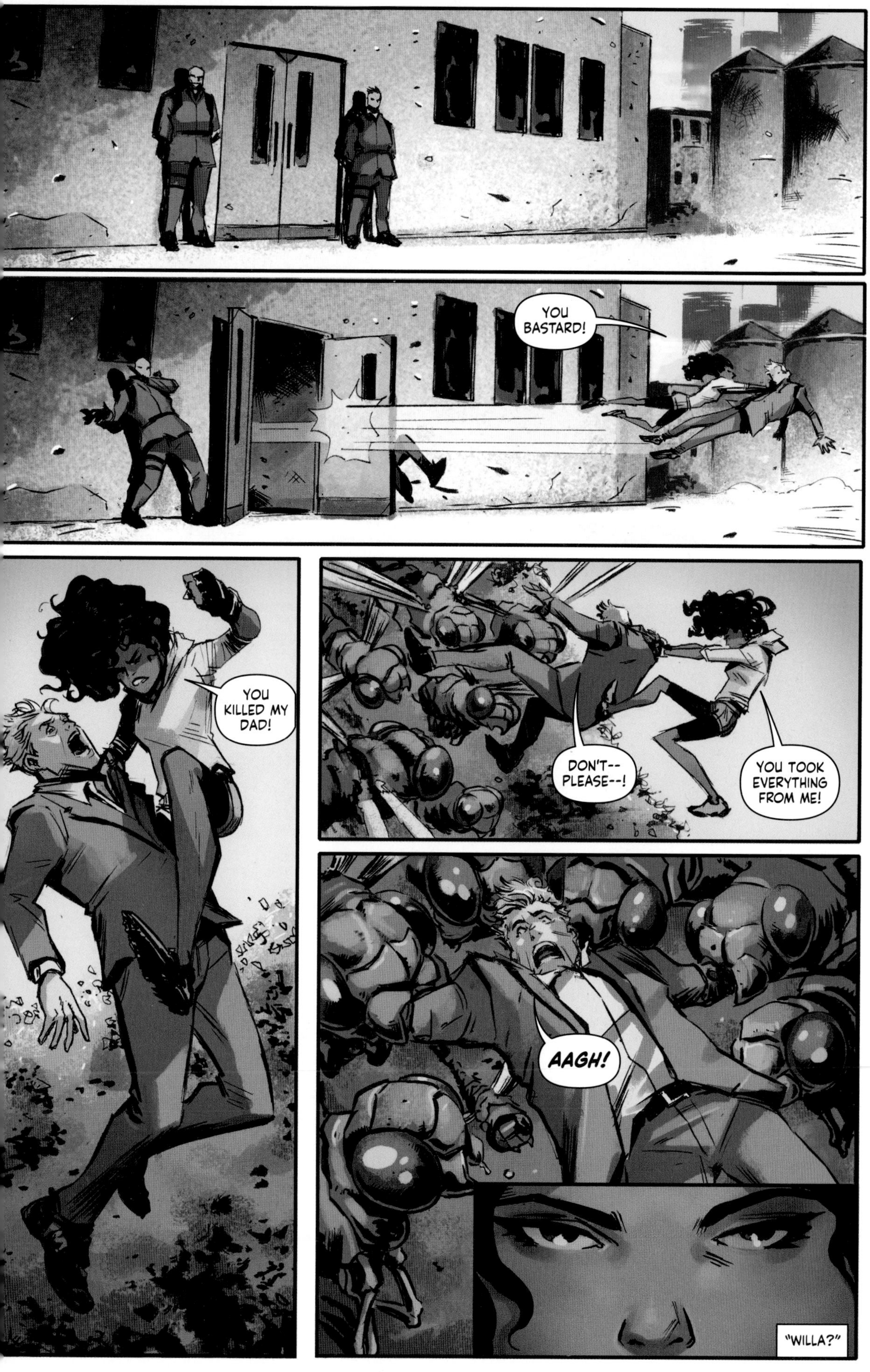
YOU BASTARD!
YOU KILLED MY DAD!
YOU TOOK EVERYTHING FROM ME!
DON'T-- PLEASE--!
AAGH!
"WILLA?"

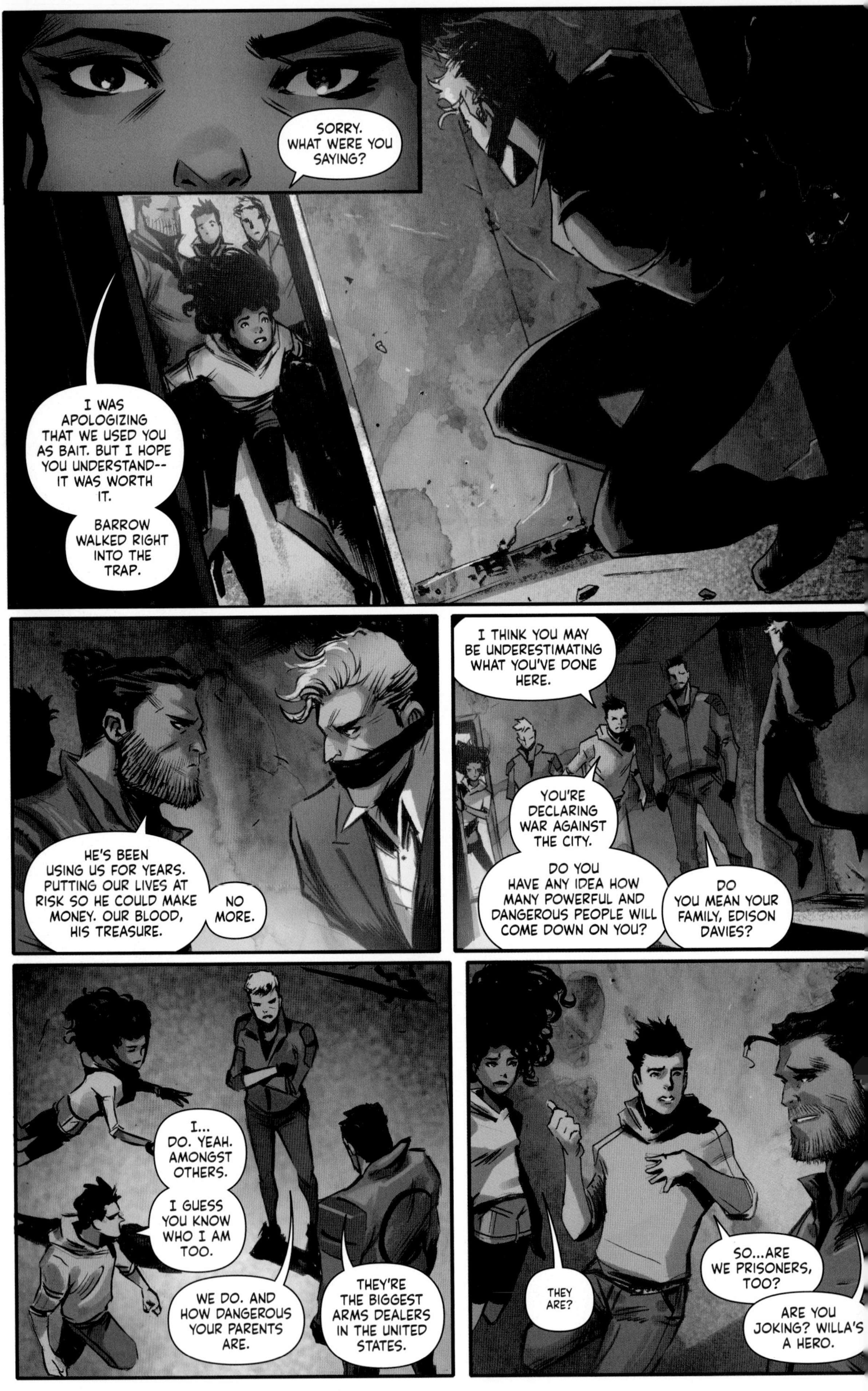
SORRY. WHAT WERE YOU SAYING?
I WAS APOLOGIZING THAT WE USED YOU AS BAIT. BUT I HOPE YOU UNDERSTAND-- IT WAS WORTH IT.
BARROW WALKED RIGHT INTO THE TRAP.
HE'S BEEN USING US FOR YEARS. PUTTING OUR LIVES AT RISK SO HE COULD MAKE MONEY. OUR BLOOD, HIS TREASURE.
NO MORE.
I THINK YOU MAY BE UNDERESTIMATING WHAT YOU'VE DONE HERE.
YOU'RE DECLARING WAR AGAINST THE CITY.
DO YOU HAVE ANY IDEA HOW MANY POWERFUL AND DANGEROUS PEOPLE WILL COME DOWN ON YOU?
DO YOU MEAN YOUR FAMILY, EDISON DAVIES?
I... DO. YEAH. AMONGST OTHERS.
I GUESS YOU KNOW WHO I AM TOO.
WE DO. AND HOW DANGEROUS YOUR PARENTS ARE.
THEY'RE THE BIGGEST ARMS DEALERS IN THE UNITED STATES.
THEY ARE?
SO...ARE WE PRISONERS, TOO?
ARE YOU JOKING? WILLA'S A HERO.

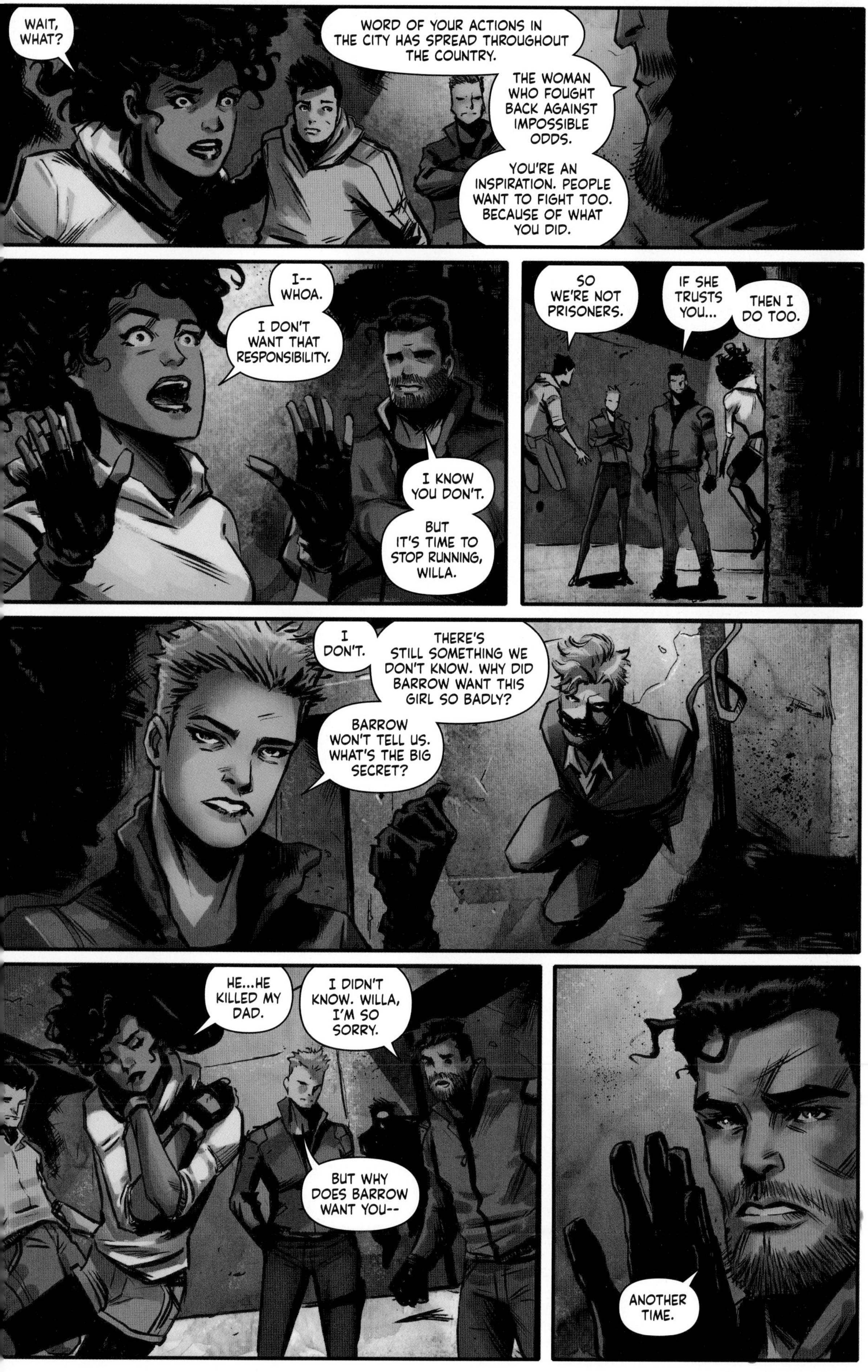
WAIT, WHAT?
WORD OF YOUR ACTIONS IN THE CITY HAS SPREAD THROUGHOUT THE COUNTRY.
THE WOMAN WHO FOUGHT BACK AGAINST IMPOSSIBLE ODDS.
YOU'RE AN INSPIRATION. PEOPLE WANT TO FIGHT TOO. BECAUSE OF WHAT YOU DID.
I-- WHOA.
I DON'T WANT THAT RESPONSIBILITY.
I KNOW YOU DON'T.
BUT IT'S TIME TO STOP RUNNING, WILLA.
SO WE'RE NOT PRISONERS.
IF SHE TRUSTS YOU...
THEN I DO TOO.
I DON'T.
THERE'S STILL SOMETHING WE DON'T KNOW. WHY DID BARROW WANT THIS GIRL SO BADLY?
BARROW WON'T TELL US. WHAT'S THE BIG SECRET?
HE...HE KILLED MY DAD.
I DIDN'T KNOW. WILLA, I'M SO SORRY.
BUT WHY DOES BARROW WANT YOU--
ANOTHER TIME.

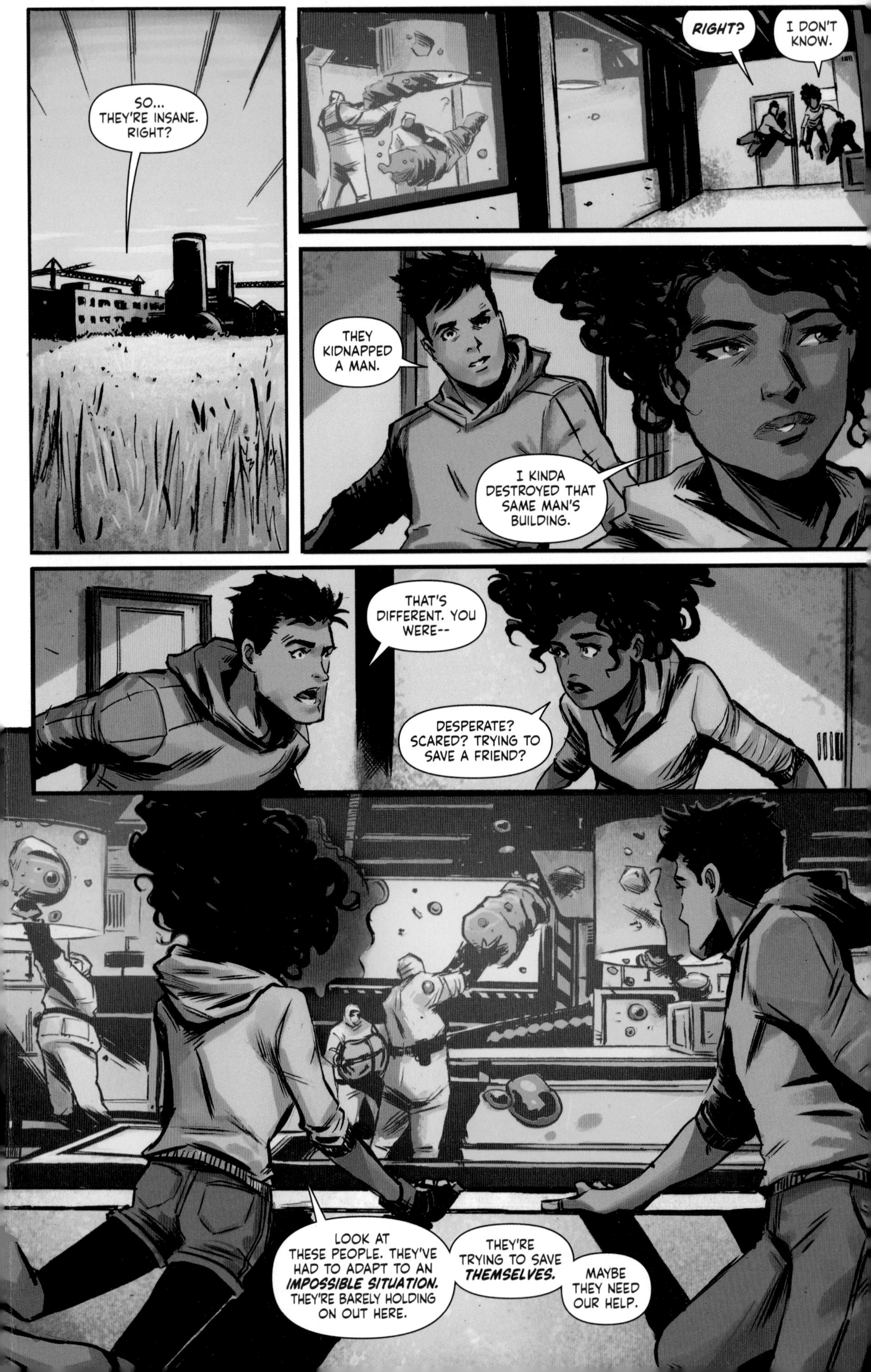
SO... THEY'RE INSANE. RIGHT?
RIGHT?
I DON'T KNOW.
THEY KIDNAPPED A MAN.
I KINDA DESTROYED THAT SAME MAN'S BUILDING.
THAT'S DIFFERENT. YOU WERE--
DESPERATE? SCARED? TRYING TO SAVE A FRIEND?
LOOK AT THESE PEOPLE. THEY'VE HAD TO ADAPT TO AN IMPOSSIBLE SITUATION. THEY'RE BARELY HOLDING ON OUT HERE.
THEY'RE TRYING TO SAVE THEMSELVES.
MAYBE THEY NEED OUR HELP.

YOU CAN'T BE SERIOUS.

THERE'S SOMETHING ELSE. I WAS TALKING TO LUCAS LAST NIGHT. AND HE SEEMED TO KNOW ABOUT--

YOU WERE WITH HIM EARLIER? WHEN?

I COULDN'T SLEEP. SO I LOOKED AROUND. RAN INTO HIM.

HE TAUGHT ME SOME MOVES.

"SOME MOVES."

NO, I MEAN, WITH HIS SWORD--

NOT WHAT I MEANT, AND YOU KNOW IT.

I GET IT. HE'S HANDSOME.

I GUESS.

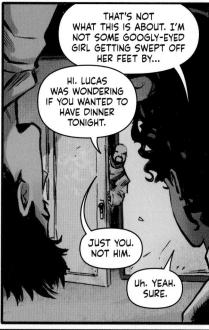

THAT'S NOT WHAT THIS IS ABOUT. I'M NOT SOME GOOGLY-EYED GIRL GETTING SWEPT OFF HER FEET BY...

HI. LUCAS WAS WONDERING IF YOU WANTED TO HAVE DINNER TONIGHT.

JUST YOU. NOT HIM.

UH. YEAH. SURE.

DON'T.

I DON'T THINK I NEED TO.

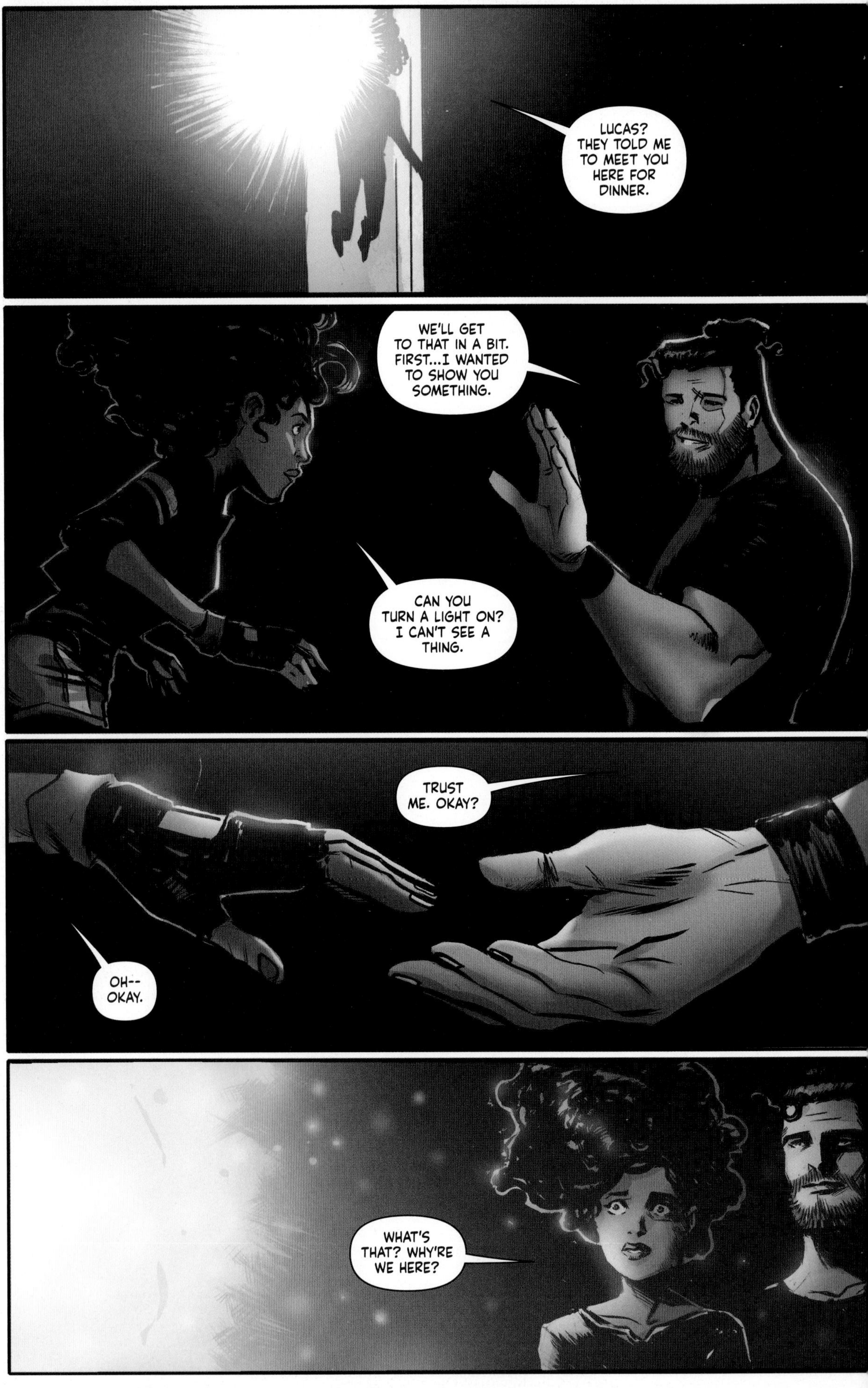
LUCAS? THEY TOLD ME TO MEET YOU HERE FOR DINNER.
WE'LL GET TO THAT IN A BIT. FIRST...I WANTED TO SHOW YOU SOMETHING.
CAN YOU TURN A LIGHT ON? I CAN'T SEE A THING.
TRUST ME. OKAY?
OH-- OKAY.
WHAT'S THAT? WHY'RE WE HERE?

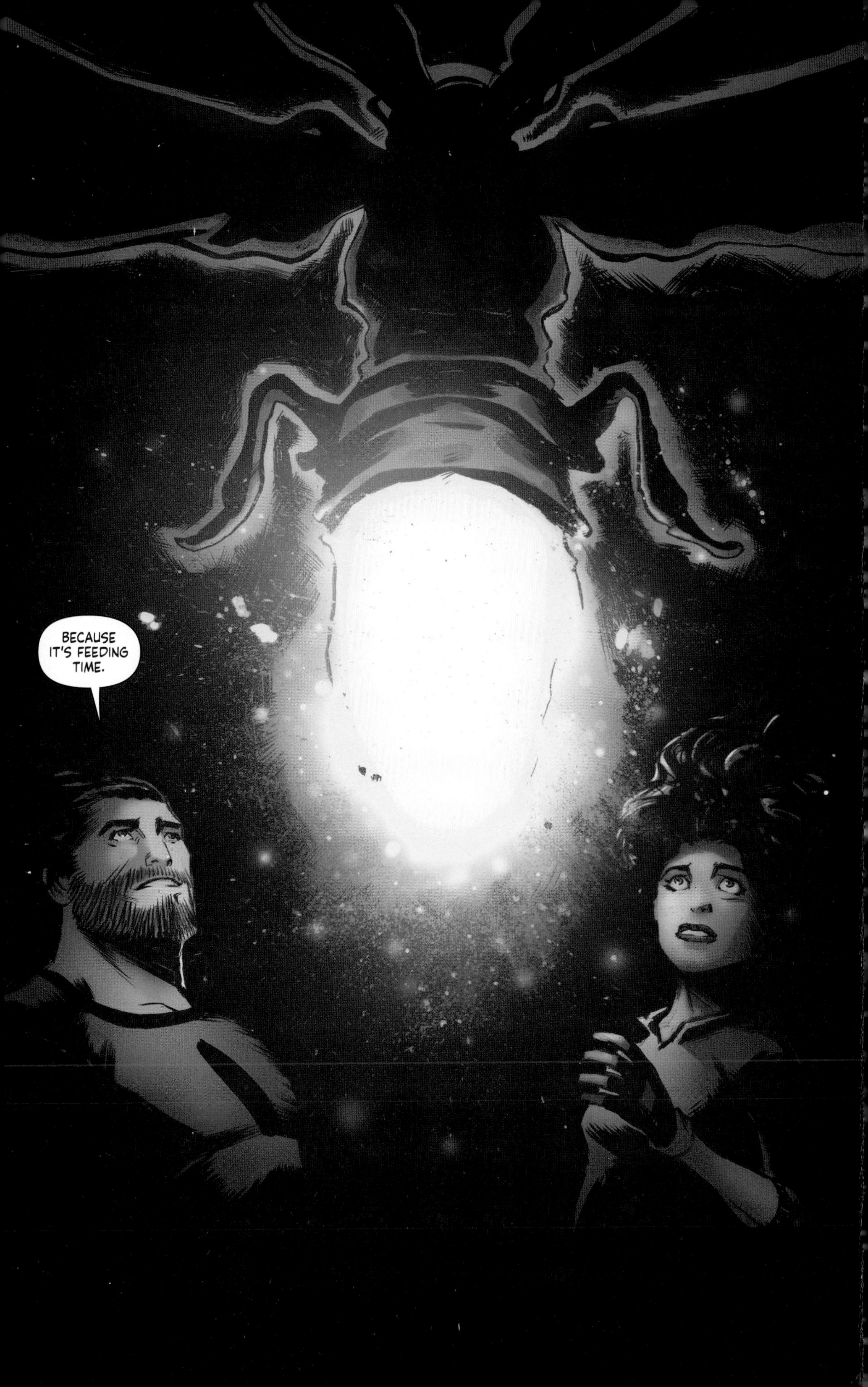
BECAUSE IT'S FEEDING TIME.

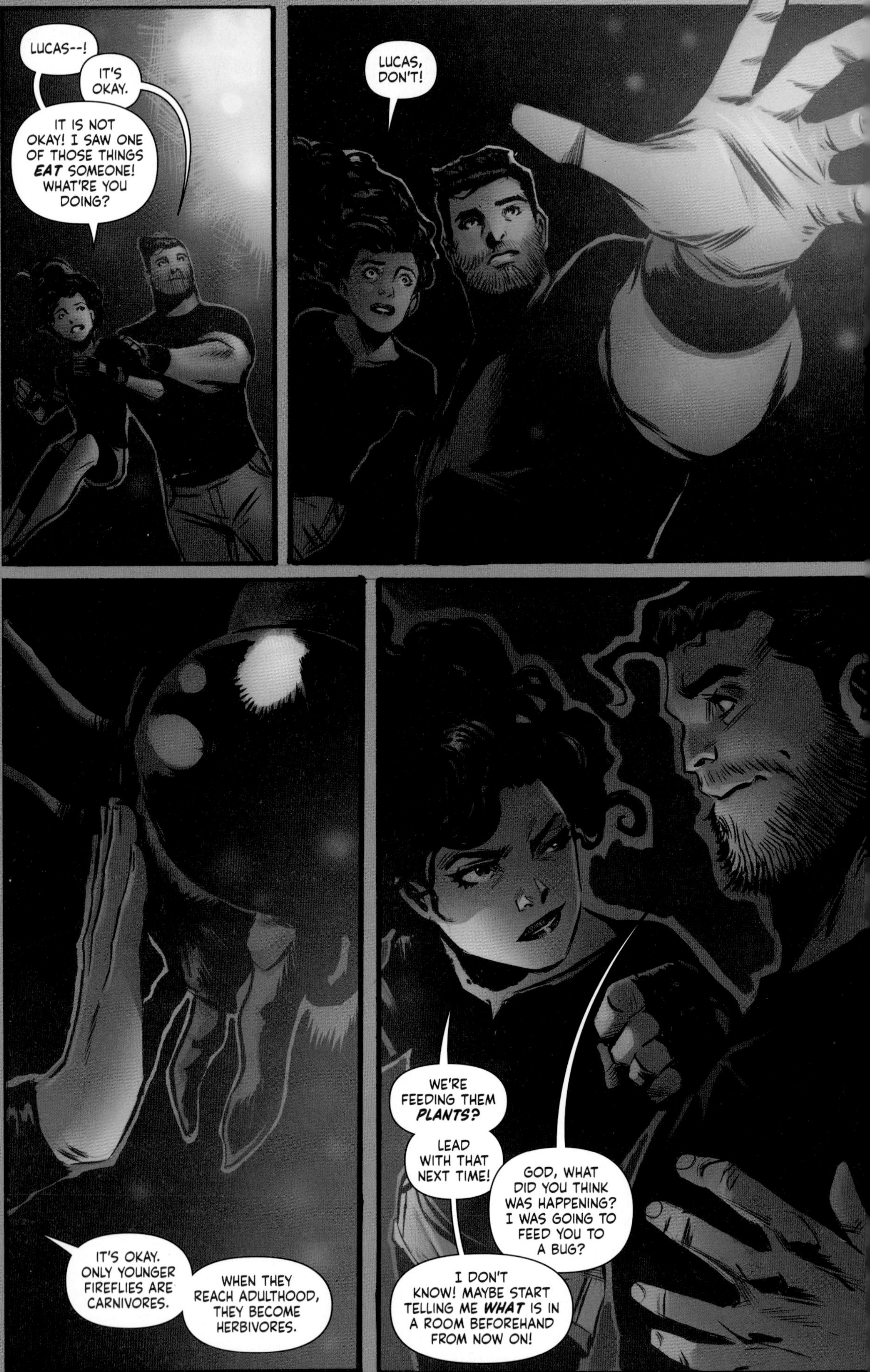
LUCAS--!
IT'S OKAY.
IT IS NOT OKAY! I SAW ONE OF THOSE THINGS EAT SOMEONE! WHAT'RE YOU DOING?
LUCAS, DON'T!
IT'S OKAY. ONLY YOUNGER FIREFLIES ARE CARNIVORES.
WHEN THEY REACH ADULTHOOD, THEY BECOME HERBIVORES.
WE'RE FEEDING THEM PLANTS?
LEAD WITH THAT NEXT TIME!
GOD, WHAT DID YOU THINK WAS HAPPENING? I WAS GOING TO FEED YOU TO A BUG?
I DON'T KNOW! MAYBE START TELLING ME WHAT IS IN A ROOM BEFOREHAND FROM NOW ON!

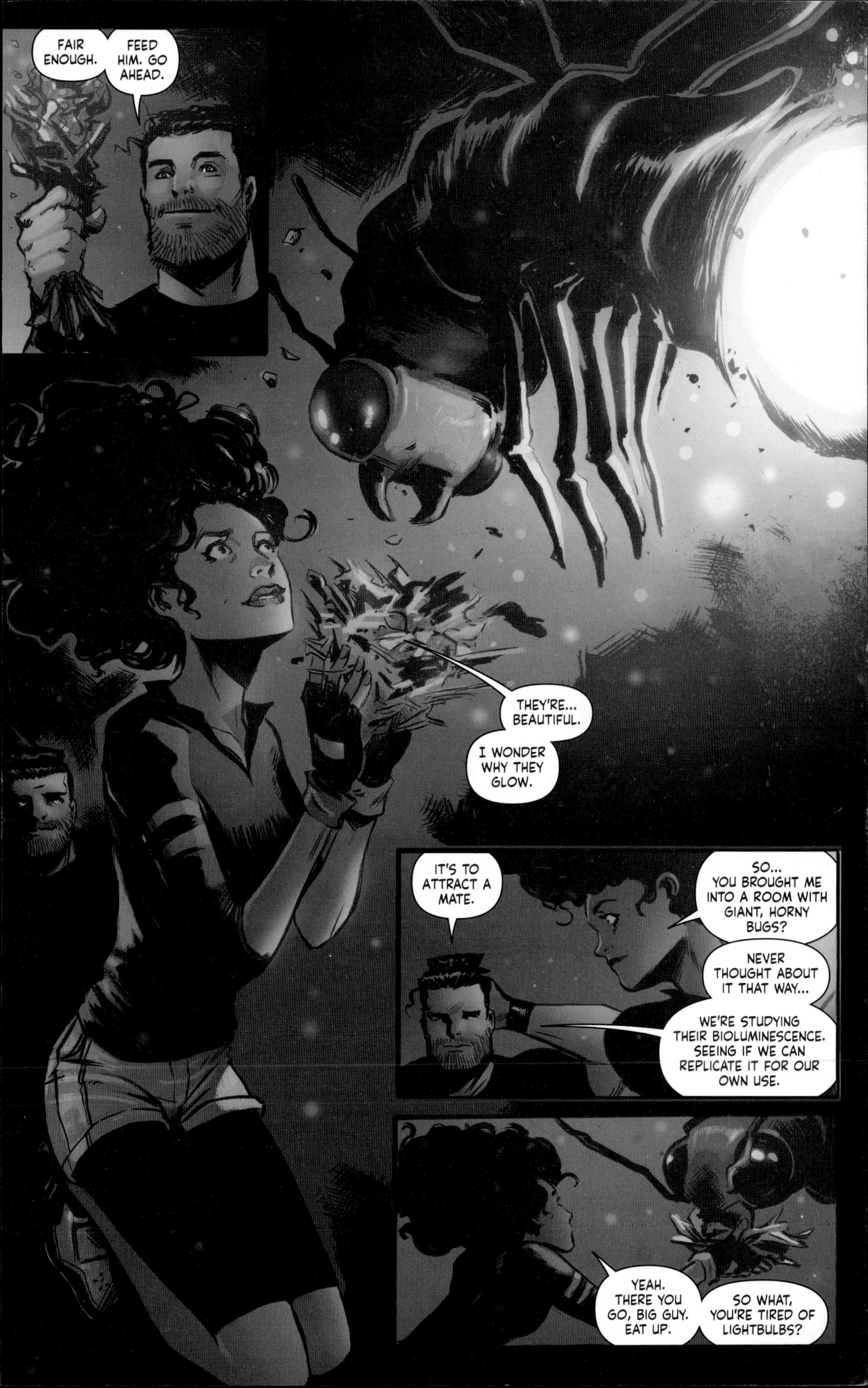
FAIR ENOUGH.
FEED HIM. GO AHEAD.
THEY'RE... BEAUTIFUL.
I WONDER WHY THEY GLOW.
IT'S TO ATTRACT A MATE.
SO... YOU BROUGHT ME INTO A ROOM WITH GIANT, HORNY BUGS?
NEVER THOUGHT ABOUT IT THAT WAY...
WE'RE STUDYING THEIR BIOLUMINESCENCE. SEEING IF WE CAN REPLICATE IT FOR OUR OWN USE.
YEAH. THERE YOU GO, BIG GUY. EAT UP.
SO WHAT, YOU'RE TIRED OF LIGHTBULBS?

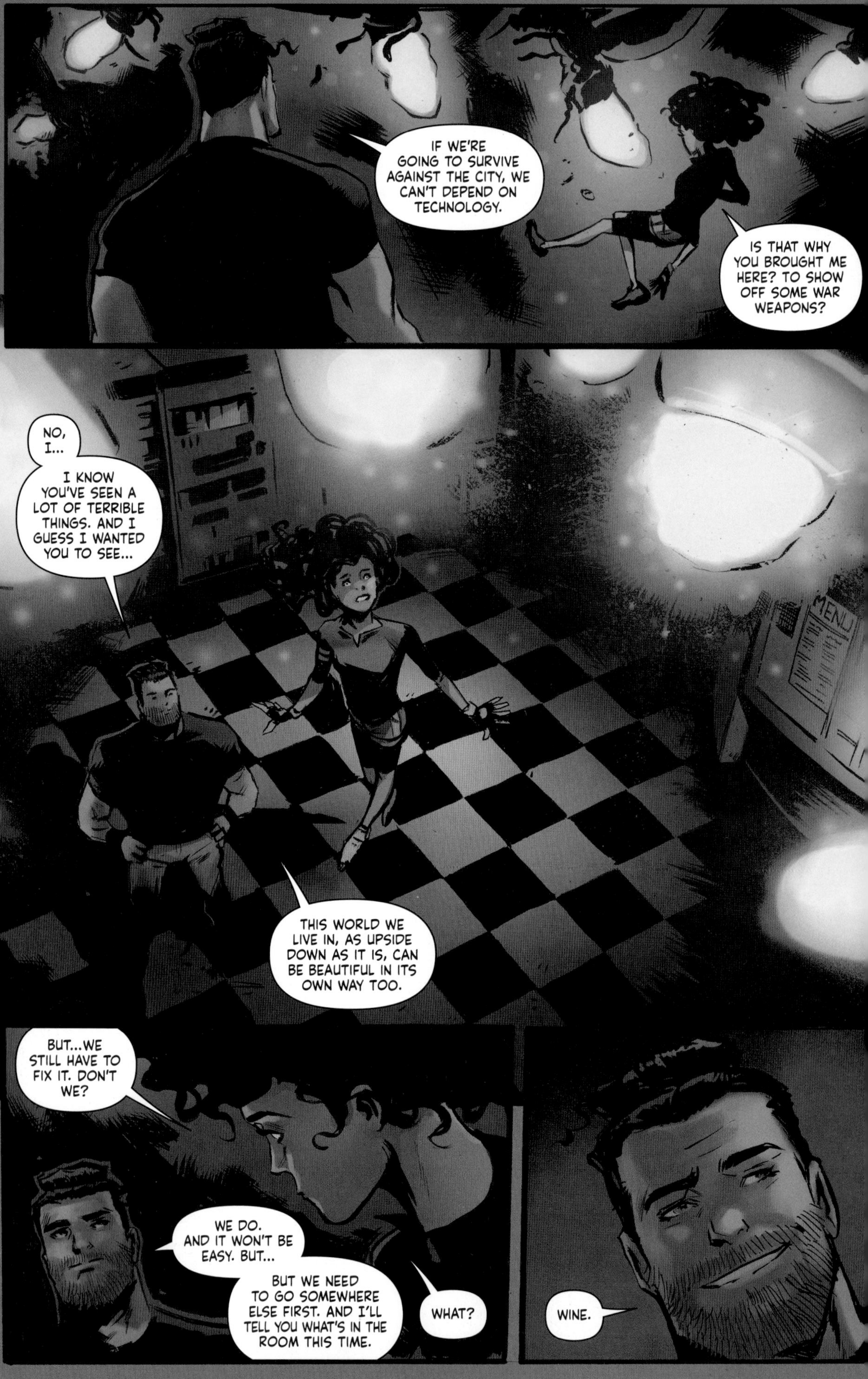
IF WE'RE GOING TO SURVIVE AGAINST THE CITY, WE CAN'T DEPEND ON TECHNOLOGY.
IS THAT WHY YOU BROUGHT ME HERE? TO SHOW OFF SOME WAR WEAPONS?
NO, I...
I KNOW YOU'VE SEEN A LOT OF TERRIBLE THINGS. AND I GUESS I WANTED YOU TO SEE...
THIS WORLD WE LIVE IN, AS UPSIDE DOWN AS IT IS, CAN BE BEAUTIFUL IN ITS OWN WAY TOO.
MENU
BUT...WE STILL HAVE TO FIX IT. DON'T WE?
WE DO. AND IT WON'T BE EASY. BUT...
BUT WE NEED TO GO SOMEWHERE ELSE FIRST. AND I'LL TELL YOU WHAT'S IN THE ROOM THIS TIME.
WHAT?
WINE.

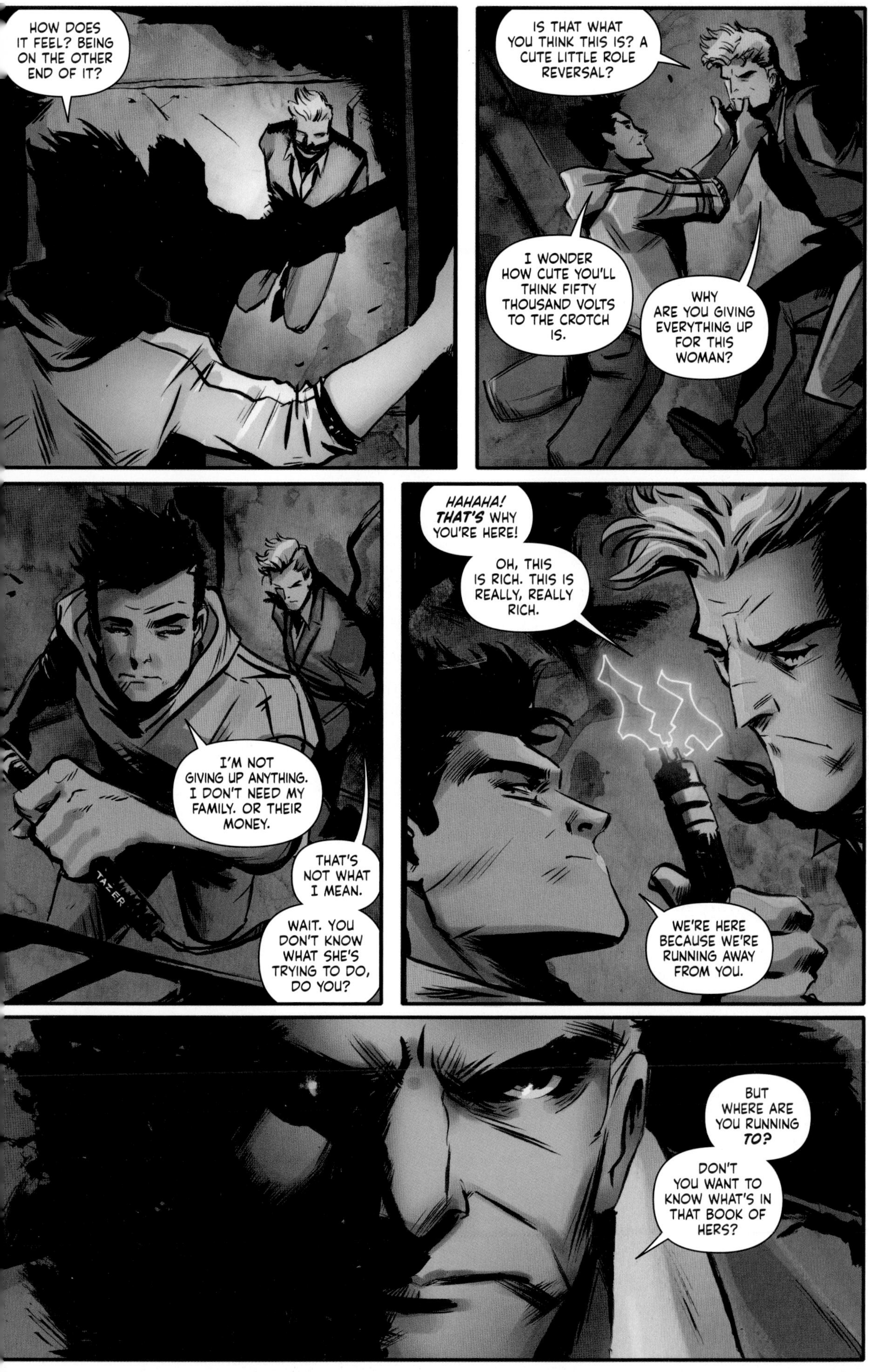
HOW DOES IT FEEL? BEING ON THE OTHER END OF IT?
IS THAT WHAT YOU THINK THIS IS? A CUTE LITTLE ROLE REVERSAL?
I WONDER HOW CUTE YOU'LL THINK FIFTY THOUSAND VOLTS TO THE CROTCH IS.
WHY ARE YOU GIVING EVERYTHING UP FOR THIS WOMAN?
I'M NOT GIVING UP ANYTHING. I DON'T NEED MY FAMILY. OR THEIR MONEY.
TAZER
THAT'S NOT WHAT I MEAN.
WAIT. YOU DON'T KNOW WHAT SHE'S TRYING TO DO, DO YOU?
HAHAHA! THAT'S WHY YOU'RE HERE!
OH, THIS IS RICH. THIS IS REALLY, REALLY RICH.
WE'RE HERE BECAUSE WE'RE RUNNING AWAY FROM YOU.
BUT WHERE ARE YOU RUNNING TO?
DON'T YOU WANT TO KNOW WHAT'S IN THAT BOOK OF HERS?

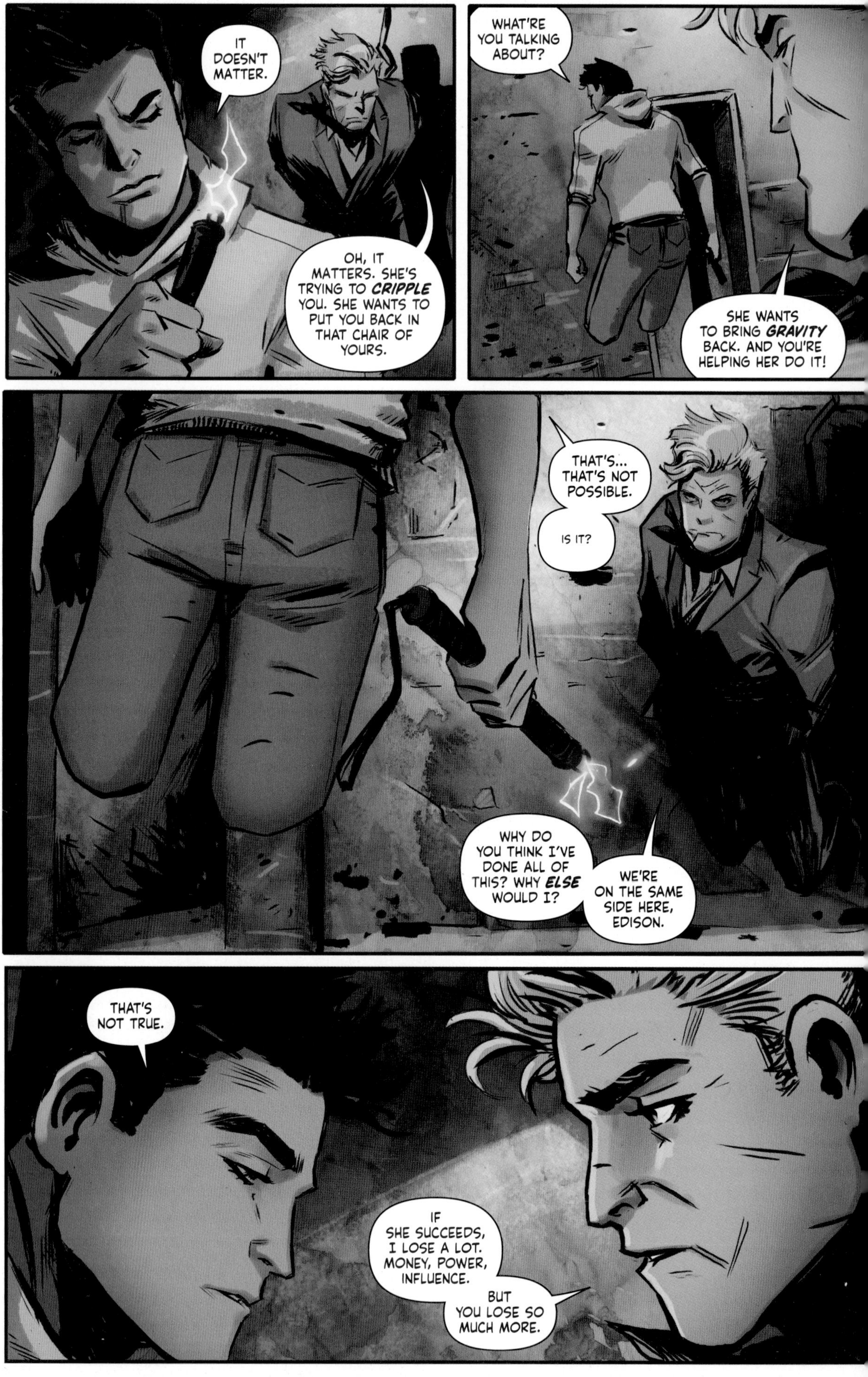
IT DOESN'T MATTER.
OH, IT MATTERS. SHE'S TRYING TO ***CRIPPLE*** YOU. SHE WANTS TO PUT YOU BACK IN THAT CHAIR OF YOURS.
WHAT'RE YOU TALKING ABOUT?
SHE WANTS TO BRING ***GRAVITY*** BACK. AND YOU'RE HELPING HER DO IT!
THAT'S... THAT'S NOT POSSIBLE.
IS IT?
WHY DO YOU THINK I'VE DONE ALL OF THIS? WHY ***ELSE*** WOULD I?
WE'RE ON THE SAME SIDE HERE, EDISON.
THAT'S NOT TRUE.
IF SHE SUCCEEDS, I LOSE A LOT. MONEY, POWER, INFLUENCE.
BUT YOU LOSE SO MUCH MORE.

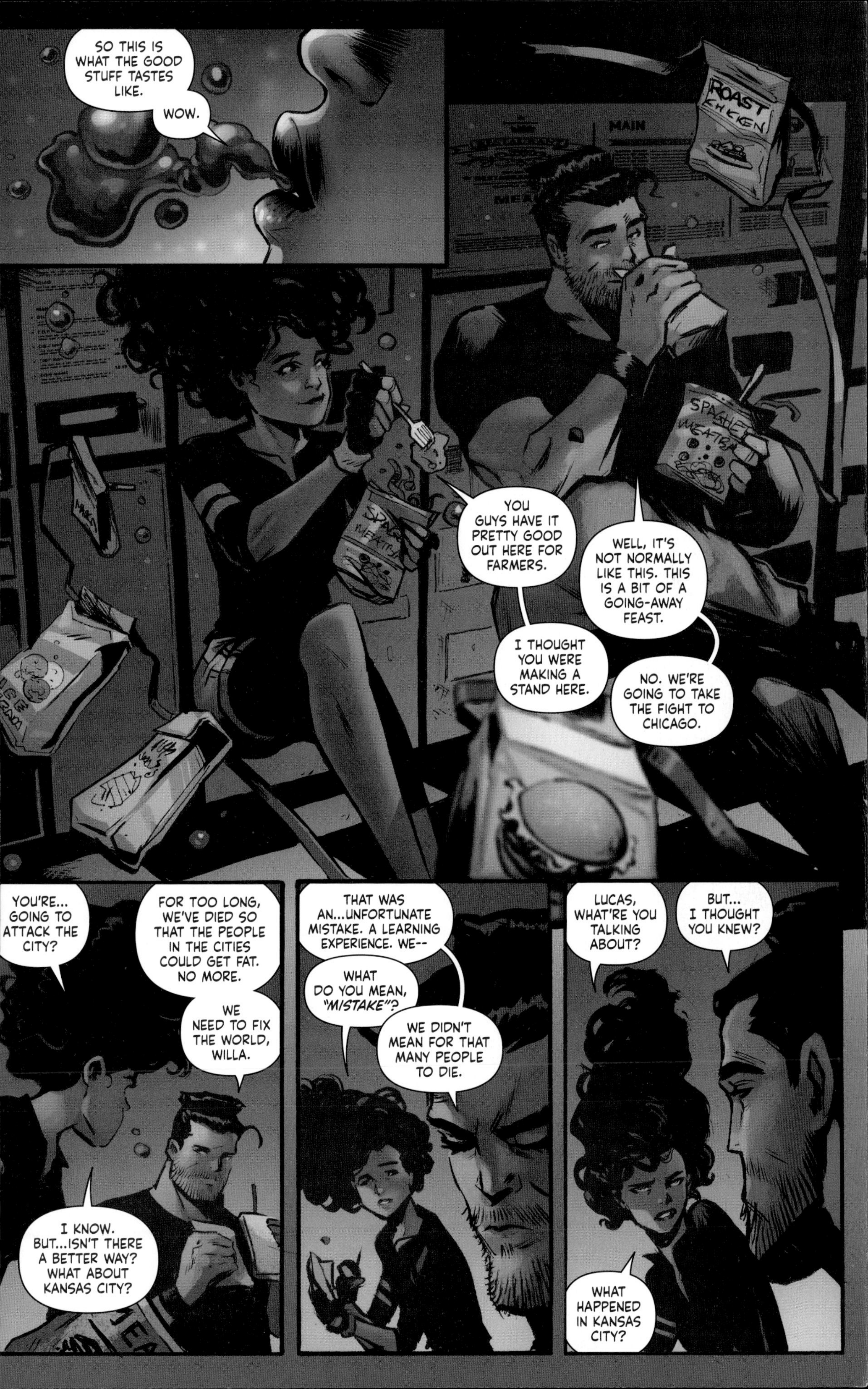
SO THIS IS WHAT THE GOOD STUFF TASTES LIKE.
WOW.
ROAST CHICKEN
YOU GUYS HAVE IT PRETTY GOOD OUT HERE FOR FARMERS.
WELL, IT'S NOT NORMALLY LIKE THIS. THIS IS A BIT OF A GOING-AWAY FEAST.
I THOUGHT YOU WERE MAKING A STAND HERE.
NO. WE'RE GOING TO TAKE THE FIGHT TO CHICAGO.
YOU'RE... GOING TO ATTACK THE CITY?
FOR TOO LONG, WE'VE DIED SO THAT THE PEOPLE IN THE CITIES COULD GET FAT. NO MORE.
WE NEED TO FIX THE WORLD, WILLA.
I KNOW. BUT...ISN'T THERE A BETTER WAY? WHAT ABOUT KANSAS CITY?
THAT WAS AN...UNFORTUNATE MISTAKE. A LEARNING EXPERIENCE. WE--
WHAT DO YOU MEAN, *"MISTAKE"*?
WE DIDN'T MEAN FOR THAT MANY PEOPLE TO DIE.
LUCAS, WHAT'RE YOU TALKING ABOUT?
BUT... I THOUGHT YOU KNEW?
WHAT HAPPENED IN KANSAS CITY?

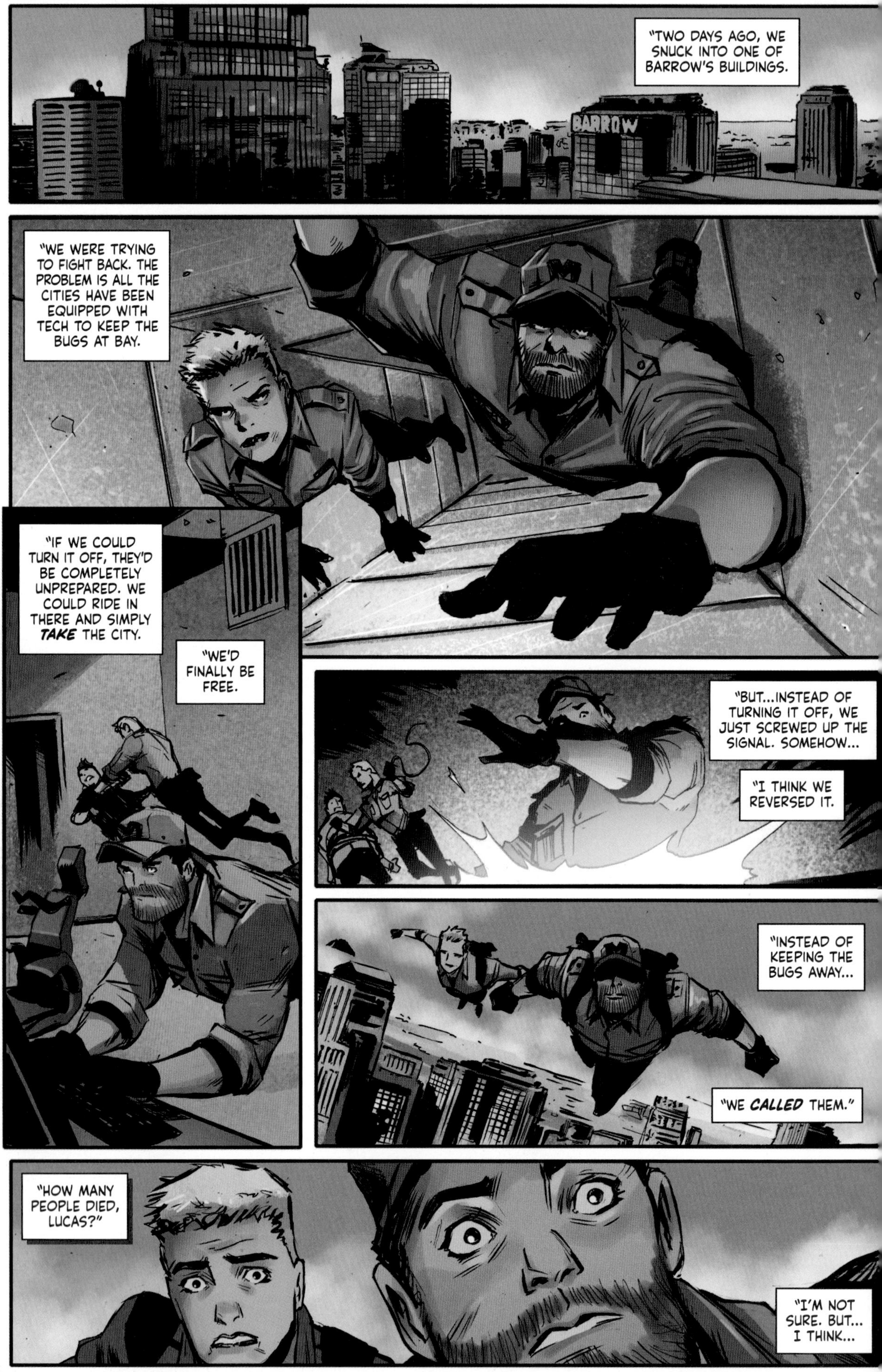
"TWO DAYS AGO, WE SNUCK INTO ONE OF BARROW'S BUILDINGS.
BARROW
"WE WERE TRYING TO FIGHT BACK. THE PROBLEM IS ALL THE CITIES HAVE BEEN EQUIPPED WITH TECH TO KEEP THE BUGS AT BAY.
"IF WE COULD TURN IT OFF, THEY'D BE COMPLETELY UNPREPARED. WE COULD RIDE IN THERE AND SIMPLY *TAKE* THE CITY.
"WE'D FINALLY BE FREE.
"BUT...INSTEAD OF TURNING IT OFF, WE JUST SCREWED UP THE SIGNAL. SOMEHOW...
"I THINK WE REVERSED IT.
"INSTEAD OF KEEPING THE BUGS AWAY...
"WE *CALLED* THEM."
"HOW MANY PEOPLE DIED, LUCAS?"
"I'M NOT SURE. BUT... I THINK...

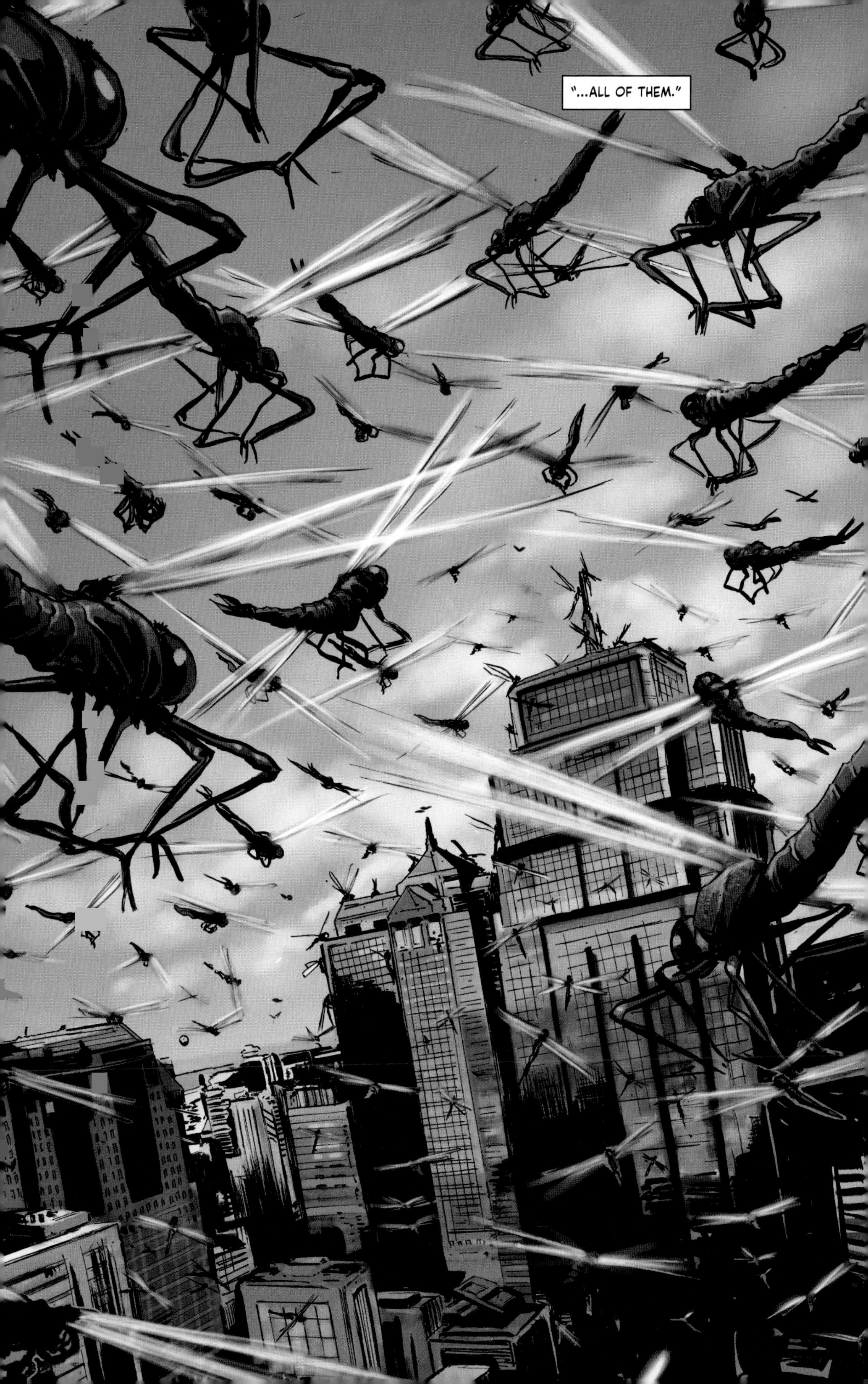
"...ALL OF THEM."

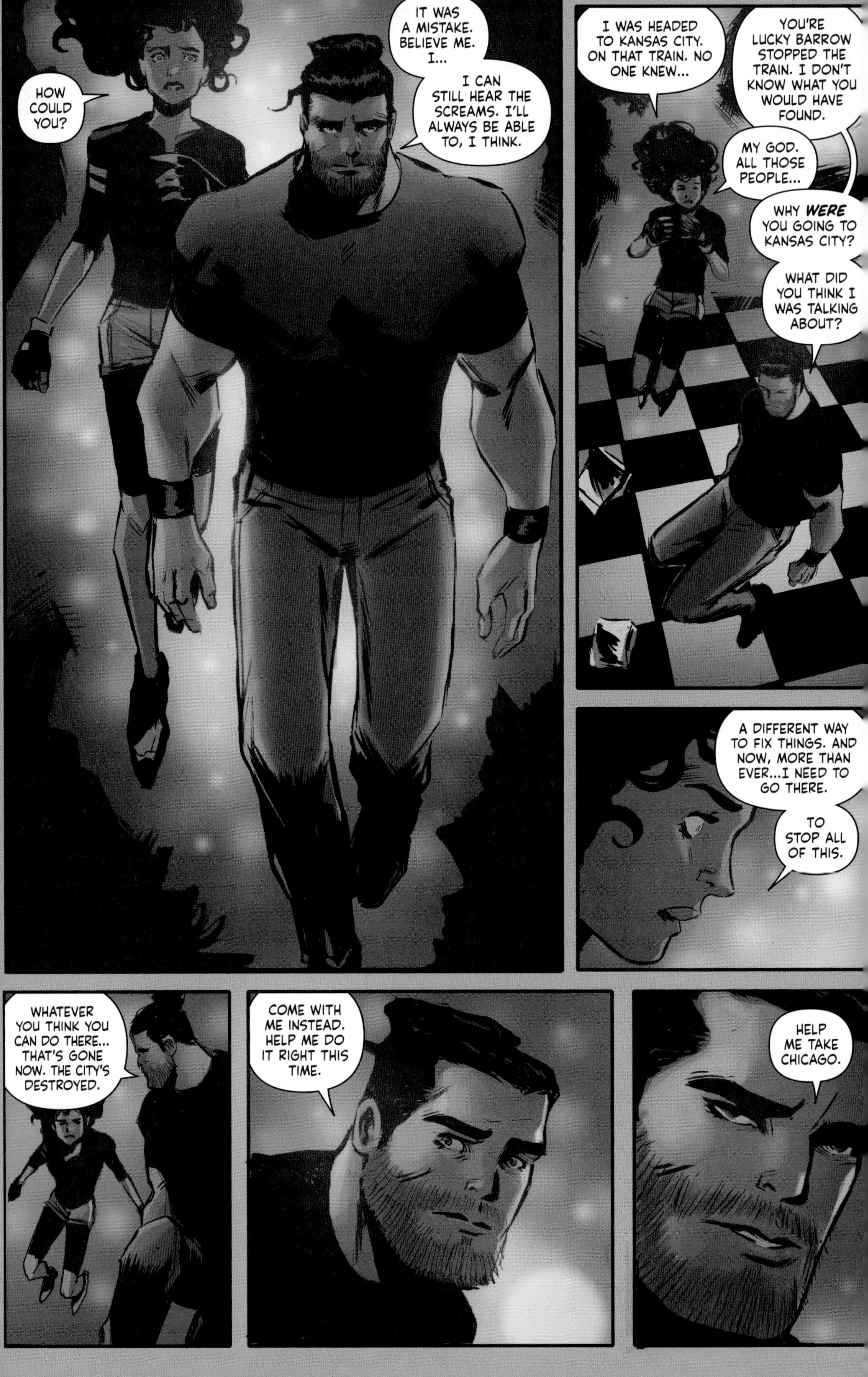
HOW COULD YOU?
IT WAS A MISTAKE. BELIEVE ME. I...
I CAN STILL HEAR THE SCREAMS. I'LL ALWAYS BE ABLE TO, I THINK.
I WAS HEADED TO KANSAS CITY. ON THAT TRAIN. NO ONE KNEW...
YOU'RE LUCKY BARROW STOPPED THE TRAIN. I DON'T KNOW WHAT YOU WOULD HAVE FOUND.
MY GOD. ALL THOSE PEOPLE...
WHY WERE YOU GOING TO KANSAS CITY?
WHAT DID YOU THINK I WAS TALKING ABOUT?
A DIFFERENT WAY TO FIX THINGS. AND NOW, MORE THAN EVER...I NEED TO GO THERE.
TO STOP ALL OF THIS.
WHATEVER YOU THINK YOU CAN DO THERE... THAT'S GONE NOW. THE CITY'S DESTROYED.
COME WITH ME INSTEAD. HELP ME DO IT RIGHT THIS TIME.
HELP ME TAKE CHICAGO.

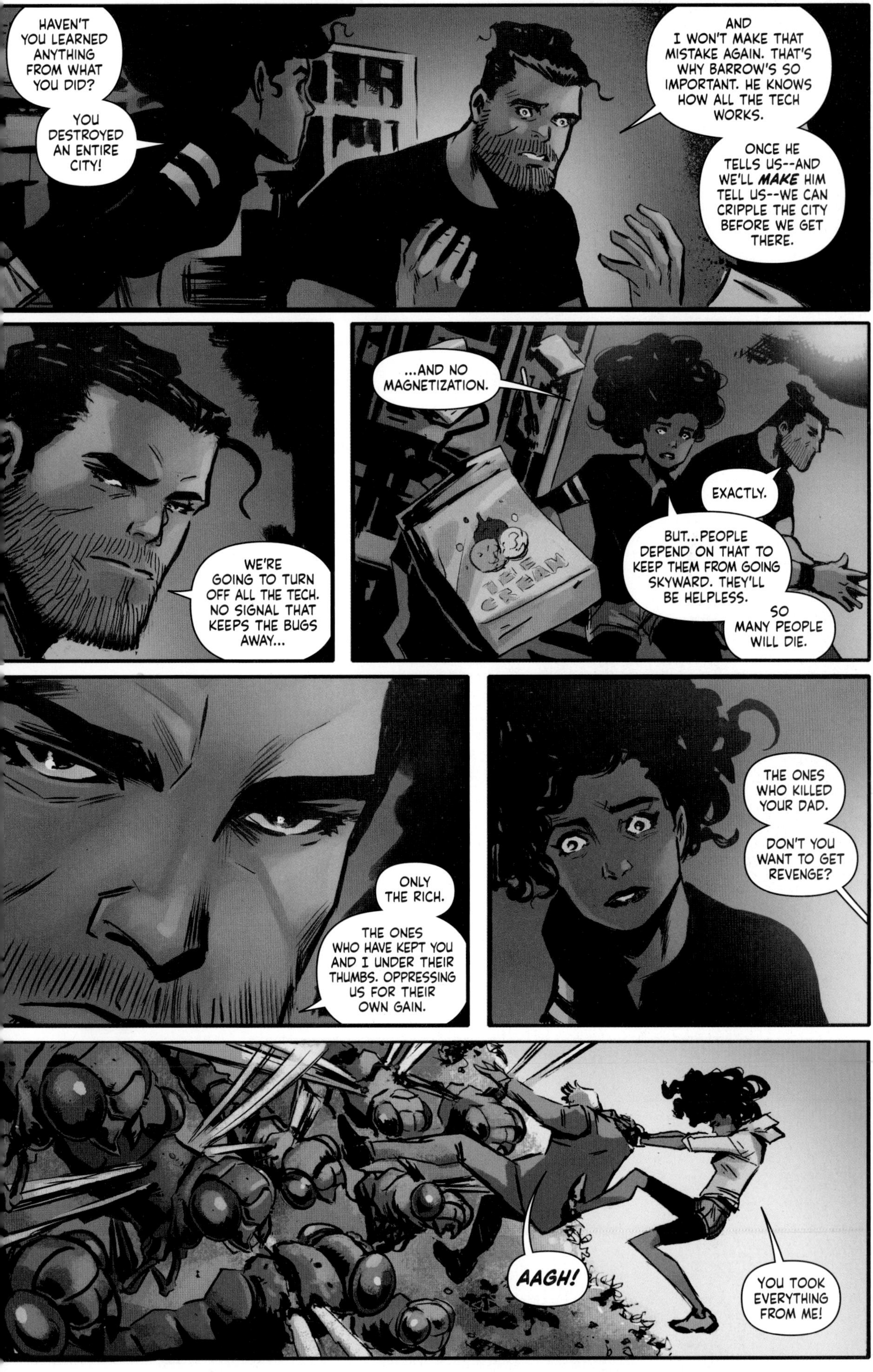
HAVEN'T YOU LEARNED ANYTHING FROM WHAT YOU DID?
YOU DESTROYED AN ENTIRE CITY!
AND I WON'T MAKE THAT MISTAKE AGAIN. THAT'S WHY BARROW'S SO IMPORTANT. HE KNOWS HOW ALL THE TECH WORKS.
ONCE HE TELLS US--AND WE'LL *MAKE* HIM TELL US--WE CAN CRIPPLE THE CITY BEFORE WE GET THERE.
WE'RE GOING TO TURN OFF ALL THE TECH. NO SIGNAL THAT KEEPS THE BUGS AWAY...
...AND NO MAGNETIZATION.
ICE CREAM
EXACTLY.
BUT...PEOPLE DEPEND ON THAT TO KEEP THEM FROM GOING SKYWARD. THEY'LL BE HELPLESS.
SO MANY PEOPLE WILL DIE.
ONLY THE RICH.
THE ONES WHO HAVE KEPT YOU AND I UNDER THEIR THUMBS. OPPRESSING US FOR THEIR OWN GAIN.
THE ONES WHO KILLED YOUR DAD.
DON'T YOU WANT TO GET REVENGE?
AAGH!
YOU TOOK EVERYTHING FROM ME!

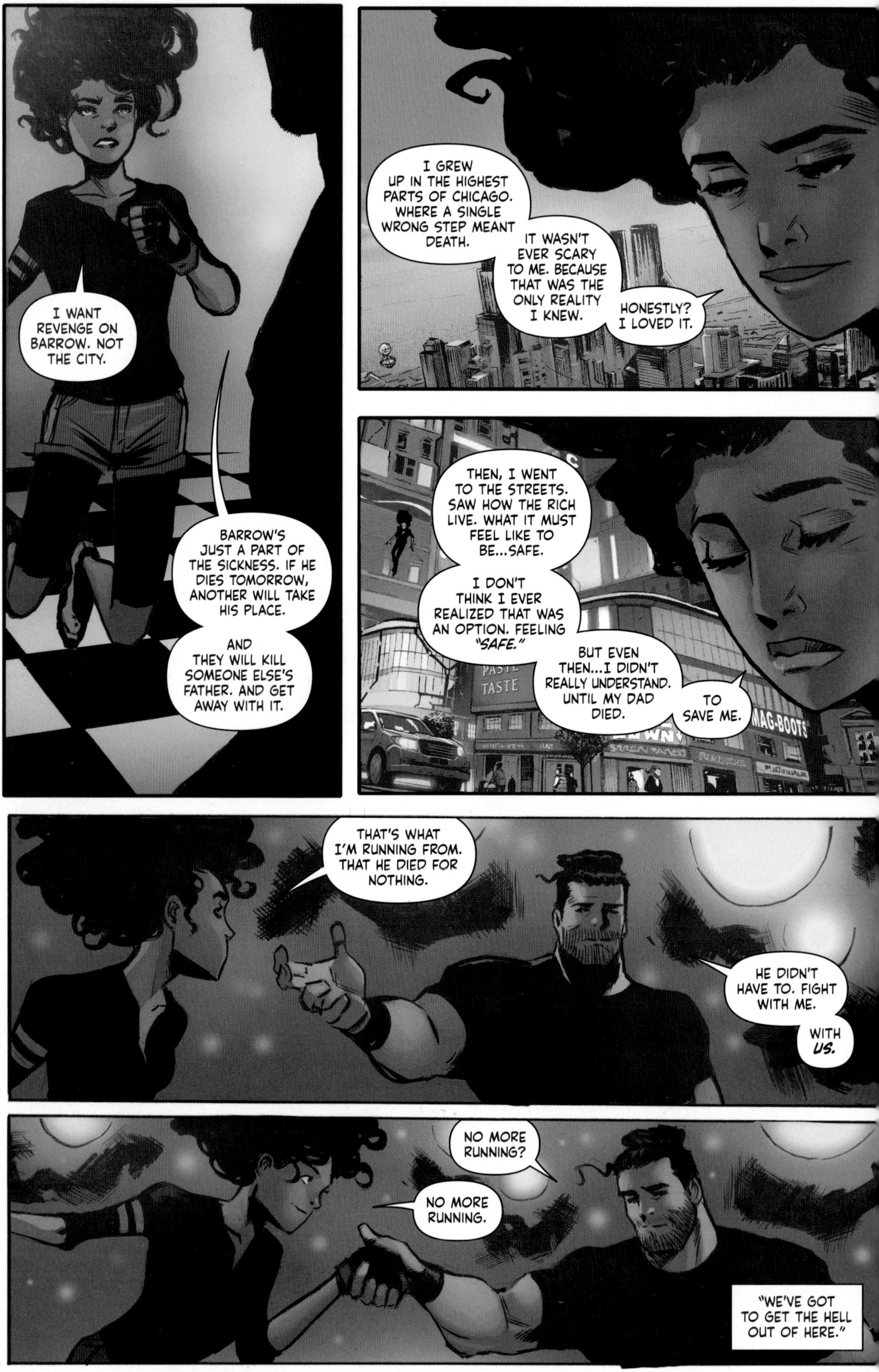
I WANT REVENGE ON BARROW. NOT THE CITY.
BARROW'S JUST A PART OF THE SICKNESS. IF HE DIES TOMORROW, ANOTHER WILL TAKE HIS PLACE.
AND THEY WILL KILL SOMEONE ELSE'S FATHER. AND GET AWAY WITH IT.
I GREW UP IN THE HIGHEST PARTS OF CHICAGO. WHERE A SINGLE WRONG STEP MEANT DEATH.
IT WASN'T EVER SCARY TO ME. BECAUSE THAT WAS THE ONLY REALITY I KNEW.
HONESTLY? I LOVED IT.
THEN, I WENT TO THE STREETS. SAW HOW THE RICH LIVE. WHAT IT MUST FEEL LIKE TO BE...SAFE.
I DON'T THINK I EVER REALIZED THAT WAS AN OPTION. FEELING *"SAFE."*
BUT EVEN THEN...I DIDN'T REALLY UNDERSTAND. UNTIL MY DAD DIED.
TO SAVE ME.
PASTE TASTE
MAG-BOOTS
THAT'S WHAT I'M RUNNING FROM. THAT HE DIED FOR NOTHING.
HE DIDN'T HAVE TO. FIGHT WITH ME.
WITH ***US.***
NO MORE RUNNING?
NO MORE RUNNING.
"WE'VE GOT TO GET THE HELL OUT OF HERE."

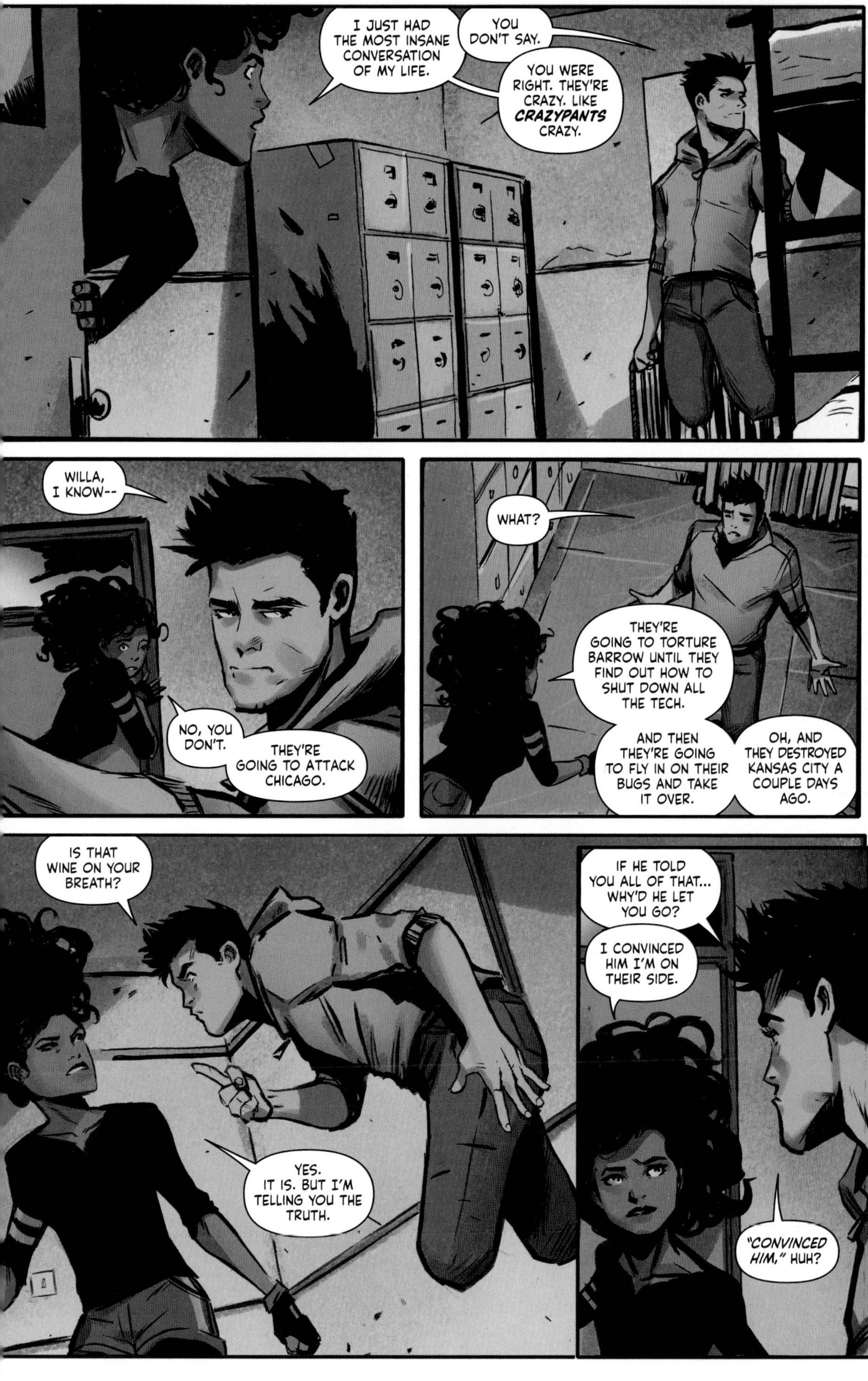
I JUST HAD THE MOST INSANE CONVERSATION OF MY LIFE.
YOU DON'T SAY.
YOU WERE RIGHT. THEY'RE CRAZY. LIKE ***CRAZYPANTS*** CRAZY.
WILLA, I KNOW--
NO, YOU DON'T.
THEY'RE GOING TO ATTACK CHICAGO.
WHAT?
THEY'RE GOING TO TORTURE BARROW UNTIL THEY FIND OUT HOW TO SHUT DOWN ALL THE TECH.
AND THEN THEY'RE GOING TO FLY IN ON THEIR BUGS AND TAKE IT OVER.
OH, AND THEY DESTROYED KANSAS CITY A COUPLE DAYS AGO.
IS THAT WINE ON YOUR BREATH?
YES. IT IS. BUT I'M TELLING YOU THE TRUTH.
IF HE TOLD YOU ALL OF THAT... WHY'D HE LET YOU GO?
I CONVINCED HIM I'M ON THEIR SIDE.
"CONVINCED HIM," HUH?

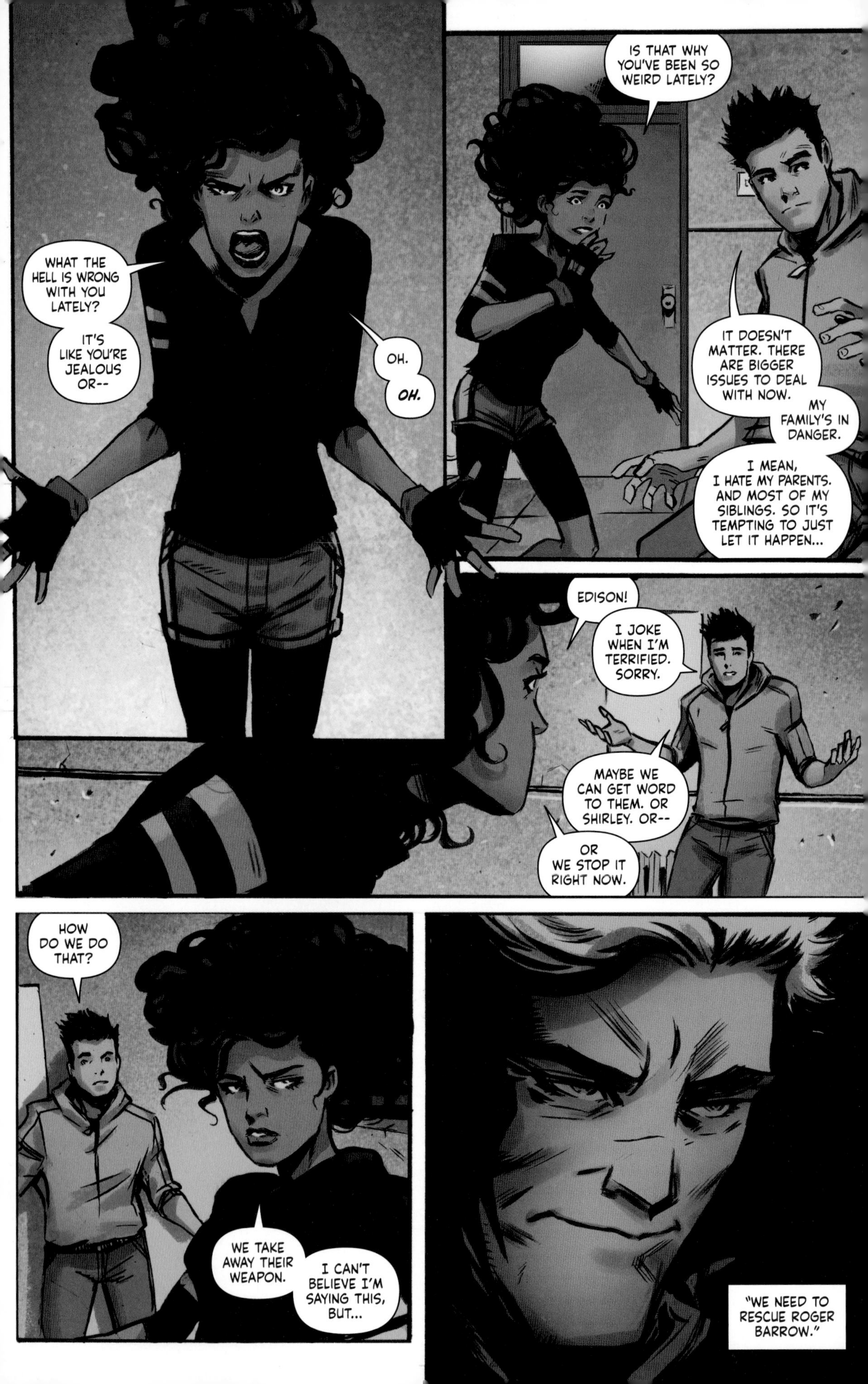
WHAT THE HELL IS WRONG WITH YOU LATELY?
IT'S LIKE YOU'RE JEALOUS OR--
OH.
OH.
IS THAT WHY YOU'VE BEEN SO WEIRD LATELY?
IT DOESN'T MATTER. THERE ARE BIGGER ISSUES TO DEAL WITH NOW.
MY FAMILY'S IN DANGER.
I MEAN, I HATE MY PARENTS. AND MOST OF MY SIBLINGS. SO IT'S TEMPTING TO JUST LET IT HAPPEN...
EDISON!
I JOKE WHEN I'M TERRIFIED. SORRY.
MAYBE WE CAN GET WORD TO THEM. OR SHIRLEY. OR--
OR WE STOP IT RIGHT NOW.
HOW DO WE DO THAT?
WE TAKE AWAY THEIR WEAPON.
I CAN'T BELIEVE I'M SAYING THIS, BUT...
"WE NEED TO RESCUE ROGER BARROW."

END CHAPTER NINE

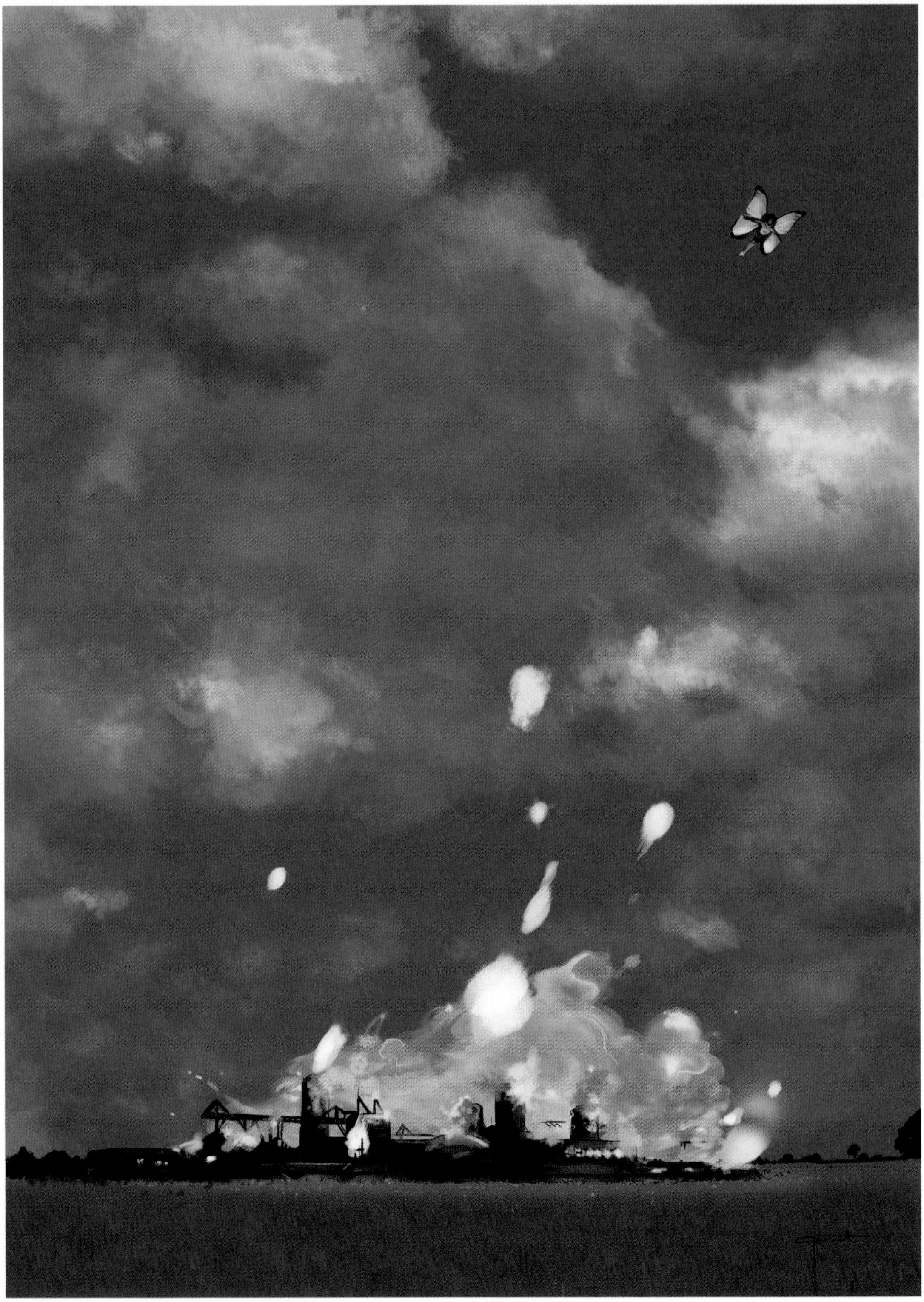

CHAPTER TEN

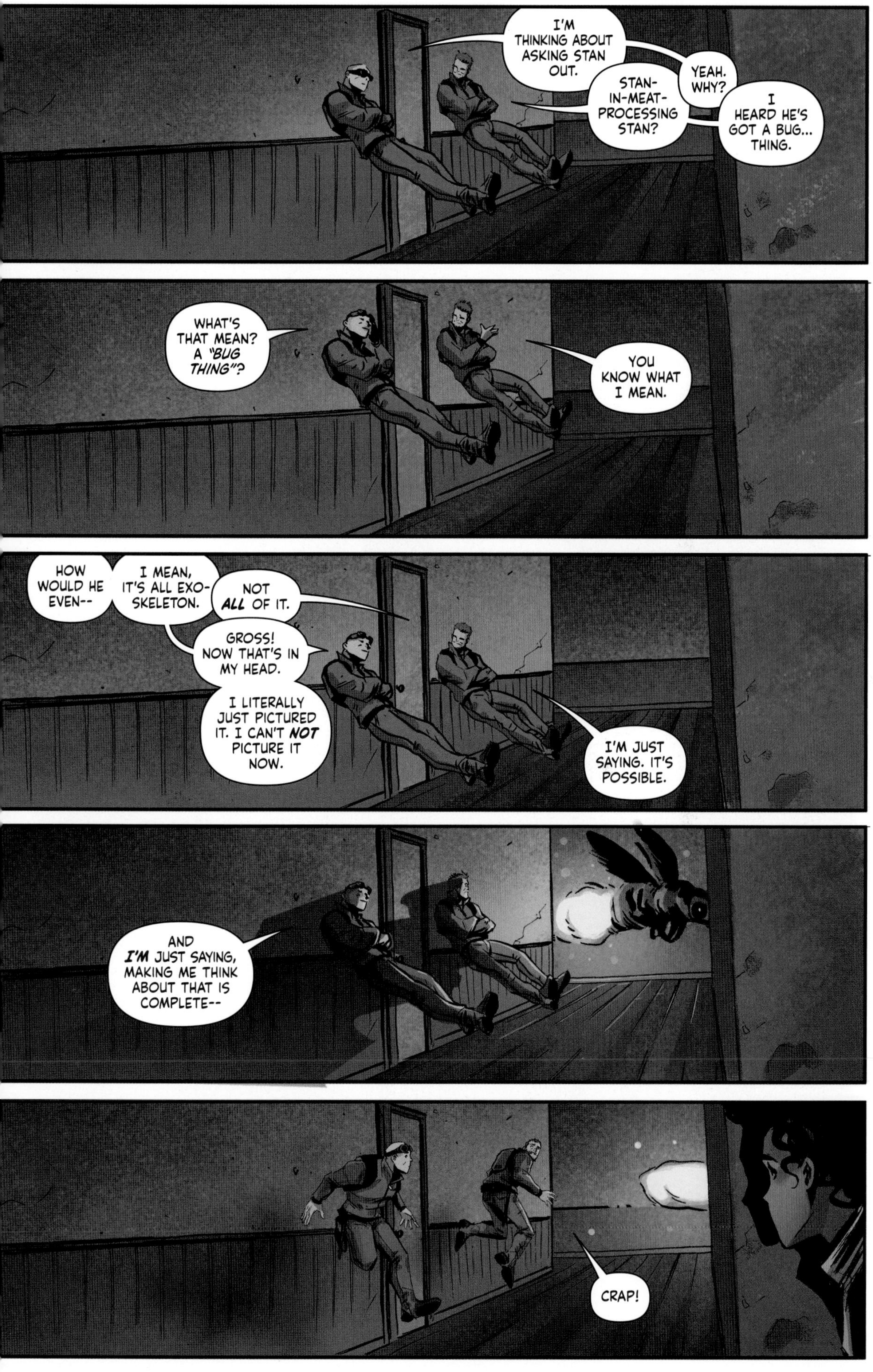
I'M THINKING ABOUT ASKING STAN OUT.
YEAH. WHY?
STAN-IN-MEAT-PROCESSING STAN?
I HEARD HE'S GOT A BUG... THING.
WHAT'S THAT MEAN? A "BUG THING"?
YOU KNOW WHAT I MEAN.
HOW WOULD HE EVEN--
I MEAN, IT'S ALL EXO-SKELETON.
NOT ALL OF IT.
GROSS! NOW THAT'S IN MY HEAD.
I LITERALLY JUST PICTURED IT. I CAN'T NOT PICTURE IT NOW.
I'M JUST SAYING. IT'S POSSIBLE.
AND I'M JUST SAYING, MAKING ME THINK ABOUT THAT IS COMPLETE--
CRAP!

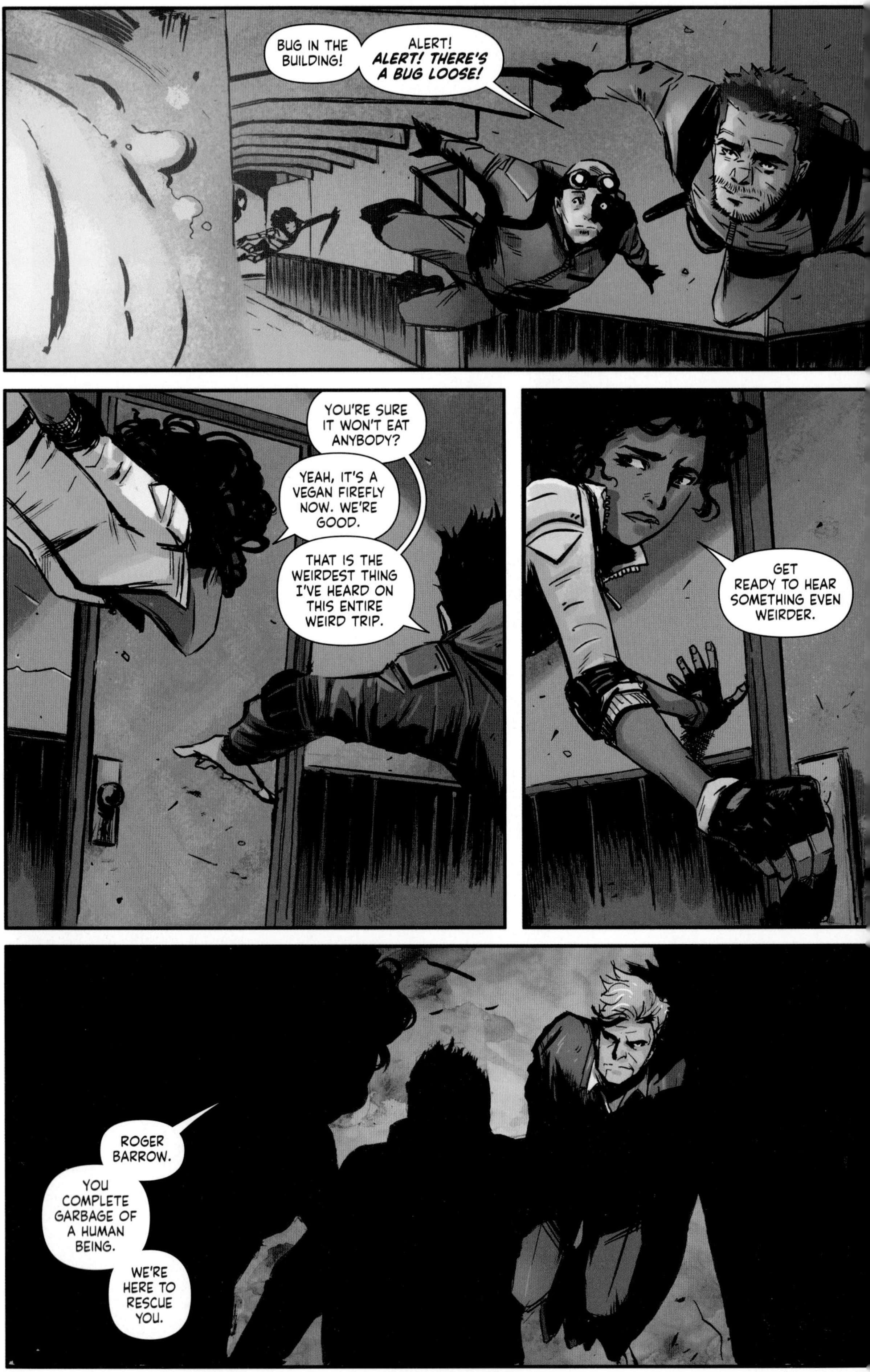
BUG IN THE BUILDING!
ALERT! ALERT! THERE'S A BUG LOOSE!
YOU'RE SURE IT WON'T EAT ANYBODY?
YEAH, IT'S A VEGAN FIREFLY NOW. WE'RE GOOD.
THAT IS THE WEIRDEST THING I'VE HEARD ON THIS ENTIRE WEIRD TRIP.
GET READY TO HEAR SOMETHING EVEN WEIRDER.
ROGER BARROW.
YOU COMPLETE GARBAGE OF A HUMAN BEING.
WE'RE HERE TO RESCUE YOU.

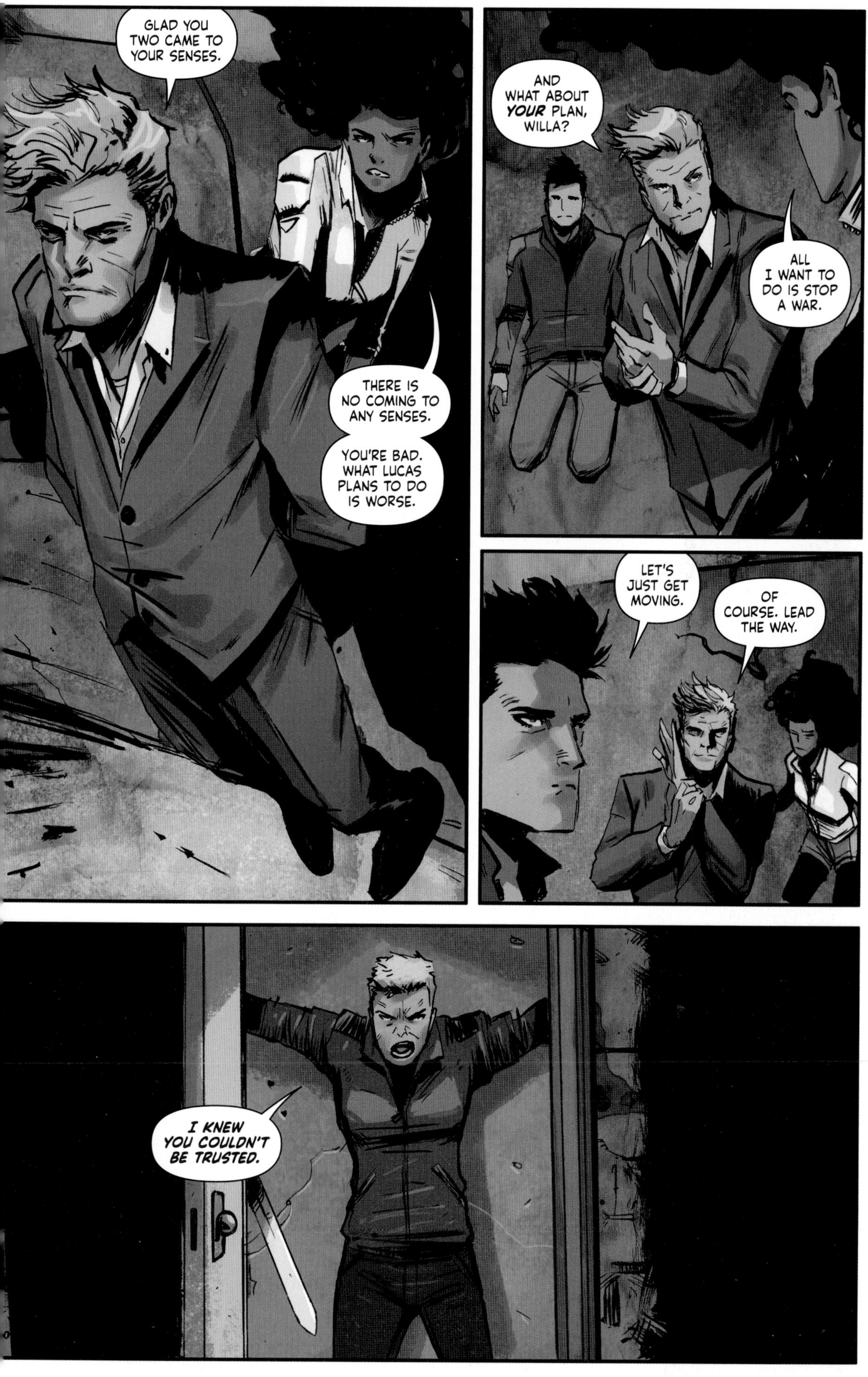
GLAD YOU TWO CAME TO YOUR SENSES.
THERE IS NO COMING TO ANY SENSES.
YOU'RE BAD. WHAT LUCAS PLANS TO DO IS WORSE.
AND WHAT ABOUT YOUR PLAN, WILLA?
ALL I WANT TO DO IS STOP A WAR.
LET'S JUST GET MOVING.
OF COURSE. LEAD THE WAY.
I KNEW YOU COULDN'T BE TRUSTED.

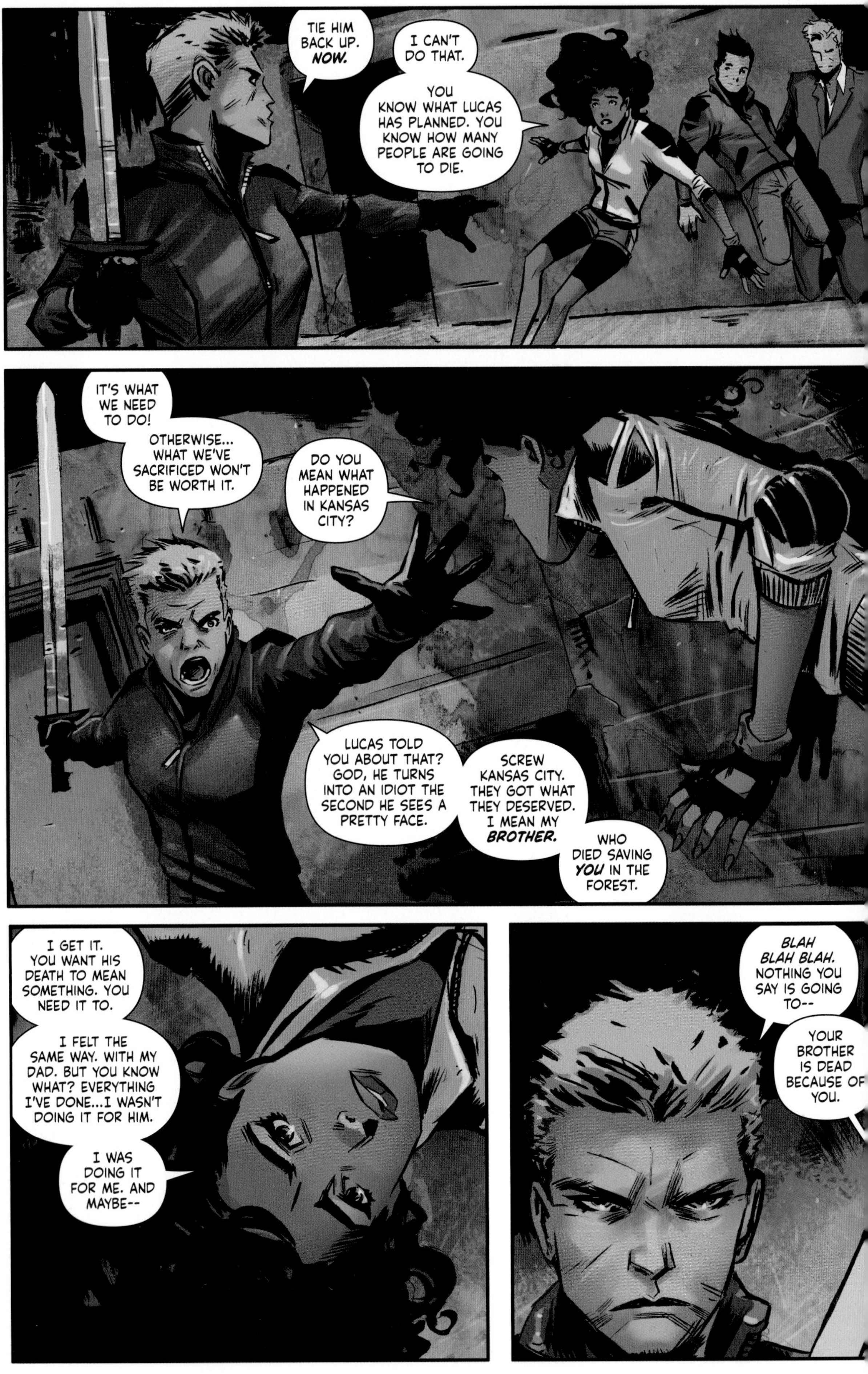
TIE HIM BACK UP. *NOW.*
I CAN'T DO THAT.
YOU KNOW WHAT LUCAS HAS PLANNED. YOU KNOW HOW MANY PEOPLE ARE GOING TO DIE.
IT'S WHAT WE NEED TO DO!
OTHERWISE... WHAT WE'VE SACRIFICED WON'T BE WORTH IT.
DO YOU MEAN WHAT HAPPENED IN KANSAS CITY?
LUCAS TOLD YOU ABOUT THAT? GOD, HE TURNS INTO AN IDIOT THE SECOND HE SEES A PRETTY FACE.
SCREW KANSAS CITY. THEY GOT WHAT THEY DESERVED. I MEAN MY ***BROTHER.***
WHO DIED SAVING ***YOU*** IN THE FOREST.
I GET IT. YOU WANT HIS DEATH TO MEAN SOMETHING. YOU NEED IT TO.
I FELT THE SAME WAY. WITH MY DAD. BUT YOU KNOW WHAT? EVERYTHING I'VE DONE...I WASN'T DOING IT FOR HIM.
I WAS DOING IT FOR ME. AND MAYBE--
BLAH BLAH BLAH. NOTHING YOU SAY IS GOING TO--
YOUR BROTHER IS DEAD BECAUSE OF YOU.

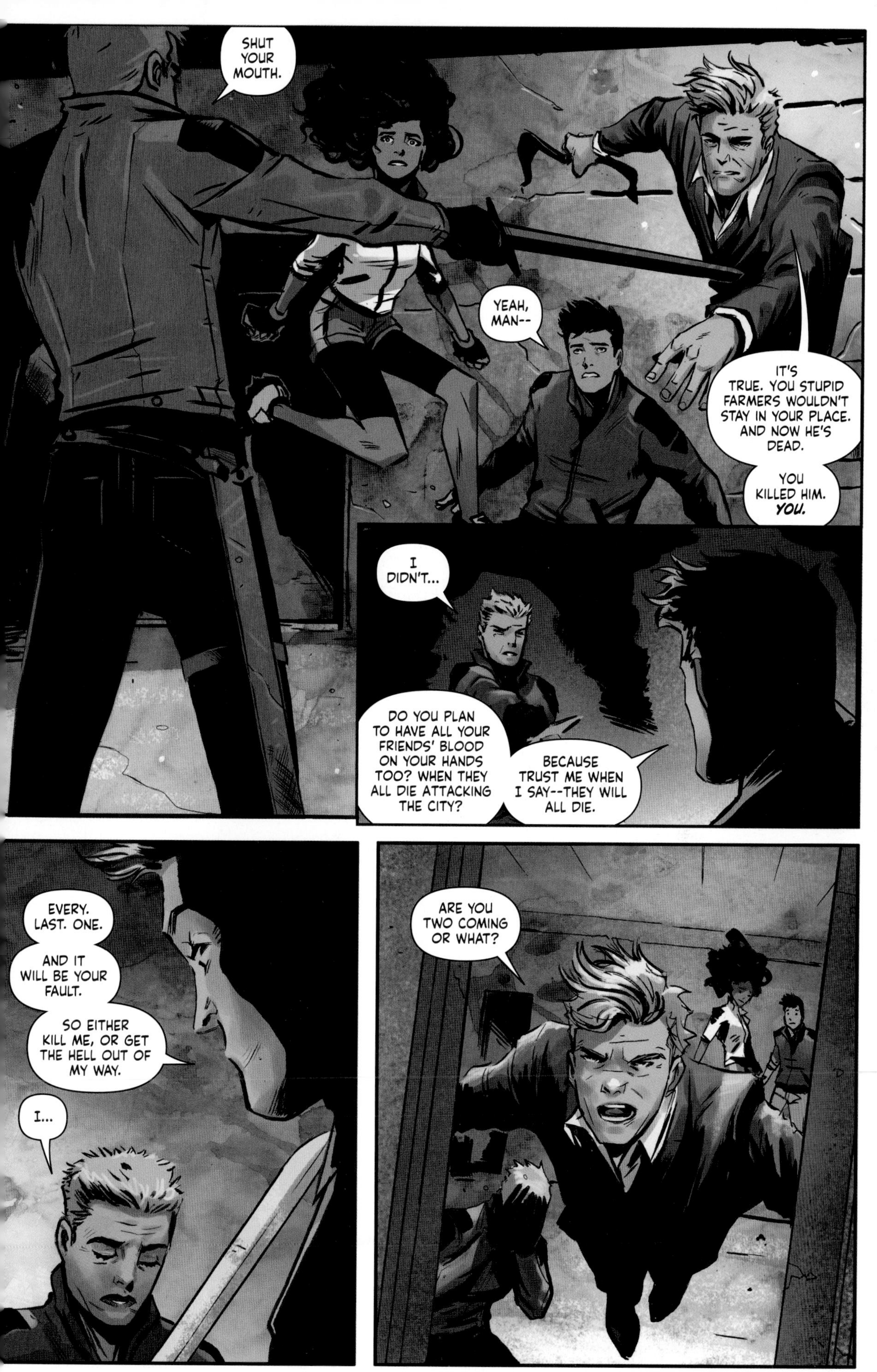
SHUT YOUR MOUTH.
YEAH, MAN--
IT'S TRUE. YOU STUPID FARMERS WOULDN'T STAY IN YOUR PLACE. AND NOW HE'S DEAD.
YOU KILLED HIM. *YOU.*
I DIDN'T...
DO YOU PLAN TO HAVE ALL YOUR FRIENDS' BLOOD ON YOUR HANDS TOO? WHEN THEY ALL DIE ATTACKING THE CITY?
BECAUSE TRUST ME WHEN I SAY--THEY WILL ALL DIE.
EVERY. LAST. ONE.
AND IT WILL BE YOUR FAULT.
SO EITHER KILL ME, OR GET THE HELL OUT OF MY WAY.
I...
ARE YOU TWO COMING OR WHAT?

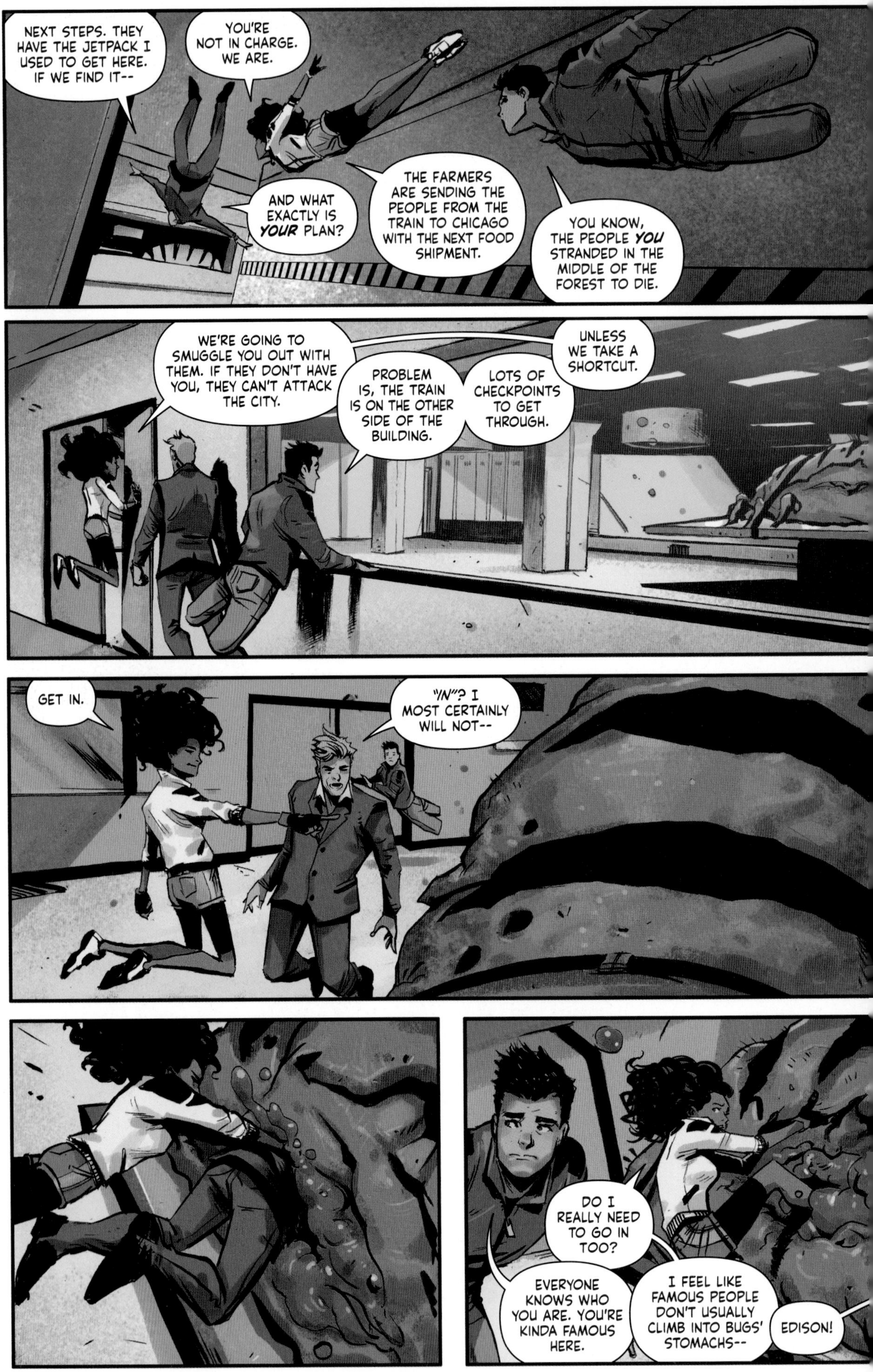
NEXT STEPS. THEY HAVE THE JETPACK I USED TO GET HERE. IF WE FIND IT--
YOU'RE NOT IN CHARGE. WE ARE.
AND WHAT EXACTLY IS *YOUR* PLAN?
THE FARMERS ARE SENDING THE PEOPLE FROM THE TRAIN TO CHICAGO WITH THE NEXT FOOD SHIPMENT.
YOU KNOW, THE PEOPLE *YOU* STRANDED IN THE MIDDLE OF THE FOREST TO DIE.
WE'RE GOING TO SMUGGLE YOU OUT WITH THEM. IF THEY DON'T HAVE YOU, THEY CAN'T ATTACK THE CITY.
PROBLEM IS, THE TRAIN IS ON THE OTHER SIDE OF THE BUILDING.
LOTS OF CHECKPOINTS TO GET THROUGH.
UNLESS WE TAKE A SHORTCUT.
GET IN.
"IN"? I MOST CERTAINLY WILL NOT--
DO I REALLY NEED TO GO IN TOO?
EVERYONE KNOWS WHO YOU ARE. YOU'RE KINDA FAMOUS HERE.
I FEEL LIKE FAMOUS PEOPLE DON'T USUALLY CLIMB INTO BUGS' STOMACHS--
EDISON!

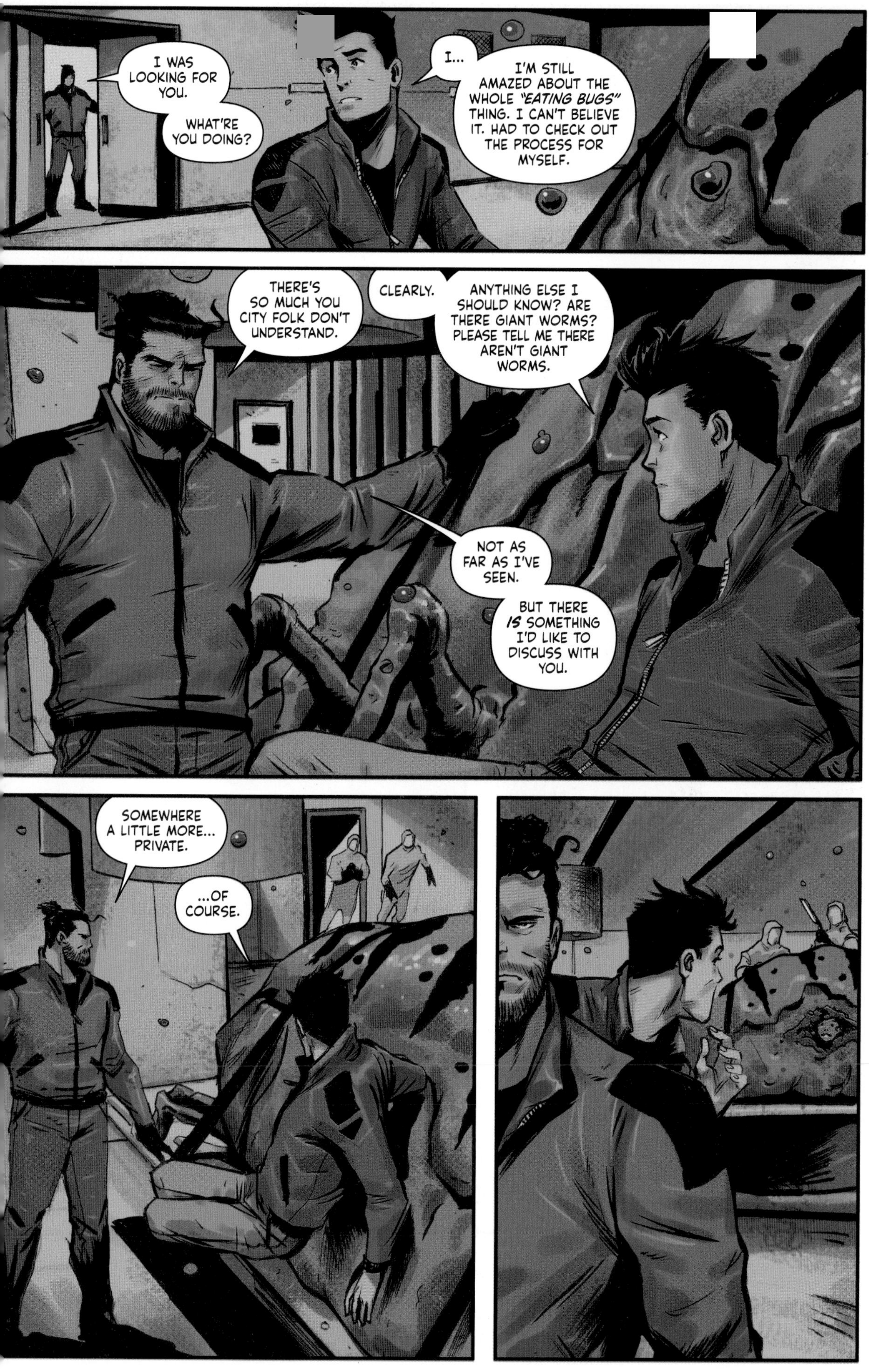
I WAS LOOKING FOR YOU.
WHAT'RE YOU DOING?
I...
I'M STILL AMAZED ABOUT THE WHOLE "EATING BUGS" THING. I CAN'T BELIEVE IT. HAD TO CHECK OUT THE PROCESS FOR MYSELF.
THERE'S SO MUCH YOU CITY FOLK DON'T UNDERSTAND.
CLEARLY.
ANYTHING ELSE I SHOULD KNOW? ARE THERE GIANT WORMS? PLEASE TELL ME THERE AREN'T GIANT WORMS.
NOT AS FAR AS I'VE SEEN.
BUT THERE IS SOMETHING I'D LIKE TO DISCUSS WITH YOU.
SOMEWHERE A LITTLE MORE... PRIVATE.
...OF COURSE.

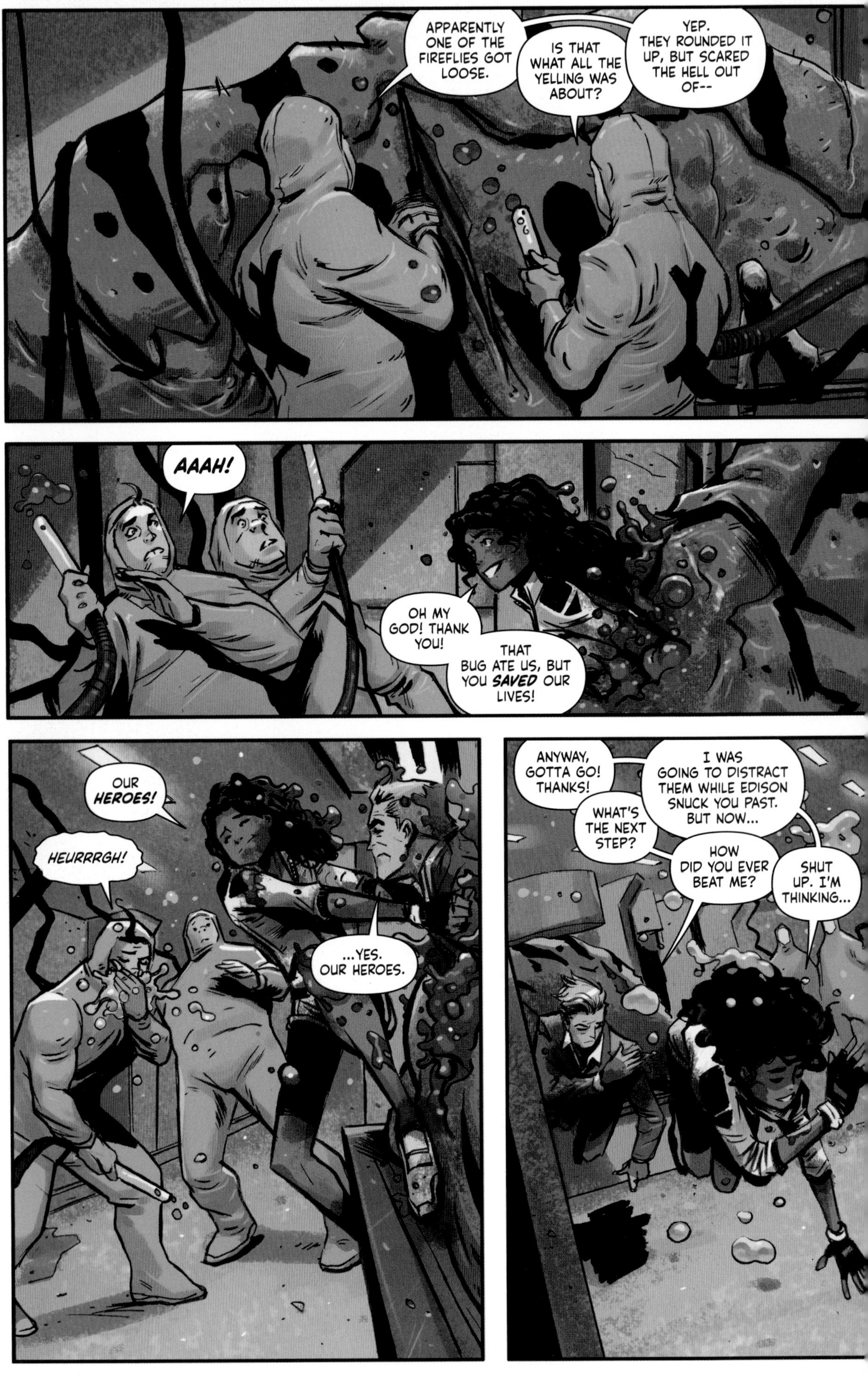
APPARENTLY ONE OF THE FIREFLIES GOT LOOSE.
IS THAT WHAT ALL THE YELLING WAS ABOUT?
YEP. THEY ROUNDED IT UP, BUT SCARED THE HELL OUT OF--
AAAH!
OH MY GOD! THANK YOU!
THAT BUG ATE US, BUT YOU *SAVED* OUR LIVES!
OUR *HEROES!*
HEURRRGH!
...YES. OUR HEROES.
ANYWAY, GOTTA GO! THANKS!
I WAS GOING TO DISTRACT THEM WHILE EDISON SNUCK YOU PAST. BUT NOW...
WHAT'S THE NEXT STEP?
HOW DID YOU EVER BEAT ME?
SHUT UP. I'M THINKING...

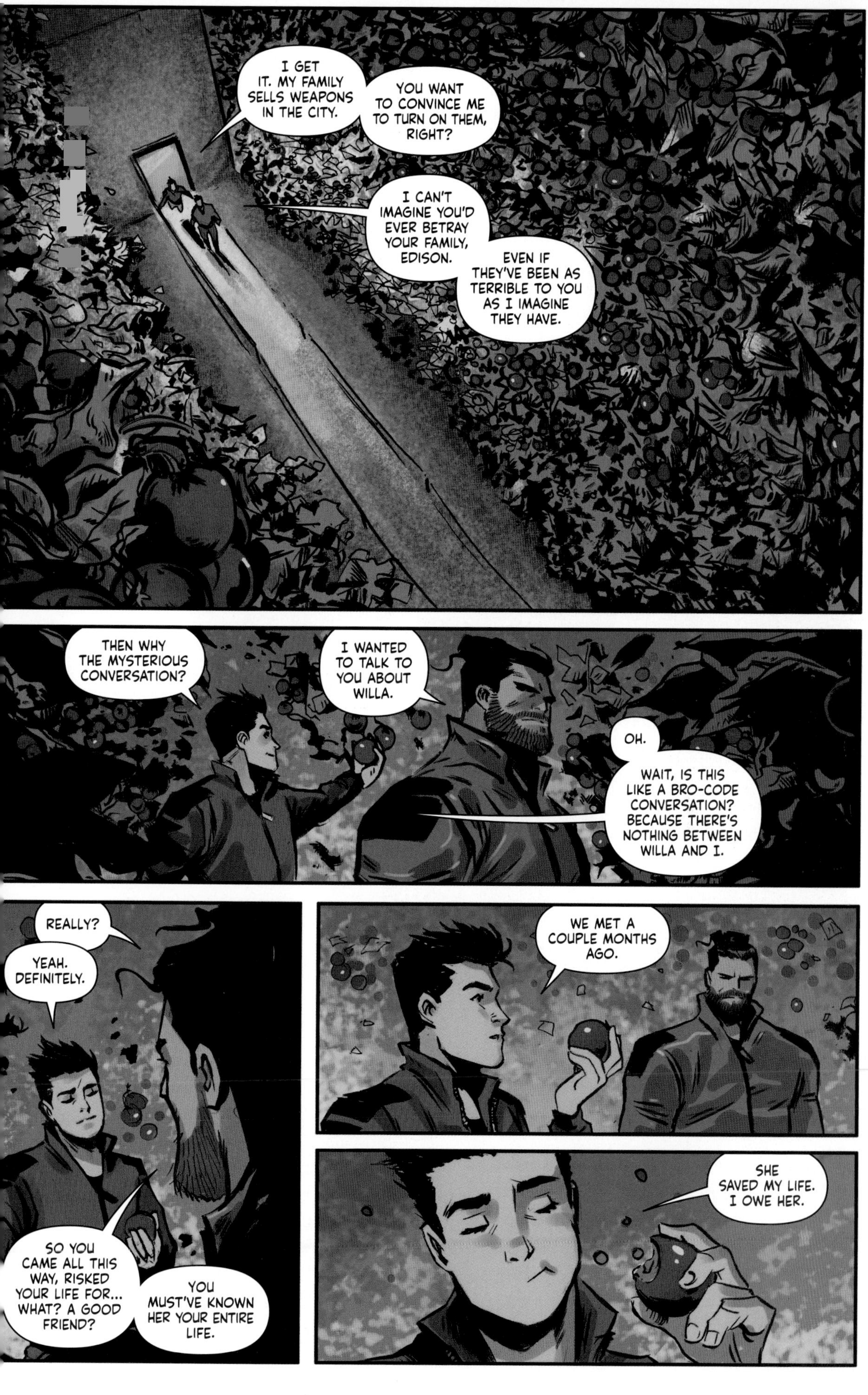
I GET IT. MY FAMILY SELLS WEAPONS IN THE CITY.
YOU WANT TO CONVINCE ME TO TURN ON THEM, RIGHT?
I CAN'T IMAGINE YOU'D EVER BETRAY YOUR FAMILY, EDISON.
EVEN IF THEY'VE BEEN AS TERRIBLE TO YOU AS I IMAGINE THEY HAVE.
THEN WHY THE MYSTERIOUS CONVERSATION?
I WANTED TO TALK TO YOU ABOUT WILLA.
OH.
WAIT, IS THIS LIKE A BRO-CODE CONVERSATION? BECAUSE THERE'S NOTHING BETWEEN WILLA AND I.
REALLY?
YEAH. DEFINITELY.
SO YOU CAME ALL THIS WAY, RISKED YOUR LIFE FOR... WHAT? A GOOD FRIEND?
YOU MUST'VE KNOWN HER YOUR ENTIRE LIFE.
WE MET A COUPLE MONTHS AGO.
SHE SAVED MY LIFE. I OWE HER.

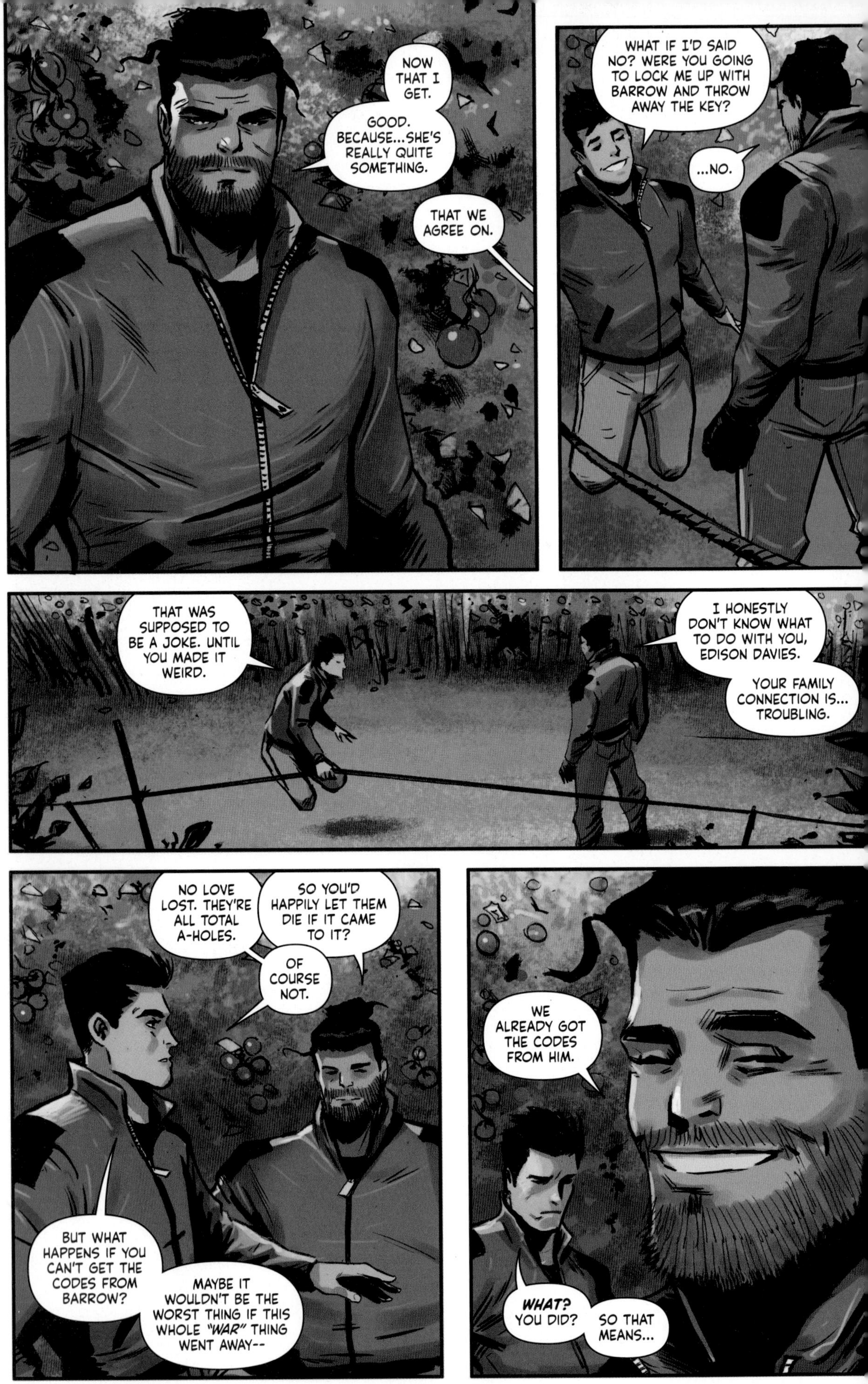
NOW THAT I GET.
GOOD. BECAUSE...SHE'S REALLY QUITE SOMETHING.
THAT WE AGREE ON.
WHAT IF I'D SAID NO? WERE YOU GOING TO LOCK ME UP WITH BARROW AND THROW AWAY THE KEY?
...NO.
THAT WAS SUPPOSED TO BE A JOKE. UNTIL YOU MADE IT WEIRD.
I HONESTLY DON'T KNOW WHAT TO DO WITH YOU, EDISON DAVIES.
YOUR FAMILY CONNECTION IS... TROUBLING.
NO LOVE LOST. THEY'RE ALL TOTAL A-HOLES.
SO YOU'D HAPPILY LET THEM DIE IF IT CAME TO IT?
OF COURSE NOT.
BUT WHAT HAPPENS IF YOU CAN'T GET THE CODES FROM BARROW?
MAYBE IT WOULDN'T BE THE WORST THING IF THIS WHOLE *"WAR"* THING WENT AWAY--
WE ALREADY GOT THE CODES FROM HIM.
WHAT? YOU DID?
SO THAT MEANS...

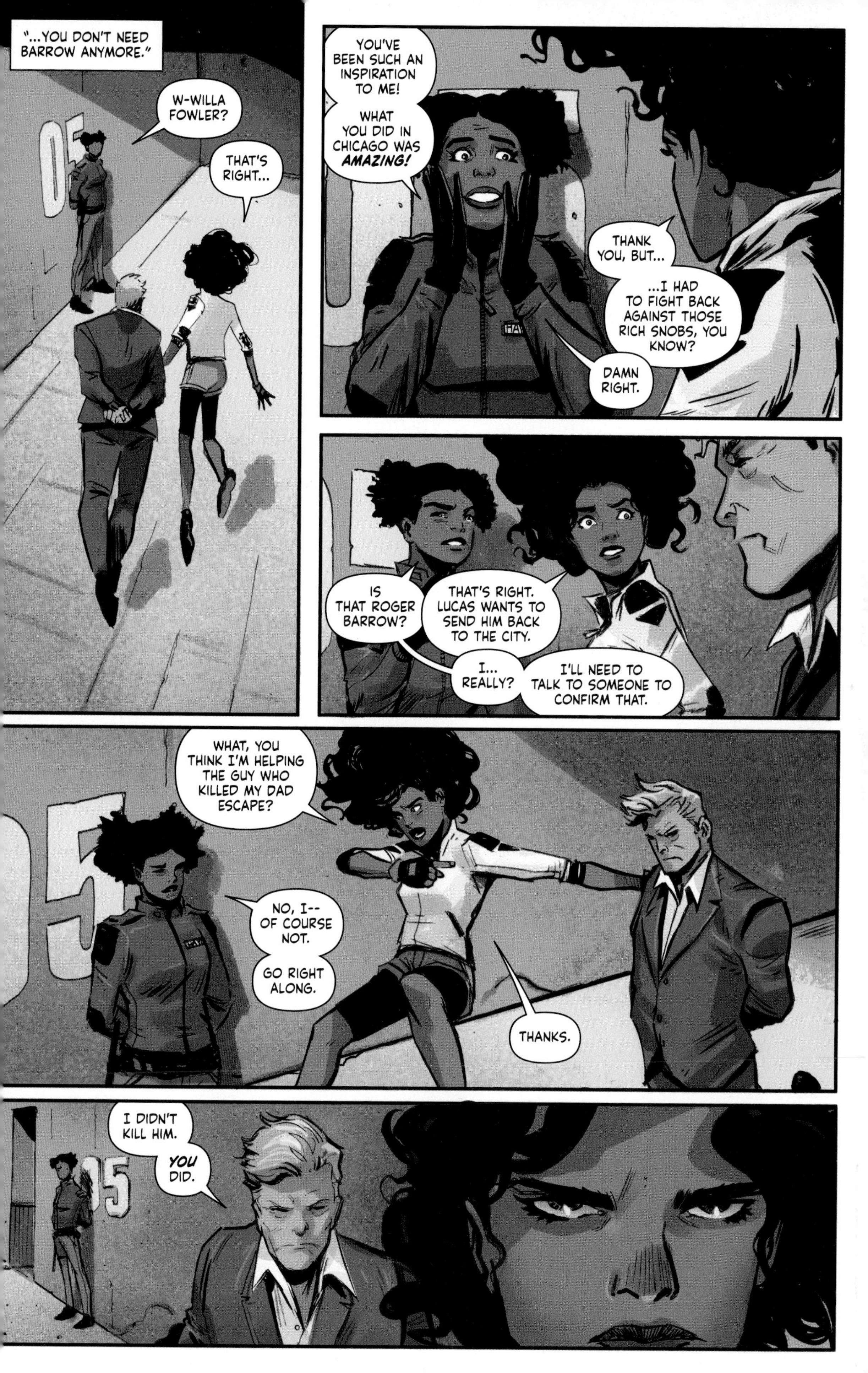
"...YOU DON'T NEED BARROW ANYMORE."
W-WILLA FOWLER?
THAT'S RIGHT...
YOU'VE BEEN SUCH AN INSPIRATION TO ME!
WHAT YOU DID IN CHICAGO WAS *AMAZING!*
THANK YOU, BUT...
...I HAD TO FIGHT BACK AGAINST THOSE RICH SNOBS, YOU KNOW?
DAMN RIGHT.
IS THAT ROGER BARROW?
THAT'S RIGHT. LUCAS WANTS TO SEND HIM BACK TO THE CITY.
I... REALLY?
I'LL NEED TO TALK TO SOMEONE TO CONFIRM THAT.
WHAT, YOU THINK I'M HELPING THE GUY WHO KILLED MY DAD ESCAPE?
NO, I-- OF COURSE NOT.
GO RIGHT ALONG.
THANKS.
I DIDN'T KILL HIM.
YOU DID.

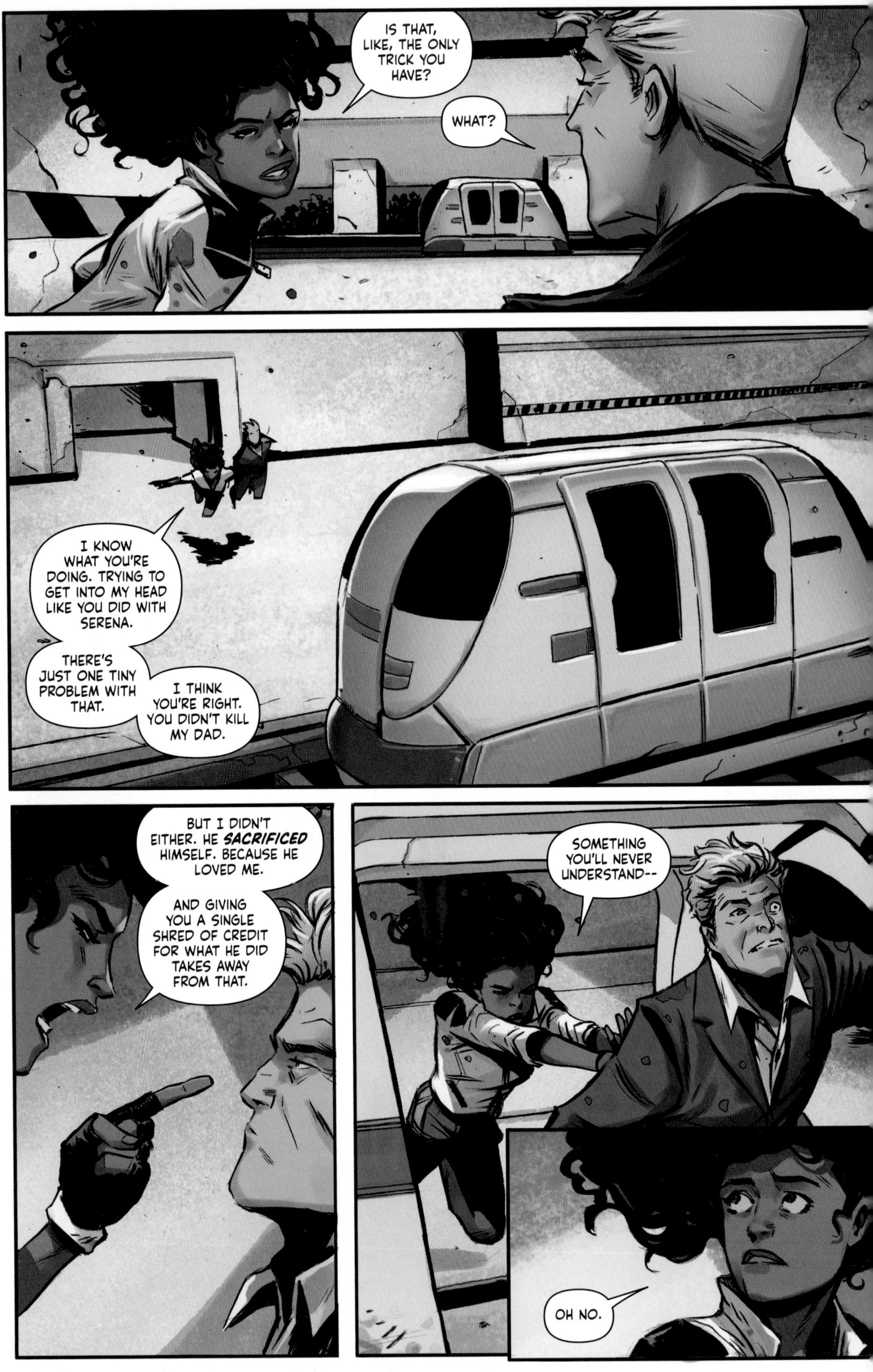
IS THAT, LIKE, THE ONLY TRICK YOU HAVE?
WHAT?
I KNOW WHAT YOU'RE DOING. TRYING TO GET INTO MY HEAD LIKE YOU DID WITH SERENA.
THERE'S JUST ONE TINY PROBLEM WITH THAT.
I THINK YOU'RE RIGHT. YOU DIDN'T KILL MY DAD.
BUT I DIDN'T EITHER. HE *SACRIFICED* HIMSELF. BECAUSE HE LOVED ME.
AND GIVING YOU A SINGLE SHRED OF CREDIT FOR WHAT HE DID TAKES AWAY FROM THAT.
SOMETHING YOU'LL NEVER UNDERSTAND--
OH NO.

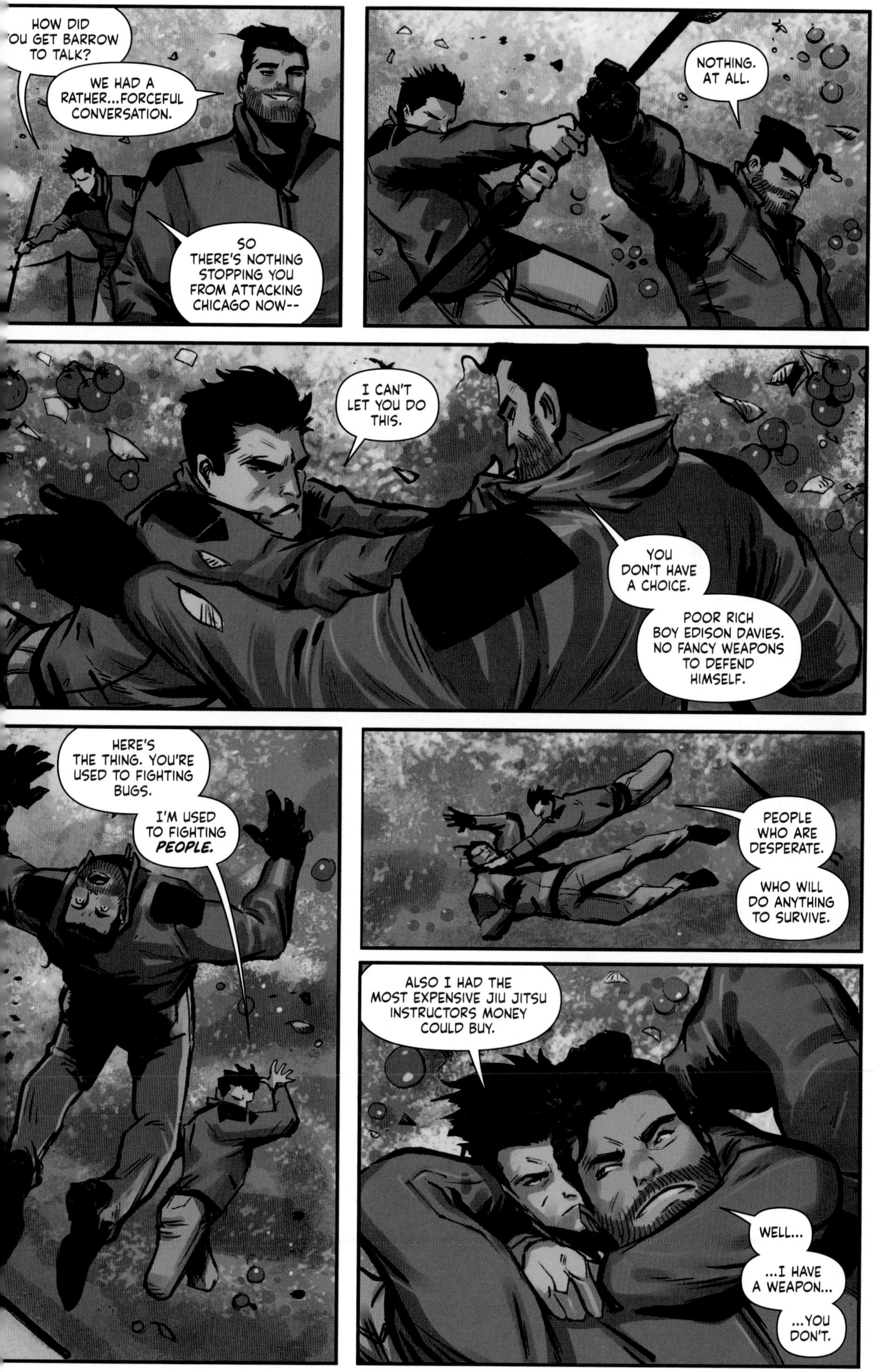
HOW DID YOU GET BARROW TO TALK?
WE HAD A RATHER...FORCEFUL CONVERSATION.
SO THERE'S NOTHING STOPPING YOU FROM ATTACKING CHICAGO NOW--
NOTHING. AT ALL.
I CAN'T LET YOU DO THIS.
YOU DON'T HAVE A CHOICE.
POOR RICH BOY EDISON DAVIES. NO FANCY WEAPONS TO DEFEND HIMSELF.
HERE'S THE THING. YOU'RE USED TO FIGHTING BUGS.
I'M USED TO FIGHTING ***PEOPLE.***
PEOPLE WHO ARE DESPERATE.
WHO WILL DO ANYTHING TO SURVIVE.
ALSO I HAD THE MOST EXPENSIVE JIU JITSU INSTRUCTORS MONEY COULD BUY.
WELL...
...I HAVE A WEAPON...
...YOU DON'T.

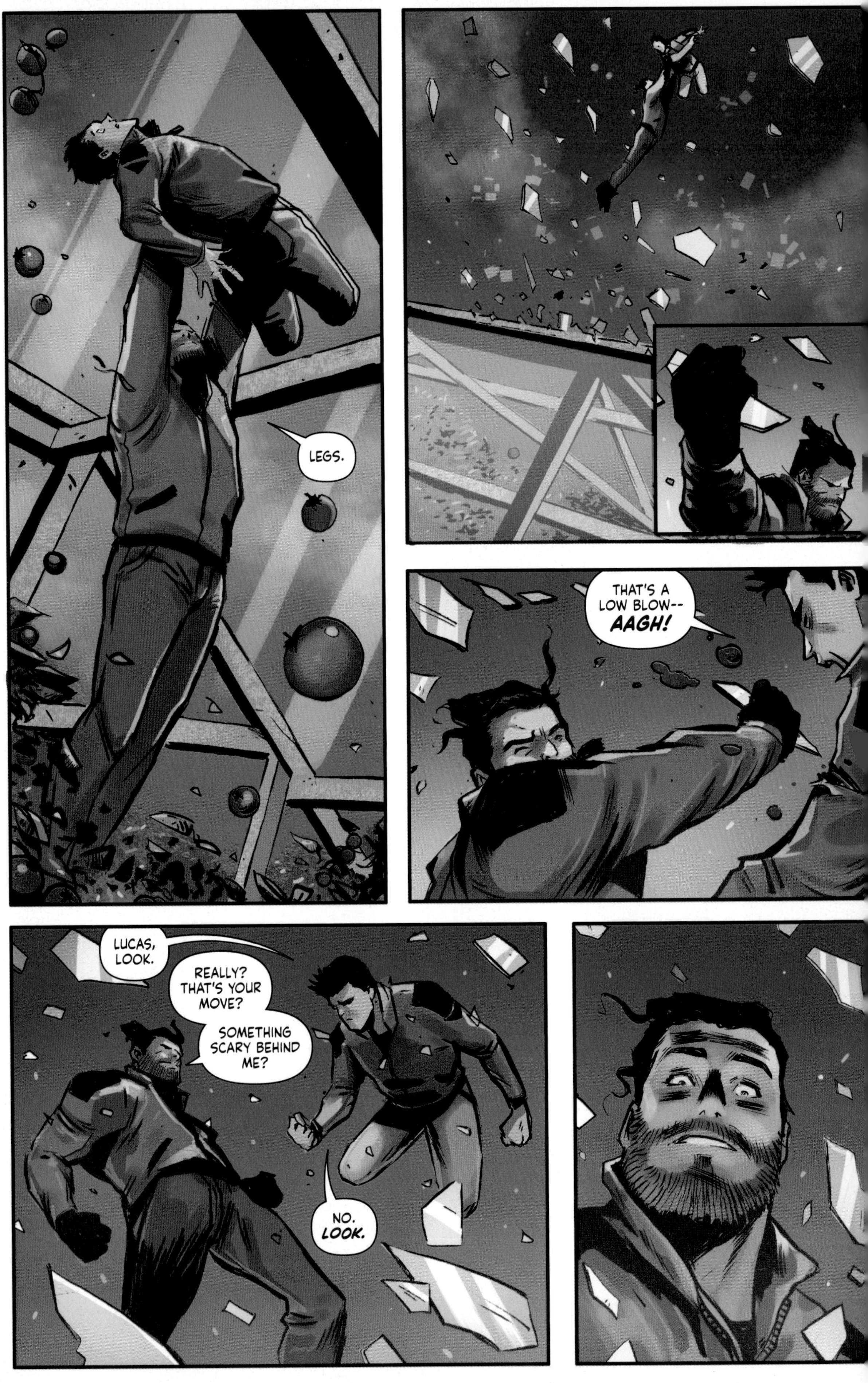
LEGS.
THAT'S A LOW BLOW-- AAGH!
LUCAS, LOOK.
REALLY? THAT'S YOUR MOVE?
SOMETHING SCARY BEHIND ME?
NO. LOOK.

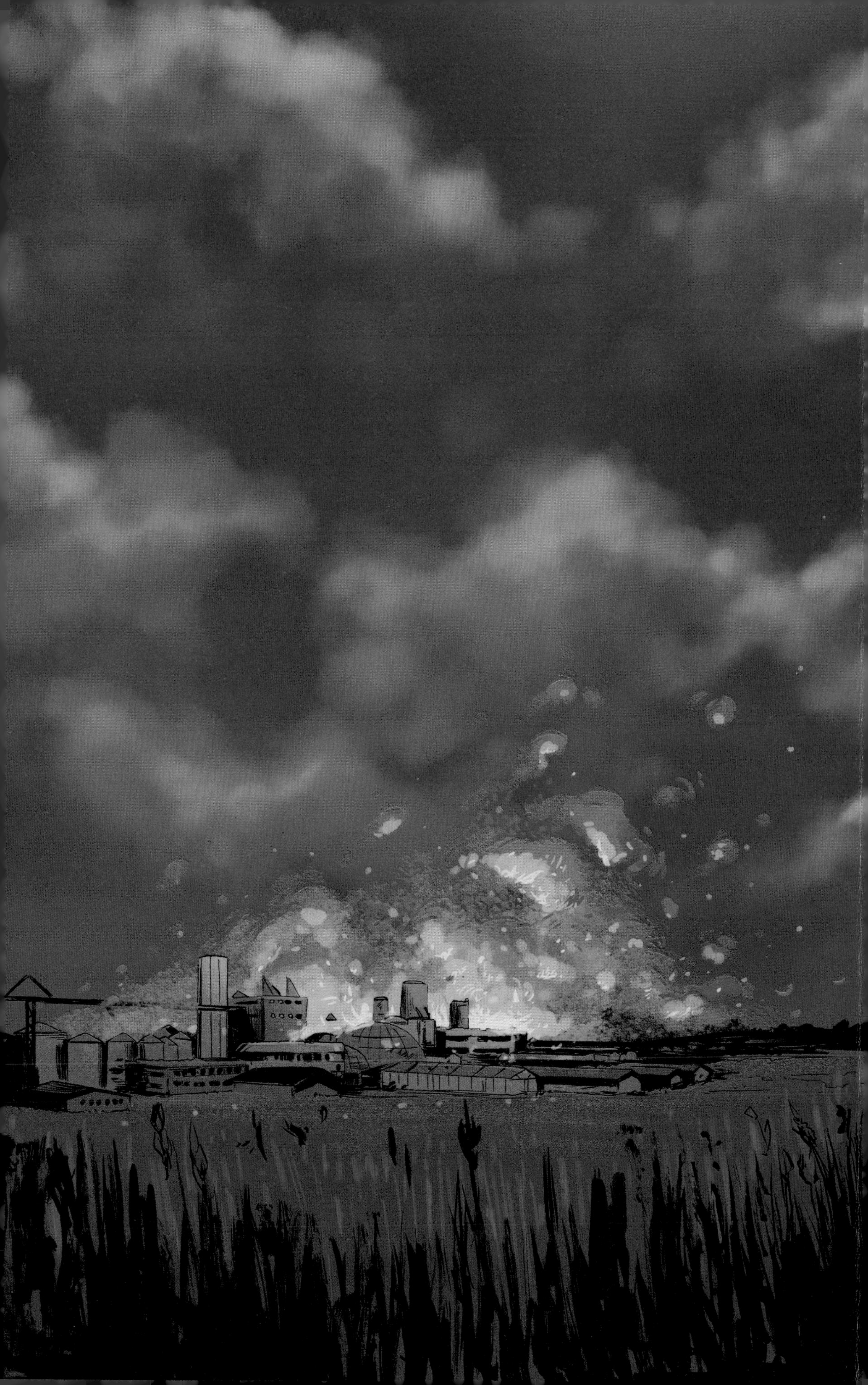

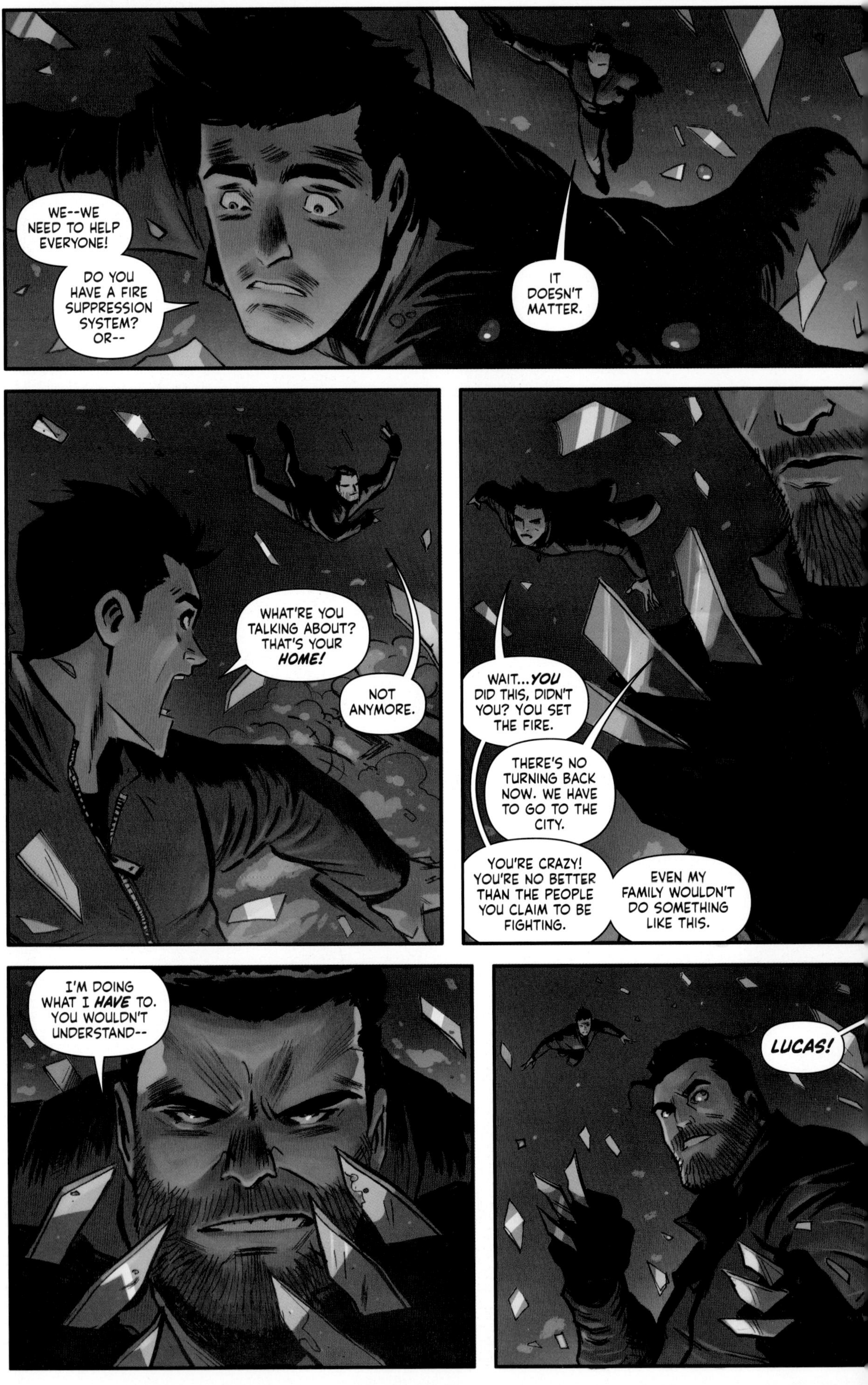

WE--WE NEED TO HELP EVERYONE!
DO YOU HAVE A FIRE SUPPRESSION SYSTEM? OR--
IT DOESN'T MATTER.
WHAT'RE YOU TALKING ABOUT? THAT'S YOUR *HOME!*
NOT ANYMORE.
WAIT...*YOU* DID THIS, DIDN'T YOU? YOU SET THE FIRE.
THERE'S NO TURNING BACK NOW. WE HAVE TO GO TO THE CITY.
YOU'RE CRAZY! YOU'RE NO BETTER THAN THE PEOPLE YOU CLAIM TO BE FIGHTING.
EVEN MY FAMILY WOULDN'T DO SOMETHING LIKE THIS.
I'M DOING WHAT I *HAVE* TO. YOU WOULDN'T UNDERSTAND--
LUCAS!

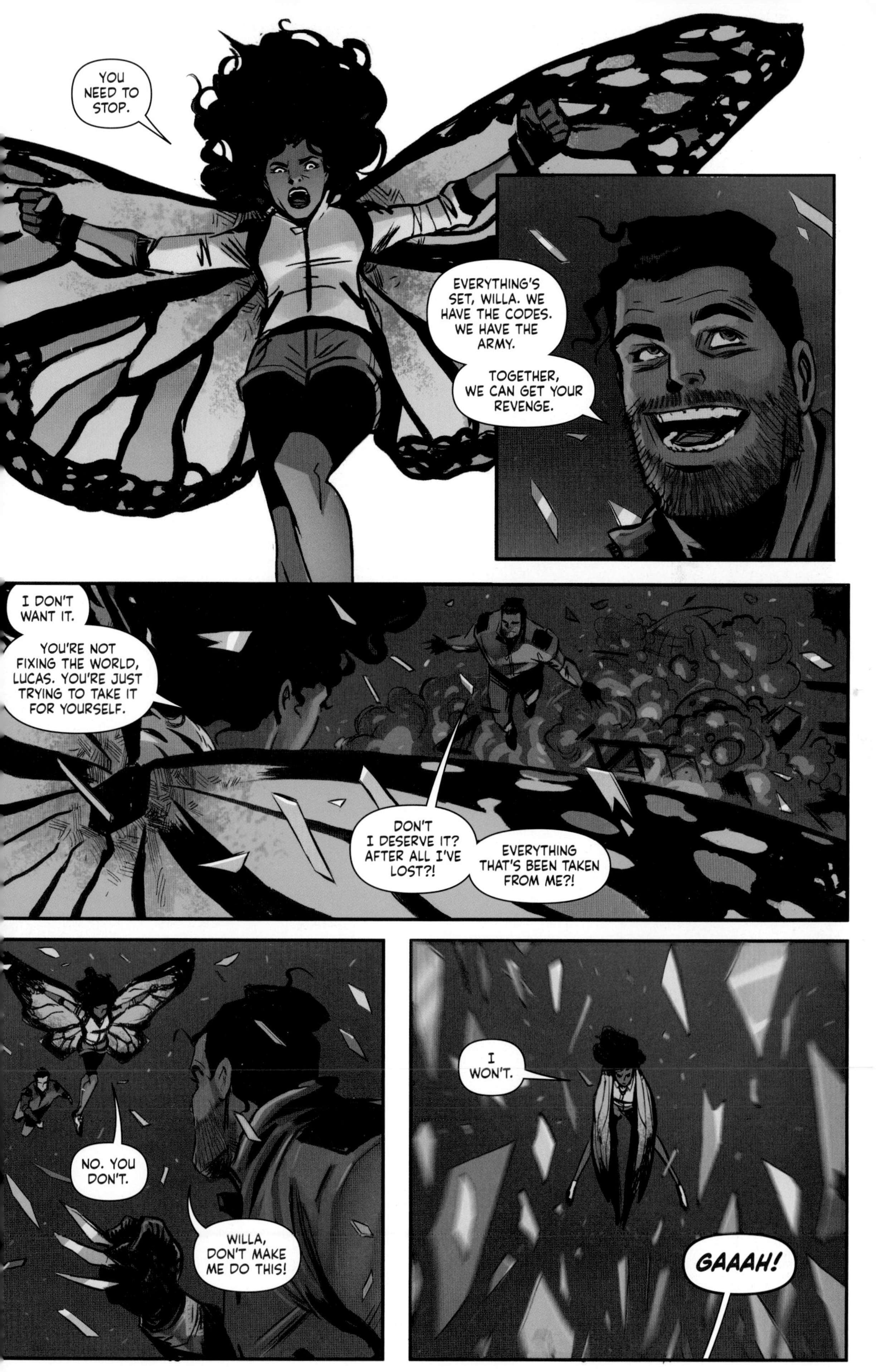
YOU NEED TO STOP.
EVERYTHING'S SET, WILLA. WE HAVE THE CODES. WE HAVE THE ARMY.
TOGETHER, WE CAN GET YOUR REVENGE.
I DON'T WANT IT.
YOU'RE NOT FIXING THE WORLD, LUCAS. YOU'RE JUST TRYING TO TAKE IT FOR YOURSELF.
DON'T I DESERVE IT? AFTER ALL I'VE LOST?!
EVERYTHING THAT'S BEEN TAKEN FROM ME?!
NO. YOU DON'T.
WILLA, DON'T MAKE ME DO THIS!
I WON'T.
GAAAH!

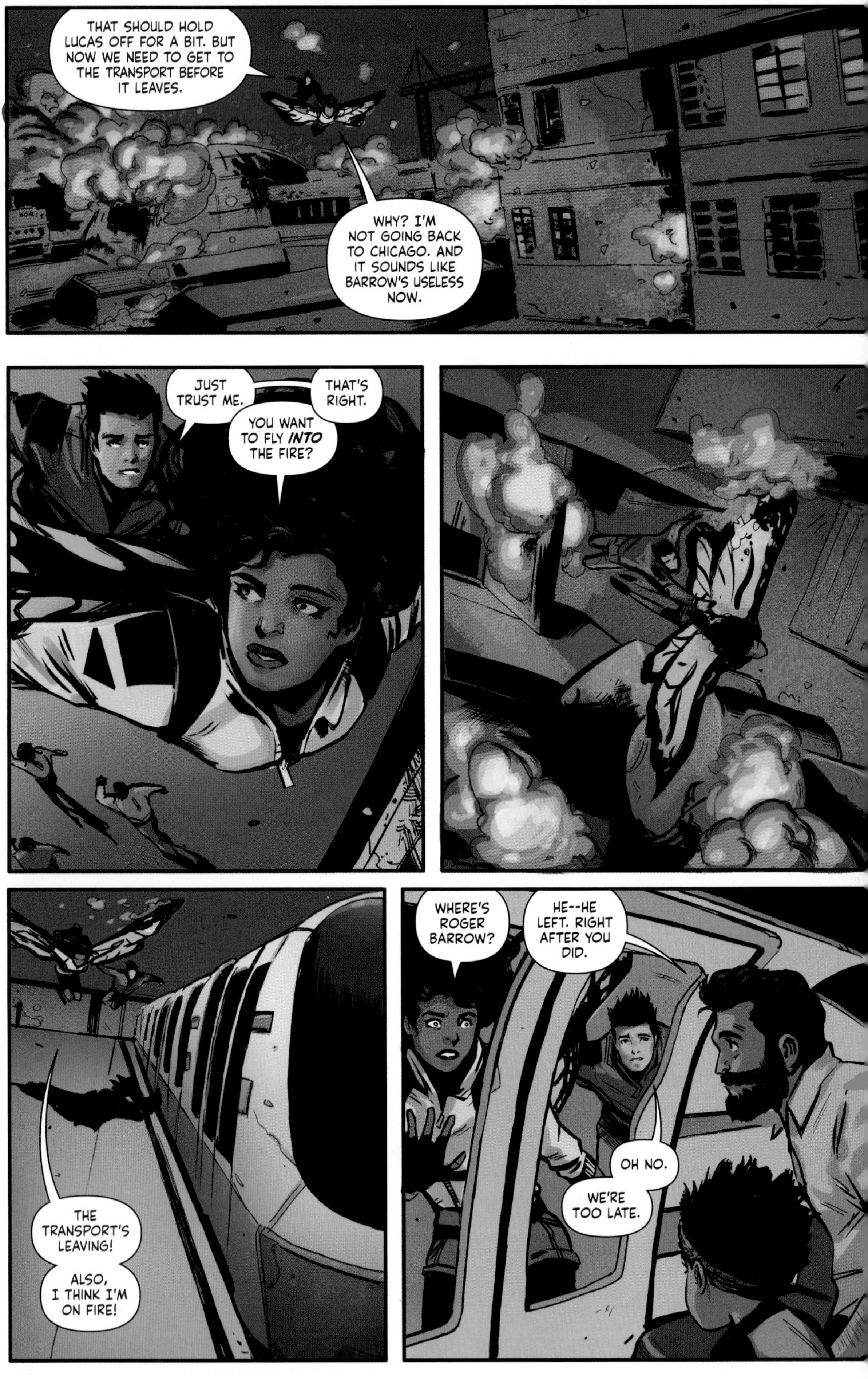
THAT SHOULD HOLD LUCAS OFF FOR A BIT. BUT NOW WE NEED TO GET TO THE TRANSPORT BEFORE IT LEAVES.
WHY? I'M NOT GOING BACK TO CHICAGO. AND IT SOUNDS LIKE BARROW'S USELESS NOW.
JUST TRUST ME.
YOU WANT TO FLY *INTO* THE FIRE?
THAT'S RIGHT.
THE TRANSPORT'S LEAVING!
ALSO, I THINK I'M ON FIRE!
WHERE'S ROGER BARROW?
HE--HE LEFT. RIGHT AFTER YOU DID.
OH NO.
WE'RE TOO LATE.

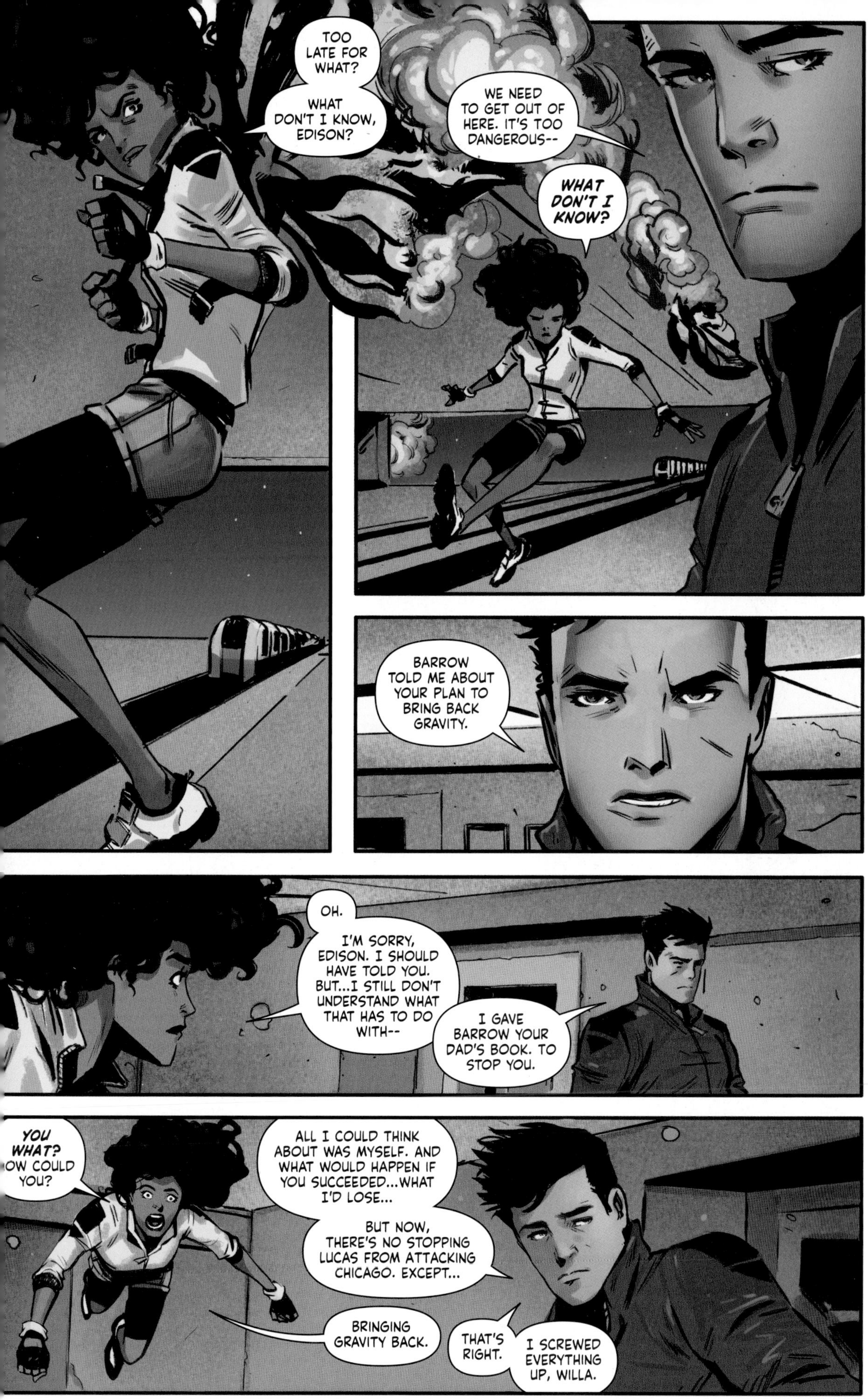
TOO LATE FOR WHAT?
WHAT DON'T I KNOW, EDISON?
WE NEED TO GET OUT OF HERE. IT'S TOO DANGEROUS--
WHAT DON'T I KNOW?
BARROW TOLD ME ABOUT YOUR PLAN TO BRING BACK GRAVITY.
OH.
I'M SORRY, EDISON. I SHOULD HAVE TOLD YOU. BUT...I STILL DON'T UNDERSTAND WHAT THAT HAS TO DO WITH--
I GAVE BARROW YOUR DAD'S BOOK. TO STOP YOU.
YOU WHAT? OW COULD YOU?
ALL I COULD THINK ABOUT WAS MYSELF. AND WHAT WOULD HAPPEN IF YOU SUCCEEDED...WHAT I'D LOSE...
BUT NOW, THERE'S NO STOPPING LUCAS FROM ATTACKING CHICAGO. EXCEPT...
BRINGING GRAVITY BACK.
THAT'S RIGHT.
I SCREWED EVERYTHING UP, WILLA.

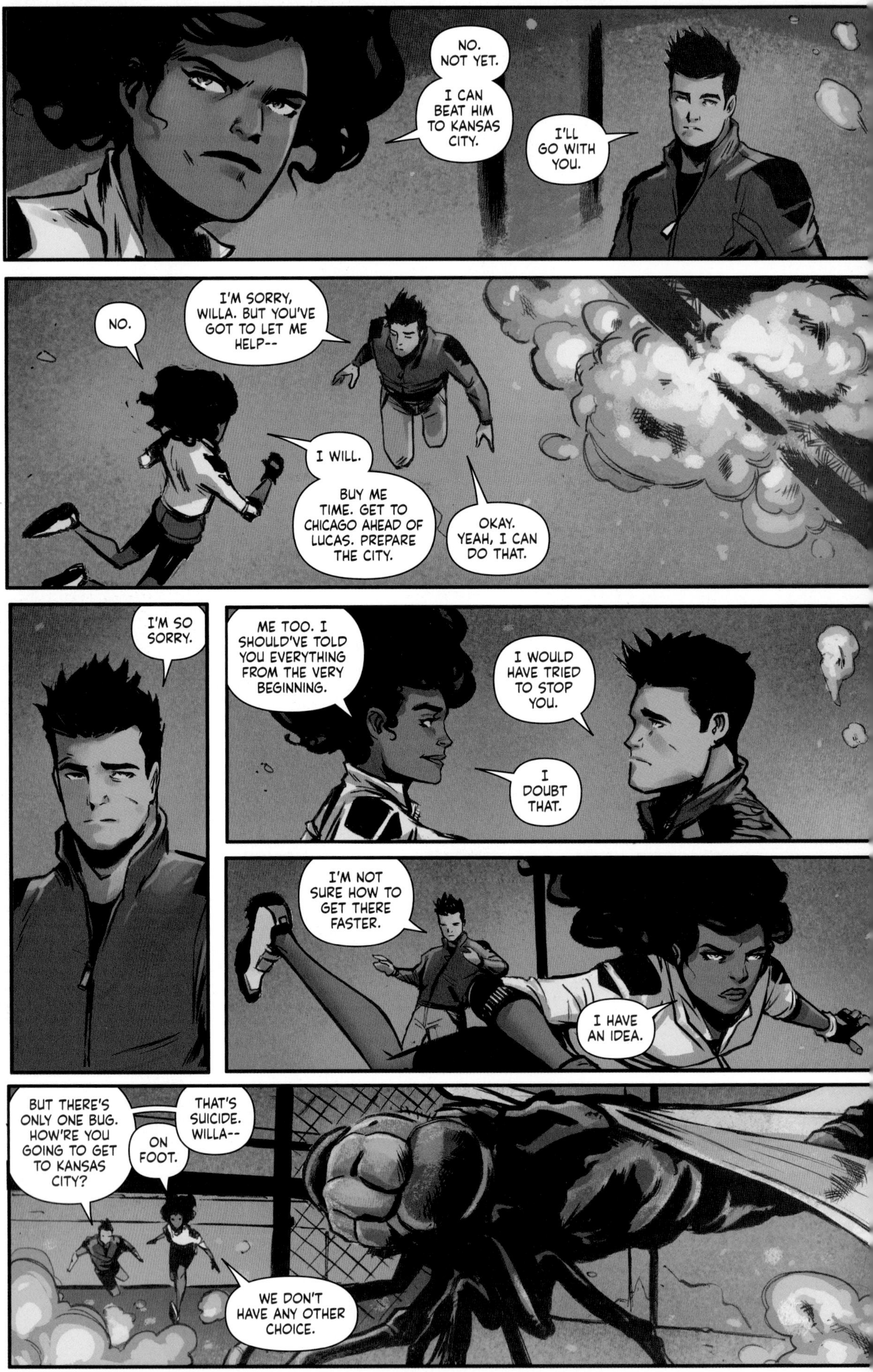
NO. NOT YET.
I CAN BEAT HIM TO KANSAS CITY.
I'LL GO WITH YOU.
NO.
I'M SORRY, WILLA. BUT YOU'VE GOT TO LET ME HELP--
I WILL.
BUY ME TIME. GET TO CHICAGO AHEAD OF LUCAS. PREPARE THE CITY.
OKAY. YEAH, I CAN DO THAT.
I'M SO SORRY.
ME TOO. I SHOULD'VE TOLD YOU EVERYTHING FROM THE VERY BEGINNING.
I WOULD HAVE TRIED TO STOP YOU.
I DOUBT THAT.
I'M NOT SURE HOW TO GET THERE FASTER.
I HAVE AN IDEA.
BUT THERE'S ONLY ONE BUG. HOW'RE YOU GOING TO GET TO KANSAS CITY?
ON FOOT.
THAT'S SUICIDE. WILLA--
WE DON'T HAVE ANY OTHER CHOICE.

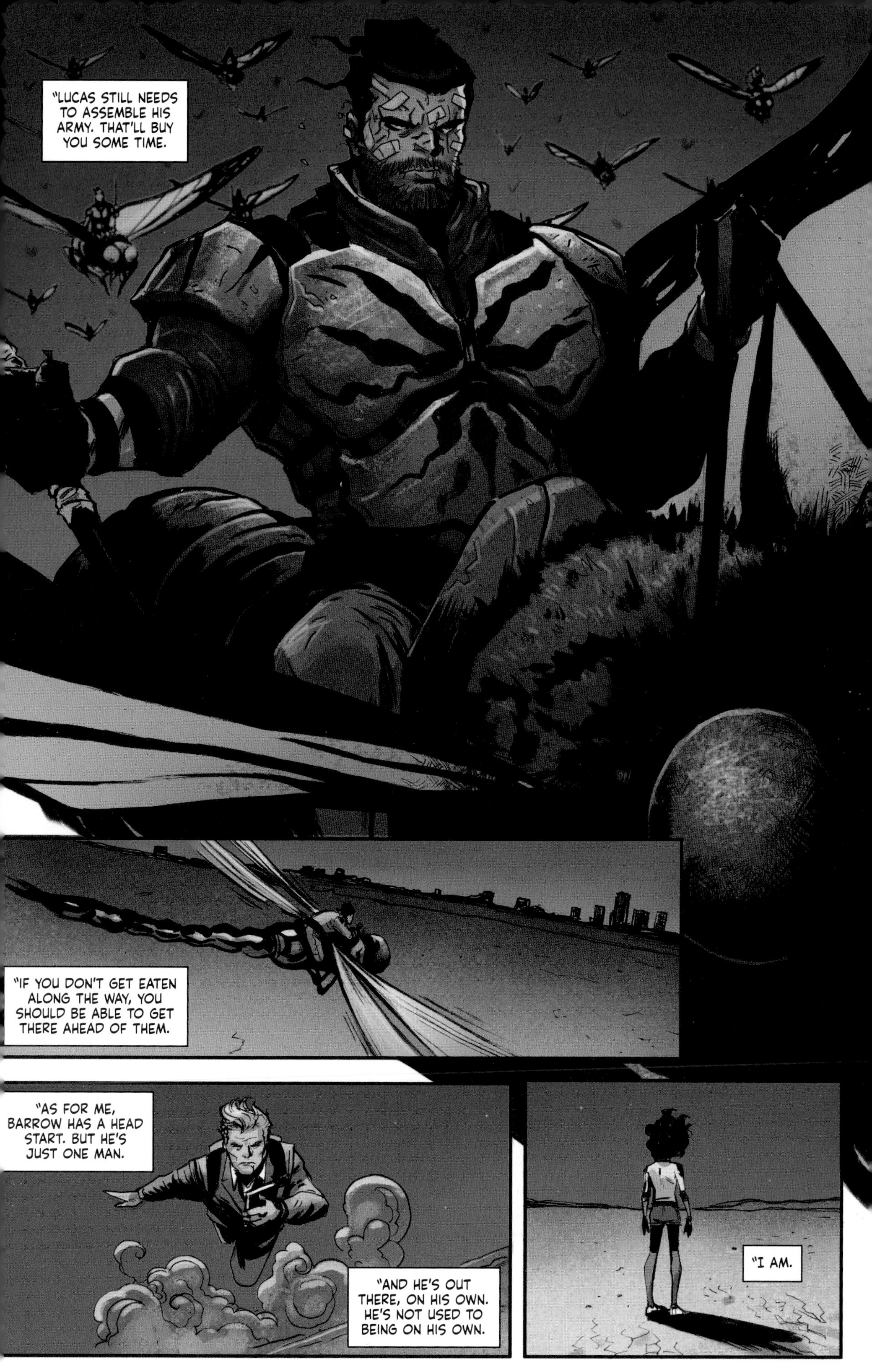

"LUCAS STILL NEEDS TO ASSEMBLE HIS ARMY. THAT'LL BUY YOU SOME TIME.
"IF YOU DON'T GET EATEN ALONG THE WAY, YOU SHOULD BE ABLE TO GET THERE AHEAD OF THEM.
"AS FOR ME, BARROW HAS A HEAD START. BUT HE'S JUST ONE MAN.
"AND HE'S OUT THERE, ON HIS OWN. HE'S NOT USED TO BEING ON HIS OWN.
"I AM.

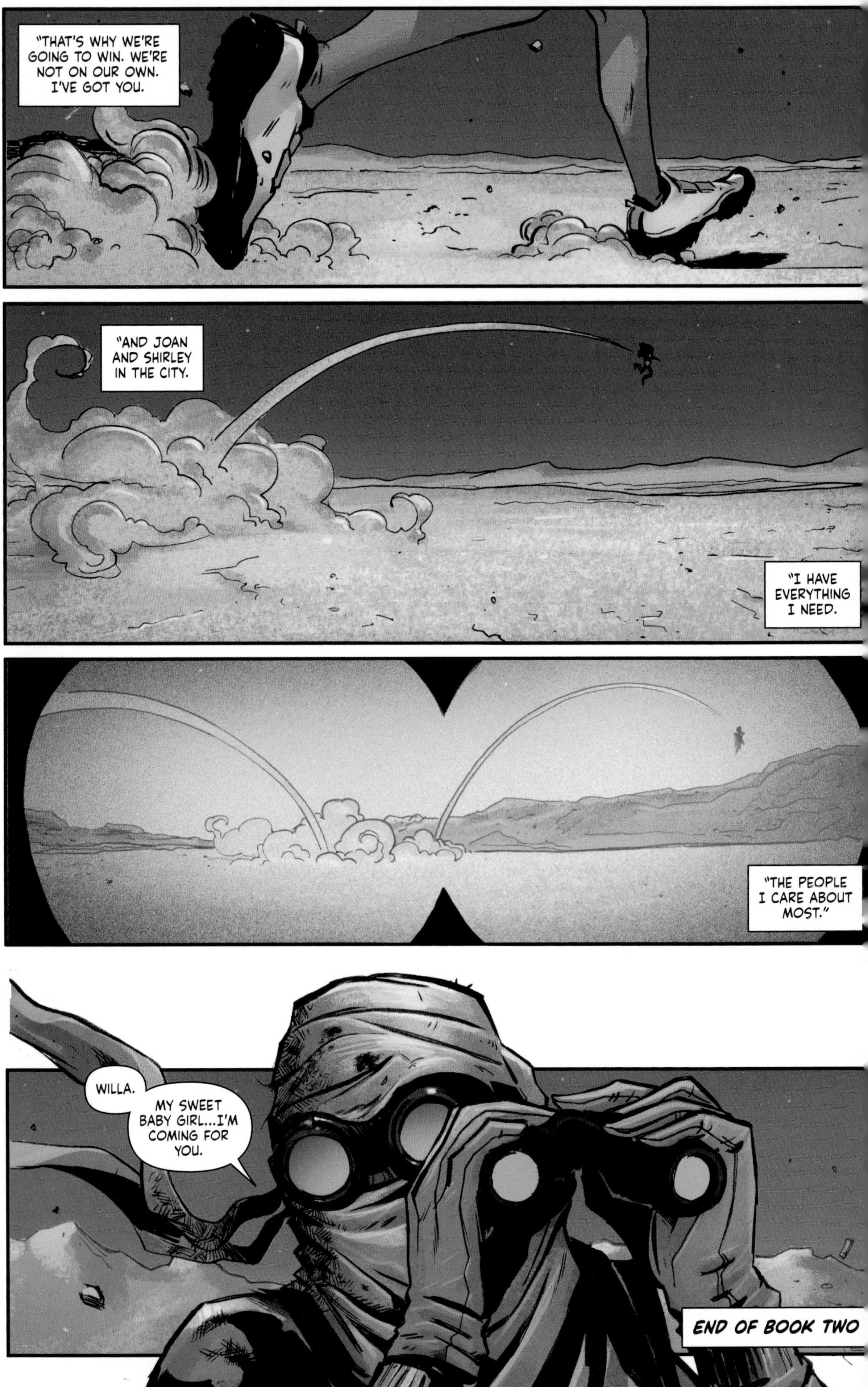
"THAT'S WHY WE'RE GOING TO WIN. WE'RE NOT ON OUR OWN. I'VE GOT YOU.
"AND JOAN AND SHIRLEY IN THE CITY.
"I HAVE EVERYTHING I NEED.
"THE PEOPLE I CARE ABOUT MOST."
WILLA.
MY SWEET BABY GIRL...I'M COMING FOR YOU.
END OF BOOK TWO

END CHAPTER TEN

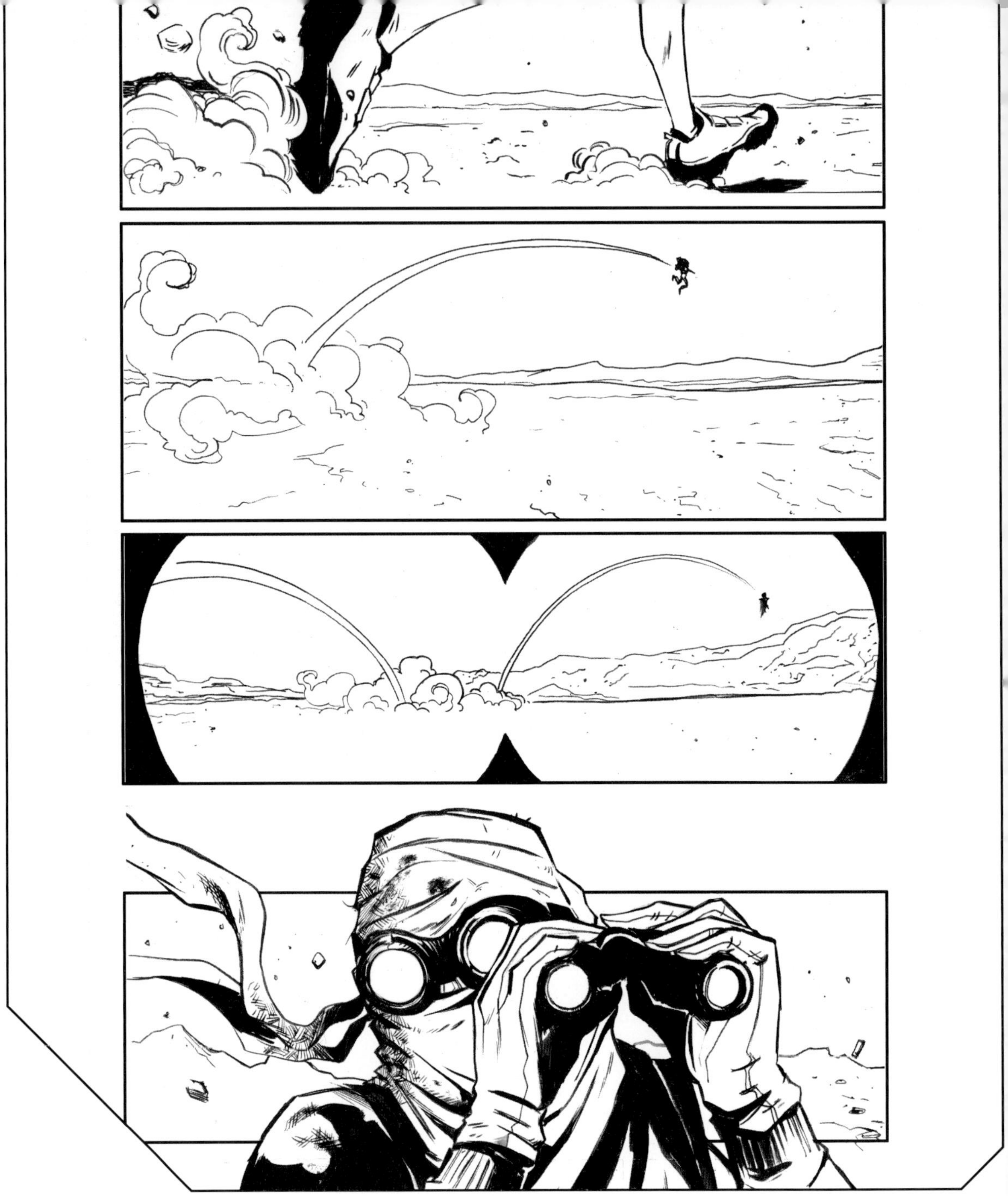

As I was writing issue 10, I felt like something was missing. I had all the big pieces, and I knew where Willa had to end up emotionally. She needed to deal with the devastating events of the first arc and overcome the fear she was finally facing. Come out stronger for all the terrible things she saw. Tested and triumphant.

And I knew where she was heading - I'd already figured out the crazy journey Willa's about to embark on for the third arc. I had all the pieces figured out. And yet... something wasn't right.

It reminded me of issue 5, when I suddenly realized Nate wasn't going to continue on the journey with Willa. When their story told me that Willa needed to explore this leg on her own. That time, something had to be removed. It broke my heart... but it was necessary for Willa to truly grow as a person. To stand on her own two legs (or at least float on them).

This time, something was missing that needed to be there. And then it hit me like a lightning bolt. It wasn't something... it was someONE. I texted the idea to Lee, and he voiced the same concern I was feeling. If we do this, we need to earn it. So I went to work trying to do just that.

And suddenly, a whole bunch of new story for the next arc opened up. Not changing Willa's story, but deepening it. So get ready for the biggest, craziest, most heartfelt arc of Skyward yet.

It's called Fix the World. And it changes everything.

—JOE

SKYWARD

supplemental

3

PAGE 3:

PANEL 1: She's JERKED back as the Bug won't let go. The Dad still held in its clutches.

> WILLA (CONT'D)
> OOOF!

PANEL 2: The Dad stares at her, amazed. She PULLS at him, but the Dragonfly's got a strong hold.

> DAD
> Oh my God, thank you! I can't believe
> you --

> WILLA
> Don't thank me yet.

PANEL 3: The Dragonfly brings them both towards its face to eat. The Man looks terrified; Willa's reaching for her gun.

> DAD
> This can't be real this can't be
> happening --

PANEL 4: Close Up as the Dragonfly opens its insect maw, and Willa aims her GUN right down it:

> WILLA
> Close your eyes and hold on tight.

SFX: BLAM!

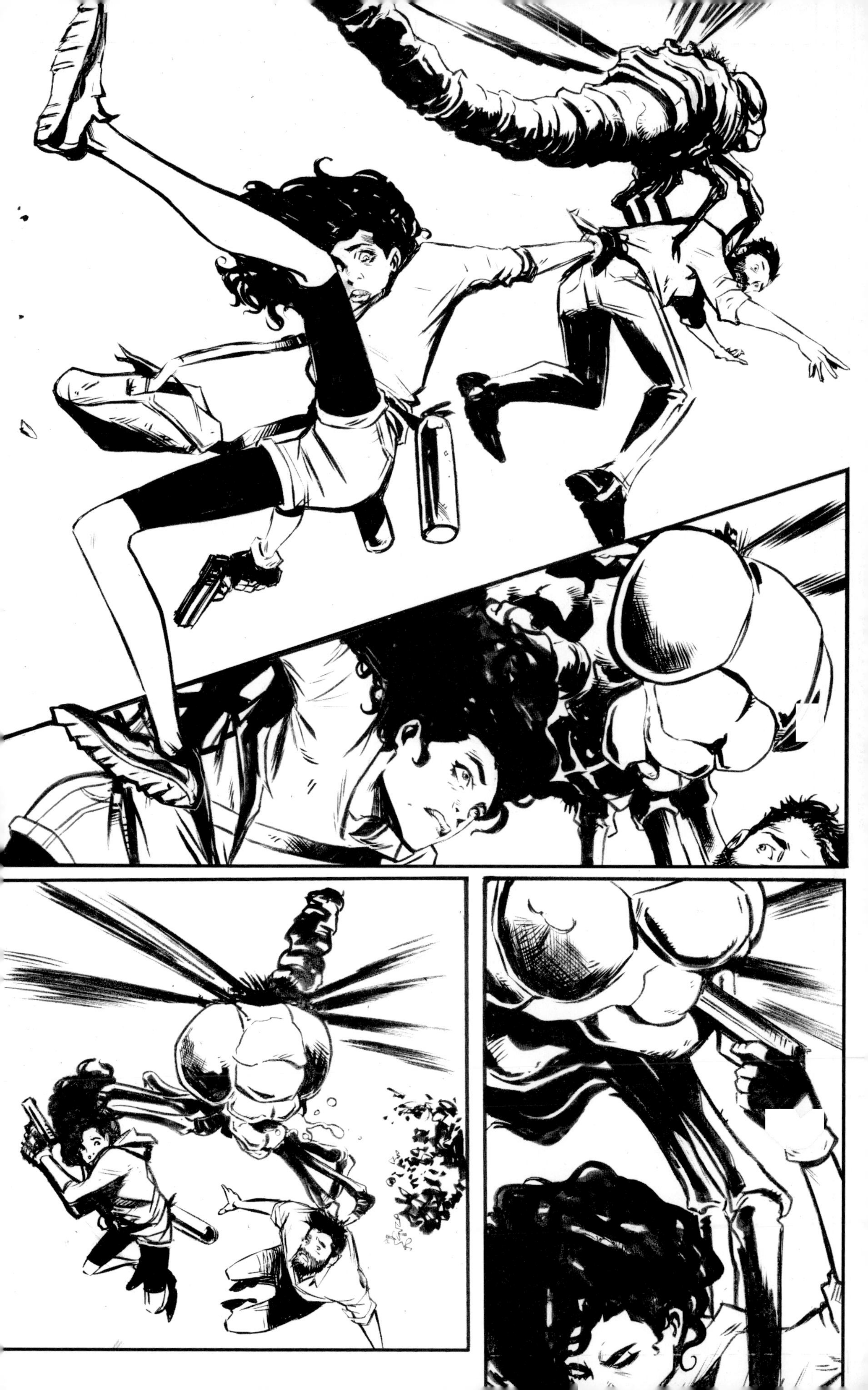

4

PAGE 4:

PANEL 1: Grossness FLOATS through the air where the dragonfly's head just to be. Make it disgusting without being too graphic, and embrace the zero-G ick of it. The Dad looks like he's going to be sick. Willa's just relieved. (Also, either their back should be against something, or the Bug's hold on the Dad's shirt is enough that they didn't go flying. Dealer's choice).

                    WILLA (CONT'D)
          Okay, now --

PANEL 2: The Bug's HEADLESS BODY JERKS around violently, BASHING them against a tree. It should look like it HURTS.

                    WILLA (CONT'D)
             UNGH!

PANEL 3: Willa aims the gun at the mandible holding the DAD, PULLING THE TRIGGER.

                    WILLA (CONT'D)
          Come on! You don't have a head!!
          That's not fair!

SFX: BAM!

PANEL 4: Willa and the Dad go flying into another tree, COLLIDING with it, half of the mandible (or whatever's holding the Dad) still attached to him.

PANEL 5: Willa looks at the Dad.

                    WILLA (CONT'D)
          Okay. Well at least we're...

PANEL 6: Bugs all TURN their heads, having heard the commotion. Willa sees it.

                    WILLA (CONT'D)
          ...Screwed.

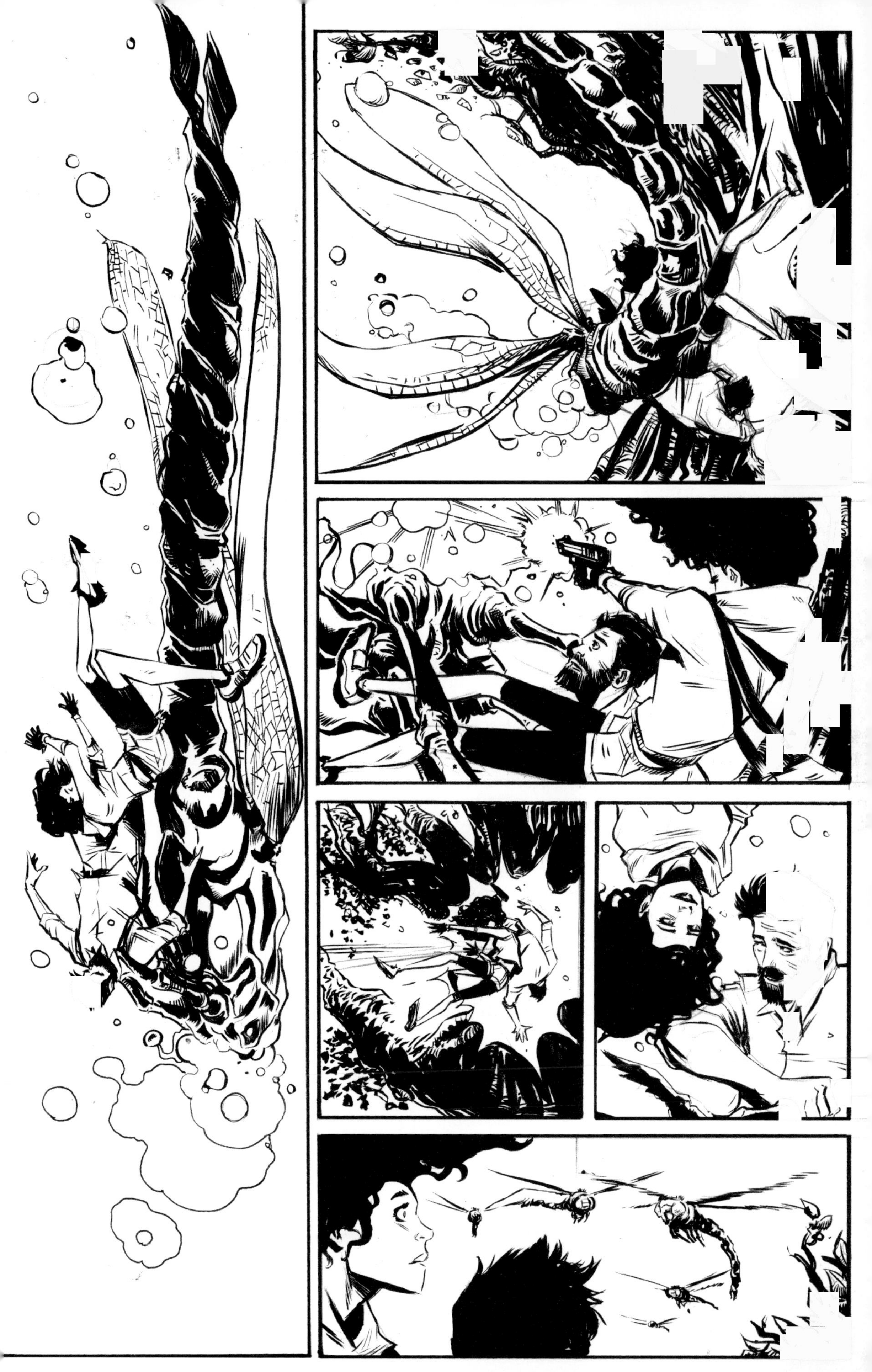

5

PAGE 5:

PANEL 1: Willa SHOVES the man deep into the foliage of the tree. Willa has a fiery intensity to her. The Dad is listening like a school kid getting lectured.

>   WILLA (CONT'D)
>   Stay here. Don't move.

>   DAD
>   But --

>   WILLA
>   You are NOT leaving your daughter
>   alone. You are NOT. Understood?

>   DAD
>   Yes ma'am.

PANEL 2: Willa DARTS away, waving her arms as the Bugs follow.

>   WILLA
>   Hey bugs! Follow me! I'm delicious!

PANEL 3: Willa grabs her extinguisher, uses it to propel herself in front of the bugs. Willa, telling herself to make herself feel better:

>   WILLA (CONT'D)
>   Relax. Those aren't impossibly
>   gigantic bugs.
>   (another balloon)
>   You're back in high school. It's
>   dance class. That's all this is.

PANEL 4: Willa shoots herself up, barely dodging a BUG.

>   WILLA (CONT'D)
>   Just a dance.

PANEL 5: Willa shoots herself down, dodging another (or its mandibles).

>   WILLA (CONT'D)
>   Oh yeah. I'm a terrible dancer.

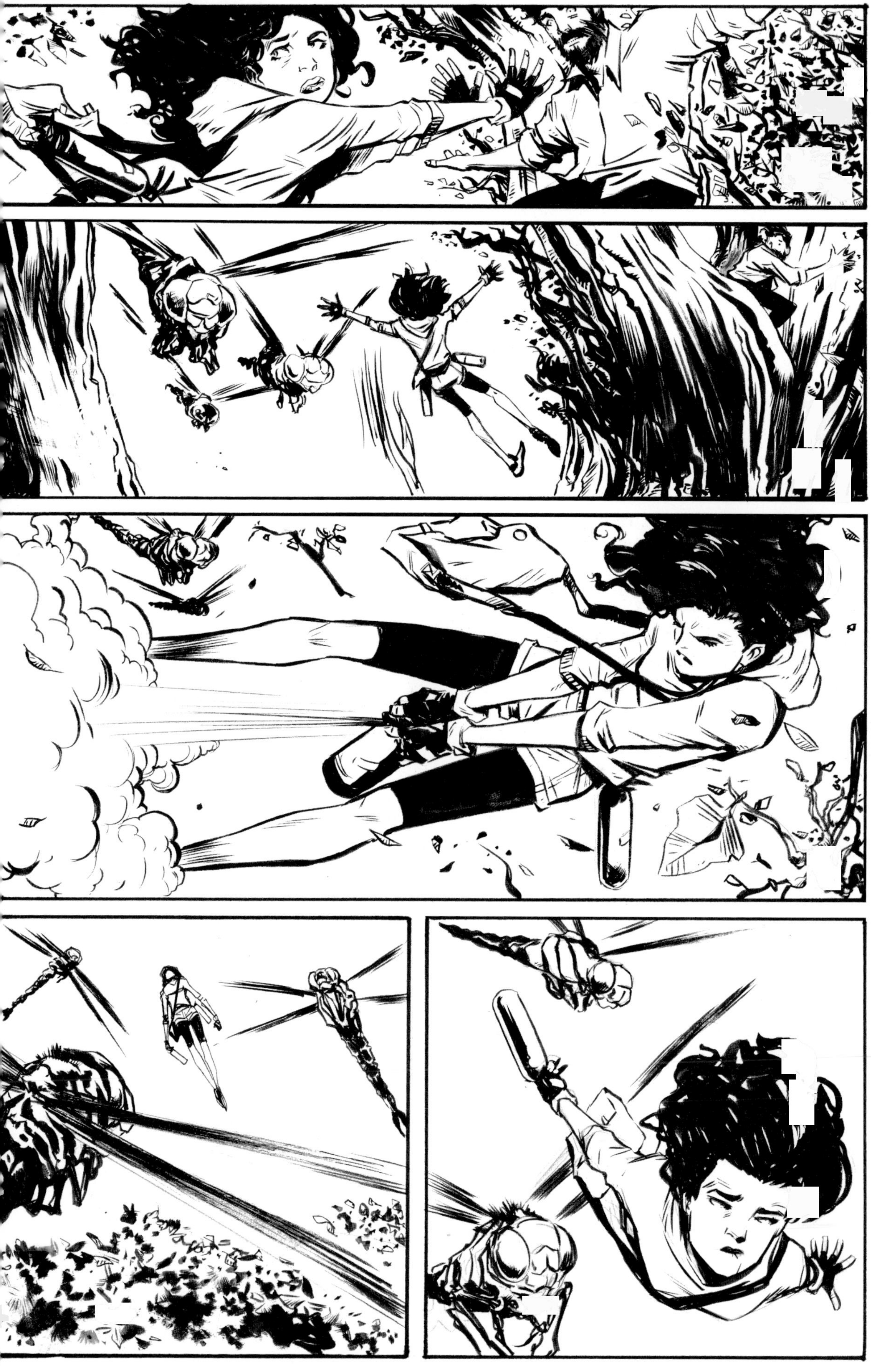

PAGE 6:

PANEL 1: A BUG's close to her. She gives it a face full of
EXTINGUISHERS.

                              BUG
              SKKKKRK!

PANEL 2: Another bug GRABS her leg. She struggles, pulling
the extinguisher off her back.

                            WILLA
              GAH!

PANEL 3: Willa JAMS her extinguisher in its mouth.

                         WILLA (CONT'D)
              Eat THIS!

PANEL 4: It EXPLODES, freeing Willa and blowing up the bug's
face. Willa goes flying.

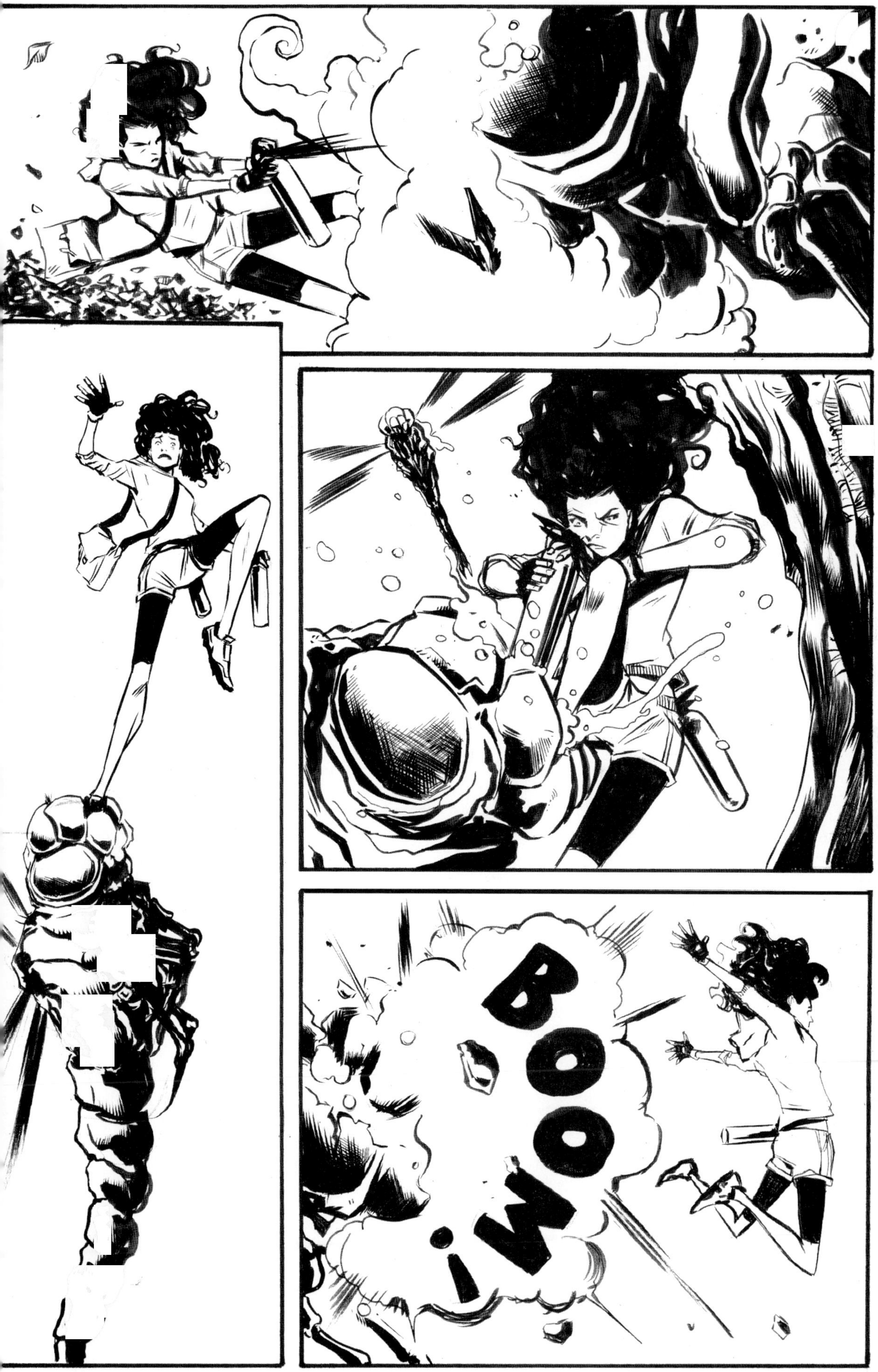
BOOM!

PAGE 7:

PANEL 1: Willa HITS the ground, skidding across it. Her gun's already out, held above her as BUGS approach. She's barely keeping it together. She's LOSING this fight.

PANEL 2: The bug's MOUTH is almost on her as Willa pulls the trigger:

SFX: CLICK

PANEL 3: Willa PANICKS as a bug is inches away from eating her, still pulling away at the trigger. The Bug's MOUTH starts to cover her feet. She's DEAD. SHE'S DEAD.

                    WILLA
          Come on come on come on --

SFX: CLICK CLICK CLICK

PANEL 4: Willa hasn't moved, but the Bug's entire head floats PAST her. We see that the head's been severed directly from the neck. Bug gore floats around it. Willa looks completely bewildered.

PANEL 5: Willa's POV -- a silhouetted figure stands over her. Her hero. Willa stares:

                    WILLA (CONT'D)
          Edison... ?

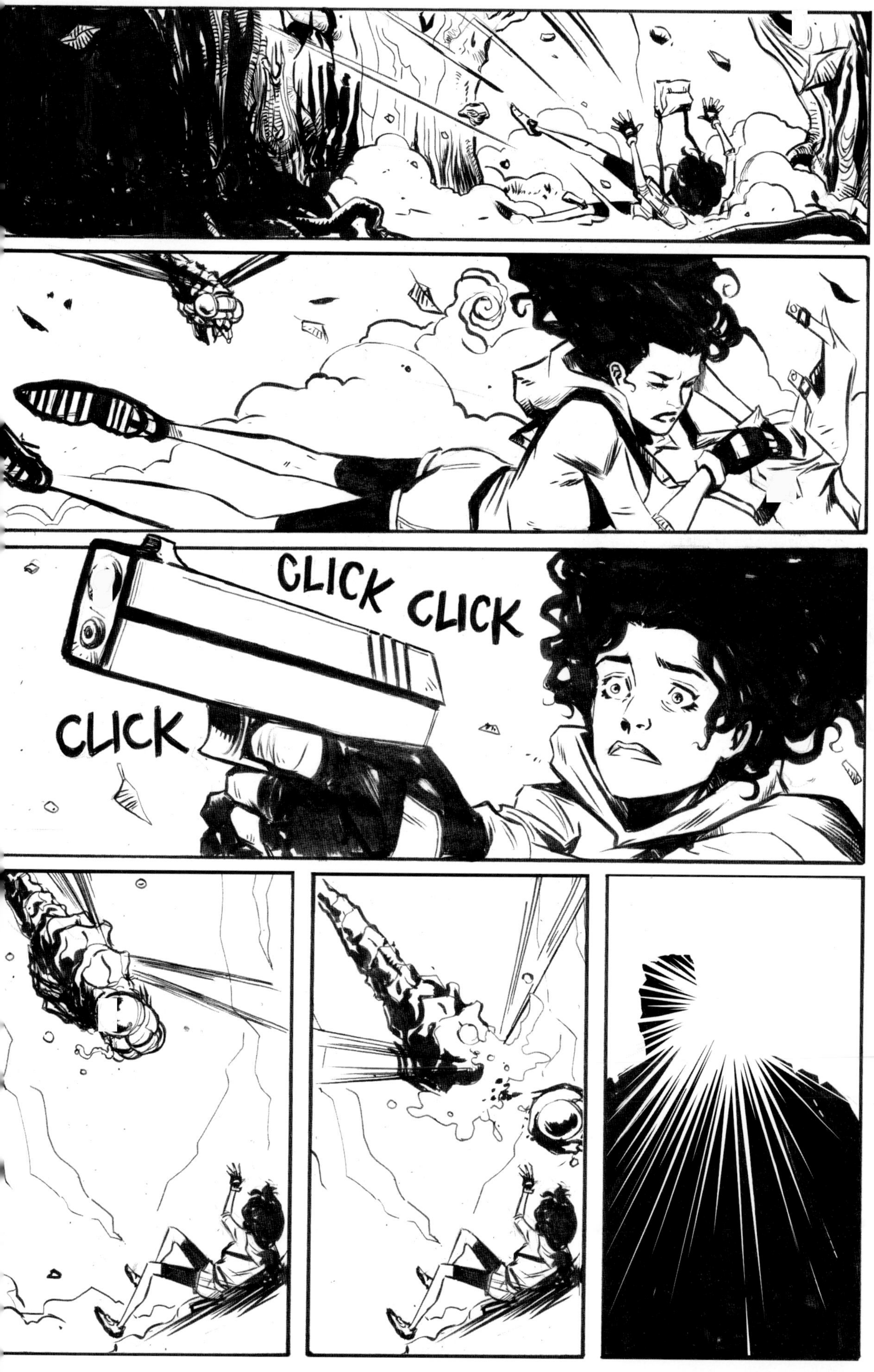
CLICK CLICK
CLICK

PAGE 8:

PANEL 1: Hero shot! This is LUCAS SERRANO (Hispanic). He's handsome in a rugged way. And he's holding A SWORD. Basically, think how to make him look as different from Edison but feel like a proper rival. Whereas Edison is slight, this dude should be beefcake and bearded. A MAN who has had to survive.

> LUCAS
> Hi.

PANEL 2: Willa stares up at him. She's immediately besotted.

> WILLA
> You saved my life.
> (another balloon)
> You have a sword.

PANEL 3: Lucas looks amused. Willa's in shock.

> LUCAS
> I do.

> WILLA
> That's an actual sword.

> LUCAS
> Yes. Yes it is.

> WILLA
> Giant bugs and swords. Sure. Okay.

PANEL 4: Lucas wipes bug gore off the sword.

> LUCAS
> The key is to sever the spinal cord.
> Otherwise the body still kicks for a
> bit.

> WILLA
> (still processing)
> I'll remember that the next time.

PANEL 5: Willa looks over his shoulder. He turns to see what she sees:

> WILLA (CONT'D)
> Oh no.

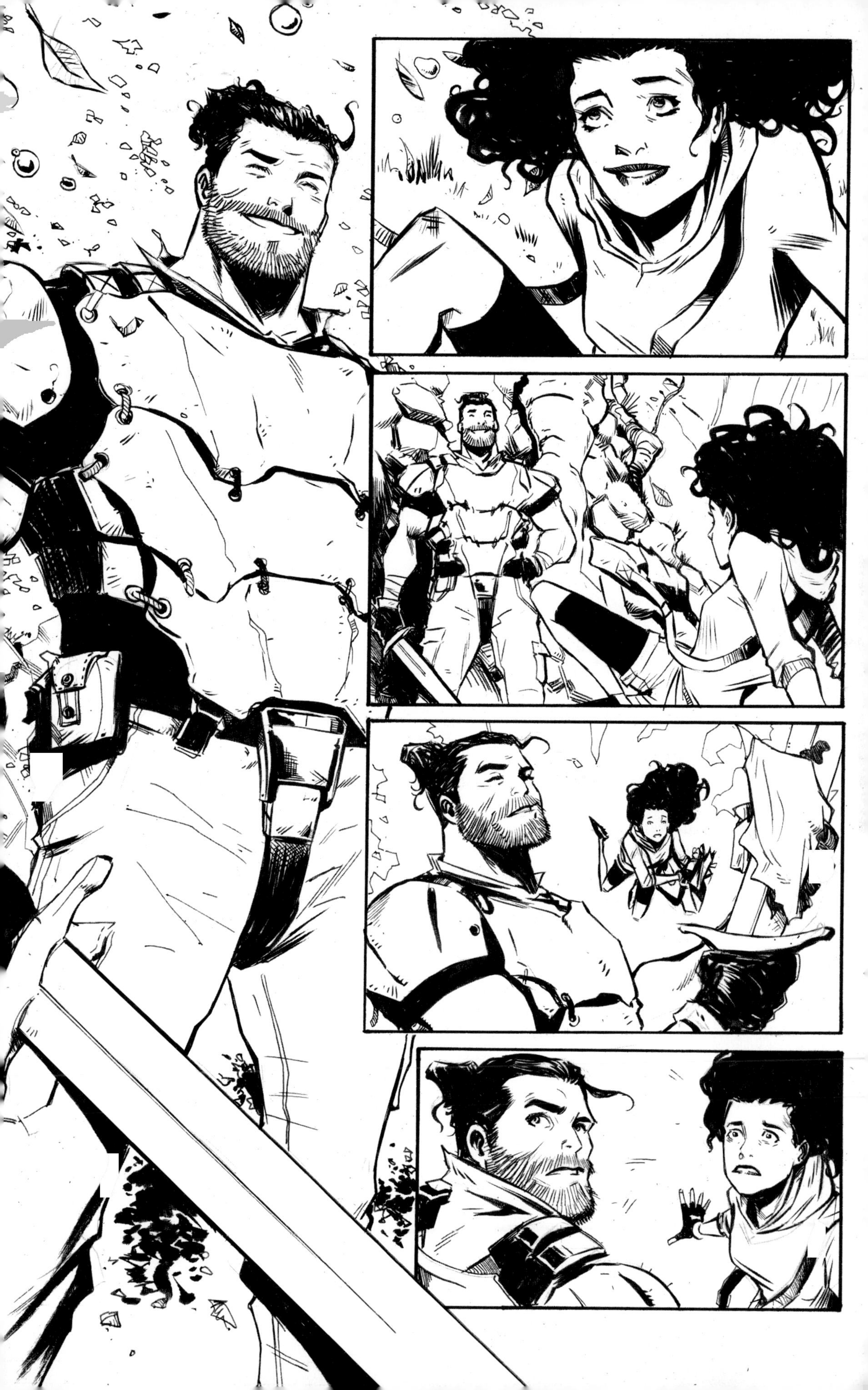

PAGE 9:

PANEL 1: It's a GIANT BUTTERFLY. It looms over them, beautiful but terrifying. She GRABS him.

> WILLA (CONT'D)
> Quick, come on --

PANEL 2: Lucas stops her. Not worried at all.

> LUCAS
> Relax. She's with me.

> WILLA
> Wait, that's YOUR butterfly?
> (another balloon)
> Is a sentence I didn't think I'd be
> saying today.

PANEL 3: Lucas floats up to its back. We see: There's a SADDLE back there, as well as a contraption to hang MEAT in front of the butterfly's face.

> LUCAS
> Don't get me wrong, she'll tear your
> arms off and eat them if she gets
> the chance.
> (another balloon)
> So don't give her the chance.

PANEL 4: He holds out a hand.

> LUCAS (CONT'D)
> Need a lift?

PANEL 5: off Willa, holy crap, taking his hand --

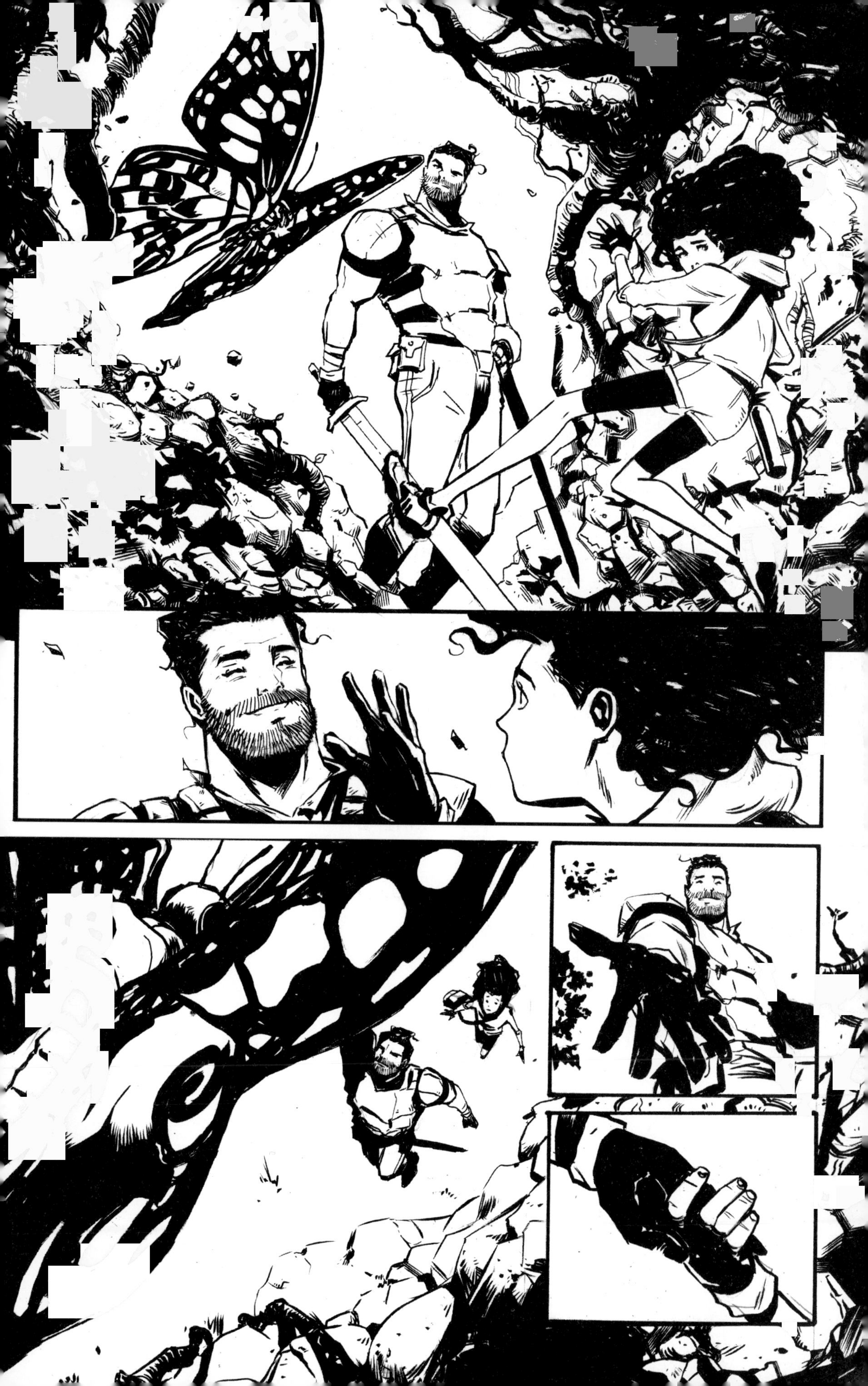

PAGE 10:

PANEL 1: The PASSENGERS stand near the door.

> PASSENGER
> I haven't heard anything out there
> for a little bit.

> PASSENGER 2
> Maybe they just went away.

> PASSENGER
> Or followed that crazy lady.

PANEL 2: Edison moves towards them, insistent. He's getting ready for a big speech. The Passengers are already ahead of him.

> EDISON
> Let me go out there and check. Worst
> case, I die. Best case, I can still
> save my friend.
> (another balloon)
> Please, you need to --

> PASSENGER
> Sure.

> PASSENGER 2
> Yeah, go ahead. Better you than us.

PANEL 3: Edison's surprised. He moves towards the door and everyone moves to the OPPOSITE SIDE (play it for comedic effect, everyone basically throwing Edison to the wolves).

> EDISON
> Oh. Great. Okay. Get ready Edison.
> (another balloon)
> Deep breath --

PANEL 4: Edison opens the door. Over his shoulder, he sees: Willa, riding on the back of a butterfly, sitting behind Lucas. The Dad holds on behind her in FEAR. She waves.

> WILLA
> Hey Edison! I'm riding a butterfly!

PANEL 5: Edison stares in shock. Both at the butterfly, and the annoyingly handsome dude she's with.

> EDISON
> You... sure are.

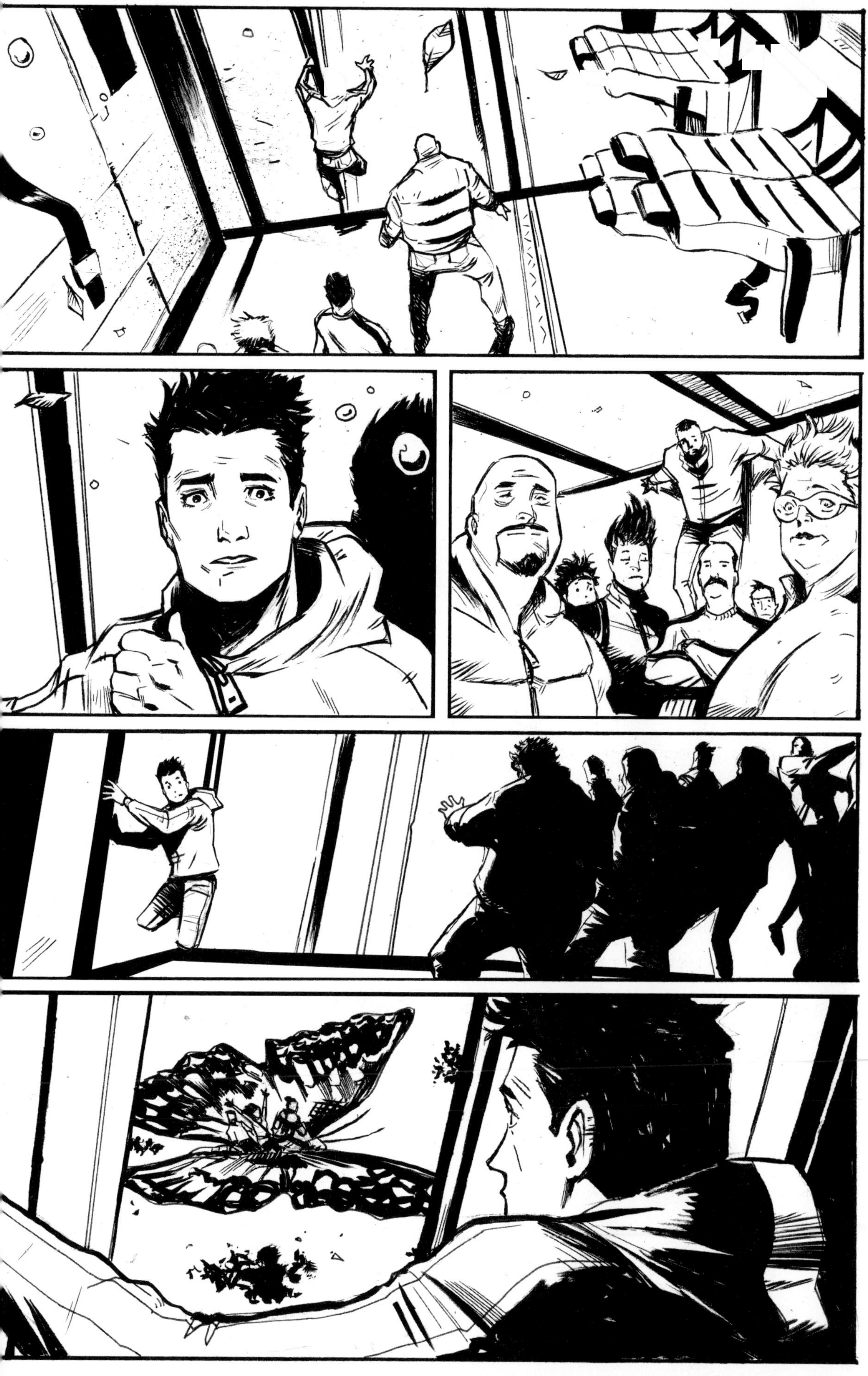

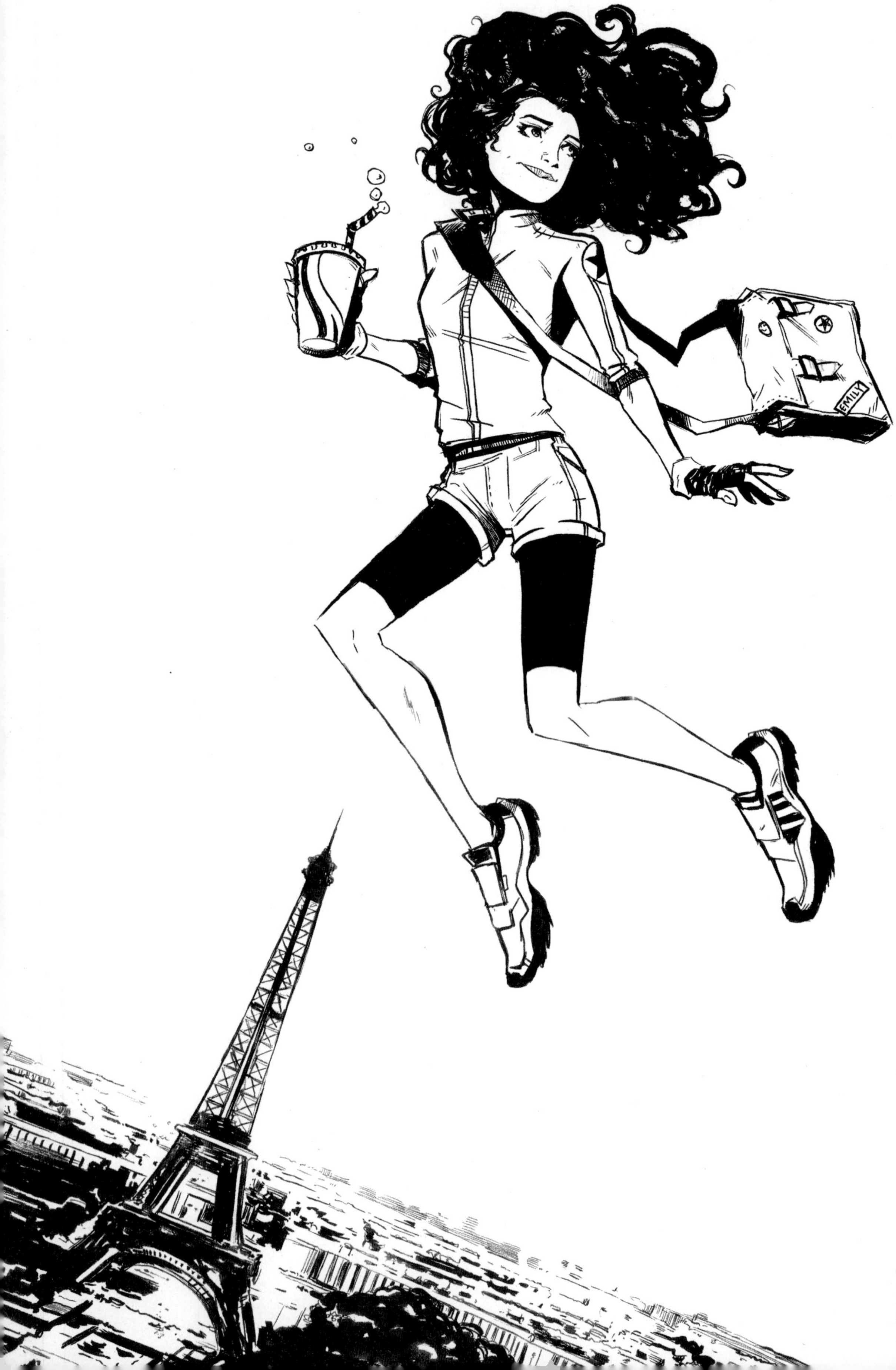
EMILY